SELECTED PRAISE FOR

THE MOUNTAIN'S CALL

"Definitely a don't-put-this-down page-turner!"
—*New York Times* bestselling author
Mercedes Lackey

"A riveting plot, complex characters, beautiful
descriptions, and heaps of magic."
—*Romance Reviews Today*

"Caitlin Brennan has created a masterpiece
of legend and lore with her first novel. Hauntingly
beautiful and extremely powerful...Take Tolkien and
Lackey and mix them together and you get this new
magic that is Caitlin's own. You will stay enthralled
with each page turned."
—*The Best Reviews*

"Caitlin Brennan is a fantastic world builder who
creates a world where magic is an everyday
occurrence.... There is plenty of action and romance
in this spellbinding romantic fantasy."
—*Paranormal Romance Reviews*

CAITLIN BRENNAN

SONG OF UNMAKING

LUNA™
www.LUNA-Books.com

LUNA™

First edition October 2005

SONG OF UNMAKING

ISBN 0-373-80232-3

This edition published by arrangement with Harlequin Books S.A.

® and TM are trademarks of Harlequin Books S.A., used under license. Trademarks indicated with ® are registered in the United States Patent and Trademark Office, the Canadian Trade Marks Office and in other countries.

www.LUNA-Books.com

Printed in U.S.A.

For Shenny
Maybe now your friends will believe
that your aunt writes books!

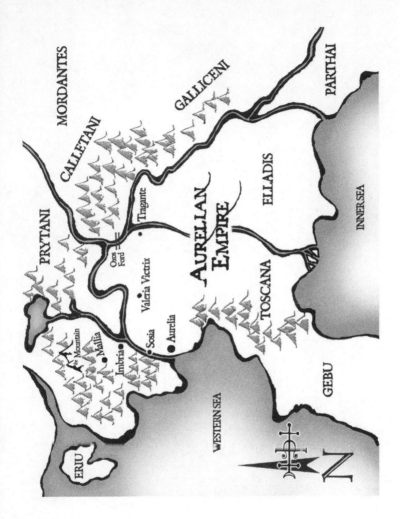

One

The sky was raining stars.

Euan Rohe lay in the frozen sedge. The river gleamed below, solid with ice from bank to bank. The brighter stars reflected in it as they fell, streaks of gold and white and pallid green.

He was dizzy with cold and hunger and long running—and there were the damned imperials, yet again, between him and his hope of escape. Though winter had set in early and hard, the border was crawling with them. Every ford, every possible crossing was guarded.

For days Euan had been struggling along the river, while the hunting grew more and more scant, and the cold set in deep and hard. He was ready to swear that the emperor's patrols were waiting for him, even herding him, driving him farther and farther downriver. His own country seemed to mock him, rising in steep slopes black with pine and white with snow, so near he could almost reach out and touch, but impossibly far.

He could appreciate irony. He had come out of the heart of the empire, a big redheaded man in a world of little dark people, with a price on his head and a cry of treason that echoed still, months after his stroke against the emperor had failed—and none of the emperor's hounds had been able to find him. But then, why would they trouble themselves? All they had to do was close the border.

He was trapped like a bear in a pit. They would herd him all the way down to the sea, then corner him on the sand—or they would catch him much sooner, when cold and starvation and sheer snarling frustration made him drop his guard.

Maybe he would die and cheat them of their revenge. They could do what they liked with his corpse—he would not be using it any longer. Even soft imperials might turn savage toward the man who had reduced their emperor to impotence, disrupted their holy Dance, and come near to destroying their herd of horse mages.

His lips drew back from his teeth when he thought of those stiff-necked fools with their overweening arrogance and their worship of fat white horses. At least six of them were dead, and good riddance, too.

One of them was still alive, and that might be good, or it might be very, very bad. If he closed his eyes, he could see her face. Its lines were burned in his memory, just as he had seen her in that last, desperate meeting. Black hair in tousled curls, smooth rounded cheeks and firm chin, and eyes neither brown nor green, flecked with gold. She was bruised, filthy, staggering, with one arm hanging limp—but she held his life in her one good hand.

She could have killed him. He would have bared his throat for the knife. He could have killed her—and by the One God, truly he should have, because she had betrayed him and broken her word and brought down his plot against her empire.

She had let him go. And he had let her live. Because of her he had failed, but also because of her, he had escaped.

That might have been no mercy. He had won through to the border, but the border was closed. The emperor's legionaries would do her killing for her.

Twenty of them camped now between him and the river. He was not getting across tonight.

His belly griped with hunger. He did his best to ignore it. There were no villages or farmsteads within a day's hard slog— more than that for a man as worn down as he was. The last rabbit he had managed to snare was long since eaten, down to the hide and sinew. He would be starting in on his boots next, unless he went mad and tried to raid the patrol's stores.

Maybe that was not so mad. Most of the patrol were asleep. Their sentries were vigilant—and well hidden—but he knew where each of them was.

There was a light in the captain's tent, but no movement. Probably the man had fallen asleep over his dispatches.

Euan gathered what strength he had. He had to do it soon or he would freeze where he lay. Slip in, snatch what he could, slip out and across the river. He could do that.

He could die, too, but he would die if he stayed where he was. Die doing something or die doing nothing—that was not a choice he found difficult.

He flexed his stiffened fingers and rose to a crouch. He had to stop then until the world stopped spinning. He drew deep breaths, though the air burned his lungs with cold.

When he was as steady as he was going to get, he crept forward through the sedge. The moonlight was very bright and its color was strange—as if the moon had turned to fire.

The hairs of his nape stood on end. He flung himself flat, just as the fire came down.

It struck with a roar that consumed everything there was. The earth heaved under him. A blast of heat shocked him, then a squall of scalding rain. He gagged on the reek of hot metal.

He lay blinded, deafened, and soaked through all his layers of rags and leather and furs. His skin stung with burns. For a long while he simply lay, clinging to the earth that had gone mercifully still again.

He suspected that he might be dead. Every account of the One God's hell told of fire and darkness, heat and cold together, and the screams of the damned rising to such a pitch that the ears were pummeled into silence.

If he was dead, then the dead could feel bodily pain. Shakily he lifted himself to his elbows.

The sky was still raining stars. The river's gleam was dulled— spattered with earth and mud and fragments that must be ash. The camp was a smoldering ruin.

All the horses were dead or dying, and the men were down in the ashes of their tents, writhing in agony or else terribly still. Even Euan's dulled ears could hear the screams of the wounded—and from the sound, those wounds were mortal. The tents were shredded or, on the upriver side, completely gone. The earth gaped where they had been.

Euan's clothes had been a mass of tatters even before the fire came down. What was fabric was scorched and what was fur was singed, but most of it was intact. Snow and sedge between them had protected him.

He bowed to the strength of the One God who had hurled a star out of the sky to defend His worshipper. He only had to hope that there was enough of him left to make it across the river—and enough provisions left in the camp to feed him before he went.

If nothing else, he could feast on horse meat. There would

be a certain pleasure in that, considering how the imperials worshipped the beasts. He staggered erect and made his wobbling way down the hill to the remains of the camp.

None of the legionaries had escaped. Those few who had not died outright, Euan put out of their misery.

The stink of roasted meat made his stomach churn. When he sliced off a bit from a horse's haunch, he found he could not eat it. He put it away thriftily in his traveling bag, then tried to forget he had it.

There was bread in the ashes of one of the fires on the camp's edge. It was well baked and savory—a miracle of sorts. He disciplined himself to eat it in small bites, well spaced apart to spare his too long deprived stomach, as he prowled the ruins.

The blasted pit was still smoldering. Every grain of sense shouted at him to stay far away, but he could not make himself listen. It was as if a spell drew him to the place where the star had fallen.

Amid the embers and ash in the heart of the pit, something gleamed. It was absolute stupidity, but he found a way down the crumbling sides into the new-made and intoxicatingly warm bowl.

The star lay in the center in a bed of ash. In spite of the light he had seen, it was dark, lumpen and unlovely, an irregular black stone half the size of his clenched fist.

The heat of its fall was still in it. He had a firepot, stolen from a trader outside a town whose name he had never troubled to learn, and it was just large enough to hold the starstone.

The thing was shockingly heavy. He almost dropped the pot, but he caught it just in time. The weight of the heavens was in it.

It was much harder to climb out of the pit than it had been

to go down into it. The sides were steep and slippery with mud and melting ice. Euan came dangerously close to surrendering—to sliding back to the bottom and lying there until death or daylight took him.

In the end it was not courage that got him out. It was pride. However he wanted to be remembered, it was not as the prince of the Calletani who gave up and died in a hole.

He lay on the edge, plastered with mud and gasping for breath. He had no memory of the climb, but his arms and legs were aching and his fingers stung.

Gingerly he rolled onto his back. The stars had stopped falling.

The one in his bag weighed him down as he rose. Wisdom might have persuaded him to drop it, but he had paid too dearly for it already. He stood as straight as he could under it.

There was still food to find and a river to cross. He scavenged a bag of flour that had been shielded by a legionary's body, a wheel of cheese that was only half melted, two more loaves of bread that had been baking under stones and so were preserved from destruction, and a jar of thick, sweet imperial wine. There was more, but all the horses were dead and that was as much as he could carry.

He stopped to eat a little bread and nibble a bit of cheese. Near where he was sitting, the captain's tent still stood, scorched but upright. The captain had come out when the fire fell—his body lay sprawled in front of the flap, crisped and charred, with the marks of rank still gleaming on his coat.

Inside the tent, something moved.

Euan sat perfectly still. It was only the wind. But if that was so, then the wind blew nowhere else. The night was calm. Even the moon seemed to be holding its breath.

A shape rose up out of the ashes. It was clothed in a glimmering garment, like something spun out of moonlight. When it stood upright, it stretched long arms and groaned, shaking off a scattering of ash and cooling embers.

The shimmer tore and slid away like the caul from a newborn calf. A man stood in the ashes, whole and unharmed, fixing glittering eyes on Euan. "You're late," he said.

Two

Euan was not often speechless. He did not often find himself face to face with a man he had never expected to meet in this of all places, either—still less a man who should have been dead a dozen times over.

"Gothard," he said. His tone was as cold as the air. "There was a meeting? I must have missed the messenger."

His sometime ally and cordial enemy looked him up and down with that particular flavor of arrogance which marked an imperial noble. By blood and looks he was only half of one, but his spirit did nothing by halves. "One of the patrols should have captured you days ago. How did you manage to escape?"

"Apologies," said Euan, dry as dust. "Clearly I failed to do my duty—whatever that was."

Gothard was barely listening, which did not surprise Euan in the least. "Every stone I scried showed the same thing—you in the legions' hands, ready to be taken back to Aurelia for trial and inevitable execution. And yet you eluded them all. That's interesting. Very."

"I'm sure," said Euan. He rose carefully, and not only because he was still weak. He did not trust this man at all. "I take it you weren't a captive, either? Don't tell me you've got the legions in your pay. That's a fair trick, considering what you tried to do to their emperor."

Who, he did not add, happened to be Gothard's father. That particular family quarrel served Euan well. He was not about to take issue with it.

Gothard's lip twisted. "Clearly you don't understand how easy it is to get possession of legionaries' gear if you happen to have allies in the ranks. Those were my men. I don't suppose you've found any of them alive?"

"None who would want to stay that way," Euan said. "Was that your star? Did you call it down?"

"Would I had such power," Gothard said with an edge of honest envy. "This is a stroke of the gods. It cost me twenty men—but it gained me you. Maybe you'll prove to be worth the exchange."

Euan's lips drew back from his teeth. "What makes you think I want anything to do with you?"

Gothard's grin was just as feral and just as empty of humor. "Of course you do. I'm your kinsman—and I know the empire well. You can use me, just as I can use you."

"I'm not taking you across the river," Euan said. "You're a traitor to your kin already. I doubt you'll be any different on the other side of the border."

"You know what I want," Gothard said.

"You wanted to be emperor," said Euan. "Now that's failed. What's next? A plot against the high king?"

"I don't want to be king of the tribes," Gothard said. "I'll leave that for you. I want the throne of Aurelia, just as I always have. We haven't failed, cousin. We've merely suffered a setback."

Euan threw back his head and laughed until he choked. "A setback? All our men dead, the emperor not only alive but well, and the two of us hunted with every resource the empire can command—I call that a crashing defeat."

"Do you?" said Gothard. "The emperor's alive but not entirely well, the hunt has not succeeded in finding, let alone capturing either of us, and the empire's magic is wounded to the heart. Do you know what it means that half a dozen horse mages are dead? They still have their Master, but only one other of the highest rank still lives, and I broke him before the Dance began."

"Then he took your magic stone and drove you out," Euan said. "That's not as broken as I might like."

Gothard's face flushed dark in the moonlight, but he did not give way to his fit of temper. "Yes, I underestimated him, and that was a mistake. But that won't give back what I took away. His powers are in shards. Maybe he'll be of some use as a riding master, but as a master of the white gods' art, he's done for. And so, for all useful purposes, are the horse mages. They'll be years gaining back even a portion of what they lost."

"I do hope you're right," Euan said, "because there's a war coming, and now we have an enemy who's not just defending his lands against invasion. He's out for vengeance."

"All the better for us," said Gothard. "Anger blinds a man— as I know better than any."

"So you do," said Euan sweetly. He turned on his heel. It was a somewhat longer way to the river than if he walked by Gothard, but he was not eager to risk a blade in the belly.

Unfortunately for his hopes of escape, he was much weaker than he wanted to be—and Gothard was well fed and armed with magic. His hand gripped Euan's arm and spun him back.

Euan struck it aside with force enough to make Gothard hiss with pain, but the moment for escape had passed. He was not going anywhere until this was over.

"Suppose I take you with me," he said. "What's our bargain? You help me become high king and I help you become emperor? What guarantee does either of us have that we'll get what we wish for?"

"There are few certainties in life," Gothard said. "Don't you love a good gamble? There's a crown for you and a throne for me, and power enough for the two of us. Or we're both dead and probably damned."

"I can't say I dislike those odds," Euan said. "Come on, then. Take what you need and follow. I want to be well away from the river by sunup."

"In a moment," Gothard said. "Wait here."

Euan considered telling him what he could do with his damned arrogance, or better yet, walking away while Gothard did whatever he had taken it into his head to do. But curiosity held Euan where he was—and weakness, if he was honest with himself. The heat of the star's fall was nearly gone. The cold was sinking into his bones.

Gothard strode directly toward the pit where the star had fallen. Euan knew what he was looking for. He was a mage of stones, after all, and the star was a stone.

It weighed heavier than ever in Euan's traveling bag. A hunted renegade, stripped of his warband, needed every scrap of hope or glory that he could get his hands on if he wanted to stand up before all the tribes and declare himself fit to be high king. This was a gift from the One, a piece of heaven. It carried tremendous power.

How much more power might it carry if a stone mage wielded it—and if that stone mage was sworn to Euan?

Gothard was a wrathful man and a born traitor, and he was probably mad. But he had powers that Euan could use—if Euan could keep him firmly in hand.

This was a night for taking risks. Euan stood on the edge of the pit and looked down. Gothard was crawling on hands and knees, muttering what might be spells, or more likely curses.

The firepot was cold. The starstone felt as if it had turned to ice. It was so cold it burned Euan's hand as he held it up. "Is this what you're looking for?"

Gothard's back straightened. The pale oval of his face turned toward the moon. His eyes glowed like an animal's.

His voice echoed faintly against the sides of the pit. "Where did you find that?"

"Not far from where you're standing," Euan said. "It was hotter than fire then. Now it's bloody cold."

"What were you thinking to do with it?"

"Make myself high king," Euan said.

"Are you a stone mage, then?"

Euan refrained from bridling at his mockery. "No, but you are. What will you give in return for this?"

"What do you want?" Gothard asked. "We've already bargained for the high kingship."

"Now I'm assured of it," said Euan. "Wield your powers for me. Help me win the war that's coming. Then we'll talk about the empire we're going to take."

"All with a single stone," Gothard said, but Euan could hear the yearning in him.

Euan could feel the power in the stone, too, though thank the One, he had no magic to work with it. His soul was clean of that.

"This is a star," he said. "There's nothing stronger for your kind, is there? I see it in your eyes. You've never lusted for a woman the way you lust for this. This is every bit of magic you lost when your brother took your master stone—and as much again, and more that I'm no doubt too feebleminded to comprehend. I want my share of it, cousin. Swear by it—swear you'll wield it in my cause."

"I swear," Gothard said. His eyes were on the stone.

It was growing warmer in Euan's hand, or else his fingers were too numb to tell the difference. It seemed both heavier and lighter.

Its power was changing. Gothard was changing it—without even laying a hand on it.

Euan refused to give way to awe. He would use a mage for his purposes, but this was still a half-blood imperial with the taint of treason on him. Gothard would keep his oath exactly as long as it served his purpose, and not a moment longer.

Euan would have to make sure that that was a very long time. He was aching, frozen, dizzy with hunger and exhaustion, but he laughed. He was on his way home, and he was going to be high king.

Three

Euan Rohe walked into his father's dun a handful of days before the dark of the year. A bitter rain was falling, but the west was clear, a thin line of pale blue beneath the lowering cloud.

The dun was older than the Calletani, a walled fort of rammed earth and weatherworn stone. The wall enclosed a half-ruined tower and a clutter of round houses built like the traveling tents of the people. The king's house was built around the tower, with his hall in the center. All of it sat on a low hill that rose abruptly out of a long roll of downs.

In milder seasons it was a vast expanse of grass and heather shot through with the silver lines of rivers. Now it was a wilderness of ice and drifted snow, whipped with wind and sleet.

Gothard could have brought them there on the backs of dragons, or conjured chariots out of the air around the starstone. It was Euan who had insisted on taking the hard way on foot over the mountains and through the forests into the heartlands of the Calletani. It was a long road and grueling, but it was honest.

It had also given Gothard ample time to learn the ways and powers of the stone. Euan had no objection to the provender it brought, either the game that walked into his snares or the wine that appeared in his cup. It kept them both alive and walking. It protected them against either discovery or attack, and smoothed their way as much as Euan's scruples would allow.

"You're as stubborn as the damned horse-gods," Gothard had muttered one evening, while a blizzard howled outside the sphere of light and warmth that he had conjured from the stone. "They won't fly, either. The harder their worshippers struggle, the happier they are."

"That's the way of gods," Euan said.

Gothard had snarled at that, but Euan refused to change his mind. Magic was a dangerous temptation. He would use it if he had to, but he refused to become dependent on it.

They walked, therefore, and Gothard played with the stone, working petty magics and small evils that made him titter to himself when he thought Euan was asleep. Gothard had never been what Euan would call sane, but since he had gotten hold of the starstone, he had been growing steadily worse. He was not quite howling mad, but he was on his way there.

He had been talking to himself for two days when they passed the gates of the dun—a long ramble that Euan had stopped paying attention to within the first hour. Part of him listened for signs of immediate threat, but it all seemed to be focused on the riders and their fat white horse-gods, Gothard's dearly loathed brother, his even more dearly loathed father, and occasionally the sister whom he direly underestimated. Gothard, in true imperial style, had convinced himself that the females of his kind had neither strength nor intelligence.

At last, under the low and heavy lintel of Dun Eidyn's gate, he stopped his babbling. There were no guards at the gate, and only a single sentry snoring on the wall above. The two wanderers went not only unchallenged but unnoticed.

Euan resolved to do something about that at his earliest opportunity. Winter it might be, but armies could still march and raiding parties rampage through unprotected camps and ill-guarded duns.

There was no one abroad within the walls. Smoke curled from the roofs of the round houses, and lights glimmered beneath doors and through cracks in shuttered windows. Even the dogs had taken shelter against the storm, which with the coming of dark had changed to sleet.

The door to the king's house was unbarred, and also unguarded. The guard who should have been there was inside with the rest, in the warmth and the smoky firelight of the hall, finishing the last of the day's meal and passing jars of wine and skins of ale and mead. The songs had begun, the vaunting that would bring each warrior to his feet with the tale of his own exploits and those of his ancestors for as far back as the rest would let him go.

Euan stood in the shadow of the doorway, letting it sweep over him. Five years he had been away, fighting his father's war and living as a hostage among the Aurelians. He needed time to believe that he was back at last—and to see what had become of his people in the time since he was gone.

He recognized many of the faces, though some had gone grey and not a few had gained new scars or lost an eye or a limb. Too many were missing, and a surprising number were new— young, most of those. They had been in the children's house when Euan left, or had come to the tribe as hostages or in marriage alliances.

There were more than he remembered. They filled the circle of the hall, overflowing to the edges. There were more shields and weapons hung on the walls, and a good number of those were bright and new, not yet darkened with smoke or age.

He had feared to find a weakened clan and a faltering people, but these were strong. They were eating well for the dead of winter—the remains of an ox turned on the spit in the center, and the head of a wild boar stood on a spear beside the high seat. The king was wearing its hide for a mantle over a profusion of plaids and a clashing array of golden ornaments.

The old man was gaunt and the heavy plaits of his hair and mustaches had gone snow-white, but his back was still straight and his hand was steady as he drank from a skull-cup. The pale bone was bound with gold and set with chunks of river amber, and the wine inside was as red as blood. It was imperial wine— drinking defiance, the king liked to call it.

He was arrogant enough to leave his dun unguarded and his doors unbarred. Some downy-cheeked stranger was chanting, badly, the lay of a battle Euan himself had fought in. People were already hooting and pounding the tables to make him stop.

Euan raised his voice above the din, drawling the words as if he had all the time in the world. "Now, now, that's not such a bad vaunt for a stripling. He's even got his father killing three generals, and there were only two that I remember—and I killed them both. Look, that's old Aegidius's skull my father's drinking from, and there's the nick where I split it, too."

While he spoke, he moved out into the light. He knew what he looked like, wrapped in rags and filthy tatters, with ice melting and dripping from his matted beard. He allowed a grin to split it, flashing it over them all, until it came to rest on his father's face.

It was expressionless, a schooled and royal mask, but the yellow wolf-eyes were glittering. Euan met them steadily. "Good evening, Father," he said.

The hall had gone silent except for the crackling of flames on the hearth. No one even breathed. Out of the corner of his eye Euan caught the flick of fingers. Someone was trying to expel him as if he were a ghost or a night spirit.

That made him want to laugh, but he held the laughter inside. He had played his hand. The next move was his father's.

Niall the king studied him for a long while. Euan knew better than to think that slowness was the wine fuddling the old man's brain. Niall was clearer-headed with a bellyful of wine than most men were cold sober.

At last he said, "So. You made it back. Took you long enough." He filled the late General Aegidius's skull to the brim and held it out. "This will warm your bones."

That was a great honor. Euan bent his head to acknowledge it, but he did not leave the door quite yet. "I brought you a gift," he said.

He held his breath. Gothard might choose to be difficult—it would be like him. But he came forward at Euan's gesture.

He was even more rough and wild a figure than Euan, with his mad eyes and his pale, set face. He stank of magic, so strong it caught at the back of Euan's throat.

"Uncle," Gothard said in his mincing imperial accent. "I'm pleased to see you well."

The king did not look pleased, but neither would Euan have said he was displeased. The bastard son of the Aurelian emperor and a Calletani princess was a potent hostage—even without the starstone.

Niall would have to know about that, but not in front of the whole royal clan.

Maybe he caught a whiff of it. Anyone with a nose could. His eyebrows rose, but he asked no questions.

"Nephew," he said. He beckoned to the servant who stood closest. "Take him, feed him. Give him what he wants to drink."

Gothard had been disposed of, and he could not fail to know it. Euan did not find it reassuring that he bowed to the king and let the servant take him to a lower table—not terribly low, but not the king's table, either. A flare of temper would have been more honest, and a blast of magic would have been almost comforting.

Now Euan would have to watch him as well as the rest of them. But then, that had been true from the moment Gothard shed the skin of his magical protection and stood up in the camp he had failed to save. Gothard was no more or less untrustworthy than he had ever been.

For Euan there was a place beside his father and the best cut of the ox that remained. Tomorrow he would be looking out for daggers in the back, but tonight he was the prince again, the king's heir. He was home.

Four

Euan woke in bed with no memory of having been brought there. He had lasted through four cups of the strong, sweet wine and uncounted rounds of bragging from the king's warband. They were courting him—eyeing the king's age and his youth, and reckoning the odds.

The wine was still in him, making his head pound, but he grinned at the heavy beams of the ceiling. He was in the tower, in one of the rooms above the hall—he recognized the carving. Rough shapes of men and beasts ran in a skein along the beam. Like the tower, they were older than his people. He had known them since he was a child.

His face felt different. His hand found a cleanly shaven chin and tidily trimmed mustaches. The rest of him was clean, too, and the knots and mats were out of his hair.

He sat up. He was still bone-thin—no miracles there—but months of crusted dirt were blessedly gone. He was dressed in finely woven breeks, green checked with blue in a weave and a pattern that he knew. The same pattern in rougher and heavier wool marked the blanket that covered him. There was a heavy torque around his neck, and rings swung in his ears and clasped his arms and wrists. He was right royally attired, and every ornament was soft and heavy gold.

He hardly needed to look toward the door to know who stood there, waiting for him to notice her. She was nearly as old as his father, but where age lay on Niall like hoarfrost, on Murna his first wife and queen, it was hardly more than a kiss of autumn chill. Her hair had darkened a bit with the years, but it was still as much gold as red. Her skin was milk-white, her features carved clean, almost too strong for beauty. They were all the more beautiful for that.

She looked like a certain imperial woman—not the coloring, the One God knew, but the shape and cast of her face and the keenness of her moss-green eyes as they studied him. It startled him to realize how like Valeria she was.

Well, he thought, at least his taste was consistent. He let the smile escape. "Mother! You haven't changed a bit."

"I would hope not," she said. "Whereas you—what have you been living on? Grass and rainwater?"

"Near enough," he said. "I'm home now. You can feed me up to your heart's content."

She frowned slightly. "Are you? Are you really home?"

"For good and all," he said. "I'll tell you stories when there's time. I've seen the white gods' Dance, Mother. I've brought an empire to its knees. It got up again, staggering and stumbling, but it was a good beginning."

"All men love to brag," she said.

"Ah," said Euan, "but my brags are all true."

"I'm sure," she said as if to dismiss his foolishness, but her eyes were smiling. "There's breakfast when you're ready. After that, your father will see you. Something about a gift, he said."

Euan nodded. "You'll be there for that?"

"Should I be?"

He shrugged. "If it amuses you."

"It might."

She left him with a smile to keep him warm, and a parcel that proved to be a shirt and a plaid and a pair of new boots, soft doeskin cut to fit his feet exactly. Someone must have been stitching all night long.

It was bliss to dress in clean clothes, warm and well made and without a rip or a tear to let the wind in. There were weapons, too, the bone-handled dagger that every man of the Calletani carried, the long bow and the heavy boar-spear and the lighter throwing spear and the double-headed axe, and the great sword that was as long as a well-grown child was tall.

He left all but the dagger in their places. The day was dark as he went out, but the sun was well up—somewhere on the other side of the clouds. Last night's glimmer of clear sky had been a taunt. Snow was falling thick and hard, and wind howled around the tower.

It could howl all it liked. Euan was safe out of its reach.

There was food in the hall, barley bread and the remains of last night's roast, with a barrel of ale to wash it down. Euan ate and drank just enough to settle his stomach. If he had been playing the game properly, he would have lingered for an hour, bantering with the clansmen who were up and about, but he was still half in the long dream of flight. His feet carried him to the room where the king slept and rested and held private audiences.

It was the same room he remembered. Just before he went away, the trophies of two legions had been brought there. They were still standing against the wall. The armor of the generals, their shields and the standards with their golden wreaths and remembrances of old battles, gleamed as if they had been taken only yesterday.

They struck Euan strangely. For most of five years he had lived in the empire, surrounded by guards in armor very like that. Seeing them, he understood, at last, that he had escaped. He was free.

Maybe it was only a different kind of bondage. His father was sitting in the general's chair that he had taken with the rest of the trophies. Away from the clan and its eyes and whispers, Niall allowed himself to feel his age. He slumped as if with exhaustion, and his face was drawn and haggard.

He straightened somewhat as Euan came through the door. The gladness in his eyes was quickly hooded.

That might have been simply because other guests had arrived before Euan. Two priests of the One stood in front of the king. Gothard perched on a stool, more or less between them.

Euan tried to breathe shallowly. No matter their age or rank, priests always stank of clotted blood and old graves. These were an old one and a young one, as far as he could tell. They stripped themselves of every scrap of hair, even to the eyelashes—or their rites did it for them—and they were as gaunt as the king and far less clean. Bathing for them was a sin.

The one who might have been older also might have been of high rank. He wore a necklace of infants' skulls, and armlets pieced together of tiny finger bones. The other's face and body were ridged with scars, so many and so close together that there was no telling what he had looked like before. Only his hands and feet were untouched, and those were smooth and seemed young. He was very holy, to have offered himself up for so much pain.

Euan's mother was not in evidence, but there was a curtain

behind his father, with a whisper of movement in it. She was there, watching and listening.

He breathed out slowly. Gothard grinned. He had been washed and shaved and made presentable, just as Euan had. Oddly, in breeks and plaid and with his chin shaven but his mustaches left to grow, he looked more like an imperial rather than less. In that country he was taller and fairer and blunter-featured than the rest of his kin. Here, he was a smallish dark man with a sharp, long-nosed face, playing at being one of the Calletani.

He seemed to be enjoying the game. "Don't worry, cousin," he said. "I've told them all about it. You don't have to say a thing."

"Really?" said Euan. "About what?"

"Why," said Gothard, opening his hand to reveal the starstone, "this." He flipped it into the air, then caught it, laughing as the priests flinched. "I know you thought we should bring it on gradually, but I think it's better to have it out in the open. All the better—and sooner—to get where we want to go."

"And where is that?" Euan inquired.

Gothard's eyes narrowed. "So you're going to play stupid? I told them who found it, too. You're a great giver of gifts, cousin. The stone to me, and me—with the stone—to your father. Your people will love you for it."

"They'll love me more when I help them conquer Aurelia," Euan said. "You are going to do that, yes? You won't renege?"

"I'll keep my word," said Gothard, "as long as you keep yours."

"We are all men of our word," the king said. "Tell us again, nephew, what a starstone can do for us besides be an omen for the war."

"It's a very good omen," Gothard said. "So is the fact that it came into the hands of a stone mage. The One is looking after you, uncle. This is going to win your war for you."

"I hope we can believe that," said Niall.

"Look," said Gothard. He held the stone in his cupped hands. It never seemed heavy when he held it, but it was getting darker—Euan did not think he was imagining it. It looked like a piece of sky behind the stars, or a lump of nothingness.

Things were moving in it. They were not shapes—if anything they were shapeless—but they had volition. There was intelligence in them. They groped toward anything that had light or form, and devoured it.

The priests had gone perfectly still. Euan had seen fear before. He was a fighting man. He had caused it more times than he could count. But to see fear in the eyes of priests, who by their nature feared nothing, even death itself—that gave him pause.

Gothard smiled. The movements of the dark things were reflected in his face. His eyelids were lowered. His eyes were almost sleepy. He had an oddly sated look. "Yes," he said softly. "Oh, yes."

The stone stirred in his hands. Euan's eye was not quite fast enough to follow what it did. It did not move, exactly. It *reached*.

The younger priest had no time to recoil. Formlessness coiled around him. When he opened his mouth to scream, it poured down his throat.

It ate him from the inside out. There was pain—Euan could have no doubt of that. The eyes were the last to go, and the horror in them would haunt him until he died.

When the last of the priest was gone, the thing that had consumed him flowed back into the stone. Gothard's hands that held it were unharmed. His smile was as bright as ever. "Well?" he said. "Do you like it? We can do it to a whole army if we like, or the whole world. Or just the generals. You only have to choose."

"The greatest gift of the One is oblivion," Niall said. "Would you give such a gift to our enemies?"

"Would you give such a gift to your people?"

"It's a strong thing," the king said, "and it's victory. It's also magic. We don't traffic with magic here."

"Even if it will win the war?"

"Some victories are not worth winning." Niall bent his head slightly. The remaining priest stiffened, but he laid a hand on Gothard's shoulder.

Euan watched Gothard consider blasting them both. Then evidently he decided to humor them. He let the priest raise him to his feet and lead him away.

For a long while after he was gone, Euan had nothing to say. Niall seemed even more stooped and haggard than he had when Euan came in.

At last the king said, "That's a troublesome gift you've given me."

"You're refusing it?"

Niall drew a deep breath. It rasped in ways that Euan did not like. "I'd be a fool to do that. But I don't have to let it turn on me, either."

"You know we're going to have to use him," Euan said. "Every time the Aurelians have raised armies against us, we've won a few skirmishes, even taken out a legion or two—then they've won the war. We can out-fight and out-maneuver them, but when they bring in their mages, we have no defense."

"We have the One," Niall said. "He exacts a price, but he protects us."

"The price is damnably high," said Euan.

"He takes blood and pain and leaves our souls to find their own oblivion. This thing will take them all—down to the last glimmer of existence."

"Isn't that what we want?" Euan demanded. "Isn't the Unmaking our dearest prayer?"

"Not if magic brings it," his father said. "I thank you for the gift of our kinsman. As a hostage he has considerable worth. For the rest…the One will decide. It's beyond the likes of me."

"You are the king of the people," Euan said. "Nothing should be beyond you."

"You think so?" said Niall. He seemed amused rather than angry. "You're young. You have strong dreams. When I'm gone, you'll take the people where they need to go. Until then, this is my place and this is my decision—however cowardly it may seem to you."

"Never cowardly," Euan said. "Whatever else you are, you could never be that."

Niall shrugged. "I'm what I am. Go now, amuse yourself. It's a long time until spring."

Not so long, Euan thought, to get ready for a war that had been brewing since long before either them was born—the war that would bring Aurelia down. But he kept his thoughts to himself. The winter was long enough and he had a great deal of strength to recover. He could forget his worries for a while, and simply let himself be.

But first he had a thing he must do. The women's rooms were away behind the men's, well apart from the hall. They were much smaller and darker and more crowded, and they opened on either the kitchens or the long room where the looms stood, threaded with the plaids and war cloaks of the clan.

His mother's room lay on the other side of the weavers' hall. He had to walk through the rows of weavers at their looms, aware of their stares and whispers. He was a man in women's country. He had to pay the toll accordingly.

She was not in the room, but he had not expected her to be. The bed was narrow and a little short, but it was warm and soft. He lay on it and drew up his knees. The smell of her wrapped around him, the clean scent of herbs with an undertone of musk and smoke.

He did not exactly fall asleep. He was aware of the room around him and the voices of women outside, rising over the clacking of the looms.

Still, he was not exactly awake, either. The bed had grown much wider. Someone else was lying with her back to him. Her breathing was deep and regular as if she slept, but her shoulders were tight.

Her skin was smooth, like cream, and more golden than white. Her hair was blue-black, cropped into curls. He ran his hand from her nape down the track of her spine to the sweet curve of her buttocks. She never moved, but her breathing caught.

He followed his hand with kisses. She was breathing more rapidly now. He willed her to turn and look into his face. Her name was on his lips, shaped without sound. *Valeria.*

Five

"You're not Amma."

The voice most definitely was not Valeria's, nor was it Murna's. It was a child's, sharp and imperious.

The golden-skinned lover was gone. Euan's mother's bed was as narrow as ever. A child was standing over him, glowering.

It was a young child but long-legged, with a mane of coppery hair imperfectly contained in a plait, and fierce yellow eyes. By the single plait and the half-outgrown breeks, it was male—too young yet for the warriors' house, but old enough to be well weaned.

Euan shook off the fog of the dream. "I'm not your *amma,*" he agreed. "I'm waiting for my mother."

"Wait somewhere else," the child said. "This is Amma's room."

"Not unless she shares it with my mother," Euan said. His eyes narrowed. "My name is Euan. What is yours?"

"No one's named me yet," the child said.

Euan's brows rose. A child without a name was a child without a father—because it was the father who raised the child before the clan, gave him his name and bound him to the people. This one seemed not to find any shame in it.

"Who is your mother?" Euan asked him.

"Mother's dead," the child said. "Where's the other one?"

"What—"

"The lady. Where did she go?"

Euan's nape prickled. "You saw her?"

"She's pretty," the child said.

"Very pretty," Euan said a little faintly.

He was beginning to think this was a dream, too. A child of the people who saw the unseen was either fed to the wolves or handed over to the priesthood. Somehow he could not see this bright child as a priest.

He seemed very solid, but then, so had Valeria. Maybe this was all a delusion, some sleight of Gothard's to trap Euan in the starstone.

If he let his mind run that way, he would turn as mad as Gothard. He sat up and breathed deep. The air smelled and tasted real. The child in front of him did not go away.

He was real, then. So was Euan's mother, coming up behind him. "Ah, wolfling," she said, "there you are. Brigid's looking for you."

The child shrugged that off. "There's a man in your bed, Amma."

"So I see," Murna said. "Go on now. I'll find you later and we'll visit the hound puppies."

This child was not easily bribed. His jaw set and his eyes narrowed. But Murna had raised many a child. Her own eyes narrowed even more formidably than his.

He was headstrong but he was no fool. He sulked and dragged, but he went where he was told.

The fog was leaving Euan's wits—and none too soon, either. "I don't suppose that's mine," he said.

"So his mother said." Murna sat on the stool that stood at the end of the bed.

"Who was she?"

"Her name was Deira from Dun Gralloch," Murna said. "Her father was—"

"I remember," Euan said.

That had been another winter before another war. There was a gathering of the clans around Dun Eidyn, to celebrate the dark of the year and plan the spring's battles. It would be far from Euan's first battle, but it would be his first war against the empire.

He was full of himself that night, and full of honey mead, too. He looked up from his newly emptied cup to meet a pair of eyes the color of dark amber. Gradually he took in the rest of her, smooth oval face, neatly braided hair the precise color of her eyes, and tall body, well rounded, with deep breasts and broad hips.

When he smiled at her, she did not smile back. She lowered her eyes as a modest woman should do, but she watched him sidelong.

He found her in his bed that night, curled up, asleep. When he touched her, she woke completely. She was older than he was but still a maiden—though he did not know that until after it was done. He did not know her name, either, not for the nine nights she spent in his bed.

They spoke of everything but that—the world and the people in it, the One, the empire, the dreams they had and the life they hoped for. She was the first mortal creature he told of his dearest dream, not only to be high king but to sit in the throne of the emperor in Aurelia. She did not laugh at him, either. She said, "I'll make you a son to give you strength, and to stand beside you when you take that throne."

"I'm going to do it," he said.

"I know you are," she said. Her eyes were dark in the lamplight, drinking in his face. There was something odd about her expression—not sad, exactly, but somehow wistful.

Then she kissed him and he forgot everything else. Five years after, he remembered little of that night but warmth and laughter and such pleasure as a man could never forget.

Toward dawn, she kissed him one last time, letting it linger, then drew away as she had done at the end of each night. But she paused, bending down again. Her voice was soft in his ear. "Deira," she said. "My name is Deira."

He reached for her to keep her with him. He opened his mouth to ask her the rest of it—her father's name, her clan, everything—but she slipped away. That day the people of Dun Gralloch left the gathering. That night, his bed was empty. Deira was gone.

He meant to find her. But first there was the war, then they lost it, then he was sent as a hostage into Aurelia. He had not forgotten her, but five years was a long time. He would have expected that she had married and borne another man sons— that was what any sensible woman would do.

Now that he knew what had become of her, he surprised himself with grief. Out of it, he said to his mother, "She really is dead? Was it the child?"

Murna shook her head. "There was plague the year after he was born. He lived. She died. Her father sent him to me as her last gift, with a message. *Keep him until his father comes for him.*"

"Was she dishonored? Was she mistreated? Did—"

"She was treated as well as she had a right to expect," his

mother said. "The child was allowed to live. He was sent to the king's house for fostering. That's more than most fathers would do for a daughter who despoiled herself."

"I would have asked for her as a wife," Euan said.

"I'm sure you would," said Murna without expression. "Will you give the child a name, then?"

"Of course I will," he said. "I'll do it today."

That surprised her. He did not see why, but there was no denying it. "Are you sure?"

He frowned. "Why? Is there a reason why I shouldn't?"

"No," said Murna. "No reason."

That was not the truth, but something kept him from challenging her. There would be time later, he told himself. He had come here to ask her advice, not to find a son—and those other matters were pressing.

It was odd how, after all that had happened, even to the unmaking of a priest, Euan remembered little of what he said to his mother or she to him. But he remembered every moment of the exchange with his son.

That was his son—the child of his body. He was as sure of that as he was of his own name and ancestry. He would give the boy a name of his own and the life that went with it, first-born son of a prince of the Calletani.

Murna brought the boy into the hall after the men had gathered there but before the day's meal had been spread on the tables. That was the time for petitions and disputes, for men to come to the king with things that needed doing or settling.

Euan had been listening carefully to each one. Some needed his father's decision, others the warleaders' or the priests'. As he had when he was young, he committed each to memory.

He did not hold his breath waiting for his mother to bring

the child. She might make him send for the boy—and he was prepared to do that.

Late in the proceedings, as two men of the warband argued heatedly over the ownership of a crooked-horned cow, Euan saw his mother standing among the rest of the petitioners. There was a plaid over her head as if she had been a common woman. The child was too small to see among so many grown folk, but Murna looked down once and said something.

Euan did not need that kind of proof. The boy was here. He knew it in his gut.

His heart was racing. For a man to claim a son was a great thing. For a man to do it the day after he had come home from a long exile was greater still. It was like an omen, a promise that his dream would come true.

The petitions that had fascinated him now seemed terribly tedious. There were so many and they were so trivial. If they stretched out much longer, there would be no time.

Just as he was about to rise up and roar his mother's name, the last petitioner finished his rambling tale and received quick justice from the king. Euan paid no attention. His eyes were on the child, whom at last he could see.

His child. His son. No one could mistake it. There was no sign of his mother in him except for a certain air, a deep and inborn calm. He was long-limbed and rangy like a young wolf, and his eyes were wolf eyes, amber-gold and slanting in the long planes of his face.

He was royal-clan Calletani, like his father and grandfather and all their fathers before them. The One himself had marked him for what he was.

He stood straight beside his grandmother. There was no fear in him, only curiosity. His eyes were wide, taking in everything.

When those eyes fell on Euan, they brightened. He pulled

free from his grandmother, who was just beginning to bow in front of the king, and sprang into Euan's arms.

Euan was as startled as everyone else. The child was heavier than he looked, and strong.

"No need to guess whose litter *that* cub came from," someone said.

Euan readied a glare to sweep across the hall, but the child laughed. His mirth was rang out in the silence. Euan swung him onto his shoulder and said so they all could hear, "You guessed right. I'm claiming him. He's my blood and bone, the wolf-cub of the Calletani. I name him Conor, and bid you all name him likewise."

The name ran around the room in a low roll of sound. *Conor…Conor…Conor.*

Euan looked up into the boy's face. His head was tilted. He was listening hard. When the sound of his name had died down, he nodded. "That's my name," he said. "My name is Conor."

"That was well done," Gothard said.

Conor was back among the women again. The night's meal had turned into a celebration, welcoming a new man-child to the clan. Euan staggered out of it, aswim with the last of the wine, to find Gothard squatting in front of the jakes.

He or someone had made a cage of gold wire for the starstone and hung it around his neck. It swung as he rocked, drinking darkness out of the air. "Well done," he repeated. "Oh, so well done. Show the people you've got what a king needs—balls and gall and enough sense to get yourself an heir before it's too late."

"I'm glad you approve," Euan said. He made no effort to sound as if he meant it.

"I only wonder," Gothard said, rocking and smiling, with the starstone swinging and swinging, "seeing how strongly all the people resist the very idea of magic, how you managed to beget a child who fairly crackles with it."

Euan had no memory of movement. One moment he was standing on one leg, wondering if he should piss in the bastard's face to relieve himself and shut him up. The next, his hand was locked around Gothard's throat.

The stone did not blast him. He found that interesting.

He spoke very carefully, enunciating each word. "My son is not a mage."

"You know he is," Gothard said.

Euan's fingers tightened. Gothard turned a gratifying shade of crimson. "Whatever you think he is," Euan said, "or think you may turn him into, you will keep your claws off him. If I find even the slightest hint that you have touched him or burdened him with so much as a word, I will flay you alive and bathe you in salt."

He saw how Gothard's eyes flickered. His own stayed fixed on that purpling face. "Don't think your stone will save you. It was mine first. It remembers. And so should you. Hands and magic off my son. Do you understand?"

Gothard's eyes had begun to bulge. It was a pity, Euan thought, that he needed a stone mage to exploit the full power of the stone. This was the only one he was likely to get. Gothard had to go on breathing—as much as Euan might wish otherwise.

He let Gothard go. Gothard fell over, gagging and choking, wheezing for breath. Euan left him to it.

He could feel Gothard's eyes on his back as he went into the jakes. The hate in them was strong enough to make his skin twitch.

He shrugged it off. As long as they needed each other, there would be no killing on either side, and no Unmaking, either. After that, the One would provide. It would give Euan great pleasure to finish what he had begun.

Six

The Mountain was singing. It was a deep song, far below the edge of hearing, but it thrummed in Valeria's bones. When she looked up from the shelter of the citadel toward that jagged peak, gleaming white against the piercing blue of the sky, and heard the great sound that came out of it, she knew a profound and almost unbearable joy.

The Mountain was locked in snow. Winter, like the claws of grief and irretrievable loss, gripped the school as if it would never let go. Yet the sun was just a fraction stronger and the air just a whisper warmer. And the Mountain sent out the Call.

It was strange to hear it and know what it was and feel the power of it, but to be no part of it. She had been Called a year before, and now the Mountain had her. This new compulsion, renewed every spring for a thousand years, was meant for someone else. Many someones, she hoped. The school needed as many new riders as the gods would deign to send.

* * *

When the first of the Called came in, she was schooling Sabata in the riding court nearest the southward gate. It was the first day in months that anyone had been able to ride under the sky. The grass around the edges of the court was just beginning to show a glimmer of green.

The raked sand of the arena was a little damp from the winter's rains, but Sabata moved lightly on it. He liked its softness and its slight springiness.

In fact he was moving a little too lightly. He was fresh and not particularly obedient, and there was a twitch in his back that warned her to be alert.

Sabata was a god and a Great One, but he was also a stallion, and spring was in his blood. He could smell the mares on the other side of the school, in the School of War. If he had had his way, he would have gone courting and won himself a band of them.

"You have a high opinion of yourself," she said as he tried for the dozenth time to veer off toward the gate. He had not succeeded yet, but he was determined to keep trying. Discipline was the last thing he wanted to think about just then.

"Discipline is the first virtue of a rider," Valeria said.

Sabata shook his head and snorted. There was a distinct hump in his back under the saddle. *He* was not a rider, and very glad he was of it, too.

Just as he left the ground, a stranger's startled face blurred past her. It was only an instant's distraction, but that was enough for Sabata. He exploded in more directions than she could count.

It was a long way to the ground. She had ample time to tuck and roll. She also had time to contemplate the virtue of discipline, and to be struck by the humor of it all.

She tumbled to a halt with a mouthful of sand and a collection of entirely new bruises, and no breath for the laughter that was trying to bubble out of her.

Two faces stared down at her. One was long and silver-white and gratifyingly embarrassed. The other was oval and brown and incontestably human.

"Rider?" the boy said. "Are you dying?"

She did not want to sit up. She wanted to lie in the sand and count her bones and try not to think about how it would feel when she moved. Still, there was Sabata, belatedly appalled at what he had done to his rider, and this child whom she had never seen before, whose eyes looked ready to pop out of his head.

She sat up very carefully. Her head stayed on her shoulders. All the parts of her moved more or less as they should. Nothing was broken, even the arm that still ached when she moved it just so. There was a ringing in her ears, but that was the Mountain.

It was also the boy who had startled her into falling off her stallion. He was so full of the Call that she was amazed he could walk and talk.

He was otherwise perfectly ordinary, with a smooth, olive-skinned face and big dark eyes and curly black hair. His clothes were plain and had seen a great deal of use. He looked as if he had been traveling for days without enough to eat.

"You're not dying," he said. He sounded relieved. He held out a grubby hand.

She let him pull her to her feet. He was stronger than he looked. "How did you get here?" she asked him.

"I walked through the gate," he said.

"Nobody met you?"

He shook his head. "There were people, but nobody said anything. I kept walking until I came here." His eyes turned to Sabata and melted—there was no other word for it. "Is he—is that—"

"That is Sabata," Valeria said.

The boy's hand stretched out as if he could not help himself. Valeria made no effort to stop him. Sabata did not move away, either, which was interesting. No one could lay a hand on Sabata unless he wanted it—and mostly he did not.

He suffered this child to stroke his neck and find the particular spot in the middle and rub it until his lip stretched and began to quiver. The boy was enthralled. "Beautiful," he said dreamily. "So beautiful."

"*He* certainly thinks so," Valeria said. "We have exercises to finish. If you can wait, I'll show you where to go."

"Oh, yes," the boy said. "I can wait. You'll let me watch?"

"I won't be falling off again," Valeria said firmly. She lowered a glare at Sabata. "Here, sir."

Sabata had had his fill of defiance for the day. He came to her hand and stood perfectly still for her to mount. That was not as graceful as usual—some of her bruises were in difficult places—but she managed.

All the while she rode, the boy watched, rapt. He was not only full of the Call. He was full of magic. He had control over it—not like one of last year's Called, whom she still remembered with pain. This one would not give way to temper and lash out with killing force.

It was not the best ride she had ever had. She was stiff and sore, and Sabata was trying a little too hard. She finished on as good a note as she could, then with the boy trailing blissfully behind, took Sabata to his stable.

Some of the stallions were in their stalls, sleeping or chewing drowsily on bits of hay. Most were out with their riders in various of the halls and riding courts, or enjoying an hour's liberty in one of the paddocks. By that time Valeria had learned that the boy's name was Lucius, that he came from a town not far from the Mountain, and that he was a journeyman of the order of Oneiromancers.

He was helping Valeria take off Sabata's saddle and bridle and brush out the stallion's moon-colored coat. She paused as he told her what he was, staring at him over the broad pale back. "You're a dream-mage? What are you doing *here*?"

"I dreamed that I was Called," he said.

"Obviously," said Valeria. "Mages have been Called from other orders before. But just Beastmasters, I thought, and the occasional Augur. I didn't think—"

"I didn't, either," he said, "but here I am. Like you. Is a woman supposed to be a rider?"

"No," said Valeria.

"Well," said Lucius, "there you are."

He seemed to think that her existence explained his. She did not see what that had to do with it, but she was disinclined just then to argue. She went on with what she had been doing, frowning slightly.

When Sabata was clean and brushed and content with a manger full of hay, and the saddle and bridle were cleaned and put away, Valeria took the visibly reluctant Lucius to the rider-candidates' dormitory.

He was not the only one there after all. Two more had come in while he was basking in Sabata's presence. They both wore the uniform of the legions, and they were older than Valeria would have thought a rider-candidate could be. One must have been well up in his twenties.

First Rider Andres, who had taken charge of the rider-candidates in her year, as well, had them in hand. He raised a brow at Lucius's escort, but he did not say anything in front of the candidates except, "Three on the first day. That's a good number."

"Let's hope it's an omen," Valeria said. The legionaries were staring at her as if they not only knew who and what she was, they were in awe of her.

That was not comfortable. She could call it a strategic retreat, or she could regard it as a rout. Either way, she escaped those wide eyes and worshipful faces.

Valeria came to bed late. There had been lessons in history and politics and various facets of the horse magic, and a session in the library that had run through dinner. Then she had gone with a handful of riders to raid the kitchens. By the time she left the last of them at his door, the hour was well on its way toward midnight.

The lamp by the bed was lit, its flame trimmed low. The fire was banked in the hearth, but it shed just enough heat to take the edge off the chill.

Kerrec was in bed and apparently asleep. All she could see of him was a heap of blankets.

She dropped her clothes, shuddering as cold air touched her skin, and slid in beside him. His back was turned to her, his face to the wall. She pressed herself softly against him and kissed his nape where the black curls were clipped short.

He lay perfectly still. Her hand ran down his side, tracing the familiar gaps and ridges of scars. They were all healed now, the deep pain gone, and some had begun to fade.

She let her touch bring a little more healing, a little more warmth. He should have roused then and turned, but he never moved.

She sighed inaudibly. She had been full of things to tell him, but he was obviously determined not to wake.

Well, she thought, he worked hard these days—harder than she. He was the only First Rider left from the time before—that was what everyone called it now. Before the Great Dance that had ended with six riders dead and the empire's fate so nearly turned toward destruction. It was only six months ago, just half a year, but it divided the world.

He had been the youngest. Now he was the chief of the First Riders. The others were all new to their office, and none too ready for it, either. They were doing well enough now, all things considered, but it had been a bitter winter. The school still mourned its dead, and would mourn them for a long while yet.

Much more than lives had been lost in that Dance. Strong magic and great art were gone, the province of masters who had devoted decades to the mastery of the stallion magic. Nothing but time could bring that back—if it could be brought back. Some of what was gone might never be recovered.

Valeria laid her cheek on Kerrec's shoulder and closed her eyes. She wanted to hold him tight, but she knew better than to try that. He had paid a high price to be here, alive and safe. The scars on his body were the least of it. His heart and soul had been taken apart and were still healing slowly. His magic…

It was mending. He was strong. He worked harder than anyone and tested himself more sternly. He was thriving.

She had to believe that. They had done no more than sleep in each other's arms—or he in hers, if she was going to be exact—for weeks. Months? She did not remember, probably because she did not want to.

She was still here. That was enough. He was first among the First. He could order her out and she would have to go, because she had sworn herself to a rider's discipline, and obedience was part of it.

He had done no such thing. He wanted her here, even if he did not want her the way he had in the autumn and through the early winter, night after night. The memory of those nights could still warm her.

They would come back. He was tired, that was all.

So was she. She should sleep. She had another long day tomorrow, and long days after that.

A rider's discipline could accomplish this as well as anything else. She closed her eyes and willed herself to sleep. After a while, she succeeded.

Seven

Kerrec lay motionless. Valeria was at last and mercifully asleep.

Her dream brushed the edges of his awareness. It was a dim thing, tinged with unease, but the white power of the stallions surrounded it. They guarded her even in dreams.

She could never know how much he wanted to turn and take her in his arms and kiss her until she was dizzy. But if he did that, he would have to open himself to her, and she would know.

She could not know. No one could. They had to believe that he was whole. He had to be. He could not afford to be broken.

During the day he could hold himself together. Much of what he did required no magic, or could be done with what little he had. He could still ride—that much had not left him. He could teach others to ride, and through the movements see the patterns that shaped the world.

The nights were another matter. He had to sleep, but in sleep were dreams.

At first he had been able to keep them at bay, even change them. His stallion had helped him. As winter went on, the dreams had grown worse.

Now he did not even need to sleep to hear that voice whispering and whispering, or to see the featureless mask of a Brother of Pain. Sometimes there was a stranger's face behind it. More often there was one he knew all too well.

He never dreamed, awake or asleep, of the body's pain. That had been terrible enough when it happened, and the scars would be with him until he died, but it was not his body that the Brother of Pain had set out to break. He had been commanded to break Kerrec's mind and destroy his soul.

He had had to leave the task unfinished, but by then it was too far along to stop. What had been carried out of that place which Kerrec still could barely remember, had been the shattered remnants of a man.

The shards had begun to mend themselves. Kerrec's magic had grown again, slowly but surely. He had dared to hope that he would get his old self back.

Then the healing had stopped and the edges of his spirit had begun to unravel. It was as if the Brother of Pain had reached out from the other side of the dream world and set his hooks in Kerrec's soul again, even deeper than before.

Every night now, the whisper was louder, echoing inside his skull. *What use is a dead prince in a living world? What purpose is there in this magic that you pride yourself in? What is order, discipline, art and mastery, but empty show? The world is no better for it. Too often it is worse. Give it up. Let it go. Set yourself free.*

Every night he struggled to remember what he had been before. He had been a master of his art, endowed with magic of great power and beauty. His discipline had been impeccable. He had mastered the world's patterns and could bend them to his will.

That was gone. The whole glorious edifice had fallen into ruin. All that was left was a confusion of shards, grinding on one another like shattered bone.

Very carefully he eased out of Valeria's arms. It hurt to leave her—but it hurt more to stay. She was everything that he had been and more.

It was not envy that he felt. It was grief. He should have been her match, not a broken thing that she could only pity.

He was unprepared for the wave of sheer, raw rage that surged through him. The rage had a source—a name.

Gothard.

He could name the red blackness that laired in the pit of his stomach, too. It was hate. Gothard had done this to him. Gothard had given the Brother of Pain his orders. Gothard's malice and spite had broken Kerrec's mind and shattered his magic.

Gothard his brother, Gothard the half-blood, had nothing but loathing for his brother and sister who were legitimate as he was not, and for his father who had sired him on a hostage. He wanted them all dead—and he had come damnably close to succeeding.

He had escaped defeat and fled from the reckoning. No one, even mages, had been able to find him. But Kerrec knew where he was. He was in Kerrec's mind, taking it apart fragment by fragment.

Somewhere, in the flesh, he was waiting. Kerrec had no doubt that he was preparing a new assault on everything and every person who had ever dealt him a slight, real or imagined. Gothard would not give up until they were all destroyed.

With shaking hands, Kerrec pulled on breeches and coat and boots. It was halfway between midnight and dawn. The school was asleep. Even the cooks had not yet awakened to begin the day's baking.

In the stillness of the deep night, the Call grated on his raw edges. He had enough power, just, to shut it out.

He went to the one place where he could find something resembling peace. The stallions slept in their stable, each of them shining faintly, so that the stone-vaulted hall with its rows of stalls glowed as if with moonlight.

Petra's stall was midway down the eastern aisle, between the young Great One Sabata and the Master's gentle, ram-nosed Icarra. Kerrec's friend and teacher cocked an ear as he slipped into the stall, but did not otherwise interrupt his dream.

Kerrec lay on the straw in the shelter of those heavy-boned white legs. Petra lowered his head. His breath ruffled Kerrec's hair. He sighed and sank deeper into sleep.

Even here, Kerrec could not sleep, but it did not matter. He was safe. He drew into a knot and closed his eyes, letting pain and self-pity drain away. All that was left behind was quiet, and blessed emptiness.

Valeria knew that she was dreaming. Even so, it was strikingly real.

She was sitting at dinner in her mother's house. They were all there, all her family, her three sisters and her brothers Niall and Garin, and even Rodry and Lucius who had gone off to join the legions. The younger ones looked exactly as they had the last time she saw them, almost a year ago to the day.

She was wearing rider's clothes. Her sister Caia curled her lip at the grey wool tunic and close-cut leather breeches. Caia was dressed for a wedding in a dress so stiff with embroidery that it could have stood up on its own. There were flowers in her hair, autumn flowers, purple and gold and white.

She glowered at Valeria. "How could you run away like that? Don't you realize how it looked? You ruined my wedding!"

"There now," their mother said in her most quelling tone. "That will be enough of that. You had a perfectly acceptable wedding."

Caia's sense of injury was too great even to yield to Morag's displeasure. "It was a solid month late, and half the cousins couldn't come because they had to get in the harvest. And all anyone could talk about was *her.*" Her finger stabbed toward Valeria. "It should have been *my* day. Why did she have to go and spoil it?"

"I didn't mean—" Valeria began.

"You never do," said Caia, "but you always do."

That made sense in Caia's view of the world. Valeria found that her eyes were stinging with tears.

Rodry cuffed Valeria lightly, but still hard enough to make her ears ring. "Don't mind her," he said. "She's just jealous because her lover is a live smith instead of a dead imperial heir. That's how girls are, you know. Princes, even dead, are better than anything else."

"Kerrec is not dead," Valeria said.

"Prince Ambrosius lies in his tomb," said Rodry. "It's empty, of course. But who notices that?"

"That was his father," Valeria tried to explain, "being furious that his heir was Called to the Mountain instead of the throne. He declared him dead and stopped acknowledging his existence until there was no other choice. Isn't that what Mother has done to me? I'll be amazed if she's done anything else."

"Mother knows you're alive," Rodry said. "She's not happy about it, but you can hardly expect her to be. She had a life all planned for you, too."

"So did the gods," said Valeria. "Even Mother isn't strong enough to stand in their way."

"Don't tell her that," her brother said, not quite laughing.

He bent toward her and kissed her on the forehead. "I'll see you soon."

She frowned. "What—"

The dream was whirling away. The end of it went briefly strange. It was dark, a swirl of nothingness. She dared not look into it. If she did, she would drown—all of her, heart and soul and living consciousness. Every part of her would be Unmade.

The Unmaking blurred into the bell that summoned the riders to their morning duties. Valeria sat up fuzzily. The dream faded into a faint, dull miasma overlaid with her family's faces.

Kerrec was gone. He had got up before her, as all too usual lately.

She would be late if she dallied much longer. She stumbled out of bed, wincing at the bruises that had set hard in the night, and washed in the basin. The cold water roused her somewhat, though her mind was still full of fog. She pulled on the first clean clothes that came to hand and set off for the stables.

Half a dozen more of the Called came in that morning, and another handful by evening. There had never been that many so soon after the Mountain began its singing. Some of the younger riders had a wager that the candidates' dormitory would be full by testing day.

That would be over a hundred—twelve eights. One or two wagered that even more would come, as many as sixteen eights, which had not happened in all the years since the school was founded.

"We'll be hanging hammocks from the rafters," Iliya said at breakfast after the stallions had been fed and their stalls thoroughly cleaned. The thought made him laugh. Iliya was a singer and teller of tales when he was not studying to be a rider. He found everything delightful, because sooner or later it would go into a song.

Paulus was as sour as Iliya was sweet. He glared down his long aristocratic nose and said, "You are all fools. There has never been a full complement of candidates, not in a thousand years."

"There was never a woman before last year," Batu pointed out from across the table. He was the most exotic of the four, big and broad, with skin so black it gleamed blue. He had never even seen a horse before the Call drew him out of his mother's house, far away in the uttermost south of the empire.

Valeria, most definitely the oddest since she was the first woman ever to be Called to the Mountain, offered a wan reflection of his wide white smile. "Are you wagering that more will come?"

"That's with the gods," he said.

"*More* females." Paulus shuddered. "Even one is too many."

"Everything's changing," Batu said. "We'll have to change with it. That's what we were Called for."

"We were Called to ride the white gods in the Dance of Time," Paulus said stiffly. "That is all we are for. Everything leads to that. Nothing else matters."

"I'm rather partial to wine and song myself," Iliya said. He drained his cup of hot herb tea and licked his lips, as satisfied with himself as a cat.

Valeria was long accustomed to his face, but once in a great while she happened to notice that in its way it was as unusual as Batu's. In shape and coloring it was ordinary enough, with olive-brown skin and sharply carved features, but he was a chieftain's son from the deserts of Gebu. The marks of his rank were tattooed in vivid swirls on his cheekbones and forehead.

The Call had brought them here from all over the empire.

They had passed test after test, and were still passing them—as they would do for as long as they served the gods on the Mountain.

She looked from her friends' faces to others in the hall. Most of the lesser riders were there this morning. The four First Riders dined in their own, much smaller hall, usually with the Master of the school for company. Today Master Nikos was here, sitting at the head table with a handful of Second Riders.

He caught her glance and nodded slightly. Valeria's existence was an ongoing difficulty, but after she had brought all the stallions together to mend the broken Dance, he had had to concede that she belonged among the riders. To his credit, he had accepted the inevitable with good grace—which was more than could be said for some of the others.

He was probably praying that all of this year's Called were male. She could hardly blame him. They had troubles enough as it was.

She pushed away her half-full bowl and rose. The others had had the same thought. There was a classroom waiting and a full morning of lessons, then a full afternoon in the saddle.

Iliya danced ahead of her, singing irrepressibly, though Paulus growled at him to stop his bloody caterwauling. Batu strode easily beside Valeria. He was smiling.

It was a good morning, he was thinking, clear for her to read. Most mornings were, these days, though the school had come through a hell or two to get there.

Maybe there were more hells ahead. Maybe some would be worse, but that did not trouble him, either. Batu, better than any of them, had mastered the art of living as the stallions did, in the perpetual present.

Eight

When winter's back broke, so did the king's spirit. He had been fading since the dark of the year, as if he had hung on until his heir came back. Now that Euan Rohe was here, with an acknowledged son of his own, he could let go.

It was soft and slow, as deaths went. He slept more and more and sat in hall less and less. Little by little the king's various offices fell to Euan.

There were guards on the gates now, inner and outer. The roads were watched and the borders guarded. Nothing could take the clan by surprise.

Spring came with the breaking of ice and the howling of wind, and storms that lashed sleet and rain instead of sleet and snow. The clan began to emerge from its winter's idleness. The hall became a practice ground. Even when the storms raged, men of the clan went out hunting or raiding.

Scouts were coming in, nearly as ragged as Euan had been.

The empire was moving. The emperor and his legions were gathering for war.

Gothard spent most of his time with the priests as either their prisoner or their pupil—or maybe he was their master. Euan was not minded to inquire. Gothard stayed out of Euan's way, and that suited Euan perfectly.

On the day when the last of the ice broke in the rivers, the latest storm had blown away. Sun shone dazzling bright on the winter-wearied dun. Euan thought he might go hunting boar. He was tired of stringy roast ox and even more tired of being penned up in walls.

On his way to the hall to call up a hunt, he came face-to-face with Gothard. If he wanted to give himself a fit of the shudders, he could reflect that he had been looking straight down the passage and seen Gothard nowhere until he appeared directly in front of Euan.

"It's happening," Gothard said.

Mages, Euan thought sourly. "What is happening? War?"

"Among other things." Gothard smiled. Whatever he was thinking, it gave him great pleasure. "You'd better be ready. As soon as the weather breaks, the high king's calling the muster."

"Tell me something I don't know," Euan said—unwisely, maybe.

"I don't think so," Gothard said.

"I command you."

"I'm sure you do."

The skin tightened between Euan's shoulder blades. He was not sure what he wanted to say yet. When he was, he would say it, no matter what it cost.

At this particular moment, he pushed past Gothard. He had a boar to hunt, and the men were waiting.

* * *

Euan's uneasiness stayed with him through the hunt and the killing of the boar and the return to the dun. Nothing there had changed. The king was a little weaker, a little greyer, but that had been going on for months.

Every night, no matter the hour, he looked in on Conor first, then his father. Tonight he found himself turning toward his father's sleeping room. He refused to call it a premonition. Gothard had raised his hackles. He had to be sure there was nothing in it.

Niall was asleep. Lamps burned in a cluster, spoils of the last war with Aurelia. Murna sat beside the bed, stitching at a linen shirt.

Euan wanted to believe in that quiet ordinariness, but he kept seeing Gothard's face. There was nothing ordinary here. The quiet was a lie.

His mother looked up. Her eyes were somber. "Tomorrow you should send out the summons to clan gathering," she said.

Euan nodded. That was the king's duty, but the king was past performing it. The clans should have gathered to plan this year's war before Euan came back—and here it was nearly spring.

"Better late than never," he said. Then, "How long do you think he has?"

"The One knows," she said.

Euan suspected that one other was privy to that knowledge. He bowed to his father, though Niall was too far gone to see. "I'll be back," he said to his mother. "Don't let anyone else near him while I'm gone."

Her eyes widened slightly, but she asked no questions. She took up her stitching again.

It was only after Euan had passed the door that it dawned on him. That was not a shirt she was making. It was a shroud.

* * *

Euan had a fair hunt to find Gothard. He was not in the priests' house—as far as Euan dared to enter it—nor was he in the guesthouse or the young men's house or the hall. At last, in the darkness before dawn, Euan clambered up the crumbling stair to the top of the tower.

It was a steep and dangerous way in the dark, but Euan had climbed it often enough when he was younger. His feet still remembered which steps were safe and which were rotten. There were more of the latter now, one or two of which nearly cost him his neck, but he made his way past them.

The tower's roof had once been higher—by how much, even legend was not sure. It was high enough now that if Euan stood at the parapet he could see clear across the moor to the low squat of hill that was Dun Gralloch.

Gothard was in the middle of the roof, lying on his back with his eyes full of starlight. Euan considered throttling him, but that could grow tedious with repetition. He stood over Gothard instead, blocking the starlight, and said, "Take your spell off my father."

Gothard blinked as if he had roused from a dream. "What? Spell? There is no—"

"Poison, then. Whatever it is, undo it."

"I've done nothing," Gothard said.

"I don't believe you."

"I can see why not," said Gothard, "but it is true. He's dying all by himself."

"He was before you came here," Euan said. "You've been kindly helping him on his way. Don't try to deny it again. I can smell magic. He reeks of it."

"Therefore it must be my magic?" Gothard inquired.

"Who else would it be? And don't," said Euan through clenched teeth, "go blaming my son."

"I wouldn't dream of it," Gothard said. He sat up. "I have something for you. Look."

He tossed it toward Euan. Euan caught it before it could fall.

It was a stone, round and flat and polished smooth. His hand tingled when he caught it. He almost flung it down, but his fingers closed over it instead. "What's this? A spell to finish my father off?"

"It's a seeing-stone," said Gothard. "Look in it. Think of what you want to see, and there it will be. Wouldn't you like to know where the emperor's armies are?"

"You know I would," Euan said. "What's the price?"

"It's part of our bargain," said Gothard. "If it helps you win the war, so much the better."

Euan looked down at the stone. It was the size and shape of the mirror that an imperial lady would carry with her to ascertain that her face was properly painted. Not, he thought, that one particular imperial woman would care for such a thing.

The stone shimmered as if reflecting starlight. Before he could turn his eyes away, the shimmer brightened and cleared. She was there, with the glow of lamplight on her face, turning the pages of a book.

Her hair was longer than he remembered but still cut short. She was wearing the grey coat of a rider-candidate. That was what, more than anything else, she had wanted. It seemed that she had won it.

He could have reached out and touched her. It was a great effort to resist.

She seemed unaware of his eyes on her. When he wondered who else was in the room with her, the stone showed him an empty room and, more to the point, an empty bed.

It surprised him how glad he was to see that. Euan was alive and standing on this tower because of her, but he was not the man she had chosen. That one...

The vision in the stone began to shift. Euan wrenched his mind away from Valeria's lover. He did not want to see the man or know where he was or even if he was alive. He turned his thoughts to the emperor instead.

And there was Artorius to the life, asleep in a lofty bed, not only alive but clearly well—despite what Gothard had said of him.

"You see?" Gothard said in his ear. "Ask it to show you armies and it will—and all their plans and strategies, too. Imagine a king of the people with such a toy. For once in all the years of war between the people and the empire, one of our kings will have the same advantage as the emperor and his generals."

"'Our' kings?" Euan asked. "You've taken sides, have you?"

"It's not obvious?"

"With you, I never know." Euan covered the stone and slipped it into his belt. "I don't suppose there's a way to stop the enemy from seeing what we're up to."

"There might be," said Gothard. "It's more magic. What will your father say to that?"

"When he wakes, I'll ask him," Euan said.

Gothard smiled. The words hung in the air, though he had not said them. *Ah, but will he wake?*

"If he doesn't," Euan said very softly, "I will know whose fault it is."

"And then what will you do? Hand me over to the priests all over again? They're afraid of me, cousin. They worship oblivion but none of them is in a great hurry to get there."

"I am reminded," said Euan, "of the man who took a snake for a wife. She cooked his dinner, wove his war cloaks, and bore his children for other women to suckle—because after all, snakes have no breasts. She was all the wife a man could ask for, and she served him in every way. Then one night, after she had fed him his dinner and made love to him until he roared like a bull, she sank her fangs in his neck."

"And so he died," said Gothard, "but he died happy. He had everything he wanted."

"Except his life," Euan said.

Gothard shrugged. "What's life for a man who has to live weak, sick and old? Maybe she was giving him a gift. You worship the One, whose dearest child is nothingness. You should understand that."

"Not when it comes to my father."

"Is that sentiment, cousin?" said Gothard. "I'd never have thought to see it in you. The old man is dying of his own accord and in his own time. When he's gone, you'll be king of the Calletani—which is halfway to where you want to be. I should think you'd embrace it."

Euan's head was aching. Gothard's voice buzzed in his ears. It was a webwork of lies and half lies and twisted truth, but he could not muster an answer to it. It wanted him to give up, lie back, and let it happen.

What else could he do? He had taken this snake to wife. He used it, just as it used him. He had to hope that when the fangs flashed toward his neck, he was fast enough to get away.

Nine

When Euan came down from the tower, the king was dead. He had no need to hear the wailing of the women from the hall. He felt it in his gut, a deep emptiness that left him cold and still.

It did not matter then who was to blame. The king was dead, and the clans must gather as soon as they could come to Dun Eidyn—not only to make war but to make a king.

By the evening of the day after the king died, Dun Gralloch's chieftain and his warband had come in, and Dun Brenin's warriors were close behind. By the third day, seven of the nine clans of the Calletani had gathered, including the royal clan. The others had sent messengers to promise that they would be there within a day or two.

Euan was still numb. He was doing what needed to be done, but he felt nothing. The women wailing, the men chanting death songs, left him cold.

Tomorrow they would lay the king in his barrow. Tonight the feasting grew raucous, with the clansmen draining barrels of ale as if it had been water. Euan had had a cup or two, but he had barely tasted it.

He left the high table and the emptiness of the royal seat to wander through the hall. Down past the hearth, some of the young men were dancing. It was a war dance, with stamping feet and flashing blades—perfectly suited to his mood.

He seized a blade from a willing hand and leaped into the dance. His blood thundered in his ears. He stamped, slashed, spun.

He came face to face with his image, armed as he was, laughing as he met blade with blade. The others drew back, clapping and beating time with their feet. To that rough and potent music, the two of them fought the battle through to the final crossing of blades.

Euan was breathing hard. Sweat ran down his back and sides. He dropped his sword and roared. "Conory! By the One—you're alive!"

"Hell wouldn't have me," his cousin said in mock regret.

They stood grinning at one another. Conory looked so like Euan that he had, more than once, claimed Euan's name and place—a useful skill for eluding nursemaids and imperial guards. Euan seized him by the shoulders and shook him. "Damn your eyes, man. Where have you been? Dun Carrig came in yesterday."

"And so did I," said Conory. "Damn *your* eyes. I was right in front of you."

"Then I'm a blind man," Euan said, "and you are a reprobate. I mourned you all for dead."

"Not likely," said another voice he knew well.

He squinted in the firelight. "Cyllan? You, too?"

"And Donal and Cieran and Strahan," said Conory.

They were all there, drawing in from the edges of the circle—the friends of his youth, his fellow hostages, his old warband. Only one was missing, and that one Euan himself had cast out while they were still in the empire.

The numbness left him. In its place was a most peculiar mingling of grief and gladness. It felt like ice breaking in the rivers and spring storms roaring down on the frozen moors.

It was dangerous because it was so strong. It was a marvel, a miracle—a sign. It made him laugh from the depths of his belly, down below the sorrow.

With his warband around him, he had his balance. He could look at the world and see it clearly. He felt as if he had lost an arm but then found it again. He was finally whole.

Now he could claim the kingship. He swept them with him, back into another dance, a spring dance, half war and half exuberant mating.

As he danced, he saw in his head the Dance of the white stallions in Aurelia. The patterns they traced were almost the same as those his feet were beating out on the floor of this hall—his father's hall. His hall.

He could shape time and fate, too. Why not? He was king. Now that he had his warband again, out of all hope and expectation, the rest would follow.

They raised the old king's barrow down below the dun, in the dark valley where the kings of the Calletani had lain since they first came to this country. Far down the valley, the oldest barrows had grown into the earth, covered over with grass and heather. Here at the valley's head, almost out into the light, the new barrow rose up, its lines as raw and harsh as grief.

The priests made the sacrifice, the bodies of nine battle captives and nine fair women. The women died quietly, like the good handmaidens they were meant to be. The men screamed and fought and called down curses.

Their death was slow and hard, a death of tiny cuts and minute scraps of skin peeled off slowly, one by one. Multiplied nine times, it opened the way for the king's spirit, freeing it to seek oblivion in the One.

It was a long ritual, and not easy to watch. Euan, with his warband around him like a well-loved cloak, endured it as they all did, to honor the king.

Niall lay on his bier, covered with a blood-red mantle—the cloak of an imperial general. His shrunken body barely lifted the pall.

His weapons were laid beside him and his shield was at his feet. They would go into the barrow with him, along with a great store of gold and precious things. The standards of the two legions were among them, and enough imperial gold to ransom a king.

There was no ransom that would bring a man back from the dead. Euan felt the grief rising to choke him. For once he let it. Today it could rule him as it would. Tomorrow he had to be king.

When the rite was finished and the bodies of the captives had stopped twitching, the king went at last into his barrow. No living man went with him. The men who carried him down, and after him the bodies of his escort, stayed in the barrow when their task was done. Each had a knife for his own throat, or else he would die when the air ran out, buried under earth and stone.

Euan lent his hand to the sealing of the tomb. The stones were heavy. He was glad of the pain and the grueling effort. They cleansed him in spirit as well as body.

It was dark when they finished. The stars were fiercely bright. The ground crackled with frost. It crunched underfoot as the whole long column of them, clan upon clan, walked away from the valley and the barrow.

No one spoke or sang. That was their last tribute, that gift of silence.

The sun rose with a blaring of trumpets and a thunder of drums. The long dark night was over. Mourning would go on for the women, but for the men it was a new day.

Today they would make a king. In other times or other clans there would be a great contest, a battle among all presumptive heirs. Whoever won the battle could call himself king.

When Euan Rohe came out of his room after a sleepless night, the warbands of all the clans were waiting in the hall, watchful and silent. Here and there, someone twitched, thinking maybe to raise the challenge—but the men around him cuffed him into submission.

Euan's own warband stood like a guard of honor. Cyllan and Strahan had bruises and satisfied expressions. The others looked merely satisfied.

Euan would beat the story out of them later. His eyes took in the mass of faces.

They were taking him in, too, and rightly. He had been away for years, living among imperials, learning their ways and their language and their arts of war and peace. Maybe his own people could no longer trust him. Maybe he had changed too much to rule them as they needed to be ruled.

He had to answer that—the sooner, the better. He sprang up onto the nearest table and stamped his foot. The sound of boot-heel on hollow planks boomed through the hall. He raised his voice to its strongest pitch. *"Calletani!"*

That brought them all up short. He raked his eyes across them, noting who flinched and who looked down and who met him eyes-on. When he had them all, he spoke more softly. "Well, tribesmen. You know who I am. If you stay with me, you'll learn what I am. I'll fight your champions if I have to, and kill them if that's what it takes. I'd rather not. If we're going to take down the empire, we need every man. It's imperial blood we should be thirsting for—not the blood of our own."

The sound that rose in response to that made a shiver run down his spine. It began as a growl and rose to a roar. It was pure lust for blood—imperial blood, blood of the enemy who had barred the gates of the south since the people first came out of the dawn lands.

That gate would fall. That was Euan's oath and his promise.

They raised him up in the hall of his fathers, lifting him high on an imperial shield. The chieftain of Dun Gralloch clasped the heavy gold torque about his neck, and the lord of Dun Carrig weighted his arms with gold.

He stood at that dizzy height, supported on the shoulders of his warband, with his head brushing the beams, and allowed himself to savor the moment. It would not last long. The One knew, there was trouble enough waiting.

But not today. Today, he would let the sun shine. Today, he was king.

Ten

Iliya won his wager—almost. By the first day of the testing, six-teen eights of the Called had come in, less one. They had had to open one of the long-unused dormitories, and all the First and Second Riders were called on to oversee the testing of each eight and the final, anomalous seven.

There had never been anything like it. They were all male—that was a relief to the older riders—but they were not all boys or very young men. Some were older than Kerrec. One was a master of the sea magic. Several were journeymen of various magical orders, and some of those were close to mastery.

"The gods are in an antic humor," Master Nikos said the night before the testing began.

He had invited the First Riders to dinner in his rooms. That was tradition, but this year the celebration was overlaid with grief. A year ago, three of the four had been Second Riders. Their predecessors had died in the Dance of the emperor's jubilee.

Tonight they had saluted the dead, then resolutely put the memory aside. This was a time for thinking of the future, not the past.

"It's good to know we have a future," Andres said.

He was the oldest of them, and he seemed least comfortable in the uniform of a First Rider. He had been a Second Rider for twenty years and would have been content to stay at that rank for another twenty. His gift was for teaching novice riders and overseeing the Called.

He did not know how valuable he was. That was humility, Kerrec thought. Kerrec was sadly deficient in that virtue. He had not been born to it and he had shown no aptitude for it since.

Tonight Andres was more at ease than he had been since Nikos ordered him—on pain of dismissal—to accept his new rank. The Called were his charges, and he had come to know them all well. "They are remarkable," he said. "There's more raw power in them than I've ever seen."

"More trained power, too," said Gunnar. He had been a Beastmaster when he came, one of the few before this year who had had training in another order. He had just made journeyman when he was Called. "The Masters of the orders may take issue with it, if it seems they're going to make a yearly habit of losing their best to the Mountain."

"This may be an anomaly," Curtius said. Next to Kerrec he was the youngest, but as if to compensate for that, he tended to take the reactionary view in any discussion. "After all we lost in the emperor's Dance, the gods are giving us this great gift. Next year, maybe, we'll be back to four or five eights each spring, and the usual range of ages and abilities."

"Or not," Gunnar said. "The world is changing. It's not going back to what it was before, no matter how hard any of us tries."

"You don't know that," said Curtius.

Gunnar glared at him under thick fair brows. He was a huge man from the far north. People there had accepted the empire, but they shared blood with the barbarian tribes. Some said they shared more than that—that they were loyal not only to their wild kin but to the One God who stood against the many gods of Aurelia.

Gunnar was a devoted son of the empire in spite of his broad ruddy face and his mane of yellow hair. "Have you been blind when you ride the Dance? Even in schooling, the patterns are clear. They're not the same as before."

"They'll shift back," Curtius said stubbornly. "They always do. We'll make sure of it ourselves, come the Midsummer Dance."

"Will we want to?" Gunnar demanded. "Think for once, if you can. We were locked into patterns that almost cost us the empire. It took a terrible toll on the school. Maybe we need to change."

"Change for the sake of change can be worse than no change at all," Curtius said.

Gunnar rose to pummel sense into him, but Nikos's voice quelled them both. "Gentlemen! Save your blows for our enemies."

"Gods know we have plenty of those," Gunnar said, subsiding slowly. He kept a grim eye on Curtius.

Kerrec sat in silence. He had learned long since that wine did not blunt the edges. It made them worse. It helped somewhat to focus on the others' voices, even when they bickered.

This would end soon enough. Then there would be the night to endure, and after that the days of testing. He did that now. He counted hours and days, and reckoned how he would survive them.

* * *

Master Nikos caught Kerrec as they were all leaving, slanting a glance at him and saying, "Stay a moment."

Kerrec sighed inwardly. The others went out arm in arm, warm in their companionship. Watching them made Kerrec feel small and cold and painfully alone.

He stiffened his back. That was his choice. He had made it because he must.

Master Nikos had stood to see his guests out of the room. Once they were gone, he sat again and fixed Kerrec with a disconcertingly level stare.

Kerrec stayed where he was, on his feet near the door. He was careful to keep his face expressionless. So far he had evaded discovery, but this was the Master of the school. If anyone could see through him, it would be Nikos.

"You're looking tired," the Master said. "Will you be up for this? It's a lot of candidates to test—and as skilled as the others are, they haven't been First Riders long. It's all new to them."

"Not to Andres," Kerrec said. "Gunnar is the best trainer of both riders and stallions that we have. They'll do well enough."

"And Curtius?"

Kerrec lifted a shoulder in a shrug. "He'll rise to it. If he doesn't, we'll find a Second Rider who can take his place."

The Master sighed. They both knew that was not nearly as easy as it sounded. But when he spoke, he said nothing of it. "There's something else."

Kerrec's back tightened. Valeria, of course. The rider-candidate who could master all the stallions. The only woman who had been Called to the Mountain in a thousand years.

They had been evading the question of her all winter long.

In the meantime she had settled remarkably well among the rest of the candidates of her year. Sometimes the elder riders could almost forget that she was there.

Now spring was past and the Called were ready to be tested. For that and for the Midsummer Dance that would follow, they needed their strongest riders. She was the strongest on the Mountain—not the most skilled by far, but her power outshone the greatest of them.

But Nikos said nothing of that. He said, "One of the guests for the testing has asked to see you."

Kerrec had not been expecting that at all. Of course he knew that the guesthouses were full. So were all the inns and lodging houses. Half the private houses in the citadel had let out rooms to the friends and families of the Called.

They were all there to witness the final day of the testing. Kerrec could not imagine who would be asking for him by name. There were noblemen among the Called, but none related to him.

Maybe it was someone from his travels for the school, back before the broken Dance, when a First Rider could be spared to ride abroad. "So," he said, "where can I find this person?"

"In the guesthouse," Nikos answered. "The porter is expecting you."

Kerrec bent his head in respect. Nikos smiled, a rare enough occasion that Kerrec stopped to stare.

"Go on," said the Master. "Then mind you get some sleep tonight. You'll be needing it."

Sometimes, Kerrec thought, this man could make him feel as young as Valeria. It was not a bad thing, he supposed. It did not keep him humble, but it did remind him that he was mortal.

* * *

Once Kerrec had left the Master's rooms for the solitude of the passage and the stair, he gave way briefly to exhaustion. Just for a moment, he let the wall hold him up.

He should go to bed. The guest, whoever it was, could wait until he had time to waste. He needed sleep, as the Master had said.

He needed it—but it was the last thing he wanted. In sleep was that hated voice whispering spells that took away yet more of his strength. Every night it was stronger. It seemed to be feeding on the Mountain's power—but surely that was not possible. Apart from the white gods, only riders could do that.

Kerrec shuddered so hard he almost fell. If an enemy could corrupt the Mountain itself, even the gods might not be able to help the school. They would be hard put to help themselves.

Resolutely he put that horror out of his mind. The riders were weakened—perilously so—but the white gods were still strong. None of them had been corrupted or destroyed.

For now, he had a duty to perform. The Master had made it clear that he was to oblige a guest.

He straightened with care. If he breathed deeply enough, he could stand. After a moment he could walk.

Once he was in motion, he could keep moving. The guesthouse was not far at all, just across the courtyard from the Master's house. A lamp was lit at its gate, and the porter was waiting as Nikos had said.

The old man smiled at Kerrec and bowed as low as if Kerrec had still been the emperor's heir. "Sir," he said. "Upstairs. The tower room."

It was a nobleman, then. Kerrec wondered if he should be disappointed.

He bowed and thanked the porter, though it flustered the

man terribly, and gathered himself to climb the winding stair. It was a long way up, and he refused to present himself as a feeble and winded thing. He took his time and rested when he must.

He was almost cool and somewhat steady when he reached the last door. The doors along the way had had people behind them, some asleep and snoring, others talking or singing or making raucous love. There was silence at the top, but a light shone under the door. He knocked softly.

"Enter," said a voice he knew all too well.

His sister was sitting in a bright blaze of witchlight, with a book in her lap and a robe wrapped around her. She bore a striking resemblance to Valeria—much more so than he re-membered. Valeria had grown and matured over the winter. Bri-ana was some years older, but in that light and in those clothes, she could have been the same age as Valeria.

"What in the world," Kerrec demanded, "are you doing here?"

"Good evening, brother," Briana said sweetly. "It's a pleasure to see you, too. Are you well? You look tired. How is Valeria?"

Kerrec let her words run past him. "You should never have left Aurelia. With our father gone to war on the frontier and the court being by nature fractious, for the princess regent to come so far from the center of empire—"

"Kerrec," Briana said. She did not raise her voice, but he found that he had nothing more to say.

That was a subtle and rather remarkable feat. Kerrec had to bow to it, even while he wanted to slap his sister silly.

She closed her book and laid it on the table beside her chair, then folded her hands in her lap. "Sit down," she said. "I sup-pose you've had enough wine. I can send for something else if you'd like."

"No," Kerrec said, then belatedly, "thank you. Tell me what you're doing here."

"First, sit," she said.

Kerrec sighed vastly but submitted. Briana had changed after all. She was more imperious—more the emperor's heir.

Once he was sitting, stiffly upright and openly rebellious, she studied him with a far more penetrating eye than Master Nikos had brought to bear. "You look awful," she said. "Haven't you been healing? You should be back to yourself by now. Not—"

Kerrec cut her off. "I'm well enough. I am tired—we all are. We lost a great store of power when our riders died. Now with so many of the Called to test, we're stretched to our capacity."

Briana's eyes narrowed. He held his breath. Then she said, "Don't push yourself too hard. You'll make everything worse."

"I'll do," Kerrec said with a snap of temper. "Now tell me. What brings the regent of the empire all the way to the Mountain when she should be safe in Aurelia?"

"I'm safe here," she said. "I rode in with the Augurs' caravan. There's a flock of imperial secretaries camped in a house by the south gate. We're running relays of messengers. And if that fails, there's a circle of mages in Aurelia, ready to send me word if there's even a hint of trouble."

Kerrec had to admit that she had answered most possible objections—except of course the most important one. "The imperial regent is required to perform her office from the imperial palace."

"The palace is wherever the emperor or his regent is." Briana leaned toward him. "Come off your high horse and listen to me. I was summoned here. I had a foreseeing."

That gave Kerrec pause—briefly. "You are not that kind of mage."

"I am whatever kind of mage the empire needs," Briana said.

She was running short of patience. "I have to be here for the testing. I don't know why—I didn't see that far or that clearly. Only that I should come to the Mountain."

"What, you were Called?"

"You, of all people, should not make light of that," she said. "And no, I am most definitely not destined to abandon my office and become a rider. There's something in the testing that I'm supposed to see. That's all."

Kerrec wondered about that, foolishly maybe, but maybe not. His power was broken but not gone. Flashes of understanding still came to him.

He let go his attack of temper. Much of it was fear, he had to admit. He was afraid for her safety and terrified that she would see what had become of him.

She saw no more clearly than anyone else—and as she had said, she was safe on the Mountain. He sighed and spread his hands. "Well then. You're here. There's no point in sending you away."

"Even if you could," she said.

He was sorely tempted, again, to hit her. He settled for a scowl.

She laughed. "You're glad to see me. Admit it. You've missed me."

He refused to take the bait. She kept on laughing, reminding him all too vividly of the headstrong child she had been before he was Called from the palace to the Mountain.

When finally she sobered, she said, "You should go to bed. You have three long days ahead of you."

"I do," he said. But he did not leave at once. It was harder to go than he would have thought. Even as annoyed as he was with his sister, he felt better than he had since he could remember.

"Listen," she said. "Why don't you stay here? It's ungodly late, and there's a maid's room with no one in it. I promise I'll kick you out of bed before the sun comes up."

The temptation was overwhelming. He could think of any number of reasons to resist it. Still, in the end, weakness won. "An hour before sunup," he said as the yawn broke through.

"An hour before sunup," she agreed with a faint sigh. Maybe she was regretting her impulse.

Or maybe not. He never could tell with any woman, even his sister. Women were mostly out of his reckoning.

He knew already that with her there to watch over him, he was going to sleep well, maybe even without dreams. That alone was worth a night away from his too-familiar bed.

Eleven

Valeria had been dreaming of her family again, her mother and father and particularly her brother Rodry. For once, mercifully, she roused before the Unmaking came to mar the dream.

Something else had come instead—something that she was not sure she wanted to examine too deeply. It, or he, had been coming to her more and more often lately. At first the guilt had been so sharp she had fled the dream. Then little by little its edge had blunted.

Last night there had been no guilt. There had been a great deal of laughter and a burst of pleasure that went on and on.

When it was past, her body still thrummed with it. She let herself linger in the dream. She deliberately forgot dark hair and olive skin and keen hawk's face and reveled in milk-white skin and fire-red mane and eyes as yellow and slanted as a wolf's.

If that was a betrayal, then so be it. It was not she who had blown cold.

There was certain irony in waking from that dream, in that mood, to find Kerrec's sister sitting cross-legged at the foot of her bed. Briana had a book in her lap and was reading quietly by witchlight.

She looked as if she had been there for quite some time. Since the sun was not even up yet, she must have come in very early.

Valeria enjoyed the luxury of waking slowly. Briana did not melt into the edges of her dream. She was really here.

"You heard the Call," Valeria said.

Briana started a little. She had herself under control quickly, enough to say, "No. It was a premonition, that was all."

Indeed, Valeria thought. But she only said, "It is good to see you."

Briana smiled. She was much less obsessively dignified than her brother. "And you. I asked Master Nikos if I could accompany you for a day or two. He said that if you agreed, he had no objection."

Valeria sat up. The rush of delight startled a grin out of her. "Really? He said that?"

"Would I lie?"

"Not you," said Valeria.

"So? May I impose myself on you?"

"Of course," Valeria said. "Though following a very junior rider about might not be—"

"It would be a complete pleasure," Briana said. She paused. "If it would be more trouble for you than it's worth—"

"Oh, no," said Valeria, and she meant it. She had not known until she said it, how much she had missed Briana. It might be absurd and presumptuous, since Valeria was a soldier's daughter and Briana was the emperor's heir, but this was a friend. Better yet, she was a woman—and Valeria had been living with men for much too long.

She sprang out of bed and dived for her clothes. She was grinning so widely her jaws hurt. "Come on. Let's appall the riders."

Briana grinned back. She laid her book aside and went willingly where Valeria led.

At this hour, just before sunup, most of the riders were at breakfast in the dining hall. Valeria had stopped attracting attention some time since, but when she appeared with another woman behind her, the silence was abrupt.

They did not recognize Briana. She was dressed like one of them, and she was making no effort to look familiar.

That was an art. Valeria resolved to study it.

Breakfast was plain but plentiful, as always. Valeria dipped herself a bowl of hot porridge with a handful of berries sprinkled on it and a drizzle of cream. After a moment's perceptible thought, Briana did the same.

Iliya and Batu were sitting at their usual table. They were halfway through a platter of sausages and bread and cheese, while Paulus watched them with his usual expression of faint disgust. Paulus was much too haughty to eat like a drover as any sensible rider learned to do.

"Riders work hard," Iliya was reminding him between bites of sausage. "They earn their provender."

"Not *that* hard," Paulus said.

He had his back to the door. Iliya saw Valeria first, and then Briana.

His eyes widened. Unlike the other riders, he recognized the emperor's heir. He opened his mouth to say so.

Batu elbowed him into silence. When that threatened to fail, he stuffed half a sausage into Iliya's mouth and smiled at the women. "Good morning," he said in his deep beautiful voice.

Valeria smiled back. "Good morning," she answered. "The Master's given us company today. Will we all be civil? Is it possible?"

Paulus was refusing to turn and see who was with Valeria. His shoulders were stiff with it. Briana, who was his cousin and knew him very well, slid onto the bench beside him and set down her bowl. She began to eat as if she belonged there.

Paulus choked on nothing at all. Briana pounded his back until he stopped, crimson-faced and with his eyes streaming. "What in the gods' name are you doing here?" he demanded when he could talk.

"My brother asked the same thing," Briana said. "You two are terribly alike."

"Your brother is less stuffy," Iliya opined. He grinned at Briana. He was a prince where he came from, and imperial rank did not impress him in the slightest. "The Master really gave you to us?"

"For a day or two," said Briana. "I can fork hay with the worst of them. I even know how to groom a horse."

"That's more than Paulus did," Iliya said, then added, "He's better now."

"I would hope so," Briana said.

Valeria had noticed the year before when she was in the imperial city, how Briana seemed to know how to talk to anyone of any rank. She seemed perfectly at ease here, as she was everywhere that Valeria had ever seen her. She had the least pretension of any noble Valeria had yet met—not that Valeria had met many, but between Paulus and Kerrec, she had seen plenty of the less comfortable sort.

There was no point in being envious. Valeria could study and learn, if she could not exactly imitate. She doubted that Briana was even aware of what she did. She simply did it.

Still, Valeria found her mood a little sour as she finished breakfast. She stood up without looking to see if Briana was ready and made for the door, dropping her bowl in the cleaners' barrel as she went by.

Briana caught up with her just outside the door, somewhat out of breath but not apparently offended. Valeria pushed down the uprising of guilt and sat on it.

All the teaching masters were busy with the Called, but there were still stalls to clean and water buckets to be filled and horses to exercise. The Third and Fourth Riders and the older candidates were detailed to oversee the first- and second-year candidates.

What the day lacked for time in the schoolroom, it easily gained in physical labor. It must have been grueling for an imperial princess.

Briana never so much as whimpered. She even rode with the others.

She was hesitant about that, but when older stallions were brought out for the candidates' instruction, there was one more of them than usual. Some of the candidates growled. At least one of them yelped: a large hoof had come down on his foot.

The stallion who presented himself for Briana to ride was Kerrec's own Petra. He slid a bland dark eye at Valeria and studiously ignored the rest of the students.

Briana greeted him with visible gladness. She mounted easily, like the lifelong rider she was.

If she was a little breathless, that was no wonder. No one outside the school ever sat on one of the white gods. It simply was not done.

The gods did as they pleased. Today, that was to teach the emperor's daughter the beginnings of their art.

It was deceptively simple. They were asked to ride quietly in exact circles without variation of rhythm or figure, over and over until they had perfected the movement. The stallions would give nothing that the riders did not ask. That was the gods' pleasure and their challenge.

Sabata was unusually tractable today. He walked and trotted and cantered politely, did precisely as Valeria asked, and offered none of his usual opinions on the subject.

Maybe he was ill. He might be a god, and a Great One at that, but his body was mortal.

When the lesson was done, Valeria examined him thoroughly. He seemed well enough. He was pensive, that was all—most unusual for him.

Something was brewing. Valeria paused with her hand on Sabata's neck, searching the patterns that shaped the world. There was nothing there, nothing clear. The only word she could find for it was *imminence*.

Sabata shook his mane and snorted. Humans had to attach words to everything. It was a flaw in their creation.

So it was. Valeria dug fingers into his nape until his neck flattened and his lip wobbled in ecstasy. It was revenge of a sort—reminding him that he, too, in this form, had weaknesses.

He was in no way disconcerted by it. That was the trouble with gods. Nothing human could really touch them.

He nipped her, a sharp and startling pain, and departed at the trot for his stable. She stood gaping after him. In all his fits and fusses, he had never bitten her before.

Who could understand a god? She trudged in his wake, slightly humiliated but beginning in spite of herself to be amused.

* * *

"Testing isn't only for the Called, is it?" Briana asked.

She had survived the day in remarkably good condition, considering. At dinner the riders' stares had changed. Word was out. They knew who she was.

It seemed only reasonable, after dinner, for Valeria to divert Briana from the guesthouse toward the rooms she shared with Kerrec. "He's gone for the testing," she said, "and there's more than enough room. Why be all alone in a cold tower when you can be comfortable?"

Briana needed a little persuasion, but Valeria persisted until she gave in. Now they were sitting by the fire in the study, sipping hot herb tea with honey and talking drowsily. They were both bone-tired, but neither was quite ready to sleep yet.

That was when Briana asked her question. "Even after you pass the testing of the Called," she said, "the testing goes on. Doesn't it? It never stops."

Valeria nodded. "Even the Master is still tested. There's never any end to it."

"Magic is like that," Briana said. "It never lets you rest."

"Even you?"

"My magic is the empire."

Briana said it simply, but it meant more than Valeria could easily grasp. Briana tucked up her feet and curled in the big carved chair, watching the dance of the flames. If Valeria opened her eyes just so, she could the patterns there. She wondered if Briana could.

Briana had been Called. That was not the name she gave it, but it was the truth. It was a different Call than Valeria's or Kerrec's. The empire was in it somehow.

One of the logs in the fire collapsed on itself, sending up a shower of sparks. The patterns broke and fell into confusion. Valeria's sigh turned into a yawn.

She did not get up and go to bed just yet. "You're resting here," she said.

Briana smiled. "Better than I ever have. I could love this life. This place—these people. The stallions. To ride Petra, it was…" She trailed off.

"But you can't stay," Valeria said, "can you?"

Briana shook her head. She did not seem terribly sad, but her smile had died. "The Call takes you away from whatever order of magic you might have been sworn to before. The empire takes me away from everything. I was born for it. I belong to it."

"Your brother—" Valeria began.

"My brother was born for the Mountain," Briana said. "Even when he was a child, he'd run away from his duties to be with the horses. I ran away from lessons to hide behind my father's chair and listen to councils."

"Even lessons with horses?"

Briana's lips twitched. "Well. Not those. But everything else. I'd bring one of my books sometimes and do my lessons during the dull parts."

That made Valeria laugh. "Your father knew, didn't he?"

"Of course he knew," said Briana with the flash of a grin. "He never said a word—except years later, when he named me his heir. Then he said, 'You've studied for this all your life. Now be what you knew you would be.'" She went somber suddenly. "I didn't know. Not that my brother would be Called and the office would come to me. But the gods knew."

"The gods make me tired," Valeria said, yawning hugely. "Here, you take the bed. I'll take the cot in the—"

"Nonsense," Briana said, and would not hear of taking the

larger bed even when Valeria pointed out that she had slept on the servant's cot for most of last year. "Then I'll be perfectly comfortable in it. Go on, you're out on your feet."

Valeria gave way. She was too tired to fight over it. Briana went off yawning, radiating a quiet happiness that made Valeria smile in spite of herself.

The bed was too large without Kerrec in it. Valeria lay on his side, hugging the pillow to herself and breathing deep.

It smelled of herbs and sunlight. She groaned. The servants had been there while Valeria was out, changing the sheets. There was not even his scent to wrap around her and help her sleep.

She did not want to dream of someone else tonight. She wanted Kerrec.

She had a wild thought of finding him in the First Riders' hall. But she knew better than to try that. The riders scrupulously ignored certain facts of Valeria's existence, one of which was that she did not sleep in the servant's room in Kerrec's quarters. There were no laws against it, since there had never been a woman rider, but there were proprieties—and those took a dim view of what the two of them were to each other.

Mostly she did not care. Now, in the middle of the candidates' testing, she found she did. The testing was more important than her comfort.

If she wanted to be honest, tonight was no lonelier than the past few months of nights had been. It was colder without his warmth beside her, but his heart and mind had been elsewhere for longer than she had wanted to accept.

Twelve

The first two days of testing went on apart from the rest of the school. Valeria realized as the first day began that she was knotted tight.

There was no eruption of magic from the quarter of the citadel where the testing was being done. No word came of any candidate hurt or killed. The disaster of her year, when three of her group of eight died—one by magic, two put to death for causing it—had not happened again. As far as she could tell, the testing was going on without trouble.

It was maddening not to know what they were doing behind those walls. No one was supposed to know but the candidates and the riders who tested them. It was a mystery.

It was building up to something. What it was kept eluding Valeria, slipping into the core of her, hiding behind the Unmaking.

Sometimes she almost had it. Then it slithered away. It made her think of blind wriggling worms and flyblown corpses.

She almost would rather have the Unmaking than that. There was no one she could tell, because if she told, then she would have to confess the rest of it. Even Kerrec could not know what was inside her. No one could know.

All she could do was watch and wait and be ready for whatever came.

The last day of the testing, the one day that was open to the world, dawned clear and bright. "It's never rained on a testing day," Iliya said at breakfast. "Not in a thousand years."

"Legend and exaggeration," Paulus said with his customary sourness.

Iliya mimed outrage. "You doubt the gods?"

Paulus snarled into his porridge. Iliya grinned and declared victory.

Their banter was familiar and somehow poignant. Valeria ate distractedly. She could feel the power rising under her, the Mountain preparing to complete what it had begun. That other thing, the thing she could not speak of, had gone quiet—which did not reassure her at all.

The testing ground was crowded already when Valeria came to it. Long rows of benches were set up along the sides of the arena, adding to the tiers of stone seats that had been built into the walls. The riders' tiers still had room and there were chairs left in the nobles' box, but people were standing everywhere else.

Briana could have claimed a cushioned chair in the nobles' box high above the eastward end, but she settled between Valeria and Batu on the lowest tier of the north side, with her feet brushing the edge of the raked sand.

Valeria took a deep breath. Countless patterns were coming together here. All the candidates, their families, the riders, the people who lived in the citadel and served the Schools of Peace and War, the stallions in whose name it all existed, the Ladies who were greater than gods, were part of this.

Every year for a thousand years, that had been true. It was truer this year, because there were so many Called. Some of the riders looked as if their heads ached. The stronger they were, the more they must be able to see.

Kerrec was not there yet. He was in charge of the candidates, along with the rest of the First and Second Riders. They would watch from the sidelines, making sure those who failed were taken care of and those who succeeded knew what to do.

The testing was devastatingly simple. For this many candidates, three eights of stallions entered in procession, saddled and bridled but unburdened by riders. The candidates came in three eights at a time.

Each candidate chose a stallion, which was a test in itself, then did his best to mount and ride. If he got as far as that, the nature of the ride itself was a test and a reckoning. The worst simply sat there, with the stallion motionless under them. The best were offered a few of the movements that, with training, would evolve into the Dance of Time.

It was a long testing—so long that they paused twice for water and refreshment. The stallions were merciless in their winnowing. By midday, twenty candidates had managed to ride their chosen stallions through some fraction of the movements. Three times that number had failed.

Many of those who passed were older, and nearly all were mages of other orders. The rest failed in various ways—failed to choose, failed to mount, failed to understand that to ride one of the white gods, there had to be complete humility. No man could master a god, but he could become that god's partner in the Dance.

Some of them left on stretchers. Others limped or walked away, but were not followed or rebuked. The Call itself was a great honor. Failure was no dishonor.

It was painful for Valeria to watch them. She could not look at Kerrec at all or let herself be aware of him. Her skin felt raw and her throat was aching. Her heart kept trying to pound its way out of her chest.

She clung for support to the stallions' calm. They knew exactly what they were doing.

As noon passed and the sun tilted toward the west, ten more received the gods' approval. The eleventh made Valeria sit up. It was the boy who had found her the day she went off Sabata. Lucius, that was his name. He looked rather small and very young, but Petra chose him and carried him well, dancing for him as the stallions had danced for few others.

The more elaborate the dance, the stronger the power. Valeria knew that. The stallion who had carried her in her testing had been a Great One like Petra and Sabata. He had danced for her a part of the Great Dance.

Lucius did not get that, but what he got was enough for a murmur of delight and a long ripple of applause. He slid to the ground and staggered, a feeling Valeria remembered well. His grin spread from ear to ear.

He was the last. Valeria remembered, too, when she was last, how the crowd had erupted, and how the riders had overwhelmed everyone who passed the test, laughing and shouting.

Today they seemed stunned by the length of it. All thirty-one new rider-candidates hung about in the arena, blinking and wondering what to do next. The stallions stood in a double line like a guard of honor, but they were not guarding the candidates.

They were waiting for something. Valeria could feel it coming. It was like a storm rising, but the air was clear and the sky cloudless blue. The white cone of the Mountain rose serenely above the eastward wall.

She lowered her eyes from it to the gate through which the stallions had entered, long hours ago. There was a horse standing in it.

It was not one of the stallions. They were all greys—shades of white or silver or dapple or grey. This was a sturdy, cobby creature like them, saddled and bridled as they were, but its color was rich deep red, its mane and tail and legs to the knee glossy black.

A distant part of Valeria named the color. *Bay.* There was a star on the broad forehead between the dark intelligent eyes.

Valeria rose and bowed low, all the way to the sand.

The bay Lady walked slowly into the arena. The sand was pocked with hoofprints. Her big black hooves dug deeper and yet danced lighter than any of the stallions'. She was lighter in the leg and slimmer in the neck, as a mare should be, but her quarters were deep and broad and she moved with soft power.

There was not a sound in that whole place. All patterns had gathered to her. Every eye was on her.

She knew it, but unlike the stallions, she did not care. Mortal foolishness was not her concern—and to her mind, awe was foolish. So was the thought that rang in the ether, that nothing like this had happened in all the years of the testing. The Ladies never came down from the Mountain. They never troubled themselves with these mortal games.

This Lady had troubled herself with parts of Valeria's testing. Now it seemed she had another testing to perform. The candidates were all standing, staring, not knowing what to do.

The riders who watched over them were in no better state. Valeria saw Kerrec near the end of the line, doing and saying nothing. His face wore no expression.

She wondered if she should move, once she had straightened from her deep bow. But the Lady's glance told her to be still.

She bent her head. The gods were incalculable. That was a commonplace of priestly doctrine—and rider doctrine, too.

The Lady came straight toward her, then veered slightly to stand in front of Briana.

Briana had been silent through the whole testing, watching as they all did, the good and the bad. She looked up when the Lady stopped. Her face was blank but her eyes were wide and bright.

She could refuse. She was given that gift.

She stepped onto the sand. The Lady turned as each stallion had done in the choosing, inviting a candidate to mount.

Briana hesitated. For an instant Valeria thought she would refuse after all. But then she took the reins in her hand and caught a hank of black mane just at the withers and set her foot in the stirrup. She mounted gracefully—of course she would. She had been riding since before she could walk.

The stallions had danced. The Lady Danced. It was a dance of cadence and of modulated paces, step by step and movement by movement. It carried Briana through the curves and swooping lines of one of the great patterns, the pattern that foretold a certainty.

What that certainty was, the Lady did not say. There were no Augurs there to interpret it. No one had expected the testing of the Called to turn into a Great Dance.

Valeria felt the pattern in the streams of magic that ran through her body. She knew better than to try to impose understanding on it. That would come when it was ready.

The last movement of the Dance, the exuberant coda after the singing power of the trot in place, was a leap higher than a man's head, body level with the earth she had scorned, and a sudden, flashing kick that made the air gasp. If any man had stood there, his skull would have burst.

Valeria knew that for a clear and terrible truth. She had seen it happen.

There was nothing but air today. This was pure delight, the joy of a god in the living flesh. Briana laughed, a whoop of joy.

The Lady came back to earth again, dancing into stillness, snorting lightly. That was laughter, too. She had changed the world in ways that no mortal was prepared to understand. Her mirth rippled through Valeria's blood and bones.

It was like a draft of strong wine. Valeria reeled, but she was grinning.

On the Lady's back, Briana was grinning, too. No one else was. All the men were blank, stunned. None of them understood. It was beyond them.

Briana dismounted as the candidates had, dizzily, clinging for steadiness to the Lady's neck. The Lady did not seem to mind. Her nostrils fluttered. She was whickering as a mare does to her foal.

The sound was so tender and yet so imperious that Valeria found her eyes stinging with tears. It was meant for her, too, in its way—and for all of them, whether or not they could understand.

Thirteen

The uproar this year was less pronounced than it had been when Valeria, having become champion of the testing, was unmasked as a woman.

Briana had never pretended to be anything but what she was. What exactly that was at the moment, no one knew, but Master Nikos decreed that the matter would be decided tomorrow. Today the Called would celebrate their elevation to rider-candidates. There would be no further distractions.

Master Nikos had learned a great deal in the past year. They all had.

Valeria had spent her own feast of celebration in Kerrec's study, cleaning and tidying. She had every intention of doing the same again, but Briana insisted that they both go. "I would really rather be in the stable," she said as they shared a bath and put on festival clothes, "but this is duty. The stable—and the Lady—will be there in the morning."

"You believe that?" Valeria asked.

Briana nodded. "She promised."

"Then it is true," Valeria said.

"All of it," said Briana. She was standing perfectly straight, not moving except to speak. Her maids had come down from the tower to dress her properly, which looked like a great ordeal.

No doubt she was used to it. Valeria, quickly and comfortably dressed in the grey coat and doeskin breeches of a rider-candidate, perched on a stool and watched. It was fascinating, the transformation of a stablehand into an imperial princess.

Briana's gown was very simple compared to some Valeria had seen in the emperor's court, but it was made of silk that shimmered now gold, now scarlet. She wore a collar of gold set with bloodred stones, and a net of gold and rubies confined the coiled mass of her hair.

Valeria sighed faintly. She never had cared for clothes and pretty things the way her sisters did, but there was something about silk.

Her fingers smoothed the wool of her coat. She had earned it with blood and tears. She would never trade it for anything. But she could be tempted—almost—by that beautiful gown.

Briana was still Briana, even in imperial splendor. She refused to mince down the corridors and across the courtyards like a court lady. She strode out with a swish and swirl of skirts, which would probably have given her maids the vapors.

It made for a grand entrance. The dining hall was full, but the diners' cheer seemed rather subdued. Briana's arrival changed that. They all stood up without prompting and applauded as she made her way to the front of the room.

The high platform had a long table set up on it, with all the new riders sitting there. The nobles were seated just below and to the right of the head table—across from the riders, whose table ran along the wall to the left. Briana would have gone to the nobles' table, but the rider-candidates came down in a mob and carried her up to join them.

They carried Valeria, too, over her vigorous protests. She could not stop them. There were too many and too determined.

When they set her on the platform, she finally got the words out. "I don't belong here! This isn't my year."

"You were cheated of it last year," Lucius said. He was the ringleader and proud of it. "We're giving it to you now."

One of the others pressed a cup into her hands. It looked and felt very old, a broad shallow chalice of silver engraved with intertwining figures of men on horses. The same image was carved on the arch of the great gate of the citadel. She wondered, rather distantly, which of them had come first.

There was wine in the cup. "Drink!" the rider-candidates said in chorus. "Drink! Drink! Drink!"

She looked down from the high table at the riders below. None of them had moved to stop this. Kerrec was not even looking at her. His head was bent and his hands wrapped around a cup, as if something fascinating swam inside it.

Her jaw hurt. She was clenching it. She relaxed as much as she could, and made herself stop caring what Kerrec did or thought.

She focused on Master Nikos instead. He had an expression almost of curiosity, as if he was waiting patiently to see how this game played out.

He was not angry. She saluted him with the champion's cup and drank as deep as she could stand.

The wine went straight to her head. Instead of making her dizzy, it made her wonderfully, marvelously happy. Nothing mattered then—not Kerrec, not the riders, not anything.

She passed the cup to Briana. That met with a roar of approval. These rider-candidates had none of the rigidity of their el-

ders. They loved a spectacle. If that spectacle shattered the traditions of a thousand years, then so it did. This was a new
world. They would make new traditions for it.

Valeria woke with the mother of headaches. She vaguely remembered leaving the hall, late and so full she could barely
move, but between the hall and her bed, she had no memory
at all.

Slowly she realized that not all the pounding she heard was
inside her skull. Someone was beating the door down.

Briana in the servant's room was much closer to the door—
and should have been rocked out of bed by the noise. But the
hammering went on and Briana made no move to stop it. Valeria staggered out of bed, cursing the arrogance of imperial
princesses, and stumped scowling toward the door.

Paulus stepped back quickly at sight of her face. He had a
healthy respect for her powers. She lightened her scowl somewhat, but there was no getting rid of all of it. That part was pain.

Paulus scowled back. "Master Nikos is asking for you," he said.

She had been expecting that. Yesterday's adventures had had
nothing to do with her, but the riders would be needing someone to blame. She left Paulus standing in the doorway while
she went to wash and dress.

On the way, she peered into the servant's room. The bed had
been slept in, but there was no one in it. Briana was gone.

That took a little of the edge off her temper, but not much.
She had to reach inside herself for calm, and then for focus.

She needed both. Paulus did not move out of her way when
she reached the door. He had a look that made her eyes narrow. "What is it?" she asked.

His face was stiff. Not that that was anything unusual—but
this was a different kind of stiffness. Valeria pulled him back

into the room and thrust him into the nearest chair. "Talk," she said.

He scowled even more blackly than before. "It may be nothing," he said. "I could be imagining it. I'm not an Augur. I was supposed to be one, but I was Called instead."

Valeria clenched her fists to keep from shaking him. "You saw something," she said. "When the Lady Danced."

He nodded tightly. "Did it occur to you to wonder why, of all the hundreds of people at the testing, there was not one Augur? You'd think *one* would come just to watch. It's not as if there were a tradition against it."

"Are you saying there's some sort of conspiracy?" Valeria demanded.

"I don't know," said Paulus. He said it without exasperation or excessive temper, which for him was unusual. "I saw things in the patterns of the Dance. It was like writing on a page."

"What did it say?" Valeria was working hard to cultivate patience. Paulus was not going to come to the point until he was ready. Considering how reluctant he obviously was, she wondered if she wanted to hear it.

"I'm not sure what it said," Paulus said. "I can tell you what I think it said. It was like a poem in a language I never properly learned. There was a stanza about the school and about change, and about how the old had to die to make room for the new. Then there was a sequence about the war. How the only way to win it was by doing nothing. Or by embracing nothingness."

Valeria's stomach clenched. "Embracing nothingness? Are you sure?"

"No, I'm not!" he snapped. "I don't know why I'm even telling you this. I should be telling the Master. Except when I try, it all seems too foolish to bother him with."

"Believe me," said Valeria, "there's nothing foolish about this. What else did you see?"

"What else should I have seen?"

She took a deep breath, praying for patience. "That's what I'm asking. You haven't said anything we haven't all seen, one way or another. What's the rest of it?"

"I don't know," said Paulus. If he had not been so consciously dignified, he would have been squirming in his chair. "I can only tell you what I think it was. There was more about the war. Kings dying and kings being made. And the Mountain. That was the leap at the end. It said, 'The Mountain is not what you think it is.'"

"That is cryptic," Valeria said.

"I told you," he said.

"What do you think it means?"

He flung up his hands. "The gods must know, because I don't. It's bad news for us, whatever it is. It says we think we're safe, but we dance over the abyss. We trust ourselves and our powers, but they're a delusion. We bury ourselves in tradition, and tradition buries us. This war isn't on the frontier at all, though there will be battles enough there. It's here, in our citadel. It will be our undoing, unless we wake up and give it its name."

Valeria had gone cold inside. Augur or not, Paulus had seen the truth. He had seen the Unmaking.

"You have to tell the Master," she said, though her throat tried to close and stop her.

"What can he do that he's not already doing?"

"He needs to know," Valeria said. "The threat's not just to the emperor or his army. It's to us. To the Mountain."

"We don't know that," Paulus said. "I could be all wrong."

"You're afraid," she said.

For once he did not give way to her baiting. She devoutly wished he would. She was afraid, too—deathly afraid. All he had to protect him was the fear that he was wrong. She knew he was right.

"Look," she said, "Midsummer Dance is in three days. There will be Augurs there. If the Lady Danced the truth, the stallions will, too. The Augurs will see it and everyone will be sure."

"And if they don't?"

"If it's there, they'll see it."

Paulus nodded. This gave him a graceful way out of his dilemma. It gave Valeria one, too—though she had far more to be afraid of than he did.

He pulled himself to his feet and smoothed his expression back into place. When it was as haughty as it usually was, he said, "We'd better go. We're keeping the Master waiting."

Valeria nodded. Neither of them would talk about this again—until they had to. That was understood.

She expected Paulus to bring her to the Master's study, but he went on past it. By that time she was almost fit for human company. The worst of her fears were buried and the rest were tightly reined in. She could face the Master with, she hoped, a suitable degree of calm.

Master Nikos was waiting for her in the riding court nearest the Master's rooms. He had been training one of the young stallions in his care and was just finishing, with a lump of sugar and a pat on the neck, when Valeria came through the arch onto the sand.

Another stallion was waiting, equipped for instruction with the heavy training headstall. His groom stood by him, holding the loops of the long soft line.

The groom took the young stallion's bridle and led him out.

Master Nikos took charge of the older stallion. He was very old, this one, so old he looked like a glass full of light.

Valeria bowed low. This one she did not know, and she had thought she knew every stallion in the citadel.

"This is Oda," the Master said. "Mount."

Valeria knew better than to argue. She was too curious in any case—and wary enough to pause before she mounted, to stroke the long arched nose and meet the wise dark eye. There was no threat of humiliation there. This was a test, but it was honest.

She mounted and settled lightly in the saddle. The back under her was broad and, for all its age, still strong.

Oda's stride when he moved out on the circle at the Master's request had a swoop and swing that made her laugh. Sabata moved like that, but he was young and still a bit uncertain. This stallion had been instructing riders for longer than Valeria or even Kerrec had been alive.

The Master stood silent in the middle of the circle. This was not his lesson, then. The stallion was teaching it.

Valeria breathed in time with those sweeping strides. She let her body flow into them, riding without rein or stirrup, legs draped softly, hands on thighs. Anger, frustration, even fear and dread of what Paulus had told her, drained away. There was only the thrust and sway of the movement, the sensation of power surging up through those broad quarters. *Follow,* was the lesson. *Simply follow.*

She had been taught this way when she first arrived in the citadel, at night and in secret, because she was not allowed the other riders' instruction. It was familiar, so much so that she forgot the man who was standing in the circle, watching. She was alone with the stallion, who was unquestionably a Great One. He felt almost as vast in the spirit as one of the Ladies.

As if the thought had brought her, Valeria opened her eyes to find the bay Lady there with Briana on her back. They were watching as the Master was, without moving or saying a word.

The Great One's back coiled. Every instinct screamed at Valeria to snap into a ball or at the very least to clamp on with her legs and cling frantically to the mane on the heavy arched neck. She breathed deep once and then again, for focus and calm. When Oda went up, she rode with him.

He was transcribing patterns in the air as the Lady, the day before, had transcribed them in the sand of the testing ground. These were a part of the whole, but what the whole was or what it meant, Valeria was too close to see.

She did her best to remember the nature and placement of each leap—not easy when she was caught up in them. It was easier if she let her memory of the Lady's Dance run in the back of her mind. They fit together.

The last leap ended in the center of the circle, directly in front of the Master. He kept rider's discipline, with his back straight and his face still, but he looked tired and old.

She had never thought of him as old before, even with his grey hair and his lined face. "Is it going to be as bad as that?" she asked him.

He shook his head. "I don't know," he said. "The emperor's Dance isn't over. You salvaged a future, but there's no telling whether that future will be worse than the one you turned us away from. And now…"

"And now it gets stranger," Briana said when he did not finish. She ran her hand down the Lady's neck. "I wasn't expecting this."

"None of us was," the Master said. "Even the Augurs are at a loss. We've always had at least some glimmer of what is to come—but now we're stepping blindly into the dark."

Valeria bit her tongue before she said, "Not the dark. The Unmaking." That was what the Unmaking did. It swept away all that was or had been or ever would be.

"It's the end of something," Briana said to the Master through the fog of Valeria's maundering. "So many changes. Do you feel them bubbling up under your feet?"

"I feel them," Master Nikos said. "I wish to the gods I did not."

Valeria swung down from Oda's back. She wanted, suddenly, to be done with this. "What is it, then? What did you call me here to do?"

"To prove something," the Master said. "I still am not sure…" He caught Oda's eye and stopped. The stallion's ears had flattened briefly. It was a warning, and one he was well trained to listen to.

He let his breath out sharply. "As you will," he said to the stallion. Then to Valeria he said, "You will ride the Dance. Oda will carry you. He insists on it."

Valeria felt her heart stop, then start again, hammering hard. "The Dance? The Midsummer Dance? But—"

"Yes," he said, and his voice was testy. "In the ordinary way of things, you would be years from earning any such honor. But the stallions have made their will known. You must ride, and Oda must carry you. No matter how dangerous that may be, they are adamant."

"'Even the Master is their servant,'" Valeria recited.

He leveled a glare at her. "This is not a game, child."

"No?" said Valeria with a flash of sudden temper. "Aren't we playthings for the gods?"

"I would hope we may be more than that," Briana said.

The air that had been crackling between Valeria and the Master went somewhat more safely quiet. Briana nodded to herself. "Good. We can't have you fighting. We need you—all of you—more than ever."

Master Nikos cleared his throat. "This is a difficult thing. What we're seeing here, and foreseeing, and dreading, is that our life, our art and magic, will never be the same again."

"Is that a bad thing?" Briana asked. "For years, you've cut yourself off from everything but your own art and knowledge and concerns. Time was when the names of the Master and the First Riders were as well known as the emperor's own. Now hardly anyone could name you, let alone the others—and few of those who know can be said to care. You are the empire's heart, and yet not only has the empire all but forgotten you, you yourselves have forgotten what you are supposed to be." She met his shock with a hard, clear stare. "In the old days, riders from the Mountain would follow the emperor to war. They fought beside him and Danced the outcome of his battles, and often won them for him—or died in the trying. The emperor has sworn that this year, this war, will break the back of the barbarian horde. Where were you when he called for his mages? What were you doing when his armies marched to the border?"

"Lady," Master Nikos said in a soft, still voice, "we have fought our own kind of battle on your father's behalf, and taken losses that will be years in the mending. If you command us to send riders to the war, we will obey. But we have precious little strength to spare."

Briana offered no apology, but her gaze softened somewhat. "If I had such authority, I would bid you continue to heal, but be prepared to open your gates and bring down your walls."

"All signs do seem to point in that direction," Master Nikos said. He sounded as exhausted as he looked. "We'll do what we can, lady."

"That's all anyone can ask of you," Briana said.

Master Nikos was clearly not happy to have been read so

harsh a lesson by a woman a third his age, but it had made him stop and think. After a while he said, "We'll perform the Dance as the gods will it. Then may they help us all."

Fourteen

There was no inquisition of riders, either to settle the question of the Lady's testing and choosing or to protest the word that came down from the Master's study. Valeria was to ride the Midsummer Dance on a stallion who had withdrawn to the high pastures before Kerrec came to the Mountain. That gave the Dance the Master, the four First Riders, two Second Riders, and one rider-candidate.

The news reached Kerrec after he left the schoolroom, late in the morning after the testing. He had thirty-one new pupils, some older than he, and they were not the easiest he had ever had. He was mildly surprised not to see a thirty-second, but his sister had been keeping out of sight since the testing.

That was a small mercy. Thirty-one men and boys had discovered that there was no reprieve from either testing or studies. Those who had come from the legions were even less inclined to suffer in silence than spoiled lords' sons or haughty journeyman mages. "It's just like the bloody army," one of them had grumbled when they straggled into the schoolroom.

"At least in the bloody army they let you sleep it off after you've won a battle," someone else said, yawning till his jaw cracked. "Up at bloody dawn to clean bloody stalls. I thought we signed on to be riders, not stablehands."

Kerrec had a lecture for that, which he decided not to deliver. They were in awe of his rank, at least, and he was kind to their aching heads and churning stomachs, though he doubted any of them was aware of it. He set them simple exercises that would engage their stumbling brains and teach them—or in many cases remind them of—the beginnings of focus.

He could use a course of that himself, he reflected grimly as the rider-candidates dispersed to their afternoon lessons. He would follow them later, to judge each one and mount him accordingly on the stallion who would be his schoolmaster.

He was on his way to Petra's stable and a lesson of his own when he crossed paths with Gunnar, who was on the same errand. Gunnar was frowning. "Bad news?" Kerrec asked him as they went on together.

"That depends," Gunnar said. "Did you know our most troublesome pupil is riding the Dance at Midsummer?"

"Valeria?" Kerrec could not find it in him to be surprised. "How?"

"Another whim of the gods," Gunnar said. "Oda is carrying her—the old one."

"I thought he had died in that body," Kerrec said.

"Apparently not." Gunnar's frown deepened to a scowl. "A Lady comes to the testing and makes an impossible choice. A Great One returns from the dead to dance the Dance with a novice barely past the Call. And we were thanking the gods that there were no women Called. We were too complacent."

So they were, Kerrec thought. Gunnar went his way, to find his lofty Alta and school the lesser figures of the Dance. Petra was waiting for Kerrec to do the same. His groom was not Valeria as it should have been—it was one of the others of that year, Kerrec's cousin Paulus.

From his expression, which was even more sour than usual, Paulus had heard the news. Valeria's way had never been easy, but this would make it even more difficult.

Kerrec wrenched himself into focus. The truth, his heart insisted on reminding him, was that of the eight who would ride the Dance, the greatest danger to it was not Valeria. It was Kerrec.

Valeria lacked training. Kerrec lacked worse. He lacked strength, focus, and full control over his magic. The voice inside him was whispering its poison even in daylight. Sometimes he could not see the sun for the cloud of hatefulness around him.

Petra would protect him, just as Oda was clearly meant to protect Valeria. This was not supposed to be a Great Dance, in which the fabric of time itself could be unraveled and then rewoven. It was a Dance of foreseeing. It opened the future, but not to alter it. It was meant to read the patterns only, then chart a course through them.

The emperor's Augurs would be there, looking for signs of hope or warning for the war. That was all they would expect and all they would see.

Kerrec turned his back on the voices inside—both the one that laughed and mocked and egged him on to death and worse, and the one that told him he was wrong to do this. He was not strong enough.

With Petra he would be. He had to be. He mounted, took up the reins and began the day's exercises.

Until the Dance was over, Valeria had no duties except to look after Sabata and Oda and learn from the old one everything that he would teach. She had more time to herself than she had ever had. She could not spend all of it meditating on the great working she was about to be a part of.

If there was anything she had learned from the stallions and their Ladies, it was that, when it came to the Dance, thinking was not a virtue. It was better to slip into the pattern and simply be.

She had to be careful of that, too. The patterns were seductive. They could lure her away from the necessities of life, from eating and sleeping and even breathing. She had to walk the middle ground, and that was hard—as hard as anything she had ever done.

People left her alone. All the riders for the Dance were caught in the same sacred half trance as she was. The others were together, she supposed, in one of the more secluded houses, with their own riding court.

She was not invited to that, but she had not expected to be. She was only a rider-candidate, and a terribly troublesome one at that. She went her own way as usual, dimly aware that there was food when she was hungry and drink when she needed it, and her bed was always ready for her when it was time to fall into it. The pattern that ran through it all bore a striking resemblance to Briana's.

Briana was a rider here. Maybe no one would call her that, but there was no denying it. The Lady had made sure of it.

The night before the Dance, Valeria should have been asleep soon after sundown. But she could not find sleep anywhere.

It was not the Dance that kept her awake—she was as ready for that as she would ever be. She was missing Kerrec. He still had not come back from his room in the rider-candidates' dormitory.

What if he never came back?

She wanted him so keenly that her body ached with it. The redheaded lover was waiting on the other side of a dream, but dreams, tonight, were not enough. She wanted—she needed—the solidity of a living body in her arms, the feel and smell and taste of him, the weight of him on her and the fullness of him in her most secret places. His absence was a physical pain.

Kerrec was cold. Nights were cool even in summer, here on the Mountain's knees. Even under a blanket he shivered.

Warmth slipped in behind him. A familiar body fit itself to his. He breathed the scent of her, horses and herbs and clean night air.

He was weak and off guard. He let himself turn in her arms. He should not—he should avoid—if she discovered—

Her lips tasted of honey and ginger—sweet and fiery. Her skin was as smooth as cream. So quick, so strong that he gasped, she took him inside her.

Some dim part of him was jabbering at him to stop this, save himself, drive her away. It was very dim and fading fast.

They made love quickly, but it felt luxuriously slow. Neither of them said a word. When it was over, she kissed him softly and slipped away.

He reached for her, but she was gone. Maybe it had been a dream. If it was, it had left her scent in his bed and the memory of her all through his body.

His mind and magic were quieter. The broken edges seemed a little less sharp.

He sighed. As the breath left him again, he slipped into sleep—blessedly peaceful and free of insidious voices.

Fifteen

Valeria woke with her heart pounding. For a long while, measured in the gallop of her pulse, she could not remember where she was.

Kerrec was not there. She had come back to her own room—their room—last night. Then she had slept. She had dreamed—

It was gone, except for the sense that the sky was collapsing under its own weight. She made herself remember that it was dawn and she had to get up and get ready for the Dance. Then after the Dance, the young stallions would come in from the Mountain, and their choosing and taming would begin.

It was a joyous day. She was trapped in old memories, that was all.

There was a bath waiting for her, with Briana still finding it amusing to play the servant. The uniform that was laid out was one Valeria had not worn before. The breeches were doeskin and the boots black leather as always, but the coat was crimson edged with gold. Each of its buttons was a golden sun. She had to stand stroking it for a little while, because it was so beautiful.

There were no marks of rank on it, since she had none. But she was riding the Dance. The gods had decreed and the Master, reluctantly, agreed.

When she was clean and dressed, Briana pulled her into a quick embrace. "We'll be there," Briana said.

She and the Lady, she meant. Valeria found that immensely comforting.

The eight stallions were waiting in the inner court behind the hall of the Dance. Valeria was not the first to arrive, but not the last, either. Master Nikos and the First Riders Andres and Gunnar were already mounted, circling the court on a long rein.

Whoever had brought the rest of the stallions, saddled and bridled, was gone. Valeria found Oda at the end of the line beside Petra. She would not have been surprised at all to find Sabata there, too, ready to do battle for his mortal property.

Although she could feel him in her heart where he always was, his presence was quiet. He was not jealous of the old one. Oda was too far above that.

It was a little disconcerting, as always, to know the truth of what the stallions were, and find herself taking the rein of a thickset grey cob with a distinct arch to his nose and a distinct expression of irony in his eye. Oda wore mortal flesh because he chose to—and whether he had died in this body and then chosen to come back, or simply retired to the high pastures after his time in the school was done, he was very much here and solidly present now.

He looked like a horse, smelled like a horse. As far as her

body needed to know, he was a horse. The rest of him was too large for her little human mind to comprehend.

She settled in the saddle. He did not give her the deep sense of coming home that Sabata did, but he was willing to carry her and his back fit her well. He was neither too wide nor too narrow. His barrel took up her leg in comfort, with room to spare.

She stroked his neck, smoothing his mane. He pawed lightly, which made her smile. Like all his kind, he was not particularly patient.

She sat a fraction deeper in the saddle. He moved out obligingly to join the rest in the court. Two more riders had come in while Valeria settled herself, the First Rider Curtius and the Second Rider Farraj. Two more had yet to come. One of them was Kerrec.

Valeria could not let herself think about him. She had to focus on the Dance—even though, when she thought about Kerrec and the Dance together, the sense of dread came crashing down.

Surely he would not try the Dance if he was not fit for it. Even Kerrec had sense enough for that.

Focus, she warned herself. She was here for a reason. She had to be ready for whatever it was. Oda was solid under her, rocking her hips with his big catlike walk. As she had when he tested her, she let herself flow into it.

The rest of the riders had come in and mounted. She felt them as she felt the horse under her. Their patterns were random still but beginning to come together.

One was more random than the others. She reached without thinking, not knowing exactly how she did it, and smoothed that one as much as she could. It was not much, but it was better than nothing.

Master Nikos spoke in her ear. He had ridden up beside her.

"Just follow," he said. "Let the old one go as he will. Don't worry about controlling him. The rest of us will be looking out for you."

Valeria opened her mouth to point out that it was she and not the Master who had, in the Great Dance, taken control of all the stallions. On second thought, she nodded without saying anything. If the Master needed to tell himself that she was a simple rider-candidate whom the gods had forced on the Dance, let him enjoy the illusion.

"Time," the Master said quietly. Riders picked up reins and straightened in their saddles, taking position two by two. Valeria was last. Kerrec rode beside her.

He was not looking at her. His eyes were fixed straight ahead. His face was still and somewhat pale.

Focus! she admonished herself. She faced forward with soft eyes as First Rider Gunnar liked to say, looking ahead through the stallion's ears. They focused on nothing in particular but were aware of everything within their reach.

Stallions ahead. Courtyard behind. Stone passage echoing as they rode through it, the sound of hooves resonating in her skull. There was a pattern in it, as there was in everything. This was like a drumbeat, a prelude to the Dance.

Sunlight blazed in front of her. The Hall of the Dance was roofed and walled, but its many tall windows let in the light. Shafts of it fell on the sand of the arena.

There were people everywhere, crowds of them ascending the walls from floor to ceiling. She was only distantly aware of them. The Mountain gleamed through glass above the royal box—which was empty. Briana was somewhere that involved the Lady.

The shape of this Dance was ordained, at least in the beginning. Entrance in stately, cadenced walk. Division into two skeins of four, flowing into slow and floating trot, curving in circles and serpentines.

So they blessed the earth and raised the gates of time. The Dance proper was not yet begun, but the powers were rising.

So was the panic in Valeria. The last time she rode the Dance, it had nearly ended in destruction. The spell of Unmaking was still in her, could still rise and devour her and all the rest of the world with her. All it needed was an instant's weakness.

This was a simple Dance, a pure Dance. No one was trying to disrupt it. No one could come near it to try. The Mountain was here, with the gods' full power. She was safe.

Oda went on calmly, carrying her through the increasing complexity of movements. They were all one, all of them—Valeria, too, once she had herself under control. The patterns were shifting as they should. Master Nikos was shaping them, discarding some, strengthening others, weaving them into a strong and coherent whole.

It was beautiful, how he did it. He made it look easy. He was drawing on them all, weaving their magic with his and binding it with the power of the stallions.

He could have done more. Some threads were not as well woven as they might be.

Valeria resisted the temptation to interfere. She was here for her raw strength, not for her skill. The Master did not need her meddling with his magic.

It was hard to simply be, to ride and follow and not try to shape the Dance. It was a test of discipline and obedience. Valeria gritted her teeth and endured.

At first, when the pattern started to fray, she thought it might be intentional. Then she was sure the flaws in the design were getting out of hand. Only last and most unwillingly did she realize what was happening.

One of the riders was losing his grip. He had given all he had to give, but the Master kept drawing from him, looking for strength where there was none. The Dance bound both of them. Valeria could feel the bonds of it on herself, but they were light, barely noticeable. They were a choice rather than a compulsion.

She tried to slip enough of herself free to feed power into the failing rider. Even before she touched him with her magic, she knew who it had to be. When she did touch him and saw the truth, she nearly broke the Dance herself.

Kerrec had been healing. She was sure he had. But what she saw now was nothing like the beautiful structure of ordered arts and powers that had been Kerrec when she first met him. This was a ruin. Walls were fallen, timbers broken. Whole expanses were nothing but flotsam and shards.

Deep down in it somewhere was the man she had known. She had set healing in him—she remembered.

It was not a false memory. He *had* been healing. But somehow, since he came back to the school, the spell had undone itself. There was very little of it left.

The Dance was crumbling. The patterns were losing their solidity. The gates of time, which should have shown the future as in a window—to study but not to touch—were beginning to open.

This could not be a Great Dance. None of the riders was ready for it.

The stallions were calm as always, but their movements were less easy now. The air seemed thick. They waded through it as if through water.

Valeria had no skill and precious little finesse. Master Nikos was doing nothing to close the gates and restore the patterns. It was all he could do to keep the remaining riders from falling apart.

Oda's back coiled. It was a warning and an instruction. He could Dance the pattern into submission, but the gates needed her to shut them. She could not do that if she was also keeping Kerrec from destroying them all.

Kerrec knew what was happening. He wanted that end, no matter what the cost.

His despair sucked Valeria down. She struck back ruthlessly. She locked him in wards, eased him out of the pattern, then as an afterthought, eased the rest of the riders out, as well. Most were too startled to fight back.

Oda danced for them all. One by one the patterns steadied. The gates opened no further.

The formlessness beyond was reaching through. It had no will or purpose. It simply was—like the Unmaking in the heart of Valeria's magic. They were the same. They called to one another.

She must not panic. She could keep the Unmaking and the Unmade apart. She could set her magic against the gates and will them to shut.

It was not as hard as controlling all the stallions at once. It was nowhere near as easy as following the Dance and letting the Master draw her power. She was tired already, overextended with saving Kerrec from himself and the rest of the riders from what he had done.

The gates resisted. She knew better than to fight. As with riding the stallions, fighting only made it worse.

She softened instead. She molded herself so that when the gates tried to open further, they could not move.

Slowly, too slowly maybe, they drew away from that resistance. The Unmade was howling, waking agony in the center of her.

She thrust with all the strength she had left. The gates of time closed. The Unmaking went silent. Oda stood still, with the sun shining in and the dust settling slowly.

Valeria's right arm was throbbing where she had broken it in the emperor's Dance. It had been healed, she thought, but the memory of its breaking had come back with full force.

The Unmaking was quiet. That was all, for the moment, that mattered.

Sixteen

This time there was a tribunal. The First Riders sat at the half-moon table in the Master's hall, surrounded by paintings and statues of old Masters and Great Ones who had left the body long ago.

The living riders had a bruised look. It might have been better for them to rest and face this confrontation tomorrow, but it was too urgent to put aside.

There had been no gathering and choosing of the young stallions today. There would be none tomorrow, either. That would have to wait until this confusion was settled.

Kerrec was there, as the cause of it. So were the Second Riders who had ridden the Dance, and Valeria. Briana had not been summoned, but she had come regardless. In Valeria's mind, she had as much right to be here as any of the rest.

There were no gods in the room, male or female, but they were watching. Valeria could feel them.

Kerrec was alive and conscious. The healers had examined him. Master Martti of that order was beside him now, looking as if he would have preferred that his charge be strapped down in bed rather than standing in front of the tribunal.

Kerrec looked much as he always did, with his windows shuttered and his doors barred. His face was somewhat paler than usual, but he was steady on his feet.

Valeria stood as far away from him as she could manage. It was not nearly far enough. All that kept her from killing him was the fact that he might die too quickly, and not suffer.

She did not need Briana's hand on her arm to keep her silent, though it helped. From the look of the riders' faces, she was not the only one who wanted Kerrec's hide on a pole. Some of them wanted hers, too, on general principles, but she was used to that.

"Well, sir," Master Nikos said after a while. He sounded exhausted in body and soul. "What do you have to say for yourself?"

"Nothing," Kerrec said stiffly. "Sir."

"You do understand what you did?"

Kerrec's face did not change, but Valeria could feel the spark of anger. "Yes, sir."

Nikos glanced at the healer—feeding Kerrec's anger. Valeria wondered if Nikos cared, or if he was too far gone.

Master Martti spread his hands. "There's nothing wrong with his body. His mind I'm not so sure of, but I reckon him sane, as riders go. His magic…"

"Sane?" one of the First Riders burst out. It was Curtius, the youngest except for Kerrec. "He nearly destroyed us all!"

"I overestimated my capacity," Kerrec said. His voice was brittle. "It was an error. I will pay whatever penalty the riders may exact."

"Even if that is expulsion?"

Kerrec met Curtius's stare until it dropped. "Whatever penalty the riders may exact." He bit off each word as he repeated it. Sometimes, Valeria thought, he remembered all too well that he was born to be emperor.

Nikos did not seem to have heard their byplay at all. His eyes were still on the healer. "How bad?"

"Bad," Martti said bluntly. "He was mending when he came back from Aurelia. That's been undone. From the signs, I'd say it's been unraveling for some time."

Nikos's glare leveled once more on Kerrec. "How long?"

"Since just after the Midwinter Dance," Kerrec answered.

"And you rode another Dance? Knowing you could break beyond repair—and take the rest of us with you?"

Kerrec's lips tightened. "I make no excuses. Obviously my judgment was impaired. I should have known, and withdrawn from the Dance."

"You knew," Gunnar said from halfway down the long curve of the riders' table. "For the gods' sake, don't lie to us. I'm at fault, too, for sensing something was wrong and not doing anything about it."

"None of us did," Nikos said. He rubbed his eyes as if they ached. "We've all been desperate. There's so much lost that we may not ever regain. We're all to be faulted for refusing to see what was in front of us. We needed him—therefore he had to be whole. Even when we knew that there was no way—"

"I think I've heard enough," Briana said. She did not say it particularly loudly, but it stopped the Master short. She stared down any other rider who would have opened his mouth.

She looked very much like Kerrec when she did that. She sounded like him, too, with her impeccably royal accent. "Master Healer, is there anything you can do?"

Martti shook his head. "Not here. The Mountain protects itself. Some workings break under the force of it. Maybe that's what happened. Though I'm not sure…" He trailed off.

"So it wasn't the first Dance? It was already breaking?"

"It is possible," Martti said. "I've never seen a working like it. It's almost like a village healer's spell, but the intricacy of it, and the way it's woven all the way to the heart of him—it's marvelous. If I could have seen it when it was new, before it unraveled…"

"Can it be woven again?" Briana asked with a touch of sharpness.

"Not here," Martti said again.

"But elsewhere?"

"It's possible," said Martti. "Away from the Mountain, in the Healers' hall in Aurelia, maybe…"

"So I had been thinking," Briana said. She turned to the Master. "Are you going to expel him?"

"I am not," Master Nikos said.

Not all the riders were pleased to hear it. Valeria noticed who was not—and who was. Was she? At the moment she could not be sure.

"He can't stay here," Briana said. "Whatever has got hold of him, it will kill him if it keeps on. Will you let me take him back to Aurelia with me?"

"It might be best," Nikos said. Valeria wondered if he meant to sound as relieved as he did. "There is even a title for him if he needs one."

Briana nodded. "Rider-envoy," she said. "He held the office before. He can take it up again. And while he's in Aurelia, with so many orders of mages besides the healers, surely one or more of them can discover what—"

"Do I get a say in this?"

Briana looked at Kerrec with complete lack of sympathy. "No," she said.

"You are not my master," he said.

"I am," said Nikos, "and I tell you also—no. You have forfeited the right to speak for yourself."

"Do I get a choice of sentences, then?" Kerrec demanded.

"No," Nikos said again.

"You won't strip me of my rank?"

"Do you want that?"

Kerrec's face was stark white. His nostrils flared. "It's what I deserve."

"It's not what you'll get." Nikos turned back to Briana. "He's yours. If you can bring him back whole, I'll thank you with all my heart and soul. If not...so be it. We may be coming to the end of our time in this world. All the omens seem to be pointing to it. But I'm not going down without a fight."

"The Augurs have said this?" Valeria asked. She did not mean to speak aloud, but there it was. Maybe Nikos would ignore her as he had been doing since this inquisition began.

Her luck in that respect had run out. "The Augurs see darkness and confusion," Nikos said, "war and terror and the fall of nations."

"No more or less than they ever see," Gunnar muttered, "and no clearer, either."

Valeria had seen more, but if they were not asking, she was not telling. She had seen the world's Unmaking.

That was the end of it. They were dismissed. For once in her life on the Mountain, Valeria was not the one called to account for her sins.

When the riders rose from the table, Briana stayed where she was. She was still gripping Valeria's arm, which kept her there, as well.

They all left, all but the Master. Kerrec had been the first to go—running away, damn him.

Valeria would deal with him later. Briana was dealing with the Master now. She let Valeria go, then braced her hands on the table and leaned toward Nikos.

"Now," she said. "Talk to me. What did the Augurs really say?"

"Very little," Master Nikos answered. If he was angry, he did not show it. "The Dance was corrupted before the omens could be read."

"You will pardon me, I'm sure, if I say I don't believe you. It was not the purest Dance there ever was, but it was completed. I saw the patterns like shapes of fire in the air. What did the Augurs say they meant?"

Master Nikos pressed his fingers to his brow as if to quell the pounding inside. "The Augurs say that there is no meaning. It's all chaos."

"The war? The empire? Everything?"

"They said," said the Master, "'All that can be done, may be done, and all that is made may be Unmade.' And they said, 'There is a worm in the Mountain's heart.'"

Briana sat back slowly. Her face had gone pale. "They said nothing about the war? Whether it will be won or lost?"

"That seems to be in the lap of the gods," Master Nikos said.

"It certainly seems to be in our hands," said Briana. She looked as if she had found strength somewhere. "We'd best get about it, then—all of us."

"What would you have us do?" he asked.

"You're asking me?"

"Lady," he said, and in that word he put a great store of meaning, "you seem to see more clearly than I. I ride the patterns—I even shape them. I do not interpret them, still less act upon them."

"Maybe you should," she said.

Master Nikos studied Briana for a long while. What he was seeing, Valeria thought she could understand. Patterns upon patterns, strands of duty and destiny and a confusion of futures, and through them all, the shock of uncertainty.

Maybe he could make more sense of it than Valeria could. Or maybe not. This was not the world he had expected or wanted to live in.

She was almost sorry for him. But he was the Master of the riders' art. He should have been better prepared.

He was no weakling even so. He straightened at last and said, "None of us pretends to know everything. We leave that to the gods. I see some of their purposes, dimly, and some of those frighten me. But I'm bound to further them as much as I can."

"No one is bound to anything," Briana said. "Even the Call leaves room at the end for a choice—to accept it or turn away. You choose to help the gods, you say. That's a great good thing if you do mean it. If you don't, you'll not be answering to me. The gods will call you to account—and maybe more to the point, the Ladies to whom they give obedience."

Master Nikos bowed his head. "If that must be so, then so be it."

"Don't be weak," Briana said sharply. "Don't give up. We need you more than we ever have. If you fail the test, there may be no empire left."

"Maybe that itself is a weakness and a failure," Nikos said. "Maybe it's time the empire had its own, human heart instead of relying on the whims of gods."

Briana raised a hand. "*Don't* say it. Try not to think it. You have to be strong. That's not a choice, Master. That's what has to be."

Master Nikos sat back in his chair. He was almost laughing—which was more alarming in its way than if he had risen up in a killing rage. "By the gods on the Mountain! I never thought I'd see the day when I was taken to task for every aspect of my tenure, and by a woman at that."

That was not well calculated. Briana's eyes narrowed. "I am the Regent of Aurelia. As such, I have no specific authority over you, but I speak on the empire's behalf. I render no formal judgment. But be aware, Master of riders, that you are under scrutiny. You are charged with the empire's fate and its future. That future demands choices that no Master has ever had to make. You must make them. If you do not, or if you choose wrongly, there will be consequences."

Nikos rose to his feet. His back was stiff. "Are you asking for my resignation?"

She met his glare. "Truthfully? No. I don't think you're incompetent. I do think you've been faced with more than you bargained for. You've lost a great deal, and I'm afraid you'll lose much more before this is over. You'll be asked to give everything you have, and then give again. I wouldn't blame you if you backed away from it. Any sensible man would."

"Sensible," Nikos said. His mouth twisted. "There's sense, and there's reality. If I go, who takes my place? The one I was grooming for it is so broken he may never be whole again. No one else has the training or the strength. The Called of the past two years have been remarkably gifted—but they're children. It will be years before any of them is ready. We need a leader now, not ten years from now."

"So," said Briana. "Will you lead?"

"I will try."

"You will do it."

That was one of the riders' own most cherished instructions. Master Nikos clearly was not pleased to be treated like a recalcitrant student. Equally clearly, he saw the justice in it.

A rider did not bow to any mortal, but he could grant the emperor's heir his sincere respect. "You've given me much to think on, lady," he said.

"I should hope so," said Briana.

Seventeen

Briana kept her royal face all the way from the Master's hall to Kerrec's rooms. He was not in them. He was under guard until he could be taken away from the Mountain.

That would have to be soon. But not today. Once the door was shut and there was only Valeria to see, Briana dropped where she stood. Valeria leaped in alarm, but her fit of shaking was neither weeping nor convulsions. She was laughing.

It was hysteria, mostly. Valeria was rather tempted herself. She filled a cup from the water jar by the bed and brought it to Briana, and persisted until she drank it.

By then she had stopped shaking. Valeria sat on the floor beside her.

"That man," Briana said, "is the most frustrating person I have ever run across—and I live in the imperial court."

"All riders are," Valeria said. "It seems to go with the gifts. The older they are, the worse they get."

"Kill me if I ever turn into one of them." Briana lay back and closed her eyes. "Dear gods. I gave the Master of the Schools of Peace and War a dressing-down as if he were one of the stableboys. Will he blast me to a cinder, do you think?"

"I think you gave him too much to think about."

"That would be a good thing," Briana said. She sighed. "And yet again, through all of this, he never once acknowledged what you did. Is that riders' discipline or is it more of their stubborn blindness?"

Valeria shrugged. "I'd rather be ignored than sent away. I was there for a reason. I did what I was meant to do. It's over."

"You know it's far from over. You're down another First Rider. That's going to hurt."

"Didn't you hear the Healer?" Valeria said. "The Mountain protects its own."

"You have a cold heart," Briana said.

"I'm a rider," said Valeria. "Which I suppose makes me blind, too."

"I don't think any of us is seeing clearly," Briana said. "All I can see is that there's a war on, and not only on the frontier. I don't think this year is going to end as quietly as it began."

"I know it's not," Valeria said, not particularly loudly. She rose to her knees. "Here, do you need help? You should rest."

"So should you," said Briana.

"I will. Just let me get you to bed first."

"I can get myself to bed," Briana said, fixing a cold eye on Valeria. "What are you plotting?"

"Nothing," said Valeria.

Briana's glare did its best to sear the truth out of her, but she was adamant. She helped Briana into bed over her protests. Then when Briana was safely settled, she went where she needed to go.

* * *

There is a worm in the Mountain's heart.

Those words had been echoing behind everything Valeria did and said since the Master spoke them. He seemed to think they pointed to Kerrec. She knew otherwise.

She also knew what she had to do. She would do it properly this time, if she could—or as properly as she dared.

Master Nikos was standing by the stallion paddocks in the evening light, watching his Icarra and Kerrec's Petra scratch one another's necks over the fence they shared. They were none the worse for their adventure in the Dance.

He kept his eyes on the stallions, but Valeria could tell he was aware of her. She leaned on the fence some distance down, in front of Sabata's paddock. He came to be petted and fed a bit of sugar, then wheeled on his haunches and erupted in a fit of bucks and caracoles. In spite of all her troubles, Valeria could not help but laugh.

Master Nikos came up beside her. He was smiling. "You've done well with him," he said.

Valeria blinked. Compliments from any of the elder riders were rare. From the Master, they were nonexistent. "He does it for himself," she said. "I'm only there to offer suggestions."

Nikos laughed. "So are we all," he said.

She eyed him suspiciously. The stallions could soothe any rider's temper. Even so, this seemed excessive. "What is it?" she asked. "What's happened?"

"No more than you already know," he said. "You acquitted yourself well in the Dance."

Valeria was immune to flattery. "Oda did most of it. I did what had to be done."

"You did it well," he said. "You do understand that this has no effect on your rank or training. There's still a great deal for you to learn."

"Why, did you think I'd demand to be made a First Rider? I'm not ready for that. I'm not ready to be even a Fourth Rider, not yet. I don't know nearly enough about training horses. Or history and strategy. Or—"

"Good," he said, and that stopped her. She was babbling. "I am sorry that you'll be losing your primary teacher, but Gunnar has agreed to oversee your education. He's not as gifted as Kerrec or as experienced as Andres. Still, he believes in your talents and he isn't dismayed by your gender—and he has more feel for the Dance, in some respects, than any other rider, even Kerrec. In that he's as nearly your equal as any of the riders."

Valeria heard him in a sort of despair. Her stomach clenched at each mention of Kerrec's name.

It was all quite reasonable. She could tell the Master had given it a great deal of thought. She should be honored, and to an extent she was.

But she had to say what she had come to say. "I do thank you—really. I like Gunnar. He's a good teacher. But I need to go with Kerrec."

Nikos frowned. "We all wish he could stay here—it wrenches my heart to send him away. But he'll destroy himself, and likely all of us, as well, if he stays. In Aurelia at least he has some hope of healing."

"I know that," said Valeria. "I need to go to Aurelia with him. If we're both away from the Mountain, I can—"

"You are not a Healer," Nikos said. "You are a rider. Your teachers and training are here."

"Kerrec can teach me," Valeria said. "He's been doing it for a year. It doesn't matter how much or how little magic he has— the knowledge is still there, and he can pass it on."

Nikos drew a breath. Valeria would wager he was praying for patience. "I understand what he is to you. Whatever you young things might think of an old man who has never had a wife, I do have some knowledge of what is between a man and a woman. Still, his destiny is elsewhere, for now. Yours is here. Without him, we need you more than ever."

That was true, and it was bitter to hear. It did not stop Valeria from saying, "At this moment, if I could wring his neck, I would. But that's not what matters. If I go to Aurelia, continue my studies, do what I can for him—"

"Valeria," the Master said. His voice was almost gentle. "You can't take the whole weight of the world. You need to be here. He needs to be away from the Mountain. There are mages by the hundred in Aurelia, and Healers of more strength and skill than any we have here. He'll be in good hands."

Valeria shook her head. "You're blinding yourself again. Can't you see how the patterns are running? My path leads away from here. It will lead back, and so will his—if the gods allow. But I have to go."

"I see the patterns," Nikos said. "I see that your greatest safety is here."

He saw nothing. He knew nothing of what was in Valeria—what she was and what she might do if she stayed.

She tried to tell him. The words were there, ready to be spoken. But when she tried, they vanished in the Unmaking. It was like a geas, a spell of binding.

If she had not been sure before that she needed to remove herself from the Mountain, that persuaded her. She had to give in to the spell—but she refused to let it stop her. She could talk about Kerrec, if not about herself.

"And his safety?" she asked. "What happens to him?"

"The hard truth," Master Nikos said, "is that his destiny is of less importance to us than yours. If we lose him forever, we won't all die. If we lose you…"

Valeria hissed in frustration. "You need us both. He needs me. I have to go."

"Child," he said, "you will not. Your place is here."

She bit her tongue until she tasted blood. All her life, her elders had done their best to keep her from doing what she was called to do. She should have known Master Nikos would forbid her—everyone else had.

She should have kept quiet and simply gone when it was time. But she had fought so hard to be a rider, and suffered so much to win it. If she did this against the Master's wishes, she would lose her place among the riders.

There was no budging him. He might have done a bit of thinking and he might be considering the uses of flexibility, but he was still a stiff-necked old man. He could only see that Valeria would be safer here and that Kerrec was safer elsewhere. One of which happened to be true, but one of which was not.

No wonder the gods were threatening to break the school apart. All the riders needed a good shaking—every last one of them.

Sabata roared up to the fence and skidded to a halt in a stinging spray of sand. He danced in place, tossing his mane and snorting.

The absolute simplicity of him brought her nearly to tears. He was a pure being. Doubt never stained him. Hesitation never sullied his spirit. He knew what he was and why, always.

He was the best of all diversions. She watched the patterns shift around the Master. Sabata was shaping them in ways Valeria could just begin to understand.

Nikos might be aware of it, somewhere deep inside, but Sabata's presence was blurring his memory. When he looked for the seeds of his argument with Valeria, he found a shimmer of white and an eye so deep a man could drown in it. There were stars there, and world upon world vanishing into the dark.

Valeria shook herself free of the vision. When she bent her head in respect and began to retreat, Nikos waved her away with an air of distraction. He was enspelled, fixed on the stallion's beauty and power.

It was hard not to feel guilty, but Sabata was losing patience. If she would not go, he would break down the fence and carry her off.

That would break the spell. For all her guilt, she did not want that. For once she had a free path ahead of her, and white gods guarding it. She would be a fool if she failed to take it.

Eighteen

The emperor's legions had camped for close on a month at the ford the imperials called Tragante. Except for dispatches of scouts, they had made no move to cross the river.

"You think they're building a city?" Cyllan asked.

Euan Rohe glanced at him. They were crouched with the rest of the warband in a fernbrake on the far side of the river, watching the little dark men come and go from their fort. It did look like a city, with its massive palisade and squat square watchtowers, but he said, "That's just a war camp. If it was a city, they'd be building in stone instead of wood."

"So why aren't they moving?" Donal demanded. "They can't just sit there until the snow flies."

"They certainly can," said Euan, "and they will, if they think they can gain something by it."

"What would that be? Months of wasted time and no battle worth the name?"

Euan shrugged. "They don't think like us. If our raiding across the river everywhere but here hasn't brought them out, I don't know what will. They're waiting for something—an alignment of the stars, a signal we're not aware of...who knows?"

"Maybe they're waiting for us to surrender," Conory said.

"Or to attack them," said Donal.

"We will," Euan said, "when the high king is ready." He pushed himself from his belly to his knees. "Come on. We're wasting daylight."

None of them argued with that. There was a herd of cattle coming in from one of the towns farther inland, and they had a hankering for the taste of imperial beef.

Conory led—he was the best tracker. Euan brought up the rear. Half a dozen Calletani against two eights of legionaries and a pack of drovers—they reckoned that fair odds.

This was good country to hunt in. Much of it was thick woodland. The legions had made a road through it, eight man-widths broad and paved with stone, and cut back the trees for a furlong on either side.

There was still plenty of cover for a raiding party. Euan and his kinsmen ghosted through the trees, staying just within sight of the road.

The shadows grew longer as the sun sank. Under the trees it was already dark. Conory led them by smell and feel more than sight.

With this many cattle to slow them down, the supply train would have to stop for the night where the woods opened into a rough-hewn field. But when the warband reached it, they were not there. The field was empty and the stream that ran through it was undisturbed since the last time a supply train had camped there.

The others wanted to continue down the road until they found the cattle, but Euan stopped them. "They'll be here," he said.

"What if they aren't?" said Strahan.

"They will be," Euan said.

They were not all convinced, and Strahan least of all, but Euan stared them down. Finally Strahan muttered, "It's on your head if you're wrong." He made himself comfortable in the undergrowth beyond the earthworks that marked every legionary camp, past or present.

They had a clear view from where they were, and ferns to lie on and water to drink from a brook that fed into the larger stream. As ambushes went, it was rather pleasant.

When the others were settled, Euan indicated a full bladder and slipped away. He did not go far, and he did not go out of sight of the clearing. If he peered around a tree, he could see the shadows in shadow that were his warband.

His excuse had been true enough. When he had taken care of that, he made sure he was well out of sight of the others. Then he slipped a packet wrapped in linen from the bottom of his traveling pack.

Carefully he uncovered the seeing-stone that Gothard had given him. One way and another, he had never got around to telling anyone that he had it. It seemed a useful secret to keep.

It was black dark where he was, though the last of the sunset light still glimmered in the clearing. The short summer night was finally falling. Yet even in the dark, and as black as the stone seemed in daylight, he could see it lying in its wrappings.

The longer he had it, the easier it was to make it work. He thought of legionaries and drovers and cattle, and the stone's surface stirred and shimmered. He looked down as if from a height onto the twilit road.

As he had expected, a herd of cattle plodded along the paving and spilled into the cleared space on either side, driven by men on horseback. The legionaries marched on foot, eight in front of the herd and eight behind.

They were moving slowly. It was late and they had been traveling for two days. Some of the cows had calves that needed to stop and nurse.

The fall of night did not urge them to greater speed. There was a moon, a few days from the full, bright enough to see by. And they had a mage.

Euan had seen mages in the stone before when he spied on the emperor's camp. He had learned to recognize the signs. There was a glimmer over the cattle like a drift of mist and moonlight. Those were wards, protections against just such a raid as Euan was contemplating.

The mage was riding with the drovers. He looked and dressed and acted exactly like them, but the moonlight glimmer flowed out of him and then back into him in a steady, circular stream.

Euan took note of the horse he was riding and the clothes he wore. Neither had any distinction. Still, it would help a little when the time came.

They were close to the camp. Euan bade the stone show the road laid out like a map. The cattle were a few furlongs down from the camp, drawing slowly closer.

He covered the stone and paused to take a deep breath. No matter how often he used the stone or how well he justified it, he still felt a sickness in the pit of his stomach. Magic was magic, whatever he wanted to call it.

This was worth it. It had saved his neck a time or two, and won him more than a few raids.

He had not led a raid against a mage before. The stone let him see, but it did not make him a mage. He had only his wits and his weapons to rely on.

Mages were mortal. Their powers had limits. They could be wounded and killed.

He rounded the tree and went back to the warband. They were lying so low that some of them were asleep.

He would sleep when the raid was over. He propped himself against a tree where he could see the camp, covered his face with his dark hunting plaid, and waited.

He could feel the mage coming. It was like a torch drawing closer to his face, first the light, then the heat. Then the cattle came jostling and lowing into the palisade, with the drovers behind and around them and the legionaries scattering to make camp.

The rest of the warband had roused. He heard the change in their breathing. Conory crawled on his belly to the edge of the fernbrake.

Euan followed suit, laying a hand on his arm. "Wait," he breathed.

Conory nodded, a shifting of shadow against shadow and a faint jingle of the rings he wore in his ears. Euan felt the others come up behind them.

They waited until the camp was made and the fires lit, dinner cooked—that made Euan's stomach growl in sympathy— and men bedded down for the night. There were guards, but they were out in the open where they could be watched.

With his own eyes, Euan could not see the wards that were on the camp—but he could smell them. They smelled like hot metal.

He followed his gut. The camp was quiet. The cattle had settled down. The mage was sleeping with the drovers outside the cattle pen.

Conory and the rest knew what to do. With a soft trilling whistle like a night bird's call, he sent them to it.

He knew from the quality of silence when the sentries fell. The mage slept on, trusting in his magic to keep the cattle safe.

Mages never seemed to remember that they were mortal. Another mage would go for the spell. Euan went for the mage.

The fool had never thought to ward himself. He trusted in legionaries and barbarian ignorance—false faith on both sides. Euan slit his throat in one swift, practiced cut.

The wards collapsed with a sound like feathers falling. Their stink lingered, but it was fading fast.

He dispatched the rest of the drovers while his warband disposed of sleeping legionaries. Strahan and Donal were the first to get to the cattle. Euan rounded up the horses.

They could all ride—thanks to the emperor who had sent them as hostages to the School of War on the Mountain. Tonight it was a useful skill. The horses were trained to drive cattle, and the cattle were used to these horses.

They left the dead as a message for the emperor. The cattle did not object too strongly to being herded off the road and into the wood. There were ways a hunter knew, that proved wide enough for one or two cows abreast.

The legions could not watch every ford, here at midsummer with the river running low. The cattle crossed in starlight a few bends upriver of Tragante, slipped through the water and up the bank and out of the empire.

Nineteen

The raiders came thundering into the high king's war camp in the hot bright morning, whooping and laughing and driving a herd of imperial cattle. Clansmen tumbled out of tents and ran from the practice grounds. Even the high king, the Ard Ri, stood up in the council circle to see what had come to disturb his peace.

Eight horses, eighty cattle—that was a fair night's work. Euan sent most of the cattle to the Calletani, but he and Conory between them herded a dozen into the high king's circle.

Old men and priests scattered, squawking in dismay. The king had to step aside briskly to keep from being run down by a spotted cow.

The people had been raiding cattle since the dawn time. They moved by instinct, inborn, to pen the cattle in the king's circle.

Euan sat on the stocky brown horse that had belonged to the

mage, and grinned at the high king. "Here's a gift from the Cal-letani," he said. "They're fine eating, these imperial cattle."

The Ard Ri was a big man, bigger than Euan, and broad as a bull. His strength was legendary. He had broken twelve men's backs over his knee to take the high king's torque.

Euan wondered how many backs he had stabbed and priests he had bribed to get that far. He looked as brainless as a bull, but there was more than muscle between those gold-ringed ears.

Euan had no doubt that he knew what his brother king dreamed of. Every king of the people did. They all wanted the torque that clasped that massive throat.

It lent a certain edge to the high king's smile as he said, "You've raided well. Was there much pursuit?"

"None at all," Euan said.

The Ard Ri hawked and spat. "They're soft. They think a line of forts and a few thousand men in armor will keep us from bleeding them dry."

"Indeed," said Euan sweetly. "You'll be leading us to battle soon, then?"

"That will come in due time," the high king said.

"I'm sure," said Euan. He wheeled his horse about—not wait-ing to be dismissed—and left the king to enjoy his new cattle.

"Rudeness can be an asset in a king," Gothard observed. He had been nowhere in sight while Euan faced the Ard Ri, but that was hardly an obstacle to a mage.

He was sitting in front of Euan's tent in the middle of the Cal-letani camp, playing a game or more likely working a div-ination with a handful of smoothly polished stones. Euan's eye slid over the patterns, refusing to try to make sense of them. If any of them was a seeing-stone, he did not want to know it.

Gothard's usual following of priests was absent for once.

They had long since stopped pretending to guard him. The stone he carried was an incarnation of the One, and he was its master. They would never worship him or any mortal man, but they bowed before the starstone.

Euan bowed to nothing—and that included the high king. He squatted beside Gothard, reaching for the jar of ale that lay between them. It was good ale, well brewed, and welcome after the night and morning he had had.

"You only gave the Ard Ri a dozen cattle," Gothard said. "He can count, you know—at least when it comes to reckoning what he thinks is due him."

"He got more than his due," Euan said. "There were eighty cattle. I gave him twelve. That's more than a tenth part."

"He'll reckon you owe him twice that," said Gothard. "You're his vassal, after all."

There was no such word in the language of the people—he had to say it in Aurelian. Euan bared his teeth at the insult. "I could have declined to give him any at all. He's been squatting on his arse up here for a solid month, while the imperials lock up the river and the people lose their edge. What's he waiting for? The same sign the emperor is?"

"His courage, probably," Gothard said. He scooped up the stones and cast them in a new pattern. It made him frown. "He says he wants all of the people to come in before he makes his move. You know that. You've heard him."

"Most of war is waiting," Euan said. It had been an axiom of his father's. "We're not barred from raiding, at least. The more we tweak the imperials' noses, the more likely they'll be to lose their tempers. Then we'll get a real war in spite of the Ard Ri."

Gothard shifted one stone, then another. He was still frowning. He slanted a glance at Euan. "What if you were the Ard Ri?"

"Oh, no," said Euan. "Not yet. I've power to build first, and allies to win. The five tribes will get cattle, with one of my own warband to give the gift. Then we'll see who comes calling."

"I could make them want to come," Gothard said, "and you wouldn't have to give up your cattle."

Sometimes, Euan thought, Gothard lost his grip on the half of him that was Calletani and turned into a complete imperial courtier. It usually happened when his magic came into it.

Euan decided to be patient—yet again. "Let them come on their own. There will be plenty for you to do once they get here."

Gothard's lip curled. "Oh? Such as? Do you want me to fetch them ices from the south and shellfish from the sea, and make them an emperor's feast?"

"You're not a servant," Euan said.

"Then what am I?" Gothard demanded. "I'm not a priest. They've made that all too clear, even if I could stomach the life they live. I'm not one of your stouthearted clansmen. No one is calling me prince in my mother's right, either. What am I, then? Your pet sorcerer?"

"What do you want to be?"

That gave Gothard pause. Imperials never asked that question—and as far as Euan could see, in spite of plaids and mustaches, this was an imperial nobleman first and foremost.

Gothard took a long time to answer. Euan waited for it. While he waited, he eyed the stones.

They were ordinary pebbles from the river, smooth and rounded. Most were grey or white. One was red, and one had bands of black and red and pale grey.

The white ones made him think of the gods on the Mountain. The banded one was like Valeria—all things in one, woman and horse mage and lover of princes. The white ones lay in a circle around it. A grey one had fallen against it. Euan stretched out a finger to separate them.

"Don't do that," Gothard said. His voice was so mild that it was frightening.

Euan drew his hand back carefully.

"I want," said Gothard, "to be emperor. In the end, and to the end."

"I know that," said Euan. "What do you want to be here, while you wait for your stars to align?"

Gothard raised the grey stone that Euan had wanted to touch, turning it slowly in the light. "The stars have aligned. It's begun. The One will come, and the world will be Unmade."

"And you will Unmake it?"

Gothard's eyes had gone as dark as the starstone. "If that grace is given me."

Euan shivered. Whether or not Gothard wanted the priest's life, he had the priest's spirit. However whole and even fair his body was, his soul was a twisted thing.

Euan was glad to leave him to his stones and his dreams. Euan's dreams were cleaner, and he lived his life in the sunlight. The dark was necessary and the Unmaking inevitable, but he did not court it.

The kings of the five tribes were duly appreciative of their six fine cattle apiece—a proper number, if the Ard Ri had twice as many. The Calletani still had the victor's share, and the horses, too, but that was not mentioned.

Better yet for Euan's dwindling patience, the glory of that raid incited other young men to try their hand at tormenting the imperials. The boldest did not stop at stealing cattle and robbing supply trains, which in any case were guarded to the hilt since Euan had shown them the error of their ways. They raided in force, and they raided well beyond the river, striking at towns and villages and despoiling fields and herds.

There were skirmishes—more heated the longer the raids went on. Some could honestly be called battles.

The emperor stayed in his fort at Tragante, warded by magics so strong they made Euan's teeth ache even from across the river. His legions went out to deal with the raids, spreading themselves gratifyingly thin.

But the Ard Ri did nothing about it. He stayed in his war camp half a day's march from the river, just as the emperor stayed in his fort. As far as Euan could see, he debated minute points of clan law with his elders, celebrated rites of the One with his priests, and amused himself by wrestling with one or more of his burly and muscle-proud warriors. Actual war, or a battle that would settle it all, seemed the furthest thing from his mind.

Half a month after Euan's raid, envoys came from the emperor. Euan had been out burning corn and barley in fields farther down the river than anyone else had gone—there was a distinct advantage in having horses—but he came back shortly before the imperials arrived in camp. He was washing off the stink of horse and salving his blisters from the saddle when they rode in.

There were two of them, with half a dozen mounted guards. One looked like an old soldier, with the scars to prove it. The other was a weathered-looking brown person in clothes too plain for a noble, who kept to the rear like a servant.

The soldier was ordinary enough, all things considered. The brown man was rotten with magic.

If that was not a spy, then Euan was an imperial noble. He cast about for Gothard, but there was no sign of him. Euan put himself in order as quickly as he could and strode off toward the council circle.

As he had expected, the soldier-envoy was sparring in

words with the high king and his elders. The brown man was his interpreter.

Euan paid little attention to the words—they were being translated accurately, which somewhat surprised him, but there was nothing in them worth listening to. The emperor wanted surrender and withdrawal—the Ard Ri wanted the same. The emperor wanted the raids to stop. The Ard Ri pretended that he had never heard of such a thing. It was all a dance, as empty and pretty as one of the warriors' dances around the fire of an evening.

Euan watched the brown man. He seemed engrossed in translating orotund Aurelian phrases into serviceable Erisian, but there was a crackle and reek of magic all around him.

The high king's priests might have done something about it, but they seemed unaware of the spy under their noses. Euan leaned toward Strahan who had followed him to the council circle. "Find Gothard," he said under his breath. "Do it quickly."

Strahan raised his brows but did as he was told. Euan worked his way up nearer to the embassy, though so much magic so close made him want to sneeze.

The kings of the Prytani and the Galliceni made room for him. He smiled and bent his head to them. They did the same in return. And that was right and proper among kings.

Gothard did not appear, nor did Strahan come back. Euan was trapped among the other kings, listening to words that meant nothing and watching a mage against whom he could do nothing.

There was no easy escape and no one else he could send to find Gothard if Strahan had not managed it. All Euan could do was keep the brown man in sight and try not to look as impatient as he felt.

If this dance went on, there would be gifts and dinner and a celebration in the envoys' honor. Euan steeled himself to endure it.

But the Ard Ri surprised him. It did not matter particularly at which step in the dance they were. He rose, looming over the imperials, and roared, "Enough!"

The brown man stopped speaking. The soldier snapped to attention. His guards' hands clapped to their belts, where the scabbards were empty—reminding them that their weapons were in barbarian hands. For safekeeping, of course.

The Ard Ri glared down from his considerable height. "I've heard enough," he said. "Whatever you came here for, it wasn't to treat for anything we would want or care to take. I'll give you bread because honor calls for it, but then you'll be on your way. You can tell your emperor we don't traffic in empty words here. When we speak, our words are to the point."

"And that point is?" the brown man inquired—not even pretending to speak for the other.

"War," said the Ard Ri. "Our raiding parties are doing a great deal of damage. They'll only get worse the longer they go on. Give us these lands and a presence in your court and we'll consider settling for that—for this year. Otherwise, we'll take them, with everything else that we can get our hands on."

"I thank you for your honesty," the brown man said. "Of course we'll give you nothing that is ours. You can try to take it. If you do, we will destroy you."

The high king laughed, booming over the crowd that had gathered. "Oh, no! Destruction is *our* province. Now take your bread and go. You have safe-conduct to the river—but after that, I can promise nothing."

The envoys retreated rapidly, ducking the hard loaves that

were flung at their heads. Euan hoped they understood how lucky they were. They could have lost those heads.

He caught himself indulging in a fit of grudging respect for the Ard Ri. The man was not nearly such a fool as he seemed.

He still had not seen the brown man for what he was. No one had. Maybe Euan was seeing things—or smelling them.

His gut knew better. As soon as he could, which was not nearly as soon as he would have liked, he escaped.

The only place Euan could get a moment to himself was in his tent—and his warband came and went there almost as freely as he did. He uncovered the seeing-stone hastily, focused as best he could, and ordered it to show him Gothard.

It showed him nothing—blankness, without even a sheen of lamplight on the polished stone. Either the stone had failed or Gothard was invisible to it.

As a test, and for curiosity, he thought of the brown man. And there he was, riding down the mountain track from the camp. His fellow envoy looked ruffled and furious, but he was smiling. There was a net of magic on him, so dense and so varied that he looked as if he were wrapped in a mantle of silver and crystal.

He had got what he came for. What it was, Euan could not imagine. He hoped to hell that Gothard could.

Twenty

Euan's hunt for his uncomfortable ally stopped short at the tent's flap, where people were already crowding to demand the king's attention. There were disputes to settle, rations to allot, the loot from the latest raids to dispense, and conversations that he could not avoid, with people who simply wanted the king to talk to them. He had to indulge them, because a king's power rested in the loyalty of his followers—and followers stayed loyal only if the king appeared to value them. If he brushed them off, they would remember. Eventually they would wonder if the tribe would be better off with a different king.

The day was well along and the day's meal over before he could escape. In the long golden twilight, Euan shed his weight of kingly gold and put on plain and tattered breeks and a much-worn plaid. Then, as just one more rangy redheaded Calletani fighting man, he set about scouring the camp for its lone and renegade stone mage.

He did not entertain the notion that Gothard had made a run for it. He was somewhere in the high king's war camp— out of sight of Euan's stone, but Euan could feel him. It was like a splinter under a fingernail, a constant, nagging discomfort.

For lack of greater inspiration, Euan tracked that sense of jabbing annoyance. He followed it through half the camp, then back again almost to where he had started.

The priests of the Calletani had their own circle of tents and rough-built huts, set apart near a dark grove of spruce and pine. The rest of the camp spread out over a long level below a steep wooded hill, but this part of it clung to the first sharp ascent. There were no guards there and no visible protections, but even the camp dogs stayed away.

Euan would have much preferred to do the same, but Gothard was up there—in the highest and least accessible hut, of course. It was older than anything else in this camp, and must have been a herdsman's hut or a hunter's blind in its day. Now it had a pair of priests sitting in front of it like figures carved in bone.

One was blind and the other had a withered arm. The blind one said, "You took your time."

"When it comes to Gothard, I usually do." Euan held his breath as he strode past them. He still caught a whiff of their inimitable stink, but not quite enough to gag him.

The inside of the hut, surprisingly, was no more malodorous than it should be. It smelled of age and damp earth and well-worn wool. There were no furnishings apart from a battered bench and a low table. There was a loaf of bread on the table, untouched, and a jar of imperial wine with the seal intact. A lamp burned beside them, casting a dim light through the hut.

Gothard crouched in the corner farthest from the door. His arms were over his head. He was shuddering as if with cold, though the night was breathlessly warm.

Euan was not fool enough to touch him. He squatted just out of reach and said quietly, "Gothard."

It took several repetitions before Gothard's arms lowered. His face was greenish white. "I'm not ready," he said.

The words were clear, at least. Euan supposed they meant something.

"I've been playing," said Gothard, "with the stone. Learning its ways. Discovering its powers. Trying a working or two. The Mountain is stone, you know. Its roots go down to the source of magic. Its crown touches heaven. A starstone, the Mountain, a broken rider…it's as easy as flying for a bird. Which made me think I knew more than I did."

Still Euan waited. Talk of magic always made his skin crawl. What he gleaned from this was little enough, though it seemed Gothard had been torturing his brother again—using the stone this time instead of a Brother of Pain.

That was hardly surprising. Gothard's hatred of his elder brother was equaled only by his hatred of their father. "What happened?" Euan asked. "Is he fighting back?"

"Gods, no," Gothard said. He seemed astonished that anyone could think such a thing. "He's dancing sweetly to my tune. You'll see what comes of that. You'll like it."

"Will I?"

Gothard squinted at him. "You're really here."

"What," said Euan, "you thought you were imagining me?"

"I couldn't tell," Gothard said. "I have to be careful. That's the trouble with magic. If you don't control it, it controls you. This kind of magic—magic that Unmakes—is worst of all. That's why your priests ban it for anyone but themselves, and raise your clansmen to fear and hate it. They worship the Unmaking. Their god is the Unmade."

Euan did not want to hear of magic and priests together. He cut it off. "What have you done? Have you put the rest of us in danger?"

"You're already in danger. You're waging a war."

"Answer the question," Euan said.

Gothard's glance was pure poison. No wonder he wanted to be emperor, Euan thought. It drove him mad to be told what to do.

Little did he know. Kings and emperors were more truly slaves to obedience than any of their subjects.

He did, eventually, answer the question. Nastily, snappishly, but concisely and, for once, to the point. "I tried to touch the heart of the stone. That's where its strongest magic lies. That's also where it's most strongly bound to the Unmaking. I wasn't ready."

"And?"

"And nothing," Gothard said, a little too quickly.

"There is something," Euan said, cursing the very existence of mages, and especially this one.

"That man," said Gothard. "The one who came with the embassy. The brown man. His name is Pretorius. Master Pretorius. He's a master of several magics."

Euan clamped his hands between his knees to keep from throttling this bloody fool. "What did you do? Did you betray us? What did you sell us for?"

"I did not turn traitor," Gothard said through clenched teeth. "There is something you don't understand. No one is a master of more than one magic—except Pretorius. He's a freak of nature. When he came, I was in the stone. I—or it—wanted to taste his power. Which I could have done, and easily, if I had been ready. And now he knows there is a mage among the people."

"How bad is that?" Euan demanded. "Does he know it's you?"

"Probably," said Gothard. "It's the logical conclusion. Although—" he brightened slightly "—as far as any of them knows, I'm broken and all but powerless. I'm hardly a threat to them."

"You may not be," Euan said, "but the starstone is."

"He doesn't know about that," Gothard said.

"Are you sure?"

"I got out before he could have sensed it," Gothard said.

"And that's why you're cowering in a corner, gibbering and crying?"

"I was not—" Gothard broke off. "My head aches like fury. I almost lost myself. What's down there—what's at the heart of the stone—you may worship it and want to become it. I want to use it. But I'm not ready."

"When will you be?"

"I don't know," Gothard said, biting off the words.

"Let's hope it's soon. You're lucky the Ard Ri isn't a man of action. Anyone else would have led us into battle long ago."

"You might have won," Gothard pointed out.

"I want to win resoundingly," Euan said. "No emperor left to challenge either of us. No army to stand in our way. A clear path to the heart of Aurelia."

Gothard eyed him in grudging respect. "You don't ask for much, do you?"

"I'll take what I can get—but the more I can get, the better."

Slowly Gothard unfolded. "You're as bracing as a slap in the face."

"As long as it works," Euan said. "Are you sure this master mage didn't detect the stone?"

"Nothing is certain in this world."

"He was spying, wasn't he? Was he looking for you?"

"He may have been," Gothard said. "If the emperor's mages have caught wind of the stone, they'd have sent him to see what's here."

"He looked satisfied when he left," said Euan. "Whatever he found, it seems he'd been looking for it."

"He didn't find the stone," Gothard said. "I would know."

"Then you had better discover what he did find."

"Maybe all he found was that the high king has no intention of offering a real battle."

The expression Euan had seen in the seeing-stone had not been that kind of satisfaction, but then as he never failed to insist, he was not a mage. What did he know of what mages wanted when they went spying in the enemy's camp?

"Find out what he was looking for," Euan said, not caring how peremptory he sounded. "And eat something. You're starting to look as bad as the priests."

He left Gothard to obey or not, whatever he chose. Euan needed a short night's sleep. Then, he thought, he would gather as many of the people as would go, and see what the legions would do if they raided in waves farther up the river than any of them had gone before. Enough of that, for long enough, and the emperor would have to come out of his hole—and so would the Ard Ri.

Twenty-One

If Kerrec sank any deeper into self-loathing, he would slit his own throat. And yet, in spite of everything, he did not want to die. He had not wanted that even when he was being taken apart down to the core of his magic.

Maybe that was cowardice. He found it difficult to care.

And now he was riding out of the school in the grey light before sunrise, creeping away like one of the Called who had failed his testing. There had been no farewells, not from any of the riders and not from Valeria.

That hurt more than he had thought it would. He might have eluded the riders to spare pain on both sides, but Valeria was there to see Briana off. She acted as if Kerrec did not exist.

He could hardly blame her. He had treated her abominably, then left her to salvage the disaster he had made of the Dance. She had done it with poise and grace that woke him to awe— and he had said not one word of thanks.

He said nothing now, either, as he mounted Petra and Briana settled in the bay Lady's saddle. There was nothing to say. He was too broken a thing for Valeria. Now she knew it, and her disgust was palpable.

Briana and Valeria exchanged one last embrace. The Lady pawed impatiently. Valeria drew back. The guards took their places around their lady and her brother and her retinue of maids and clerks. The small pack train was ready, and the gate was open.

Kerrec did not look back, no matter how strong the temptation. He might never see this place again, that was true, but it was shrouded in mist and the Mountain was hidden. There was nothing to see.

It was a familiar road he traveled, through country empty of towns or villages, on bridges across deep gorges and through forests of trees so tall they seemed to touch the sky. Maybe he was deluding himself, but the farther he rode from the Mountain, the less shattered he felt.

Maybe it was not Gothard after all who had broken him all over again. Maybe the Healer was right and the Mountain itself had blindly undone the alien spell—and Kerrec had seen and heard it as the voice he hated most in the world. Now, as the Mountain retreated behind him, so did the sickness that had gripped him for so long.

He was not healing, but he was not disintegrating, either. Parts of him were waking with pain that made him think of a frozen limb coming to life.

There was no particular order to it, no pattern he could shape to the purpose. That frustrated him—and maybe it was a good thing. He was beginning to see patterns again, if not to be able to shape them.

Every night on that road, a courier would come with dispatches for the regent. Briana stayed awake by lamplight, night after night. During the day, unless it rained, she often had a dispatch in her hand, reading it while the Lady made her agile way up and down the steep tracks.

It was a little eerie to watch them. The eye saw a rather pretty but also rather stocky bay mare carrying a rider of ambiguous gender and evident scholarship, whereas the mind knew that they were a being above gods and a woman who would, in the fullness of time, rule the empire. The outer appearance barely even hinted at the truth.

Did the Master know that one of the Ladies had left the Mountain for the first time in a thousand years? Did he understand what it signified?

Kerrec was not sure he did, either, but that it was significant, he was absolutely certain. It was yet another sign that the world—like Kerrec—was no longer what it had been.

If Kerrec had been one of his own students, he would have upbraided himself for wallowing. He was prone to that, he had to admit.

On the fourth evening after he left the school, a summer storm had blown away with winds and lightning, leaving a sharp chill behind. Their camp was in a sheltered place, a grove of trees that grew thick and tall. Long after the rest, even Briana, had gone to bed, Kerrec sat sleepless by the fire.

The horses were quiet. The pair of guards whose turn it was to stand watch were settled on an outcropping of rock, all but invisible in fitful starlight. Now and then lightning flashed away to the east.

Kerrec clasped his knees and rocked, resting his eyes on the dance of flames. The patterns there were as nearly random as anything could be, and yet, like all patterns, they had meaning for those who could see. He could, almost. It was tantalizing how close he was to making sense of them.

By now the rising of frustration was all too familiar. He breathed deep and tried to smooth it away. He was not successful, but the effort made him feel a little better.

Petra left the horselines, trailing an inexplicably loosened lead. A darker shadow followed—the Lady, also free of her tether. They settled on either side of him, sighing and groaning and lying in the soft leaf mold.

Kerrec, not quite trapped between them, went briefly, perfectly still. He would expect this of Petra, but the Lady had not come to him before. As far as he had ever known, she was barely aware of him except as yet another fool of a male.

Her eye rolled toward him. Flames reflected in it, flickering gold and red against liquid darkness. Their dance had the same sinuous, interwoven shape as the stallions' Dance.

His hands were cold. His breath came hard. The voice in his head was trying to come back, mocking his weakness and foolishness and insufferable stupidity.

The Lady's teeth snapped just in front of his face. The voice stopped abruptly. Kerrec was alone inside himself, except for the deep quiet of Petra's presence. That had always been there, even when he was altogether broken.

He lay back against the stallion's solid and breathing warmth. The Lady lipped his foot but did not nip it. Her neck angled just so. He rubbed it with toe and heel, slowly. She leaned into it, whickering with pleasure.

He relaxed slowly. He was safe between them, warm and protected. And yet, as he rested against Petra and worked his toes into the Lady's neck and shoulder, his eyes kept coming back to the fire.

The patterns were no clearer, but his mind was less foggy

than it had been in a long while. He had been drowning in confusion and self-pity—as if his broken magic was all that he was, and without it he had nothing worth keeping.

Passivity. That was the word for it. Always giving way. Never acting, always being acted upon. Dancing the Dance, following its patterns, but never living them.

If that was a vice, then every rider suffered from it. They studied their magic, trained their stallions, and rode the Dance in season. They never *did* anything. When the world crashed in upon them, they had no inkling as to how to face it. All they knew was how to be carried through patterns they seldom shaped—and then only at the emperor's will.

No wonder Gothard had captured Kerrec so easily and broken him so completely. Kerrec had let him. Even Kerrec's healing had come from outside, a spell laid in him to do its work apart from his will. He had done nothing to heal himself.

He was a weak and spineless fool. A man with a backbone would have stayed out of the Dance. For that matter he would have done something, anything, long before that, to drive out the thing in his head and force his mind and magic to heal. Even if he had failed, he would at least have tried.

It was not the Mountain's fault he had fallen to pieces. It was not Gothard's fault, either—not at the heart of things. Gothard could not have attacked him if he had not been open to it.

Magic needed two forces—a mage to perform the working and a thing or animal or human to be worked upon. Will could be broken and volition destroyed, but Kerrec had been—*was*— a master mage. He should have stood up to it.

He should stand up to it now. Here he was, yet again, being carried off in a direction not his own. Gothard's voice or spell or whatever it was was still there, eating away at him. Maybe the Mountain made it easier for a stone mage to work his petty evil, but Kerrec would not be any more or less strong in Aurelia than he had been in the school. If Kerrec was a weakling, then that was true wherever he was.

He sat up between the Lady and Petra, fists clenched, glaring at the fire. He was not going to be weak. Not any more.

By the gods, he *would* find a spine. And then…

The fire flared in a sudden gust. Sparks flew. There was darkness behind them—absolute emptiness. Except for one thing. Gothard was there, with a stone in his hand.

It was a plain stone, lumpish and rather ugly, but it had such weight that Kerrec could feel it in his own hands, dragging him down. He fought it—yes, at last, he did.

It was reaching, working, acting upon a confusion of shapes and images. Armies marching, men in armor with swords and lances and short strong bows, men naked and painted and whirling axes about their heads, screaming soundlessly in the crackling of the flames. He saw his sister sitting on a throne that crumbled beneath her, and his father on a barren hill, looking up without fear into a maw of absolute blackness. He saw blood and slaughter. He saw it all whirl away into the void, absolutely and forever Unmade.

That was the pattern of the Dance he had almost broken. The Augurs had not seen it. But the stallions knew. The Lady knew.

And now Kerrec knew. What he would do with the knowledge, he was already sure of. But he could not do it now, however tempted he was to throw saddle on Petra's back and bolt for the border. He had to put himself together first, mind and body, and find the heart of his magic. He could only pray that he could do it soon enough to stop the thing that was coming.

Twenty-Two

Valeria waited three days before she made her escape. If anyone was expecting her to run, he would be watching for it sooner than that. Therefore she gritted her teeth and hung on.

There were plenty of distractions. The Lady had gone with Briana. That did not surprise Valeria at all, but it seemed to take the riders completely aback.

Ladies never left the Mountain. That was an article of dogma so dearly held that some of the older riders seemed unable to accept any evidence to the contrary. They insisted with religious fervor that she must have returned to the high pastures or else passed out of the body. Never mind that several people, including Valeria, had seen her trot out of the gate with Briana on her back.

Fortunately for their sanity, one tradition at least remained intact. Two days after the princess regent left, the young stallions came in at last. There was no Great One among them, though there were a good number with both breeding and talent. None of them tempted Valeria to take him for training, even if she had had the rank to do it.

Even the young ones were showing her the way. In the night after their coming, while the riders slept off the wine of a belated celebration, she found Sabata waiting impatiently in his stall. The gates had no mortal guards, and the wards that were on them were no obstacle to a Great One.

It would be a while—two or three days at least—before anyone realized Valeria was gone. She had found a spell in the library when she was supposed to be searching for something much more elementary, a trick of memory like the shifting of patterns that Sabata had wielded against Master Nikos. Everyone would think she was somewhere else, with someone else, or imagine that he had seen her passing by just a moment before.

The illusion would not last. Eventually she would be expected for something too solid to elude—then someone, probably a servant, would notice that her bed had not been slept in.

By then she would hope that the Master would throw up his hands and let her go. He might even be relieved. Valeria was an endless reproach to the riders' existence.

Meanwhile she let Sabata find the road to Aurelia. It was a slow passage, because they both had to forage for food, but she was not in a great hurry. Kerrec would be settled in the city when she got there. If she dallied long enough, he might even be glad, or at least not too icily furious, to see her.

The truth of it was, she was enjoying the taste of freedom. There was joy in long days with nothing to do but ride and hunt, with no human to trouble her and no duties to disturb her peace.

Sabata was the best company she could ask for. He swung along the forest tracks and down the mountainsides, snorting happily to himself. When he stopped to graze, she slipped off to find whatever a human could eat. She came back with herbs, often, and wild roots, and fish from one of the rivers or streams, or rabbits or birds if she had time to set a snare.

She was almost sorry one day after she had lost count of the sunrises, to see the trees thinning and the land flattening, rolling down to the inner plains of Aurelia. Roads were more frequent here, with traffic on them. Towns stood on promontories or alongside rivers or at crossroads.

She avoided the towns for a while, feeling oddly shy and wild, but after a day or two she shook herself into some sort of sense. If these outland villages were too much for her, the city of Aurelia would send her screaming back into the woods.

She started small, with a village of farmers and woodsmen, where there was a tiny garrison of imperial soldiers and an inn that mostly catered to them. There was magic in the town, the subtle shimmer of a wisewoman's workings. Valeria could see their effects in the number of healthy children and the general cleanliness of the place. Except for the garrison, it reminded her of Imbria where she was born.

She surprised herself with a stab of homesickness. On the Mountain she might dream of her family, but when she was awake she never for a moment regretted leaving it. She was a rider. That was all she had ever wanted to be. She was never meant to be a village wisewoman like her mother.

And yet here in this village of wooden houses and plain people, she remembered what home had been like before it meant stone halls and white stallions. The inn was anything but luxurious, but it was clean. Its keeper took Valeria for a young man and her stallion for an ordinary grey cob, and told her what she was doing there.

"Courier for the legion, are you?" he said. "Not many of

those riding through here these days. Most of the action's gone east to the frontier."

He sounded a touch nostalgic. "Which legion was yours?" she asked him.

"Third Antonia," he said, straightening his thickened body into the sketch of a legionary's salute. "Centurion of the fifth cohort Marcus Mezentius at your service, sir."

It seemed her rider-candidate's uniform was close enough to a courier's to pass his expert muster. That could be useful. She dipped her head to him, offering the respect he deserved.

He was a fount of gossip, thanks to the garrison and a decent number of travelers between the mountains and the plain. Over venison pasties and dark ale, she heard tales from all over the north, and some even from the war—how the emperor was harrying the barbarians and they were harrying him, but neither side had as yet committed to an open battle.

There were rumors from the Mountain, too. "Some say another woman was Called," he said, "and some say it was the princess regent, though if that's the case, what was she doing all the way out there instead of staying in the royal city where she belongs? Me, I think there's more song than sense coming out of that place. What's so magical about riding a horse? Can you tell me that?"

Valeria could, given several days and a club for persuasion, but she shrugged and held her tongue.

"Look at you, now," Mezentius said. "I saw you ride in as pretty as you please. What are they doing that you can't?"

"Not much," Valeria said, and that was the truth, more or less. "So—do you think the emperor should close the school?"

"I think there's too much mystery-mongering and too little sense. Now if there was a rider or two and some of their fancy horses in every town, connected to the garrisons, maybe, wouldn't that be a good thing? The nobles' sons could learn to ride and the recruits could learn to fight on horseback, and we'd have extra defenses if we needed them. What good are they, after all, all walled in a hundred miles from anywhere?"

"They're master mages, aren't they?" one of the people in the common room said. He was local by the accent, dressed like a farmer who had done well for himself. "Maybe they need seclusion to work their magic."

"If that's true," said Mezentius, "why do they do their Dances with as big an audience as they can get, and Augurs and nobles and princes and all? Can't they do all that in a city like the other orders? Even Beastmasters have their master house in Aurelia. You'd think they'd be the ones living on a mountain."

"Horses need pasture," the farmer pointed out. "That's not easy to find in a city."

"There's plenty of room on the plains," Mezentius said. "Plenty better pasture, too, than what you find up in the mountains. You don't see the aristos running their herds up there. They're all down in the lowlands where the forage is better."

"Harsh land makes strong stock," Valeria said. "Have you ever seen the white gods?"

Mezentius shook his head. But the farmer said, "I did once. My wife's brother was Called. We went up for the testing. They're not what you'd expect at all. You look at them standing still, you think you'd have them pulling your wagon to market. But then they move." He shook his head and sighed. "I never saw anything like it. They're as solid as mud—then they turn to light and fire."

"Magic," Mezentius said.

Valeria wondered what he would think if he knew the sturdy dappled-grey cob in his own stable was one of the gods he dismissed so easily. She was only mildly tempted to enlighten him. It was more enlightening for her to hear what he had to say and ponder all the sides of it.

Maybe this was part of what the school had to become. Isolation had protected it for a long time—but as any soldier knew, the more power was concentrated in a single place, the easier it was to make it a target and destroy it.

She had much to think about that night and when she rode out in the morning. Mezentius tried to refuse the coin she offered him. "I'll put in with the garrison," he said.

It would have been easy to give way—but she was not a courier, and she could pay. She had her rider-candidate's pittance, which usually went to peddlers or alehouses, but she had seldom touched hers. She had a year's worth. She was richer than she had ever been in her life.

Just when she was ready to tell this stubborn innkeeper exactly who and what she was, he took her silver penny. He gave her a blessing, too, and wished her a good journey. Then he slapped Sabata on the rump to send him on his way.

He never knew how close he came to having his skull kicked in. Sabata was not used to living like a mortal horse.

He would have to learn. He hunched his back and flattened his ears, but he refrained from bucking. That showed great restraint on his part.

She slapped his neck, which he did not object to. *She* was allowed the occasional insolence. He settled to a more acceptable pace, with one last, irritable headshake at the human creature who had taken such liberties with his celestial self.

Twenty-Three

Kerrec refused to live in the imperial palace. "I'll live in Riders' Hall," he said. "It's there, it's suitable, and it deserves to be used for more than a few days every hundred years."

He was braced for a fight, but Briana nodded. "That makes sense. I'll send people ahead to get it ready for you."

They were eight days out from the Mountain and a short day's journey outside of Aurelia, resting for the night in one of the royal summer houses. It perched on a promontory above the river gorge, looking out over the plain to the city and the sea.

Kerrec could have lived here, high above everything, but there was no time for that now. He had to get to the city. There were things there that he needed.

The nights, here at the height of summer, were short, and dusk seemed to last forever. He sat on the terrace with Briana in the long twilight, sipping iced wine and watching the stars come out. "I do mean to do it," he said. "Not just pretend to be an envoy, to keep us all from being shamed. I'll make myself useful."

She slid a glance at him. "You really aren't pathetic, you know. Even when you try, you only manage to look constipated."

She was baiting him. He showed her his teeth and said, "What did you think I was going to do? I have no talent for idling. I'm not particularly decorative."

"The female half of the world might disagree with that," she said. "I thought you might rest. And read. And consult with mages and find ways to heal yourself. If you want to do that in Riders' Hall, I'll arrange it."

"I would like to attend councils," he said.

"Why?" she asked.

Of course she would ask that. Fortunately he had an answer ready. "Patterns are my gift," he said. "The interplay of factions, the strategies of princes, may help restore it."

She thought about that. He held his breath—because if she asked too many questions, she might discover what he was really up to. Then she nodded. "We can use you, that's true. But I want you to promise me something."

He raised a brow.

"Promise you won't overstretch yourself. You're here to heal, not make yourself worse."

"I want to heal," he said, and that was the honest truth. "I want to be whole."

"You will be," said Briana.

He did not want to think, tonight, that they both might be wishing for the impossible. Every day he fought for a little more strength, a little more wholeness. And every day, he gained—but never as much as he wanted or needed. To be himself again, to have all his arts and powers back—he dreamed of it, night after night, when he was not dreaming of the man who had destroyed him.

Gothard. Now more than ever, his brother's name made his stomach knot and his heart beat faster. Gothard had wanted him dead—but not easily and, by all the gods, not quickly.

Kerrec wanted Gothard…what? Dead? Not necessarily. Destroyed would do. Shattered as Kerrec had been, with his magic all in shards.

It was not mere revenge, he told himself. This was a worse threat to the empire than any barbarian horde. In dreams while he slept or in campfires along the road, he had seen over and over again what Gothard would do if he was not stopped. Kerrec supposed he was obsessed—but if that obsession kept the empire from being Unmade, then he would continue to indulge it.

Riders' Hall was a fortress on the outside, grey and forbidding, but the inside was surprisingly pleasant. There were two riding courts with perfectly raked sand from the harbor, a stable between them with large and airy stalls, a hall painted and carved in the ornate fashion of three hundred years ago, and suites of rooms in different styles from soldier-simple to royally elaborate.

Briana had sent a full staff of servants, including a stableman. Half a dozen of her own horses were in the stable, to keep Petra and the Lady company. Everything that Kerrec might need was there or could be had for the asking.

He had grown out of such luxury. He chose the simplest suite with the narrowest and hardest bed, and considered sending the servants back to his sister—but there was something to be said for a clean and well-run hall. For now, he let them be.

The servants knew who he was. They were much too well trained to make a fuss, but they bowed a little lower and were a little more attentive than they might have been for a First Rider who had not been born an imperial heir.

Briana left him with them. She had an empire waiting.

He felt oddly empty without her. She had been so close for so many days, and now he was alone.

That was a weakness. He thought seriously about shutting himself in his rooms, with the servants on the other side of the door. But that was a kind of weakness, too. He had to put all of that aside.

He went to the stable instead. Briana had sent mares—none of them in foal. They were all, he happened to notice, nicely matched to Petra, if the stallion had been inclined to act on it.

They were also of good age and more than adequate training. "Our lady trained them herself," the stableman said.

His name was Quintus. Something about him made Kerrec think he had been Called but had failed the testing. It was the way he moved around the horses, and the way he paid homage to the Great Ones without making a show of it.

If he had failed, it had not left him bitter. It seemed he was one of those for whom it was enough to have been Called. No matter what became of them, they had that.

Kerrec felt himself begin to relax. Here was one of his own kind, even if the stallions had sent him away. Kerrec would not have thought it could matter so much. Riders, it seemed, were herd animals—much as their stallions were.

There were horses to feed and stalls to clean. Quintus was not too terribly appalled when Kerrec fetched a pitchfork and went to work.

Here was healing. Here was rest, better than sleep. When every stall was spotless, every horse eating sweet hay and drinking clean water, Kerrec sent Quintus to bed. "I'll stay awhile," he said.

Quintus hesitated, but after a moment he shrugged and did as he was told.

Kerrec slipped into Petra's stall. The stallion was deep in earthly contentment. Kerrec sat in the clean straw, leaning against the wall, and watched Petra eat.

He closed his eyes for just a moment. When he opened them, the stable was dark but for the soft moonlight glow that always came off the stallions. Petra was down, curled like a foal, sound asleep.

Kerrec slid over toward him and lay with his back to that large and breathing warmth. Deep inside him, something that had been clenched tight was beginning to unfold. It was like a flower—or a spell of healing waking again from too long a sleep.

In the morning Kerrec woke in a circle of strangers. He was lying on the bed in his room, not in Petra's stall. He had no memory of moving from one to the other.

The strangers were both men and women. They were all wearing robes or uniforms or badges of magical orders—no two alike, and none below the rank of master.

Some he recognized. Others he knew by reputation. They were all studying him as if he had been one of the Augurs' prodigies. A two-headed calf, maybe, or a fly with a man's head.

"It's masterful work," said the Master Healer. The old man Kerrec remembered was dead. This was a much younger woman with a much less soothing presence. She reminded him of Valeria—a bracing tonic rather than a honeyed syrup. She frowned not at Kerrec but through him. "Each of the larger patterns is cracked at the base. All the rest have crumbled in response. Really, it's beautifully done."

"If you see beauty in destruction," the Chief Augur said. Him, Kerrec had known since childhood. He was taller and thinner and greyer than ever. "Look below the patterns. Something else is there, something that mends from the roots."

"Ingenious," said the chief of the Wisewomen. "Inspired. To use so simple a working in so very effective a way—that's mastery. Where is the mage who did it? Why are we here, if he's been so well looked after already?"

"Because it wasn't enough," Kerrec said.

No one seemed startled that the object of their fascination could speak. "It should have been," the Wisewoman said. "The Mountain's interference blocked it, but now that's been removed, it should be free to work again. There's nothing else that needs to be done, apart from rest and time and maybe—" she rapped him lightly on the forehead "—a little acceptance."

"So?" said Kerrec. "I should just submit?"

"It's better to bend than to break," the Healer said. "You should learn to bend. You'll be stronger for it."

"I am already broken," Kerrec said—stiffly, yes.

"Don't wallow in it," she said.

He was cursed with acid-tongued women. Just as he opened his mouth to speak, the Chief Augur said, "There is healing that can be done, and workings to soothe the soul. Surely, Master Healer, you can see to that?"

"He has to heal himself," the Healer said, but added rather grudgingly, "although there are ways to make it less difficult—if he will accept them."

"He will," said the Chief Augur.

That was high-handed of him. Kerrec held his tongue. He had had enough of all these mages. If he kept quiet and provoked them no further, maybe they would go away.

It took rather longer than his patience would have liked, but in the end they let him be. He lay for a while, counting the familiar fragments of himself and marking those that were no longer quite so fragmentary.

The deepest part of him, the part that held his plans and visions, was safe. None of the mages had touched it. Once he was sure of that, he allowed himself a moment's profound and shuddering relief before he rose to face the day.

Breakfast, a blessed hour with Petra, a regency council. People had been warned. Not too many were shocked to see the late prince sitting across the table from the princess regent. A few even seemed to find it gratifying, or at least fitting.

Kerrec paid little attention to the words they spoke. He listened to the rhythm of their voices and watched their faces, following the patterns of alliance and hostility. Those were complicated, but if he sat quiet and relaxed almost into a doze, they took shape as easily as the exercises he had ridden with Petra that morning.

He was almost sorry when the council ended. What could have been an exercise in tedium and frustration had turned out to be rather a pleasure. He had learned nothing specific, but he was fairly certain that none of them knew what Gothard was up to or even where he was. The conspiracies that surrounded them had no stink of him, though more than one was caught in a net of barbarian alliances.

Kerrec took his time standing up while the others dispersed. He was still deep enough in the patterns to see who left with whom—and who did not want to be seen leaving together, but their patterns converged once they were out of sight.

He was the last person left in the room, except Briana. She was watching him, waiting for something. An explosion? A collapse?

"Watch Cornelius and Maelgon," he said. "They're up to something. I caught a whiff of old graves—like the barbarian priests."

Briana raised her brows. "So. You weren't asleep."

"Not exactly," he said. "You can trust Gallio, and the Chief Augur is loyal. The rest will shift where the wind blows. At least one and probably more of them has ties with the tribes."

"Can you tell which?"

"No," he said, "but by tomorrow, probably yes."

"And you were afraid you wouldn't be useful," she said. "How did you do it?"

"I wasn't doing anything," he said. "I was just listening."

"Just listening." She shook her head. "Is this something a rider learns as soon as he passes the testing?"

"Not quite so soon," he said. "It's not a rider-candidate's skill, but it's simple enough. Any Third Rider can do it."

She took her time answering that. "Do you know," she said, "no one ever really thinks about what riders do. You ride—everyone knows that. And there's the Dance. But there's so much more to it. Have you ever thought that it's a waste to keep so much art and so much magic locked up on the Mountain?"

"It's all focused on the Dance," he said.

"Yes, but should it be? What you did today goes beyond magic. I've never seen anything quite like it."

"You do it yourself," he said. "It's just patterns. Everything has a pattern—a shape in space and time. We're trained to see it, that's all. Eventually we learn to control it."

"You see?" she said. "That's what I mean. You can see things in a way no one else can. As you heal, you'll be able to do more than that. And you're not the only one. There's a whole school full of mages like you."

"The gods are on the Mountain," he said. "That's the heart of our power. Some of us can leave, yes, but if too many of us go, our powers might be dissipated or our training corrupted. Then we'll be no better than that mountebank Olivet."

"The gods don't want you to stay as you've always been," she said. "Maybe this is part of what you're meant to do."

More protests came flooding, but he let them go unspoken. He was thinking like one of the riders he had always despised, looking backward instead of forward. He needed to see what Briana saw. She was a rider, too, as no rider had ever been, chosen by one of the Ladies.

It was hard. It made his head ache. Better if he chose not to think. Just as he taught his young riders—*Don't think. Be.*

He did not remember if he said anything more to Briana. There was too much on his mind. He left the council chamber, walking for the sake of walking, up stairs and down corridors and across courtyards and through glittering halls.

He was not thinking. He was letting the patterns flow over him.

A white wall rose up in front of him. Petra blew warm breath in his face. He grasped mane and swung astride.

People gaped at the sight of a rider on a white stallion, pacing calmly through the palace halls. Kerrec stared them down. If more riders lived away from the Mountain, this would be a common sight.

Maybe Briana was right. Maybe it should be. Time would tell—time and the gods.

Twenty-Four

The last time Valeria saw the royal city of Aurelia, she could not wait to get out of it. She had survived the broken Dance and saved the world. She was going home to the Mountain.

She would still much rather have been in the school, living the life she loved. But she had to do this. She paused on the long hill outside the city, looking down across the sweeping curve of the harbor, and breathed the smell of the sea.

It smelled like sorrow. Sabata pawed impatiently. He hated cities. The sooner he was in this one, the nearer he was to getting out.

Stallion logic could make a human's head hurt. Valeria let him trot briskly down the hill into the stream of traffic that flowed through the northern gate. There were other riders, mounted on mules and donkeys as well as horses, riding on the turf that edged the paved road. On the paving, wagons and carriages rattled past, while foot traffic kept to the narrow ribbons of smoothed stone between the paving and the greenway.

Valeria had forgotten how crowded that road was. There were so many people and animals. Sabata's presence was pulsing inside her. She had to keep him calm, which meant calming herself, or no one could answer for the consequences.

That gave her a focus. She fixed on it instead of the crowds and tumult around her.

Sabata settled slowly. The city drew closer. The endless confusion of patterns washed over her. She let them drown her.

They washed her up in a place she remembered rather too well. There was the back of the palace and the back of the Temple of the Sun and Moon, and the front of the riders' house in Aurelia.

There were people in Riders' Hall, servants and guards—and Petra and the Lady like a white fire in its heart.

Valeria nodded to herself. That made sense. Riders needed their own place, and room for the horses.

The servants recognized her. Either they had served in this house during the Great Dance or they had seen the Dance itself. They knew better than to bow too deeply, but their awe made her skin itch.

Kerrec was not there. "He attends council every day, lady," the chief of servants said. "He usually comes back a little after noon."

It was midmorning now. Valeria thought of going to find him, but it was much more tempting to let the servants offer her a bath and clean clothes and her choice of rooms to rest in.

"Show me his," she said.

They were good servants. They asked no questions. She considered the dark and chilly rooms and the bed that was barely wide enough for one, and suppressed a sigh.

Still, it was a bed. She was tired and overwrought. She sent the servants away and lay down.

* * *

After five days in Aurelia, Kerrec had fallen into a pattern of his own. Every night he worked through the long dark hours, finding the patterns of his magic and then rebuilding them one by one. Every day he rode Petra and, as the days passed, one and another of the mares—though never the Lady. He attended councils. He received occasional guests.

Those were courtiers looking to curry favor, or would-be enemies spying out the prospects. In the past few days, there had been young men, nobles all, wondering if the First Rider would condescend to teach them some of his art.

He might not have known about those if he had not happened to wander into the stable at midafternoon on his second day in Riders' Hall and found Quintus upbraiding a pair of wide-eyed boys. "This is not a riding academy. The First Rider is a mage and a master. He does not stoop to teach lessons to children."

"Do I not?" Kerrec asked.

His voice was as mild as he could make it, but Quintus blanched. For a moment Kerrec thought he would faint. "Sir! I apologize for these insolent boys. They seem to think—"

"What, that I can teach them to ride?" Kerrec looked them up and down. They seemed presentable enough, and not excessively overdressed. The taller seemed thoroughly cowed, but the smaller and maybe younger kept drifting off toward the Lady.

She was amused. She let the child stroke her nose and smooth her forelock.

That told Kerrec a great deal. "Saddle the roan and the chestnut," he said to Quintus. To the boys he said, "You two can sit a horse, I suppose."

Their eyes were wider than ever. They were both speechless.

So was Quintus, but for another reason altogether. "My friend," Kerrec said. "Take the magic away and all that's left is a riding master."

Quintus was still outraged, but he was also obedient. He went to fetch the mares Kerrec had chosen.

He took the boys with him. They might be noblemen, but they could learn to saddle a horse.

Kerrec found himself smiling. It was an effort to put on a stern face when the boys presented themselves to him with horses saddled and bridled and ready to ride.

Their names were Vincentius and Maurus. Kerrec chose not to care whose sons they were. Here, as if they had been Called, they were only themselves.

Someone had taught them decently. They could mount and dismount, and they could sit the common gaits. Maurus had something approaching grace. Vincentius was more enthusiastic than skilled. They were willing to work, and neither complained.

On the second day, there were three of them, with Maurus's brother Darius. By the third day, there were half a dozen. There would have been more, but Kerrec let Quintus turn the rest away. Later, with more horses, he might increase the number of riders, but for now, six were enough.

When he first came to Aurelia, he had dreaded the prospect of long empty days and lonely nights. He still spent his nights alone, but by then he needed his solitude. His days were full. Nights were the only time he had to think and plan and concentrate on the slow and grueling task of mending broken magic.

Best of all, the mages let him be. They watched him from a distance, studying him—sometimes he could feel the pricking of their power—but they stayed out of his way. He disciplined himself to ignore them.

Five days after he came to Aurelia, he spent the morning in council and most of the afternoon in the riding court. The day was hot, but the court had both shade and the sea breeze. His six students were still eager to learn, enthralled with this new and wonderful art.

Today for the first time, partly because morning council had begun early and partly because he wanted the boys to see what they were aiming for, he rode Petra in front of them. Petra was conscious of the occasion. Kerrec knew better than to ask for any part of the Dance, but the movements in themselves were beautiful.

They flowed from one to the other, beginning with the simple gaits, the walk and trot and canter that anyone could ride. Then, little by little, they transformed into art. Kerrec was absorbed in it, but he made sure to stay aware of his audience.

They did not see it, not at once. Maurus was the first to understand. "Look," he said. "It's all there in the little things we do. Like seeds—they seem so small, but they grow. If we ride our circles and watch our gaits and remember how he wants us to sit, this is what it comes to. It's magic—but it's ours. We can do it."

"We aren't riders," Vincentius said. "We weren't Called."

"It doesn't matter," said Maurus. "Maybe the gods and the magic aren't for us. But this is."

For that, Kerrec let him sit on Petra through the exquisitely cadenced trot in place called piaffe. Maurus was enchanted. To the others Kerrec said, "You'll all ride this once you've earned it. Maybe someday one of you will train it. Then you can call yourself a rider."

"Like on the Mountain?" asked the youngest of them.

"Not exactly like that," Kerrec said. "You won't be a horse mage. But you will be a rider."

* * *

Kerrec caught himself smiling as he made his way to his rooms to change out of riding clothes and join his sister for dinner.

He paused on the stair as realization struck him. He was in danger of enjoying this life.

Briana was pleased. She had brought him here to heal, and she believed she was succeeding.

He did not want to heal in that way. Not completely. Not yet. There was one thing he had to do. Until he had done it, he could not let himself lose focus.

There was someone in his bed. His heart knew who it had to be, even while his mind floundered.

Valeria was sound asleep. When Kerrec stood over her, she did not stir.

He always forgot that she was beautiful. The knowledge was in him, but it tended to slip away in memories of her strength and her skill with horses. Strangers could still take her for a boy, though her hair had grown out to her shoulders and she had stopped deepening her voice or hiding the shape of her body.

Fully dressed and asleep in his bed, she was beautiful enough to break his heart. It was all he could do not to reach out and brush his fingers across the sweet curve of her cheek. Then if he kissed her, she would open those eyes of hers that were now green, now brown, flecked with gold like dapples of sunlight in a forest pool. She would smile and say his name. And he would be happy, and they would never be apart again.

The vision was so clear that he could almost have sworn it was real. But she was still asleep, and he was stiffly upright above her. The reality of his purpose here was sitting like a stone under his breastbone.

Maybe his visions were a lie and his obsession simply that—

a blind delusion. He could let them go. He had a life here. With her to help him, he would heal and they would build their own school, and the empire would prosper.

Dreams and delusion. The empire was at war with enemies it was only imperfectly aware of. Kerrec was broken and struggling fiercely to mend before the empire broke as he had. Valeria should not be here.

He set his teeth and shook her awake—maybe not as roughly as he should. "What are you doing here?" he demanded.

She woke quickly. Riders learned to do that. It was part of their discipline. "Kerrec," she said. Her eyes took him in, and she broke out in a smile. "You look wonderful. Is it the Healers? Or did you find someone else to help you?"

That smile had been more men's downfall than Valeria would ever know. It nearly destroyed Kerrec's resolve. But he had a little discipline left. He said coldly, "I cannot imagine that Master Nikos gave you leave to go dangling after me. What possessed you? How could you abandon the school now, when it needs every scrap of power it can find?"

It tore at his heart to see her smile die and her face take on a bruised look, with blue shadows under the eyes. "Aren't you at least secretly glad to see me? I can help you. Together we can—"

"Together we are doing nothing," he said. "You do not belong here. Take a day or two if you must, to rest—but then you are going back to the Mountain."

"I don't think so," she said. "I have to be here."

Gods, she was stubborn. But so was he. "You should not be here. You'll lose everything you've gained."

"Would you rather we all lost everything?"

Kerrec turned his back on her. It was as hard a thing as he had ever done. "Keep the room," he said. "I'll find another."

"Good," she said behind him. Her voice was nasty. "The bed's like a board."

He left her there. For a while he dreaded—or hoped—that she would come after him, but it seemed he had done what he set out to do. He had driven her away from him, if not from Aurelia.

Twenty-Five

Valeria had not been fool enough to expect an effusive welcome, but this bitter coldness left her stunned. When she first woke and saw Kerrec, she had thought he looked notably better than when he left the school. He was mending. Her working was acting on him again. He was closer to the Kerrec she had first known.

Then his eyes went cold. They were odd in dark-eyed Aurelia, the color of rain or darkened silver. When he was angry or disturbed, they went as pale as water.

Before he turned away, they were nearly white. He had shut her out completely. There was nothing left for her at all.

She sat for a long while on that hard ascetic bed. She was not a woman who cried easily, but even if she had been, all the tears were frozen out of her. Her heart was still and cold.

She wrenched herself back to the warmth of the summer evening. If she had learned anything since she was Called to the Mountain, it was that the face Kerrec showed the world had little to do with what was under it. If he showed her something devastatingly like hatred, it might have nothing to do with her at all.

That did not make it easier. What she felt for him was too deep for words. What he felt for her…who knew?

For a while she had been sure he loved her. Then he had drawn away from her little by little until he was gone. The torture that had broken his magic seemed also to have shrunk and twisted his heart.

She flung herself to her feet. She would not believe that. She refused.

Kerrec had gone to the palace. The servants were obliging when she asked. "Oh, yes, lady. He's dining with the princess regent tonight."

"Alone?" she asked. "Or a state banquet?"

"Not a banquet," said the chief of the servants. "That, we're sure of. He won't go near one of those."

Valeria thanked him, flashing a smile that left him blinking.

There was a passage from Riders' Hall to the palace, which was wide and high enough for men riding four of the white gods abreast. It led to the Hall of the Dance in the palace, but there were side passages with which she had become familiar the year before.

One of those opened on the princess regent's garden. Briana was nearby—Valeria could sense her presence that in its way was so much like one of the Ladies. She made a deliberate effort not to look for the cold and guarded stillness that was Kerrec.

They were dining alone, in the way of princes. There were only half a dozen servants standing about.

The room in which they sat had wide doors, paned with glass, which were open on the garden. Roses grew inside, and a small tree with deep-green waxy leaves and blossoms sent out a dizzyingly sweet scent, and flowers in pots hung from the ceiling and marched in rows along the walls.

Valeria stood outside in the garden, hidden in dusk. They sat in a glow of lamplight, drinking wine and laughing—yes, even Kerrec. Valeria could not remember ever seeing him laugh like that, as if he had no care in the world.

She had had thoughts of joining the party, or else waiting until after he left and sharing her sorrows with Briana. But Briana seemed to have none, at least not as far as her brother was concerned.

Valeria slipped away into the darkness. It was a long way back to Riders' Hall.

It was not as if she was alone in the world. She had the stallions—all of them, a ring of calm white shapes deep in her heart—and the Ladies beyond them. But sometimes she needed her own kind.

She needed Kerrec. But he was wrong—she had not come trailing after him. She was needed here, though why or for what, she did not yet know.

She found a room to sleep in. It little mattered which. She lay awake for long hours, while the moon climbed the sky and began to sink.

Kerrec came in late. She felt him in the house.

He did not come into the room where she was lying. Part of her wished he would, but most of her was glad. If he was cruel to her again, she would finish what his brother had started.

For the second time in as many days, Valeria woke under a man's stare. The chief of servants stood waiting for her to notice him, with clean clothes—not a rider's uniform but plain riding clothes—and instructions. "You're to tend the horses, lady," he said. "First Rider's orders. Quintus in the stable will show you what to do."

Valeria supposed she should be glad. There could have been a caravan waiting and a place for her in it.

Kerrec was gone already, though it was barely sunrise. Quintus the stableman was forking hay into mangers when Valeria found him.

He nodded to her. She nodded back and set to work cleaning stalls.

He knew who and what she was. He was not awed by it, which suited her perfectly. Once the horses were fed and watered and the stalls cleaned, there was tack to clean, aisles to sweep, horses to turn loose in the riding courts for an hour or two of exercise.

By then it was past noon. Valeria shared a loaf of bread and a bowl of soft herbed cheese and a jar of well-watered wine with Quintus. He was not a talkative man, but she was not given to chatter, either. They were both comfortable with silence.

After they ate, Quintus went off on errands of his own. Valeria had nowhere to go and no further orders to obey. There was Sabata, waiting to be ridden, and the bay Lady was hinting at it. The rest of the horses seemed to be expecting guests.

As she fetched the brushes and began to groom Sabata, she heard voices out in the court—young, male, and excruciatingly aristocratic. They bubbled and babbled closer, until they stopped outside the stable.

She counted three sets of footsteps, then a fourth running quickly to catch up. That one was breathless. "Tigellus said start without him. He'll be late."

"So?" said one of the others. "Where's Maurus? They aren't together, are they?"

"Not that I know of," the newcomer said. He was breathing

a little easier now. "He's fighting his family to do this. Tig's afraid he won't be able to keep coming."

"What, his brother again?" said one who had not spoken before. "He thinks the whole Mountain ought to come down, and the horse magicians with it. They're mountebanks, he says. They've tricked the empire into worshipping their horses and manipulated the emperors into feeding their power."

"I've heard that," the newcomer said. "And now the Mountain's stealing mages from other orders. My cousin's an oneiromancer. He says the strongest Journeyman in a hundred years got the Call, and now he's gone and the order can't get him back. All the orders have to submit to the Call."

"Even the emperor had to. He lost his firstborn to it."

"Tig's brother says it's all a plot to get and keep power. He says there's a better way."

"What, the Unmaking?"

There was a moment's perfect silence. Then the newcomer said, "Don't say it! We're not supposed to know about it. We're too young, remember?"

"Who'll hear us here?" said the young person who had so alarmed him. "The horses aren't going to tell on us."

"I wouldn't bet on it," the other said darkly. "Nobody's supposed to say that word. It's too dangerous. It's everything the emperor and the riders are not. If they know we know about it, we'll be in trouble. And our brothers and fathers and uncles will be even worse off. They could die."

"Oh, come, Vincentius. That's ridiculous. It's an excuse to get together and drink wine and wink at girls, that's all. If they want to pretend they're saving the world, where's the harm in that?"

"Plenty," said Vincentius, "if it's connected to *that*." Valeria could hear the shudder in his voice. "You don't know what it is, do you? None of you was at the emperor's Dance. I was. I saw...something. It wanted to swallow us all. All that is. And nothing less."

"If it's that bad," his friend demanded, "what do you think the riders can do about it? They didn't do very well that time. How do you know they won't do even worse when it comes again?"

"I don't know," Vincentius said. "I don't want to talk about it. It makes me scared."

Somewhat to Valeria's surprise, no one mocked him for it. A few moments later, a fifth boy burst in, babbling about taking forever to get there, and the darkness dissipated.

The door to the court rattled open. Five young noblemen trooped in together as if this were a daily occurrence. Horses' heads appeared over stall doors. One or two whickered.

There was a flurry of brushes and hoofpicks and saddles and bridles. In the middle of it, a tall and lean young thing happened to glance into Sabata's stall. When he spoke, she recognized Vincentius's voice. "Hey! Who are you? Is he letting new ones in, then?"

Valeria straightened from cleaning Sabata's hoof. Sabata was mildly interested in the row of faces that appeared above the stall door, but most of his effort was going into pretending to be an ordinary dappled-grey cob with a thick short neck and a hanging lip. He found it endlessly amusing.

"I'm Vincentius," the tall boy said, then jabbed his chin at each of the others. "Short one's Maurus, pretty one's Granius, and those two with the identical stupid expressions are Titus and Tatius. They're twins," he said as if it were not obvious. "One can ride and one can't. Trouble is, we can't tell which is which."

That set off an eruption that kept them occupied for quite some time. Valeria finished grooming Sabata and reached for the saddlecloth. As she fitted the saddle to the stallion's back and reached under his ample barrel for the girth, Vincentius said, "I don't remember you from anywhere, do I? Is that your horse?"

"He belongs to himself," Valeria said. She tightened the girth carefully—Sabata would bite if she took any liberties—and reached for the bridle.

One of the boys was holding it. Maurus, that was his name. She thanked him.

Granius, who certainly was pretty, though not as pretty as Kerrec, lifted Maurus bodily and set him in front of a red mare's stall. The others were already at work, grooming horses and saddling them.

It was clear Valeria would have company in the riding court. She considered retreating to the second court, which was on the other side of the stable, but it was much smaller and less airy. At this time of day, it would be stifling.

She left the boys to their work and led Sabata into the court. He was still pretending to be a mortal horse. It was hard for him to plod as heavily as he imagined he should, but he managed. He barely even fluttered a nostril at the mares who came out one by one.

None of them scuffed the sand like a tired old plow horse. They were all ladies of lineage, glossy and sleek. At least one of their riders, once mounted, looked down on Sabata and ever so slightly sneered.

Valeria resisted the urge to mount as clumsily as Sabata was pretending to move. Once she was on him, she was having none of that. He had to move out as he well could, for the discipline and because she was not in sympathy with the game he was playing.

Sabata slanted an ear. His back tightened.

Kerrec walked into the center of the court as she had seen

him do a hundred times before. This, next to Petra's back, was his ordained place in the world. Nothing could change that.

He began the lesson calmly. The exercises he set were painfully rudimentary—which these children truly needed. The beauty of them, of course, was that every rider needed them, and Valeria as much as any.

Sabata needed them, too. Like Valeria, he was young. As great as his powers were, he had much to learn when it came to order and discipline.

Kerrec was practicing those virtues himself. He did not single Valeria out, and he certainly did not dismiss her. He taught her as he did the rest, with a keen eye and a dispassionate word.

So that was how it was going to be. Valeria decided to find it encouraging.

After their very simple lesson, even Maurus, who could almost ride, was groaning in pain. The boys creaked and limped their way through the cooling out of the horses and the removal of saddles and bridles and the cleaning of same—all part of the discipline.

They were not very good at it. Valeria would be undoing a good part of it later—as she had this morning. That was her discipline, as menial labor was theirs. They were all being taught lessons that they needed to learn.

Hers were not over, either. When she slipped away, one of the servants was waiting with new orders. There was a library in Riders' Hall, and she was to continue her studies there. He had a list, written in Kerrec's hand, and exercises that, if she did them all, would more than consume the day.

If Kerrec thought he could wear her out with tedium, he did not know her as well as he thought he did. She came prepared to find the books in boxes or on the shelves, but they were all on a table under the window, marked where he had asked her to read.

She thought for some time about throwing them at the wall. But he wanted her to do that. She sat down instead and opened the first book.

Focus was the first of all disciplines. She focused on the words. After a while, as they were meant to, they became the world.

Twenty-Six

At first when Kerrec realized that Valeria had followed him to Aurelia, he had felt such a confusion of anger and panic that he could hardly think. But after a day's reflection and a night's sleep, he came to a different conclusion. When he saw her riding with the young nobles who insisted that he teach them, he knew what to do about her.

It would have been simpler without her. With her, there was more that he could do, and more hope that he could get it done before he was hunted down and stopped. But he would have to deceive her first, and that might not be possible.

He had to try. Though it was almost physical pain to push her away, for her own safety he had no choice but to do it.

He was going to die. He had seen it in the Dance that he nearly broke. Death in the imperial family, and great magic broken and poured away in the maw of the Unmade. He had to make that death count for something—and part of that was not to lose Valeria.

He put her to work as if she had still been in the school. It was hard work and long, but she was easily capable of it. Most of it kept them apart—which he was careful to encourage.

While she was absorbed in books and horses, Kerrec went hunting in his father's treasury. He hunted not in the body but in the mind, with magic.

What he was looking for would have been easy to find if he had been whole, but his magic was still very much a broken thing. First he had to bring the shards together, then he had to smooth the ragged edges. When he had done that, he had to slip the thread of his power past the wards on the treasury without being caught. Only then could he search for what he had left there.

It was slow and often grueling. He could not ask for help. If anyone knew what he was doing, there would be a great outcry and a barrage of questions and recriminations, and time would dribble away until it was too late.

He began the working the first night after Valeria arrived. He went out into the city to a certain house that was crumbling in ruin. He shuddered to pass the sagging gate, but he forced himself through it.

It was no easier inside. This was not where he had been broken—that had happened far away from here, in a hunting lodge in the mountains. But the power that had ordered his breaking had lived in this house. Fragments of it were still here, even more scattered than the remnants of Kerrec's magic.

He only needed a little. He went as deep into the house as he could stand. There was nothing living here but the rats, and the buzz of insects in the disheveled garden. The fountain was clogged and dead and the pool stagnant, breeding slime. The corpse of a bird floated in the water.

He held his breath and hurried on past. The house beyond was deserted. Its walls were cracked and its staircases crumbling. There was nothing there that he could use.

He circled around to the outer court. It was in even worse repair than the rest. Part of the colonnade was fallen, and the paving looked as if something had blasted it with fire.

He picked his way to the center of the charred circle. Something gleamed there. Carefully he brushed away ash and broken stone.

It must have been a ring once. The gold had melted into a shape like a rough coin. A stone rested in the middle. It was a very ordinary-looking thing, like a small pebble that might appear in one's shoe, dark grey and rounded.

It was more than he could have asked for. This stone had belonged to Gothard. It had fed his magic and he had fed it, until he was much stronger than he could ever have been without it. That was what a mage of stones was, and how he performed his workings.

Maybe Kerrec would not need that other thing, if he had this. The stone was dead, having exhausted itself in some great working, but Gothard's essence was still in it. It might be enough.

Kerrec slipped it into a pouch of leather lined with silk, being very careful not to touch it with his bare hands. When he straightened he reeled, briefly dizzy. All this ruined magic put him too much in mind of his own.

He stiffened his back. It was nothing like his. He was mending. This never would. It was all turning to dust.

He brought the stone back to Riders' Hall. Dinner was waiting in the rooms he had moved to yesterday. He was not hungry, but his body needed to eat. He ate without tasting any of it.

He should rest. Tomorrow was soon enough to begin the

next step in his plan. But while he ate, he stared at the stone that he had laid on the table. The more he stared, the more he understood, and the less happy he was.

This stone could not do what he had hoped, after all. It was too small, and it was dead. He needed the master stone, the stone through which Gothard had given the lesser stone its power.

Kerrec had taken the master stone from Gothard during the Great Dance. In his mind he could still see it, dark and round and heavy in his hand, pulsing with magic.

After the Dance was over, he had surrendered it to his father's mages. They had warded and secured it, then laid it away in the treasury. They were unlikely to release it for the asking, considering the state Kerrec was in. If he wanted it, he would have to take it.

This was not a safe or easy thing to do alone. If Kerrec had caught a younger rider doing such a thing, he would have set the boy sharply to rights.

Kerrec was not alone. Petra was in his heart, as always. He had the stallion's strength if his own failed.

The stallion was thinking of Valeria. Kerrec shut himself off from the vision of her face. She more than anyone must not know what he was doing—because she more than anyone could stop him.

Tonight he set wards—that was all. He had brought books from the library to help his memory. They stayed where they were, heaped on a table, unopened.

He was proud of that. His nightly struggles were bearing fruit. The patterns were there when he looked for them. He shaped and wove them into protections for the lifeless stone and the working he was planning.

Then he had to rest. He was not as frustrated as he might

have been. He was stronger than he had been in a long while. He had not collapsed yet, nor did he feel as if he was going to.

A rider cultivated patience. Horses were not easy or simple to train, and haste or compulsion could do great damage. If Kerrec thought of himself as a ruined horse, he could see a way through.

It was three days before Kerrec's pupils realized either that Valeria was female or that she was a rider. She would have let them go on thinking she was an excessively reserved and haughty nobleman from somewhere in the provinces, but Kerrec either tired of the game or never had been playing it at all. On the fourth day since Valeria met them, while they were bringing their horses out in the court, he said, "Valeria. Come here."

His eyes avoided her face. He was as cold as he had ever been, all First Rider, with no friend or lover left.

She hardened her heart as much as she could. "Sir?" she said as a rider-candidate should.

"Take these two—" he tilted his head toward Vincentius and Maurus "—and teach them to sit a horse."

"Sir," she said.

They were all staring. Tigellus, who had appeared the second day, looked appalled. The rest were simply fascinated.

"Gods!" Maurus said in a loud whisper. "Is that—?" His eyes darted to Sabata and went wide. "Oh, gods. It is. And we never—"

Sabata arched his neck and stamped. The common little cob was gone. He laughed in the boys' faces, chasing the chosen pair to the far end of the court.

Valeria followed with their mares. The boys were mute with awe, which for Maurus was unheard of. She left Vincentius holding his mare's rein while she fastened a long line to Maurus's mare's bridle and sent her out on a circle.

They were both in sore need of education. Valeria taught them as she had been taught, but with care not to overtax them. They were soft young courtiers, not rider-candidates.

They still thought themselves hard used. The rest were done long before them. They almost fell from their horses, each one, and stumbled into the stable.

Sabata was still waiting for Valeria. He was unusually patient. She mounted him warily, but he made no attempt to punish her for all his standing about.

After three days of beginners' exercises, Sabata was ready to dance. Valeria was ready to oblige him. He was still young and his discipline was imperfect, but simple figures of the Dance delighted him.

They delighted the two boys, too. When Sabata came to a final halt, Vincentius and Maurus were standing in the stable door, grinning and applauding. "We want to do *that*," Vincentius said.

"If you listen when we teach you, you will," said Valeria.

"How long did it take you to learn?" Maurus asked.

"For this, every day and night for most of a year," she said. "And there are more years to come. This is the simplest of our arts. Sabata only came off the Mountain a year ago. He's just learning—as I am."

"A year," Vincentius sighed.

"Eight years for a stallion. Twice that for a rider." Valeria dismounted and rubbed Sabata's neck where he loved it best, feeding him his bit of sugar.

She pulled off saddle and bridle. He nuzzled her, looking for more sugar. When there was none to be had, he wheeled and leaped into a gallop. The gallop had sparks in it, sudden leaps and exuberant curvets, settling to a lofty, floating gait that made the boys' jaws drop.

Then, like any sensible horse, he dropped and rolled, wriggling in ecstasy, both sides and then his back. It was a perfectly absurd thing to do, and perfectly mortal. He came up crusted with sand, shaking from nose to tail, with mane flying and dust coming off him in clouds. He snorted and shook his head and trotted purposefully toward the stable.

Kerrec watched and listened from a window above the court. Valeria considered herself a solitary creature with few social graces, but wherever she was, whoever was there, she always knew what to do or say. She was as comfortable with the princess regent as she was with servants and stablehands.

He sighed, not exactly in envy. He could train a horse or a rider. He could lead a council or sit in judgment. But when it came to making friends, he never knew where to start.

Valeria was doing exactly what he needed her to do. While she was busy with those eager boys, she would not be wondering what Kerrec was doing.

He had a brief, piercing memory of her skin under his hand, as soft and smooth as cream, and the taste of her kiss. He shut them away. He had wards to build and a master stone to find. Then…

First things first. One step at a time—just as with the horses.

Twenty-Seven

It took Kerrec ten days to find the master stone. Half of that he spent painstakingly constructing wards and gathering his magic—and sternly refusing to reflect that it would have taken him a fraction the time if he had been what he used to be. He was slow, but he could do it. That was what mattered.

Once his wards were raised and his magic brought together as best it could be, he focused on the dead stone that he had found. It had no magic of its own any longer, but it kept a memory of the power that had been in it. With that to guide him, he searched through the maze of magics that guarded the imperial treasury.

If he had not been the emperor's son, he could never have done it. As with so many other workings on the palace, the wards of the treasury were set to respond to imperial blood. When he answered the Call, he had removed himself from the succession, but he was still royal born. The wards recognized that.

They were a powerful and complex pattern of workings, some of them centuries old. That made his task easier, somewhat. He was looking for a new working with a certain flavor to it, a taste of his brother. Gothard's blood was royal, too, but he was half a barbarian. Kerrec set the search for stone magic that was half royal and half foreign.

His days were still taken up with the palace and the riding court, but he managed little by little to pass the latter to Valeria. The former was less simple. He did not want Valeria and Briana comparing observations and deciding that something was wrong with him.

Each day he came to council later and left earlier. He let Briana think the bloom was wearing off. He had to be careful or she would subject him to another inquisition of mages, but so far she seemed unsuspicious.

On the tenth night after he began, just before he was ready to give it up and fall into bed, he felt it. It struck him with a smell of cold stone and a memory of Gothard's voice gloating over him while he lay in agony.

The rush of hatred nearly flung him out of the working— and nearly betrayed him. But in his days of restoring himself by sheer force of will, he had learned to set aside that hatred, storing it against the day when he could unleash it on its source.

Once his mind was clear again, he followed the thread of the seeking spell through the labyrinth of wards. There, at last, was the master stone that he had taken from Gothard and wielded in the Great Dance. His own presence was still on it.

Tomorrow, he thought, he would finish what he had begun. But when he rose from the chair he had been sitting in, pretending to read, and stretched every stiff and aching muscle, he knew he could not wait. If anything happened—if Briana suspected or Valeria caught him—that would be the end of it.

He would not put it past Briana to lock him up and keep him there until there was no hope of doing what he knew he must.

Tonight, then. In spite of his desperate eagerness to have it done, he slept an hour or two. He needed the rest.

He woke when he had planned to—a bit of rider's discipline. He dressed in the clothes that he had slipped out of the palace after one of his mornings there, plain shirt and breeches and soft shoes and a servant's tabard. That, he had discovered some while since, would take him anywhere unseen. Who noticed a servant, after all?

Riders' Hall was quiet. The servants were asleep. Valeria slept in her room and the horses in their stable. Petra was aware of Kerrec as always, but he passed no judgment. He was dreaming of high pastures on the Mountain and herds of Ladies, beautiful and powerful.

Kerrec shook his head and smiled as he slipped down the passage to the palace. A stallion's mind was wonderfully simple, even if he was a god.

The door to the treasury was undistinguished. There was no guard on it. The wards were subtle, but he knew already how strong they were.

His own protections were in place. He simply opened the door and walked into the maze of rooms and corridors, doors locked and warded, and stairs in unexpected places. There were no heaps of gold and jewels lying about. Those were all in chests and boxes, shut away behind those unassuming doors.

The master stone was deep inside, where the strongest and most dangerous treasures were, workings of magic that had been made for or against the empire. They were all heavily guarded, but he could feel them inside him. They made his bones thrum.

He only wanted one of them. It was his by right, because he had won it. That surety gave him passage.

He walked carefully, as he would through a herd of horses who did not know him. They were wild and skittish and deadly dangerous. None of them would threaten him unless he touched them—but they were everywhere, crowding around him.

At length he stopped. The one he needed was in front of him. He reached to take it, but then he paused. This was too easy.

He stood in a dark room, windowless, but the wards and magic together shed enough light that he could see. The box rested on a shelf in the midst of a hundred more. It was labeled in a precise and scholarly hand.

It was the master stone. He had no doubt of that. He secured his wards again, strand by strand, exactly as the pattern demanded.

All the different magics in that place tugged at the working, twisting it in unexpected places. He held on to calm and to the pattern. No matter how long it took, no matter how desperate he was to take the stone and escape, he clung to discipline.

Only when the wards were secure and the pattern firm did he take the box. The stone was singing under the lid.

It knew him. It wanted to bind to his magic. That was what it was for.

He shielded himself yet again. It was harder now. He was tiring. The impulse that had brought him here was losing strength.

Just a little longer. He opened the box. The stone was wrapped in warded silk. He slipped it under his tabard, then closed the box and returned it to its shelf.

If anyone happened to look, it would seem that nothing was disturbed. A shadow-image of the stone lay in the box, a working that echoed the song he could still hear just under his heart.

It was easier at least to go back. He had only to follow the path he had taken, slipping through the opening he had made in the wards. He was stumbling by the time he reached the last door. He nearly fell, which would have rent the wards and set off the alarms—but he caught himself. He came safe through the door.

He did fall then, dropping to his knees. His sight came and went. His ears were ringing.

The wards were secure behind him. Little by little his strength trickled back. The stone, even heavily shielded, was feeding it.

That he had not expected. He was not a stone mage. He should have been able to use the stone as a guide or a window on the future, as any mage could, but this went considerably further—as if, in rebuilding the ruins of his magic, he had changed the nature of it.

It was baffling and it might be dangerous, but for the moment it saved him. After a while he could stand, then he could walk. By the time he reached the passage to the riders' house, he was almost himself again.

He had not meant to finish what he began, not that night. But the stone had a mind of its own. That mind was to make him strong and then find the one who had made it.

He wanted both things, even without the stone to encourage him. He knew it was dangerous, but he could not manage to care. His practical self would have slept out the rest of the night, endured the day, then the following night, done what it must. With the stone close to his skin, singing its endless song, he gathered what he needed.

Most of it was ready. The rest he found quickly, filling his saddlebags.

Petra was waiting for him. Again he exercised patience,

grooming and saddling the stallion without endangering either of them with haste.

It was still some hours until dawn. A mist lay low over the land and obscured the sea, but the sky was clear, shimmering with stars. The sigh of waves followed him through the sleeping city.

The east gate was shut until sunrise, but Kerrec knew a postern. The guard just happened to be on the other end of the wall when he slipped out onto the eastward road.

Twenty-Eight

Just before the raid went bad, Euan Rohe was thinking that this would be an easy one. The legions could not protect every cot and hamlet.

This one was more or less accidental. Euan's pack of Calletani had sacked and looted a town farther west and eliminated its garrison. On their way back to the river, they caught sight of a farmstead tucked away under a hill.

The farmer must be trusting to the lie of the land to conceal his pastures full of fat sheep. From the road they were invisible, but coming overland, the raiders had a clear view.

The town had had a good store of grain and wine and oil, but not many cattle. These sheep could feed the whole tribe for a week.

No one seemed to be guarding them. There was no sign of life around the farmstead—no dogs barking or cattle lowing.

The scouts running ahead flung gates open on emptiness. The farm was deserted.

That was not uncommon, though the farmers usually took their livestock with them. This one must have left in haste.

"Stay on guard," Euan ordered his men. "Clean out the place as fast as you can."

They were already in motion, swarming over stone walls and wooden fences. Euan and his warband brought up the rear.

Suspicion stabbed first as Euan saw that the sheep seemed to be ignoring the army descending on them. Then he took in the beasts themselves. Not that Euan was likely to know one sheep from another, but there were half a dozen in front of him, and each had the same cluster of burrs in the same spot on the left shoulder. Every one of them looked exactly alike—as if the fields were full of images of a single sheep.

He opened his mouth to order his men back—just as the mage's trick fell apart. Instead of a field of sheep, the raiders found themselves face to face with an imperial cohort.

The legionaries were fresh and rested. Euan's men had been marching all night and fighting half the day. But the way home was through this cohort.

They pulled together into battle formation, shields locked and spears bristling. They left behind the wagons loaded with loot. Either they would win the fight and come back for what was theirs, or the cohort would win it.

The cohort had committed a small but significant error. In pretending to be sheep, its soldiers had scattered over the hillsides. Instead of the impregnable wall of shields that they called the tortoise, they were a scatter of armored men, running hard to form up before the wave of Calletani hit.

They were just a little too late. The attack fell on them while they were still in motion.

Euan, in the middle of the line, had to trust to ears and gut to know what was going on beyond the thick of it. He had made a mistake, too. He had not found and marked the mage before he launched his men.

He had to hope the illusion had fallen early because the mage lost control. A mage that weak was probably a trooper with a talent rather than a master of one of the orders. Because if he was not…

A pike thrust at Euan's face. He beat it aside with the haft of his war-axe and hacked the head off the trooper behind it. The body dropped, still gripping the pikestaff.

Euan kicked it aside and kept going—much like the maundering that had damned near got him killed. Fight first, brood later. That was the only sensible rule in a battle.

The cohort was fighting bitterly to form ranks. Euan roared at his Calletani, driving them in between groups and clusters of legionaries. Like ants on the march, no matter how often Euan's men scattered them, they kept coming back.

Even the dead did not stop them. They closed up what ranks they had, that was all, and kept on coming.

By the One, Euan thought. Were they a mage's trick, too?

The eyes he met under the bronze helmets seemed human enough. They bled like men and died like them. None of the dead seemed inclined to rise again.

They were gaining ground by sheer weight of their armor and heft of their shields. The Calletani, naked or dressed in breeks, could not take the blows that legionaries took and still keep fighting. They darted in, struck hard, darted out. Or a mob of them swarmed over one or two legionaries and brought them down like hounds on a boar.

Euan cut down the cohort commander, the centurion in his

cocked helmet. The man fell in midbellow, still roaring out orders—and another beyond him took up the cry.

Chain of command, they called that. Euan lunged at the cohort-second, axe swinging up.

Every hair on his body stood on end. It was not the second bellowing orders—it was—

"*Down!*" he howled. "*Down,* damn you!"

Most of the men nearest him dropped. Those farther away were still fighting, caught up in it. Euan roared at them, but they seemed to have gone deaf.

At the last possible instant, he flung himself flat.

It was not the same as when the star fell. This was like a blast of wind, but no leaves stirred and no legionary swayed, let alone toppled. Only Calletani felt it.

Euan clung for his life to the stony ground. He heard a sound that he would remember in nightmares, the sound of bodies torn apart from inside. A hot rain fell on him—blood and entrails and fragments better left unnamed.

The man next to him was mewling like a whipped dog. It was one of the young warriors, a lanky child named Fergus. Euan pulled him up.

He did not want to look too closely at the field. Others of his men were alive. Legionaries were moving in, short swords out, to dispose of them.

Euan loosed a long, low howl, the hunting cry of a wolf in winter. As he howled, he ran, with Fergus half dragging, half running beside him.

The legionaries paused—not long, but long enough for Euan's men to find their wits and their feet. More of them than Euan had expected came staggering up, got their balance and bolted.

The cohort started in pursuit, but its mage stopped them.

"Let them go," he said. "We want the rest of the tribes to hear their story."

He should have waited until Euan was well past before he said that. He would also have done well to say it from behind a wall of shields. Euan left Fergus to wobble on his own feet, darted in past the pair of legionaries who guarded the mage, and gutted the man with one swift, ripping stroke.

He darted back, ducking the wild swing of a sword, flung Fergus over his shoulder, and ran.

Euan had not lost as many men as he feared. When they were safe across the river, more than half were still alive and walking. Strahan was gone, and Donal. Cyllan had collapsed as soon as they stopped in a clearing above the ford.

He was tossing like a man in a fever. When Euan laid a hand on his forehead, it was burning hot.

Some of the others were in hardly better condition. Euan eyed the sun, which was still surprisingly high, and tried to focus on where to go next. They were four days' run from the high king's war camp, and half a day from their own hunting camp.

Conory came over to where Euan was sitting. He looked as shattered as Euan felt. "I don't think we should camp here," he said.

Euan nodded. "I doubt they'll come after us, but we don't need to tempt fate, either. Are there enough of us to carry the ones who can't walk any farther?"

"If we rest and eat a bit, there should be," Conory said.

"An hour, then," said Euan.

Conory nodded and went to tell the others. Euan leaned back against a tree trunk and closed his eyes.

He was not thinking yet, past what he had to do to get his

men home and safe. Thinking was for later. So was remembering. For now, he let it settle down deep.

Sunset found them making their way slowly, carrying the injured. Conory and Cyllan were forging ahead. Euan, as usual, brought up the rear.

He was sure there was no pursuit. A wolf tracked them for a while, drawn by the scent of weakness, but found the tracks of a herd of deer instead.

The advance stumbled to a halt. Voices rose ahead. Euan did not recognize most of them.

They had imperial accents. He darted through the line. It straggled around a jut of rock and a thicket of fallen trees.

There was a camp on the other side of the thicket. A dozen blankets were spread under the low branches of trees. Their owners lay flat in the middle of the circle.

They were all wearing the garb of the tribes, but ten of the twelve were brown-skinned, black-haired imperials. The other two were bigger and fairer, but their accents were as Aurelian as the rest.

The bigger and fairer of the latter two had Conory's foot on his neck and a spearpoint in the small of his back. "We've caught a nest of spies," Conory said. "Shall I give you the pleasure?"

"We're not spies!" shrilled one of the dark ones. He was only a boy, smooth-skinned and beardless. His voice was barely broken.

Euan strode past Conory and his captive, seized the child by the scruff of the neck and heaved him to his feet. His face had the greenish cast that passed for pallor in these olive-brown people, but his eyes were bold as they rose up and up to Euan's face.

"Prince," the boy said, "we came to fight for you."

Euan blinked. That, he had not expected. "What possessed you to do that?"

"We see the truth," the boy said. "The One—what is beyond the One. We want to make it happen."

"You're traitors to your kind," Euan said.

"We're true to the Truth," said the boy.

Euan drew his long knife. The boy tilted his chin, baring his throat.

He was like a bull calf in the sacrifice, drugged and compliant. Euan spat in disgust. He opened his mouth to order his men to kill them all, but the boy's eyes stopped him.

The boy wanted it too much. Euan heard himself say, "Bind their hands and make them walk. I know exactly where to take them."

Conory's brows lifted. He and Cyllan hauled the captives up two by two and bound them in a double line. They were all as lost in a dream as the first one—except those who were worse.

The biggest of them, who was fair enough to be a tribesman, had the feel—if not the reek—of a priest. Him, Euan determined to watch. The rest were silly children, but this one was something more.

He might be the ringleader. He might not. But whatever he was, he was neither safe nor sane.

Maybe Euan should kill them after all. At least the big one— he should go to the One before he did any more harm than he already had.

The fair man's head drooped. The moment passed. The train of captives went on in the deepening dusk, with Euan's own men stumbling behind.

Twenty-Nine

The raiders came back to the hunting camp of the Calletani well after dark. Fires were lit, shielded from easy view, and the carcasses of three fine stags hung from the trees. A fourth turned on a spit over the largest fire.

That could be taken as an omen. The hunt in imperial lands had failed miserably, but Euan's own country was generous with its gifts.

That only meant that come the next raid, they would all be forewarned. The enemy was desperate enough to resort to battle magic. But how many battle mages could he spare? How many raids could he destroy, without the advantage of surprise?

Meanwhile Euan had a gift to bestow. He saw his men settled, the wounded in the care of the healers and the rest in their beds. Then he released Cyllan and Conory from guard duty and took the captives' leading strings in his own hand.

Neither of his shieldbrothers would let Euan dismiss him.

They followed him to the camp's edge, where the priests always were—and Gothard in his tent alone.

There was no fire here, and no priests sitting out in the open, reveling in the dark. Euan stopped in front of Gothard's tent and scratched at the flap.

For a long while there was no response, but Euan could hear Gothard's breathing, caught up sharp as he flung back the flap. He squinted at Euan, disheveled as if he had been asleep.

"I believe these are yours," Euan said, stepping aside so that Gothard could see the double line of captives.

Gothard's squint turned to a scowl. Then it went blank. Euan would wager he had recognized at least one of the boys. Probably he knew them all.

"We found them on this side of the river," Euan said. "Do with them as you like. Then come to me in the morning. I have a question for you."

Gothard shrugged. "As you will."

Euan tossed the rope to him. He caught it, staring at it as if he did not know what it was.

Euan left him to it. He did not honestly care if the young idiots were all dead by morning. In fact he rather wished they would be.

Euan wanted nothing more desperately than to fall onto his heap of blankets and sleep until the sun woke him. He got as far as to strip off his clothes and crawl into his tent, but sleep was not there waiting for him.

The thing he had left behind—deliberately, foolishly—was calling. He was too weak and weary to resist. He pulled it from its hiding place.

He could have sworn the seeing-stone reproached him. Of all times for him to decide he had had enough of magic, it

would be this one. Magic had ambushed him, and half his raiding party was destroyed.

He held it in his hand. It was cool, but somehow there was
a hint that, if he let it, it could burn.

He did not ask it to show him anything. There was nothing
he wanted to see—not tonight.

It was dark and quiet, gleaming faintly like the polished
stone it was. His eyelids drooped. His sight blurred.

The stone was inside him. He was seeing it as if it were his
eyes. It was a dream, almost, but he was still awake.

It was magic. He had let it in, and now there was no getting
rid of it. For all he knew, the stone had connived with the cohort's mage to teach him a bitter lesson. It seemed preposter-
ous—but that was the nature of magic.

And now he was seeing in the stone instead of through it.
What he saw, he would remember. That was magic, too, that
preternatural clarity of mind.

Euan woke ravenous. His small wounds, cuts and bruises,
were healing. He felt fresh and strong, in spite of the night he
had had—or perhaps because of it.

There was venison on the spit and bread baking in the fire—
made with the last of the flour. There would be no more unless the next raid had better luck than the last one.

Euan sat to eat. It was still barely sunup. Most of the men
were either asleep or out hunting.

The priests' tents were as quiet as they had been last night.
He saw no sign of the captives.

He did not want to think of them this early. He concentrated
on filling his belly and getting his thoughts in order. There was
a great deal to think about, and not much time to do it.

Gothard sat beside him and reached for the other half of the loaf. He had not come from his tent, which Euan had been watching.

Euan acknowledged him with a glance. He lifted a brow in return. "You don't know what a gift you gave me," he said.

"You've eaten them all already?"

Gothard curled his lip. "They're all mages. None ever went into an order, but they all have power. Some even have some faint knowledge of how to use it."

"So they are spies," Euan said.

"No," said Gothard. "They really are what they say they are—young idiots who have fallen in love with oblivion. Noblemen's sons are prone to that. It goes with the boredom and the arrogance."

"I never will understand how a man can take pride in being completely useless."

"Ah," said Gothard, "but these are the most useful gifts you could possibly have brought me. I'm almost ready now."

"Ready to do what?"

"How soon you forget," Gothard said. "Ready to wield the starstone. I know what the mage was looking for, who came under an envoy's banner. He was looking for me. He found weakness and rancor and petty conniving—exactly what I wanted him to see. Now he's told his fellow mages I'm no threat—and I'm ready. The emperor is finally moving. So is the high king. And the One has given us these children, these mages without order, who think they worship the Unmaking. They're the key, cousin. They're my way in to the starstone."

"I know," Euan said. "I saw."

Gothard's expression was blank.

"I saw it in the stone you gave me," Euan said. "The emperor has left Tragante. He's headed toward us. The high king has finally exhausted the hunting around his camp and decided to move it—this way. They're both getting ready to cross the river. I expect they'll meet in the middle."

"Not if we attack first," Gothard said. "All the raids have taken a toll. Their supply lines are much longer than they used to be. That means the payroll caravans are slower, too—and while armies may march on their stomachs, they stay in the ranks on their purses. If there's not a real battle soon, morale will be low enough and the men hungry enough that the commanders will be hard put to keep their men in fighting form."

"If that's the case," Euan said, "we shouldn't be pushing for a fast attack. We should be dragging our feet even more."

Gothard shook his head. "That's why he has to attack soon. His men won't stand for much more lying about. We've kept our men fit with all these raids. He's had his garrisons dealing with those while his fighting legions cool their heels in a fort."

"Very well," Euan said. "Point taken. How soon can you be ready?"

"A few more days," said Gothard. "Time enough for the rest of the people to get here and for the emperor to set up a new camp. Then you'll have your battle."

"I hope so," Euan said.

"Have faith," Gothard said. The mockery in his tone set Euan's teeth on edge.

Gothard stood, brushing crumbs from his breeks—an insufferably effete and imperial gesture. He smiled down at Euan. "You really don't know what you captured, do you?"

"Not one but two sons of the commander of the Corinia," Euan said. "At least four sworn enemies of the riders on the Mountain, including one who is probably going to become a priest if you don't use him up first. Several fairly close relatives of the emperor, and therefore you." He looked into Gothard's gratifyingly startled face. "I'm not as stupid as I look."

"Evidently not." Gothard saluted him. "Hail the king of the people."

"Just make sure I stay king," Euan said. "And help me win that battle."

"As the One wishes," Gothard said.

Thirty

Valeria had not been sleeping well. The longer she stayed in Aurelia, the stranger she felt. The Unmaking was working loose from the bonds she set on it, new ones as much as the old.

The truth was becoming all too clear. The Mountain had been keeping the Unmaking under control in the same way it had suppressed the healing spell in Kerrec. For him that had been a dangerous thing. For her, she was beginning to realize, it had been a godsend.

The days were not so bad. She had more than enough to keep her busy. At night, alone in her bed, she heard the Unmaking whispering, tempting her to set it free.

At first she thought it was only that she had left the Mountain's protection, but as the days wore on, she knew there was something else. Something in the city was calling to the void in the heart of her.

Kerrec's young students, whom he had gradually and none

too subtly shifted over to her, whispered among themselves of a new order or power or even cult among the nobles. They only named it once, the first day when she overheard them, but that was enough. Tigellus had a smell of it on him, though she could not find it inside him.

The Unmaking was in Aurelia. It did not have the power it had among the barbarians, the taste of blood and iron and raw pain, but it was distinct and growing stronger.

It was clear by then that if Kerrec had his way, she would never set foot outside of Riders' Hall. She read her books and rode Sabata and instructed her pupils. After that she was to go back to the books, but she deliberately left them lying.

What she was going to do might not be possible at all. But she had to try. The Unmaking inside her was her secret and her shame. The Unmaking in the city was a deadly dangerous thing.

Valeria had thought she would need time and persistence to get through the armies of clerks and servants to the princess regent, but it seemed there was some power in her name. As soon as she spoke it, doors opened and guards withdrew.

They remembered her from the year before. She remembered most of them, some by name. They led her straight through to the regent.

She had chosen her time well. Briana was resting between duties, sitting in the garden that Valeria remembered best, with a book in her lap and a young man playing softly on a lute. With a slight shock, Valeria recognized him. Vincentius, so gawky on a horse, had a beautiful elegance in court dress with a lute in his lap.

Valeria almost backed away, but Briana had seen her. The regent's smile was as warm as ever, and her delight was clearly not feigned. "Valeria! Did my brother finally give you my message?"

"Not a word," Valeria said, relaxing in spite of herself. Briana was Briana, no matter where she was or what she was doing. "I'm playing truant now—I'm supposed to be reading about the War for the Lilies."

Briana sighed without losing her smile. "That man," she said. "Does he want an essay, too?"

"In detail," Valeria said. "With analysis of the riders' part in the resolution of the conflict. By tomorrow morning."

"You'll be up late," Briana observed. "Here, sit. Do you know my cousin Vincentius?"

Vincentius scrambled to his feet and bowed, looking more like the awkward boy Valeria knew. "I know her," he said. "She was torturing us this afternoon. She tortures us very well. We ache for hours."

"It gets better," Valeria said.

"Then you'll just work us harder," said Vincentius. He bowed again. "Cousin. Rider. Until tomorrow."

Valeria thought Briana might call him back, but it seemed he had caught a signal Valeria missed. He left as cheerfully as he did everything else—with just a hint of a limp.

"I suppose you sent him to your brother," Valeria said when he was gone.

"Along with two of his cousins and three other likely young things," Briana said with no sign of repentance. "He plays the lute well, doesn't he?"

"Much better than he rides," Valeria said, "though he is trying. The horses like him. He's clumsy, but his heart is good."

"He'll grow into himself," Briana said. "Then he'll remember what he learned. His father is one of my father's strongest allies in the court—but he's dubious about the continued usefulness of the school. He's one of those who think that while it may not need to be shut down, it does need to be different."

"Is that what you think?" Valeria asked.

"You know what I think," said Briana. "We may not want it to change, but it's going to have to. Either we do what we can to influence the change—or it will be made for us. And that may not be anything that we would want to happen."

"I know," Valeria said, dropping to the chair beside Briana. She was tired suddenly, not just from a long day and an aching heart, but from everything.

She pulled herself together as best she could. This was her opening, and she had to take it. "If you've been talking to Vincentius, you must know about the new fashion. All those children's older brothers and some of their fathers and uncles are obsessed with it."

"I know," Briana said. "Why do you think I chose those particular boys? Their families are all supposedly loyal to the emperor. But this thing that's come into the city is eating away at the young and impressionable. We thought we had got rid of it when the Great Dance was over, but it's been seeping in like acid. You saved the Dance, as little as anyone wants to remember it, but what you saved it from is still here. It's more subtle, that's all."

"You know more than I do, then," said Valeria. "You don't need me crying the alarm."

"Oh, no," Briana said. "You see differently than we do here. I want to know what you see. What brought you to me tonight?"

"I wanted to see you," Valeria said.

She could stop there, turn aside, talk of little things. Probably she should. She had kept this secret for most of a year. It was not a threat—yet. Not the way the cult of Unmaking was.

Briana needed to know. A secret kept too long had betrayed Kerrec and nearly cost more lives than his. Valeria would not make the same mistake.

This could be a worse mistake. She swallowed hard. Speaking, shaping the words, was a conscious effort. "I need to tell you something. Will you promise not to tell anyone else?"

"Unless it affects the empire's safety," Briana said, "yes."

Valeria looked down at her hands. She had a powerful desire to meet Briana's eyes, but if she did, she would not be able to go on. She could circumvent the binding, she thought—she hoped. Though the tightness in her throat made her wonder.

Briana waited patiently. She was not going to stop Valeria, but neither would she help her.

Valeria had the wards in place and the words prepared. She had done both very carefully. While she spoke, she had to turn her mind slantwise and focus on something altogether unrelated—the scent of roses in the garden and the way the leaves of the aspens above the wall trembled in the wind off the sea. Her lips moved and her voice spoke, but she was separated from it.

"You remember last year when I pretended to be on the enemy's side, to save Kerrec and because that was the only way to save the Dance. One of the things I had to do…wasn't pretense. Mestre Olivet made me learn the first spell of Unmaking. Or rather, I didn't exactly learn. The words were there in the book. I looked at them, and they were in me. Then—later—there was the second spell. I fought that one off, I thought. I think. I don't know. What I do know…it's inside me. It's down deep and warded with everything I have, but it's there."

Valeria's voice tumbled to a halt. Her awareness drifted out past the rose arbor. She hovered for a moment, perfectly balanced between the two halves of herself.

If she let go, they would never come back together. The Unmaking yawned between them.

She shut her eyes in body and spirit and leaped. There was

an instant of pure breathlessness, of complete despair. Then the light came back.

She was in her body again. She felt strange and shaky and almost transparent, but she was real.

Briana's eyes rested on her. They were narrowed slightly as if in thought. Valeria could feel the cool brush of her magic. It was hard—almost too hard—but Valeria kept herself as open as she dared. She let Briana go where even Kerrec had never gone.

Briana saw what Valeria had been trying not to look at for nearly a year. She stiffened, but otherwise her face did not change. She drew back carefully.

"I should have told someone," Valeria said in silence that had grown too large to bear. "But I couldn't—there was no way—"

"You and Kerrec," Briana said, "are damnably alike. Neither one of you can stand to show weakness. And you both keep secrets that eat you alive."

Valeria could hardly argue with that. It made her flinch, but it was true. "What would you have us do? Drive the riders into a worse panic than they're in already? I'm hard enough for them to stomach without this."

"True," said Briana. "Still, to live with that every day—"

"Mostly I try to forget it's there. There's nothing anyone can do for it."

"How do you know?"

"I asked the Ladies," Valeria said. "Ask yours. She'll tell you. She won't touch it. None of them will."

"You can talk to all of them, can't you?"

Valeria frowned. That was a change of subject. She could hardly say she was sorry, but it caught her off balance. "Yes. I can. I'm a rider. That's what we do."

"I don't think so," Briana said. "You never asked anyone, did you? I can talk to the Lady, and Petra and I understand each other. Kerrec talks to Petra. When I look inside each of the other riders, I see one of the gods standing guard. You have a whole herd. Sabata's closest, but there's Petra and my Lady and Icarra and Oda and a whole ring of them—dozens at least—all around you. That's why you can master all the stallions. They're all inside you."

"Surely the Master—" Valeria began.

"He has Icarra. That's all. No one else has all of them."

Valeria blinked. "Am I stupid, because I never knew? I just thought I was stronger. Not that—"

"Not stupid," Briana said firmly. "They're all as stiff-necked as you are. They never even thought to look, did they? They never asked how you can do what you do."

"I thought they knew."

"So did they." Briana shook her head. "They are so complacent—so sure they know all there is to know about the gods and the Mountain. But they don't know anything at all."

Valeria did not mean to laugh, but she was too startled to stop herself. "That's my lament!"

"It should be everyone's. It's too true for comfort." Briana was not laughing with Valeria. "You are alive, sane, and not Unmade because of what's in you. The gods are protecting you."

"If you see that," Valeria said, "can you also see a way out of it for me?"

"I wish I could," Briana said. "I can ask among the mages. It won't betray you—there's enough of this cult in the city that I'm very much afraid there will be others. Without your strength or your protections, they'll be in terrible danger."

"That's what I'm afraid of, too," Valeria said. "If they've got hold of these spells, and they don't know or care what can happen to them in the working, it's not just their lives and souls we need to fear for. The Great Dance was supposed to be Un-made. Do you understand what that means?"

Briana shivered. "I think I do."

"I'm sure they do not—or they would never touch it."

"Maybe," said Briana. "Maybe not. The young nobles see a dark glory in oblivion, and joy in annihilation. The world is a foul and corrupted place. They'll take it down with them into nothingness."

"They're insane," Valeria said.

"Most are just fools," Briana said. "A few are what I would call evil. I'll be watching them—and so will the orders of mages. Anything that can be done to keep them safe, we will do."

Valeria looked at Briana in amazement. "I thought you'd be talking of keeping the empire safe. These people are betraying it and threatening you. And you want to protect them."

"They're my people," Briana said. "They don't know what they're doing. To them it's just a fashion, the latest way to throw their elders into fits."

"You're too understanding for me," Valeria said.

"I'm practical. If we protect them, we protect ourselves. If we watch them, they'll lead us to the real enemy."

"You know who that is. It's the tribes. This is their religion. There must be priests in the city. They were here to break the Dance. Who's to say they didn't stay?"

"I'm sure some of them did," Briana said. "We'll be hunting."

"You weren't before?"

"I wasn't sure. You've confirmed what I suspected—this isn't just young men's foolery. This is dangerous."

"I hope I came to you in time," Valeria said.

"Don't fret," said Briana. "Go and sleep. You've done a great thing. It took a great deal of courage. Leave the rest to me."

Valeria was not used to that at all. She was the one people

left things to. But she had had it forced on her. She did not want it. Briana was born for it.

It was almost a relief to let it go. If she could have let the Unmaking go, too, she would have been completely content.

Thirty-One

Sleep was not any easier to find once Valeria confessed her long and terrible secret to Briana. She had more than enough troubles to keep her awake. Missing Kerrec was by no means the least of it.

When she did sleep, she dreamed of her family. She could not see exactly what they were doing, just their faces while they did it. In part of the dream, she was outside in the village, during a festival, maybe, or on market day. But mostly she was in her father's house, watching her father and mother and brothers and sisters live lives that were no part of hers.

She dreamed of her brothers in the legions, too, Rodry more often than Lucius. She had been Rodry's favorite since he was a small boy and she was a newborn and, he often insisted, excessively irritable baby.

Last of all, as often before, she dreamed of Euan Rohe—but this time he was not making love to her. He was riding a bloodred stallion across the wrack of a battlefield. She had never seen him ride so well in the waking world.

When she looked into Euan's eyes, she saw no one she knew. When she looked into the stallion's eyes, she saw the Unmaking.

She woke with a hammering heart. It was still dark beyond the windows, but the air had a taste of morning. As she breathed it in, the dream fled, but the mood of it lingered. She felt vaguely uneasy, restless and out of sorts.

There was something beneath the dream. A quiver of magic. An absence that was not Unmaking. That was…

Petra was not in the stable. Sabata was. He let Valeria see what he had seen, Kerrec in traveling clothes with full saddlebags.

She said a word her brothers in the legion would have slapped her silly for even thinking. In one blinding flash of Sabata's sight, she saw everything Kerrec had been hiding from her. Why he had let himself be sent to Aurelia. What he had been doing in those long nights while she lay awake, feeling him nearby and perceptibly warded.

He was going after Gothard.

The patterns unfolded in front of her. They led her back to her rooms for her traveling bag, then to the kitchens for whatever the cooks had left from the day's meals. With a full waterskin and a bag full of bread and cheese and fruit, she made her way back to the stable.

Sabata had his door open and was standing in the aisle, nobly resisting the mare who was doing her best to seduce him. When Valeria came up with saddle and bridle, he pawed impatiently. The road was calling. He wanted to be gone.

She looked up from tightening his girth to find Quintus

standing at Sabata's head. He did not seem any more surprised by this than by anything else that happened in his world.

"Tell the boys," she said. "We'll be back when we can. If you can help them with the mares…"

"I'll do my best," Quintus said.

"Good," Valeria said. "Tell the princess regent I'm leaving the rest to her, but this I have to do for myself."

Quintus nodded. It was almost a bow. "Keep safe," he said.

It was not a bad blessing to take into the rising morning. Sabata was fresh enough to keep Valeria busy for a good distance through the city. By the time he settled, they were nearly at the gate and the sun was fully up.

Kerrec's path was clear in front of them. He thought he was invisible. To human mages, maybe he was. But Sabata could see beyond mortal sight.

Valeria left Aurelia with few regrets. Except for Briana and the boys, there was nothing to keep her there. The patterns were calling her into the east, so strong and clear a call that it reminded her somewhat of the one that came from the Mountain.

She stayed behind Kerrec for three days. That was long enough to be out of the city and well on the way to the eastern frontier.

The war was still far ahead, but there were signs of it even here. Imperial couriers galloped past almost every hour, going or coming on their spotted horses. Towns were more obviously garrisoned. People were watchful, casting a wary eye on strangers.

On the fourth day, Valeria let Sabata quicken his pace. Near sundown she came in sight of the town where Kerrec had stopped for the night.

She almost turned coward and camped in a field, but she had not come this far to turn back now. She made her way to the inn where Petra's presence was as distinct as a hand on her skin, through half a cohort of legionaries and a crowd of farmers coming home from the market.

There was room in the inn. The innkeeper eyed Sabata with mild interest, but not as if he recognized what the stallion was. He would have kept Sabata apart from Petra—stallion separated from stallion, which was wise with mortal horses—but Sabata ducked, backed, and slipped out of his headstall. Before the stableman could open his mouth to cry the alarm, Sabata laid claim to the stall beside Petra's.

They were obviously not going to kill each other. When Valeria left them, they were sharing bits of hay over the stall wall while the innkeeper watched and shook his head. "Never saw anything like it," he said.

"They're from the same herd," Valeria said. "My brother said he'd meet me here. I see he came in ahead of me."

"Only an hour or so," the innkeeper said. "He didn't mention he'd be sharing the room."

"He takes things for granted," Valeria said. "He's the oldest, you know. Thinks he owns the world."

The innkeeper grinned. "He does, doesn't he? Go on, it's at the top of the stair. He ordered dinner already—I'll make sure there's enough for two."

Valeria thanked him with words and silver. There was still the stair to face, then the door, and the rumble of bad temper on the other side of it.

She took a deep breath and started up the stair.

The room was small but surprisingly light and airy, with a window that took up most of a wall. There were two beds in it, and a hearth that at this time of year was swept clean.

Kerrec was lying on the bed under the window, stretched out

on his back with his arm over his eyes. He had taken off his coat and boots but was still in shirt and breeches.

He was awake. She could feel his awareness even before he said, "Thank you, I'll take my dinner later."

He was always civil to servants—that much she could say for him. She answered equally civilly, "The innkeeper said it will be up in an hour."

He went rigid. His arm lowered. She was braced for anger, but it still shook her to see those eyes like hot silver.

She steadied herself firmly, met his glare with a calculated lack of expression, and said, "I told him you were my brother and we were meeting here. It was Sabata's idea. He horrified the stableman—he insisted on stabling himself next to Petra. There will be blood on the walls by morning, the poor man is sure."

"You're babbling," he said coldly. "You never babble."

"You noticed?" She dropped her saddlebags beside the bed opposite his and sat on it, tugging at her boots. "And before you start, no, I'm not going back to Aurelia. No, I'm not going to try to stop you. And no, I won't leave you alone."

"Are you trying to make me hate you?"

"I'm trying to keep you alive."

"I'm not helpless."

"No," she said. "You aren't. You have Petra—and the other thing. But you need someone at your back."

When she mentioned the other thing, his hand went to his breast. She could see the cord at his neck and the slight bulge under his shirt.

He was wearing the master stone in a warded pouch—wise enough, she supposed. She could still feel it. She could smell it, too. It had a faint tang of hot iron.

"You realize," she said, "that if you can track him, he can track you."

"Not necessarily," said Kerrec, "but if he does, so be it. It will save me a great deal of traveling."

"Then what? What will you do? Blast him? Stab him? Slip poison into his cup? Hope he doesn't feed you to the void first?"

"I'll know when I see him," Kerrec said.

"If he lets you."

"This time he will. I have something of his. He'll want it back."

"He'll take it back."

"Good," said Kerrec. "Let him try."

Valeria studied him as if he had been an especially difficult chapter in one of her books. "I should put a binding on you and haul you back to your sister."

"Yes," he said. "So why are you talking about it? Why don't you just do it? I'm no match for you."

She would have loved to slap the haughty expression off his face. "Because I'm called to this road, too. So are the stallions. They've told me so."

"They haven't said it to me."

"Petra would if you asked him."

"How do you know what Petra would say?"

"I hear them all," she said. "You didn't know that, did you? You never asked. I never knew to tell you."

"No one hears them all," he said.

"No one told me that," she said, "so that I could be sure to do the proper thing and stop letting them do it."

He looked so offended she almost laughed. But then he said, "Well enough. I believe you. Now will you go away? Petra will tell you where I am. If I do something unbearably stupid, you can gallop to the rescue."

"It's much easier if I'm there with you," she said. She lay back on the bed. "I don't have a choice, either, you know."

"You could sound less smug about it."

"And you could be less hateful."

She bit her tongue. That was not what she had meant to say.

It seemed to have silenced him, at least. Maybe the edge was off his anger. He was still not happy with her at all.

Dinner came while they lay in stiff silence, glaring at the ceiling. The maid set the tray on the table between the beds, curtsied to them both, and left as quietly as she had come.

Valeria would have been willing to swear she had no appetite, but the smell of roast fowl made her mouth water. Just as she sat up, so did Kerrec—which the part of her that did not want to strangle him found encouraging.

There was more than enough for two hungry men. Valeria did the best she could with her half. Kerrec ate more than she did—encouraging, again.

Except for his uncertain temper, he looked better than he had since he met the Brother of Pain. He was stronger. His color was better. Even his magic was less broken. What he had done to find the master stone and come this far had taken considerable skill.

That had been his doing without help or support, and it was impressive. But now his magic was changing. It was partaking of the power of the stone.

That was dangerous. The magic in the stone had come from Gothard. Whatever good the stone did, it might only be doing it in order to return to its maker.

Valeria would keep watch over that—and keep quiet about it. She had said enough.

Her body, in its weakness, wanted badly to cross the narrow expanse of the room and lie beside him. Her mind knew better. Even if, somewhere in the shards of his self, he still loved her, he had no room for that now. Everything he had was focused on his hunt for his brother.

Somehow she had to change that. It was not going to be easy. If she bound or forced him, she could break his mind. If she left it too long or did too little, he would break on his own— or Gothard would do it for him.

Thirty-Two

Valeria more than half expected Kerrec to slip away before she woke, but she was up first. Breakfast was stiffly silent. So was their departure from the inn.

He was freezing her out. She set her teeth and endured it.

Gothard was somewhere toward the border, and probably beyond it. He was half a barbarian. It seemed logical that he would have gone to his mother's people.

If that was so, then he was on the wrong side of a war. And there were armies between.

They followed the legions' road to the north and then east, from the heart of the empire onto open plains of grass rolling away toward the distant teeth of mountains. Those mountains were in the barbarians' country, on the other side of the river that was the empire's border.

The closer to the frontier they came, the farther apart the towns and villages were. Most of those clustered around forts or huddled behind walls. Fields were plowed and tilled, and there were guards to protect the crops.

Most of the traffic had to do with the legions. Supply trains were running constantly, and couriers were even more frequent here than nearer Aurelia. The legions themselves were not marching. Except for cohorts traveling from fort to fort, the great mass of the army was on the border with the emperor.

Everything was leading up to a battle. Rumors were flying as to where and when, but no one doubted that there would be one. There had been raids and skirmishes all summer. Bands of barbarians had come as far as three days' ride from the river, pillaging and looting and killing whatever stood in their way.

The emperor was camped near the branching of the river, where half of it turned to flow down through the province of Toscana to the sea, but the rest went on along the eastward edge of Elladis. "Your brother will be somewhere near there if he's anywhere," Valeria said.

After days of icy silence, Valeria had had enough. If Kerrec would not say a word, she would do the talking for both of them.

He had been tracking his brother through the master stone. She was careful not to touch it with her own magic, but Petra had no objection to letting her into his mind. Through him she knew what Kerrec was seeing and feeling.

The stone was not as precise as a seeker spell. All it could do was tell him that he was going toward his brother and not away. Where Gothard was exactly, he could not see. Maybe when he was closer, that would come clear.

They were a day's march from the border in a raw and rowdy town that called itself Valeria Victrix. Kerrec had no humor and was not speaking to Valeria in any case, which spared her any comparisons between her unwelcome self and the town.

The inn in which they found themselves was not the best or

the worst to be had. It was clean, which was always the first requirement for Kerrec. The stable had room for two stallions, and the stablehands did not seem perturbed that they preferred to stay together. Its sleeping rooms were tiny, hardly more than large boxes, which forced the travelers to take their dinner in the common room.

Kerrec ate in his usual grim silence. Valeria worked her way slowly through a surprisingly wonderful concoction of lamb, dried fruits and rice with spices that she had only tasted a time or two before. The cook came from Iliya's country, and he had brought its arts and flavors with him to this outpost of the northern world.

Kerrec finished long before her, but he rather surprised her by not stalking off to their cupboard of a room. He sat scowling at a cup of wine, not even pretending to drink.

Most of the traffic in the common room was local and civilian, farmers and townsmen and vendors coming in as the market wound down. There was a table full of legionaries over by the far wall, but they were unusually restrained. It was early yet and the wine had barely begun to flow.

More interesting to Valeria's eye, many of the townsfolk were tall and fair, and one or two were even redheaded. The change had been gradual, but where a few days ago Valeria had been one of many dark, wiry people, now she was dwarfed by a crowd of big, light-haired men and the occasional woman.

They were still imperial citizens, or trying to seem as if they were. No one affected the long braided hair and exuberant mustaches of the tribes, or wore gaudy checks and plaids instead of plain and serviceable browns and butternuts and greens.

Memory ambushed Valeria. A big man, bigger than anyone here, redheaded and wolf-eyed, clashing with ornaments of gold and amber. She looked into Euan Rohe's remembered face, so vivid that she almost reached up to touch it.

It vanished into Kerrec's narrow hawk-face and silver eyes. She regarded him in something very like bitterness. This, she had chosen over that. This was her life, the other half of her—this cold and cruel thing.

Sanity struck quickly enough. Even for Euan's fine white body, she could not betray her people. That was the choice she had made. Kerrec could be part of it, or he might not. It made no difference.

From that position of shaky confidence, she opened what he would probably regard as hostilities. She did not care. It had to be said. "We'll reach the river tomorrow. Then what? How are you planning to find him?"

"I'll know when I get there," he said as he had the last time she asked.

That was meant to cut her off, but she had reached her limit. "What are you going to do? Swim the river? Walk up to the nearest dun and demand that they produce the traitor?"

His brow arched. "Do you have a better plan?"

"I'll come up with one that doesn't get us both killed," she said sharply. "You really were going to do that, weren't you? Did it ever occur to you that the One would love a royal sacrifice?"

"I was not going to do that," he said tightly. "I was going to go as far as I could safely, and then scry for him. Unless you would rather do it for me?"

"I well might," she said, "though you're doing well enough for yourself."

He shook that off. "I still remember how to focus. I'm not that far gone."

"Not now you aren't," she said. "I'll be happy for you—after I stop wanting to hit you."

"If I'm such miserable company, why do you stay?"

"Because Sabata won't let me leave."

"Don't blame the horse. You'd be here even if Sabata wanted you on the Mountain."

"Believe me," she said, "I would rather be there than here."

"So would I," he said. "But I have to be here."

"So do I."

They stopped. This was an impasse. It could go on, becoming more and more hateful, or it could stop with glare meeting glare.

Or one of them could let go the offensive. Valeria knew better than to think it would be Kerrec.

"We should sleep," he said abruptly. "The earlier we get off in the morning, the better."

Valeria fought down her first impulse, which was to argue with him. The second was to finish her cup of wine.

It was nearly full, and the wine was strong. While she sipped it slowly, rather than glare at Kerrec any longer, she let her gaze wander around the tavern. There were more legionaries now that the sun was going down, and fewer farmers and merchants.

A new company of soldiers jostled through the door. The others were either auxiliaries or infantry, but these were scouts. Instead of brass and scarlet, they wore leather and blued steel, with the sun and moon of the empire at collar and belt.

They had a lighter, rangier look than the others. A bit of wildness clung to them. They were laughing and yelling for beer.

One of them looked straight at Valeria where she sat in the corner. He must be dazzled by the dimness inside after the sunset light without, but Valeria could see his face clearly.

She had dreamed this. This place, this hour. This face squinting, then opening into incredulity.

He was just about to decide that his eyes deceived him when she said, "Rodry."

His eyes went wide. "By the gods," he said. "It is you!"

Her brother left his fellow scouts to commandeer a table and start in on the beer, and made his way through the increasingly crowded room. He was grinning from ear to ear.

Valeria got halfway to her feet before he pulled her up the rest of the way and hugged the breath out of her. He set her down, still grinning. "Gods! I thought we'd never see you again."

"I dream about you almost every night," she said.

"True dreams?" he asked.

"This one was."

He appropriated a stool from the next table and sat opposite her. His eye fell on Kerrec, then flicked back to Valeria.

She almost ignored the silent question, but she was too well brought up for that. "First Rider Kerrec," she said. "My brother Rodry. He's with the Ninth Valeria."

Rodry's eyes went wide at Kerrec's rank, and he sketched a salute. Kerrec bent in his head in return. He did not glare or say something cutting, which surprised Valeria somewhat.

Rodry turned back to Valeria. "So it's true? You really did get the Call?"

She nodded. "I passed the tests. I'm a rider-candidate. Or I was."

Kerrec stirred on his bench. Valeria ignored him. So did Rodry. He was shaking his head. "Mother must have been livid."

"She locked me in the root cellar," Valeria said.

"I heard," said Rodry. "I went back on leave for Caia's wedding. The stories were wild and getting wilder. Caia was not amused."

"I don't imagine she was," Valeria said dryly. "What are you doing here? Are you with the garrison in the fort?"

"We were out on a mission," Rodry said. "We're stationed nearer the border. And you?"

"We have a mission, too," Valeria said. Kerrec was simmering to a boil, but she carried on, driven by dreams and lifelong trust. "We're hunting a traitor—an imperial prince, a mage. He tried to kill the emperor. Now we think he's up to even worse."

Rodry took his time digesting that. While he did it, the inn girl brought beer and a bowl of spiced lamb. He ate and drank methodically, still pondering.

After a while he said, "That wouldn't be the traitor who made a disaster of the emperor's festival, would it?"

"That would be the one," Valeria said.

Rodry frowned as if he was trying to reconcile the sister he remembered with whatever Valeria had turned into. It seemed he managed. He always had been quick-witted.

"There is a rumor," he said. He leaned forward and lowered his voice. "They say there's an imperial renegade among the princes of the Calletani. He's their kin, it's said, and speaks their language like one of them, but he was raised in the empire."

"Have you heard a name?" Valeria asked.

Rodry shook his head. "The rumors call him *Brenin*—but that could be a title. It means *prince*."

"That would be my brother," Kerrec said. His voice was low, hardly more than a growl. "Where is he? Do you know?"

"Somewhere among the Calletani," said Rodry, blinking slightly at who, and what, Kerrec must be if he was the traitor's brother. "That's as much as we've heard. We have found the hunting camp of the tribe—it moves constantly and sometimes vanishes altogether, but we know where it is and more or less where it goes. It's likely he's there."

"Gothard would not be able to resist the lure of royalty," Kerrec said. "Can you guide us to this camp?"

"Both of you?" Rodry asked. "It's bloody dangerous."

"So I told her," said Kerrec sourly. "It didn't stop her. Nothing on this earth can. So—can you?"

"I'm not sure—" said Rodry.

"It's dangerous for him, too," Valeria pointed out to Kerrec. "If he's caught and recognized for what he is, you know what will happen to him."

"To all of us," Kerrec said. "We won't be caught."

"If you say so, First Rider," Rodry said. Valeria listened for mockery, but she could not find any.

Rodry was in awe. Rodry had never been in awe of anything. Valeria kicked him under the table.

He never noticed. He was leaning toward Kerrec. "Any good scout can get you into the Calletani hunting runs. Though if you're really determined to get this traitor out and bring him to justice, you'd probably do better to head downriver to the emperor's camp. The best scouts are there, and mages, too. Not," he added hastily, "that you aren't a great mage, sir, but these are seekers and spies by profession. If you talk to them—"

"Not the emperor," Kerrec said almost as coldly as if it had been Valeria saying it and not Rodry. "We'll cross the river as near here as we can. Will you guide us? Can you get leave?"

"I can try," Rodry said. "We're on alert, and no one's allowed leave. But for you, First Rider—"

"Take us to your commander," said Kerrec. "I'll see what I can do to persuade him."

Rodry nodded. His eyes were shining. "I'll gladly take you there, sir."

Thirty-Three

Valeria wanted to knock their heads together. Kerrec was full of noble revenge. Rodry was brimful of hero-worship. There was no grain of sense in either of them.

Rodry went off to his lodgings. Kerrec went up to their cupboard of a room.

Valeria was hard on his heels. Once they were in the room and the door was shut, she backed him into a corner. "What were you thinking?" she demanded. "What in the world was in your head?"

He barely blinked. His nostrils had thinned and his eyes gone pale, but that was more likely to be anger than alarm. "We need a guide across the river. An imperial scout is a godsend."

"That imperial scout is my brother," Valeria said. "If you get him killed, you won't just have me to face. You'll have my mother."

"I won't get him killed," said Kerrec with teeth-gritted patience. "Can't you see the magic in him? He has the seeker's power. We'll ward him and he'll help us hunt. We'll find the traitor and do what we must before the tribes know we're there."

"You had better hope so," she said grimly.

"You'll make sure of it if I won't," Kerrec said.

"And if that fails? Even if the tribes don't find us, your brother certainly will."

He tossed his head like an impatient stallion—so rare a gesture it made her stare. "My brother thinks I'm still on the Mountain. I've done everything I can to foster that impression. If he's looking for anyone, he'll be looking for my father's mages. We're as safe as we can be—but we don't know the country we're going into, and we don't have time to learn. Wouldn't you rather have a guide we can trust?"

"Yes, but—"

"The gods sent him," said Kerrec. "You'd see that if you would look."

"I see it," she said. "I wish I didn't."

That night it was she who went to sleep in a cold fury and Kerrec who seemed determined to suffer whatever mood she happened to inflict on him. No doubt he thought it was fair. Blasted man.

Whatever dreams came to her in the night, they left her before morning. Kerrec was up when she woke, perched crosslegged on the narrow bed, with a bowl of gently steaming water and his razor and his silver mirror.

She washed sketchily in the second bowl that he had all too thoughtfully ordered for her, then pulled on her clothes and left him to be as fastidious as he liked.

Rodry waited in the room below. He was maddeningly

bright-eyed and eager. "Good morning! I've ordered breakfast. I hope he likes barley porridge and cream. They have berries, too. I wheedled the girl into letting us have a bowlful."

"You sound as if you're in love," Valeria said. She sat down gingerly. Why her head should ache when she had barely drunk a cup of wine, she could not imagine.

Rodry filled a mug from the pot on the table. The scent of herb tea tickled her nostrils. It was sharp with alien spices, and it cleared her head wonderfully.

"It really is real, isn't it?" Rodry said. "You and the Mountain. The riders."

"You didn't believe it before?"

"It's not very believable," he said.

The girl brought breakfast. There were three bowls of porridge and a pitcher of cream still fresh from the cow, and a bowl of bright red berries and a warm loaf of bread and sweet butter, and links of sausages, and eggs cooked hard in the shell.

It was a feast. It arrived just as Kerrec came down, freshly shaved and meticulously clean as always. He barely acknowledged the bounty, but sat between Valeria and Rodry and reached for porridge and cream.

Rodry's expression was pure bliss. Oh yes, thought Valeria. He was in love—with a myth and a dream. He would wake to the snarling reality soon enough.

When they had eaten all they could hold and gone to claim the stallions, Rodry stopped in the stable door. His expression was rapt. His hand crept out.

Petra was nearer and by nature more gracious than Sabata. He allowed the stranger to stroke his neck and whisper in his ear.

Petra's eye rolled toward Valeria. This was not a stranger, it said. This was her kin. Did she not see the magic that he had?

Kerrec had asked the same infuriating question. Yes, she saw it. She had always seen it. It was not rider's magic. If Rodry had been a girl, he would have done well as a wisewoman.

Magic was magic, Sabata opined, thrusting out his nose for his share of adulation. Rodry was happy to give it.

Valeria was not going to win this fight. Even the stallions were against her.

She saddled and bridled Sabata in grim silence, taking some small pleasure in seeing how shocked Rodry was that the great First Rider groomed and saddled his own horse. Dreams and legends, it seemed, should come equipped with flocks of servants.

Rodry's own horse, an impatient and somewhat headstrong grey gelding, was pawing and stamping in the courtyard. At sight of the stallions, he went perfectly still. He was not as besotted as Rodry, but he was wise enough to bow before the white gods.

Except for the wary slant of Sabata's ear, the stallions ignored him. Rodry mounted with more skill than Valeria had expected. Someone had taught him to ride, and not too badly either.

They left Valeria Victrix at sunrise of a morning that was already promising to be hot. Rodry was clearly torn between wanting to trail behind adoringly and leading them as a scout should. A sharp blow between the shoulderblades from his sister and Sabata's teeth in his gelding's rump sent him skittering none too elegantly ahead.

They settled soon enough. Rodry was a practical person. Hero-worship only carried him so far. Then he had to be himself again.

By midmorning Rodry had coaxed Valeria into telling the whole story of her journey from the village of Imbria to the Mountain, and then a good part of her life since. She slid past the precise way in which she had met Kerrec—it would do her brother no good to hear how close she had come to rape—and

Kerrec's story was not hers to tell. But there was more than enough else to keep Rodry occupied.

He was full of questions, and each answer bred more questions. Valeria did not mind answering them at all, but she had to say, "I never knew you were interested in horse mages."

He looked down at his gelding's mane, fussing with it for a while before he said, "I used to dream about becoming a rider. I listened to all the stories. When I went to fetch you from the market, I'd stay out of sight as long as I could, so I could hear everything. I grew out of the dream, but I never stopped listening."

"Maybe—" Valeria began. Maybe he would be another one of the late Called, she meant to say. But she could see the patterns around him and the magic in him, and he was not a rider. He was a seeker and a scout and a bit of a healer. The horse magic had passed him by.

Instead she said, "Maybe you had a touch of foresight, and you were seeing me. You do ride well. I didn't know you could do that, either."

"It's a different world out here," he said. "Back in Imbria I didn't want to talk about it. I just wanted to be home."

Valeria nodded. "You can go home," she said. "We're not supposed to. Once we pass the testing, that's the end of the old world. Our whole life after that is the school and the art. If we have titles or wealth or power, we give them up. Everything comes down to one name that we choose, and the magic that Called us."

"That's hard," Rodry said.

"I don't miss home," she said quickly. "I'm where I belong. Though sometimes…"

"Blood's strong," he said. He lowered his voice. His glance flicked toward Kerrec, then away. "That's why he won't go to the emperor, isn't it? And why he's—you know. Dead."

Valeria regarded him in admiration. "You're quick," she said. "It took me forever to realize who he was. Not that he helped at all. He's the most closemouthed rider on the Mountain—and believe me, for that contest, there's a large field."

"I can see why," said Rodry. "What you gave up—marrying that boy from the mill, birthing babies and brewing simples and being a power in the village—was never enough for you. He had everything, and he walked away from it. I'd keep quiet about it, too, if it happened to me."

"You couldn't be quiet if you tried," said Valeria. "You don't have an arrogant bone in your body, either."

His brows went up. "He's not arrogant. He's just…what he has to be."

"You don't know him," Valeria said darkly.

"Probably not," said Rodry, unperturbed. He urged his gelding ahead. Valeria followed, and Kerrec lagged somewhat behind. Gods knew what was in his head. For once, Valeria did not care.

Rodry's cohort was camped beside the river. It had been there for long enough to put up a palisade and begin building a stone fort.

The riders came in with a flock of sheep and cattle, lending a hand with herding them. Rodry was more than a little appalled that the stallions would stoop to such a thing, but Sabata loved to play drover, and Petra took considerable pleasure in it himself.

"They're still horses," Valeria said when Rodry's shock started to get the better of him.

That did not help much, but it stopped his sputter of protest. They clattered and rumbled and blatted and bellowed through the gate into the fort, where the herds crowded into pens and the drovers stopped to breathe.

The heat was stifling. Even the stallions were sweating, dark skin showing through the wet white coats. Kerrec looked cool and barely ruffled and disgustingly clean.

He dismounted with casual grace. "Water," he said without lifting his voice. "For the horses."

Water came in buckets, with legionaries carrying it. Valeria wondered when she would learn that art. Or was it something one was born to?

Sabata was glad to drink. So was Valeria. The water was clean and cool—not river water, Rodry said. There was a spring up in back of the fort, which was why it had been built precisely here.

The garrison drank from the spring but bathed in the river under the walls, with men on guard above. For guests there was a bath in the guest barracks, which happened to be within sight of the stable, and food and drink if they would take it.

Rodry left them there, promising to come back as soon as he could. It was still full daylight, and hot. A breeze stirred in the room, cooling it wonderfully.

Valeria eyed Kerrec. One of her first lessons was unwinding in her head. Control of elements—that was the art of the Second Rider. But he had lost so much. And yet, these past few days…

He was getting it back. Was he aware of it? There was no telling. There never was, with Kerrec.

She was not about to challenge him now and lose this lovely breeze. She lay on one of the bunks that lined the walls. It was hard, but she had lain on worse.

Kerrec would not look at her. She had her breeches on, but she had not laced up her shirt. Never mind that he had seen her naked more times than she could count—and she him. Somehow they had become strangers all over again.

That was not her fault. She stayed where she was, lying on her back, whether it tormented him or not. He sat on a bunk as far from her as he could go, tucked up his feet and folded his hands and seemed to go to sleep.

She could feel him. He was more than awake. His magic shimmered in the room. All the patterns in it wove around him.

She never could completely hate him. Not the way he sat a horse, and not now, in the midst of such magic. It was beautiful.

The master stone must be doing it, but it felt like Kerrec. This was horse magic, pattern magic. There was only a faint hint of the stone magic.

When Rodry came, he seemed a part of it somehow. These were the patterns they were to follow out of the room and into the heart of the fort.

Thirty-Four

The cohort's commander was young. Valeria had not expected that. He was younger than Rodry—who was only five years older than Valeria—and painfully aware of his position.

He was also excruciatingly aware of Kerrec's, both as First Rider and emperor's son. He scrambled up from his worktable when Rodry brought them into his office, scattering pens and parchment. "Highness! Sir. This is an honor."

"Tribune," said Kerrec. "Thank you for seeing us. We won't keep you long."

"No," the commander said. "Oh, no, sir. Take as long as you like."

"This will be brief," Kerrec said, gentle but firm. "We need to borrow your scout to guide us across the river."

The commander stiffened. His face paled a shade or two. "Ah," he said. "I see. Is there anything else I can do for you? Anything at all?"

"Thank you," said Kerrec, "no."

"Well," said the commander. "That—well. There are orders, you see—just this morning. No one is to cross the river until the emperor issues the counterorder."

Valeria felt the chill in the hot, still air. So, it seemed, did the young tribune. His face went even paler.

"Surely," said Kerrec mildly, "you can make an exception."

The commander shook his head. His expression was miserable, but there was no yielding in it. "Sir, I'm sorry. This comes direct from the emperor's hand. Look, see." He riffled among the papers on the table, plucking out one from which hung a pendant seal.

Valeria had never seen such a thing. Kerrec obviously had. His lips thinned. "Does it say how long?"

"No, sir," the tribune said. "Just that the crossings are closed and all forces are to stay on this side of the river, on penalty of being caught and hanged as a spy. Even if you know the way, sir, I can't let you cross."

"I have to cross," Kerrec said.

The commander's misery deepened. "You can't, sir. Truly, I am sorry. Maybe if you go to the emperor—"

"I am not going to the emperor," Kerrec said through gritted teeth. He drew a breath. "Your pardon, tribune. Of course you can't disobey orders. I'm at fault for even thinking to ask."

"No, no," the tribune said. "Oh, no, sir. I wish I could help you. But the emperor—"

"The emperor," Kerrec said in a still, cold voice. "Yes."

"Please, sir," the tribune said. "Accept our hospitality. Stay as long as you like. This ban won't last forever. In a day or two or eight, you'll be free to cross. Meanwhile, we'll be delighted—privileged—to have you here."

"Many thanks," Kerrec said with perfect civility. "You are generous."

"We are honored," the commander said. "Please, sir, if you will—will you dine with me tonight?"

Kerrec inclined his head. There was nothing else he could do, not if he wanted to be polite.

Valeria, safely invisible in her guise of male and servant, was glad of this obstacle. The emperor could not have known that his son was pursuing rampant insanity within reach of the war, but his order had come just in time. Kerrec could not hunt Gothard down if he could not get across the river.

She knew better than to think Kerrec had given in. But for tonight he was trapped. He had to accept the commander's invitation.

She had no such obligation. She was free to assure herself that the stallions were well looked after, and to explore the fort. Cropped hair and riding clothes served her as well here as they had while she answered the Call. Soldiers did not look for a woman and therefore did not see one.

Rodry brought dinner to the guest barracks. She had been ready to try her luck in the soldiers' mess, but this forestalled her.

She said so. He looked as if she had proposed she sell herself to the lot of them. "You can't do that!"

"Why? You don't think I can look after myself?"

"Not against five hundred randy men you can't."

"What do you think I do every day in the school?" she demanded. "I'm the only woman there."

"Those are riders," Rodry said. "They're different."

"You think so?"

"*He's* different."

"He most certainly is," Valeria said acidly. "But that's no reflection on the rest of them. I can take care of myself, elder brother."

"I'm sure you can," said Rodry, "but five hundred legionaries under lockdown…would you torture them with what they can't have?"

"Lockdown?" said Valeria. "All the commander said was—"

"Corinius was being circumspect," Rodry said. "We're all confined to quarters except for the patrols—and they're lying as low as they can. There's a battle coming. The emperor's trying to draw the main force of the enemy across the river."

"So we can't go anywhere until it's over," Valeria said. "Can we leave? Go back westward?"

"You'll have to ask Corinius," Rodry said.

Valeria shook her head and sighed—a hiss of frustration. "Kerrec won't go. He's determined to get across the river."

"Why?" said Rodry. "Does he know something we don't?"

"Maybe," Valeria said. "Maybe he's simply out of his mind."

"Then why do you follow him?"

"Because I have to," she said.

"Orders?"

She did not answer that.

Rodry, damn him, refused to let it go. "Why does he have to cross the river? Why can't he leave it to the emperor and his mages? What is this traitor, that a First Rider pursues him to the ends of the earth?"

"The traitor wants Kerrec dead," said Valeria, "and had him tortured until he was not far short of it."

"But he's alive," Rodry said. "He's walking—riding. He's not broken."

"The deepest torture doesn't break the body," she said.

"He's not broken," Rodry repeated.

"He was," she said. "Large parts of him still are."

"That can't be all it is."

"Isn't it enough?"

"There must be more," Rodry said.

Valeria took a deep breath. "The traitor wants to be emperor," she said. "We told you he tried to kill his father. He did get six riders killed in the Great Dance, and nearly destroyed us all. If he's with the tribes, and if they'll use whatever it is we think he has, the legions are in real danger. He won't care who dies or how, as long as he gets what he wants."

"And you two think you can stop him if a whole army of mages can't? Even if he won't go to the emperor, can't he tell Corinius and have him pass it up the chain of command?"

"Probably," Valeria said. "Then again, all I've seen of men in authority is that they don't listen. Here we are, a pair of riders. One has been sent away from the Mountain because his powers are so damaged he can no longer control them. The other is female, anything but submissive, and notoriously resistant to her order's discipline. The fact we're telling the truth won't matter. We're simply not respectable."

Rodry snorted the way he did when he was trying not to laugh. "When you put it that way, I see your point. Still—"

"If you have doubts," Kerrec said from the door, "by all means give in to them. Just tell us how to find the Calletani, and we'll go."

"I'll show you," said Rodry.

"Your orders—" Kerrec began.

Rodry's head shook tightly. His lips were tight, too.

Valeria knew that expression all too well. Rodry was as stubborn as a human creature could be. And he was in love with a myth and a dream.

"Protect me," he said, "and I'll guide you."

"You'll be a deserter," Kerrec said.

"I'm sworn to serve the empire," Rodry said. "The white gods are the empire's heart. You serve the white gods. Therefore—"

"Spare me your logic," Kerrec said. "Tell me where to go."

"I can't," said Rodry. "Navigating those woods is like riding. It's done by feel and art. The tribes have their ways and their logic, but it's not something I can convey in an hour. I have to show you."

"You could lose your place in the legion. At the very least."

Rodry's eyes barely flickered. "He'll go after the emperor again, won't he? Only this time there are three legions with him, and they'll all come under fire, too. That makes it worth the cost. All I ask of you, if it comes to a court-martial, is to speak for me."

"It's not going to come to a court-martial," Valeria snapped. "You're not doing this. It's insane."

"I think I have to," Rodry said with quiet obstinacy. "Just like you. What will you lose? Will they dock you? Throw you out?"

"Probably throw her out," Kerrec said. He shook his head and sighed. "Very well. If I can protect you, I will. How soon can you ride?"

"I can go now," Rodry said. "You?"

"When it's full dark," said Kerrec. "I'll get us past the sentries. We probably shouldn't try to cross right under their noses. Where do we go? Upstream or down?"

"Downstream," said Rodry.

Kerrec nodded. "You think they'll be close?"

"The main camp, no," Rodry said. "That's at least two days downriver, probably more. But I have a fair sense of where they would have to be."

"Good," said Kerrec. Valeria would have liked to slap him for it. "Go. Act casual. Come back after the second bell."

Rodry leaped up. Once he was on his feet, he stood straight and deliberately drained the eagerness out of his body. He sauntered through the door as if he had done nothing more significant than share his dinner with a guest.

Valeria packed her traveling bag in grim silence. There was precious little to pack, but she took as long about it as she could reasonably manage. Kerrec was done already—he had never unpacked at all. He lay on his distant bunk and closed his eyes.

She debated a long while before she moved. Then she stood over him, glaring down.

He spoke, still with closed eyes. "Tell me what other choice we have."

"Give it up. Go home. Let your brother dig his own grave. He will do that, you know. He won't be able to help it."

"Not before he digs my father's grave. And my sister's. And as much of the empire's as he can. Whatever he has, it's strong. Even stronger than what he had before."

He said it so calmly that he almost convinced Valeria. But she said, "If he's that much of a threat, your father knows it already. He's as powerful a mage as you ever were."

"My father should have strangled him in the cradle," Kerrec said dispassionately. "We all knew what that child was. He was born hating anyone who had what he couldn't have. I was older and my mother was empress. Briana was born after our father left his concubine and went back to his wife. Gothard hated us both—and half of it was envy. He even hated his mother, because she failed to make herself empress and him the heir, as she promised."

"Did he kill her?"

Kerrec opened an eye. It was the color of steel. "She killed herself. She was mad. So is he. It runs in the blood."

"Then how did your father—"

"My father is as mortal as the rest of us. She came as a hostage, one of many, to be educated in the palace. Even in the throes of madness, just before she died, she was magnificent. When he first saw her, she took his breath away. Hair as red as fire. Skin as white as milk. Eyes as yellow as a cat's. She was a full head taller than he was, and strong enough to flatten three of the imperial guards with a blow. He had never seen anything like her."

Valeria had no trouble imagining it. She had her own dreams of red hair and amber eyes and hands so big they swallowed both of hers in one.

She was angry enough with Kerrec to let him see what she was thinking. His stare grew a fraction colder, but that was all.

She did not want to feel what she was feeling. She wanted him to be hers again, her lover, her friend and teacher. Not this cold and remote creature who barely cared that she was dreaming of his old rival.

"Are you sure," she asked him, "that your brother is the mad one? He seemed sane enough to me. Whereas you…"

"I am what he made me," Kerrec said, so quiet it made the small hairs rise on her neck.

Valeria threw up her hands. "Well then. We'll die with both of you. Will that make you happy?"

"No," he said.

He might have said more, but they both heard Rodry coming, a quick light step and a sudden slide as he slipped through the door. "It's time," he said.

The fort was dark but for shielded lamps along the wall. The air was thick and damp and breathless. The stars were hidden in haze.

Rodry had the horses ready and waiting. They rode out with no overt attempt to be either quiet or secret. Valeria felt the magic that flowed softly over them, like mist and water and the fall of shadow.

For a broken mage, Kerrec had remarkable stores of power. He took them remarkably for granted, too. This spell of concealment was no part of the horse magic, but it came out of him as easily as he breathed.

What Valeria had said in temper, she began to believe as they rode away from the fort and down along the river. Kerrec was not sane. His magic was healing fast, but his spirit was still badly damaged.

Thirty-Five

The Ard Ri was on his way west. His messengers put him two days out, with as many men and as much baggage as he had. He had been looting in the wake of the emperor as he too moved west—stripping the frontier of every scrap of food or precious thing that earlier raids had left.

The Calletani hunting camp was three times its old size already, with outliers from the Prytani and the Mordantes and—unexpected but more than welcome—the Skaldi who lived in the far reaches of the north. They were all fresh and hungry and spoiling for a fight.

Euan Rohe knew better than to taunt them with promises. "When the high king comes," he said when they came to him, "he'll give you the word."

"How evil of you," Gothard said one bright morning. Euan had not seen him in days. He had been shut away with the priests and his captive children, working magic that, at odd moments, set Euan's teeth on edge.

He had one of the boys with him, the big fair one with the soft face and the eyes as black and bottomless as a priest's. Rumor had it that he was a gelding—and not by choice.

He followed Gothard like a dog, and like a dog, he seemed to see little else. Gothard ignored him.

"Are you ready at last?" Euan asked.

"Almost," Gothard said, by no means for the first time. But this time he added, "We'll try a working today. It may be a little startling."

"Why? What is it?"

Gothard's eyes glinted. Euan preferred him sour—when he was as cheerful as this, it boded no good for anyone but Gothard. "You'll know when you see it."

"You don't know, either, do you?"

Gothard lifted a shoulder in one of his maddening half shrugs. "I've never tried it before—bringing a dozen mages together within the circle of a stone. And this stone being what it is…I can't predict what it will do."

"You had better try," Euan said with more than a hint of a growl. "If you harm a hair of any head in this camp…"

"I'll do my best," Gothard said. He sounded remarkably unconcerned.

He was deep in the spell of the stone. His yellow dog was deeper still. Not for the first time, Euan wondered if he should have left Gothard to die where the stone fell—or at least kept the stone from him.

By nightfall the whole camp could be dead or worse. If that happened, it would be the One's pleasure. But Euan would do his utmost to assure that no such thing happened.

He stood up and walked away without the courtesy of a farewell. Gothard's laughter followed him.

Now that Euan was warned, he saw sorcery in every breath of wind that made him shiver and every cloud that crossed the sun. He thought of going out hunting, but he refused to abandon the camp. He joined the clan chieftains and the elders in their circle, though they were saying nothing they had not said a hundred times before.

The mood in the camp was strange and growing stranger. The young men had got up a mock battle, a gathering that was half dance and half war. The sounds of stamping and shouting and the beating of drums rolled steadily under the drone of the elders' conversation.

Just as Euan decided to rise and join the dancing, a shout rang out on the edge of the camp. Drums were beating and voices shrilling the war cry of the Ard Ri.

The high king had come in ahead of his army, with a dozen men of his warband and a handful of priests. They were running long and easy, as men did on the hunt or on the war trail. As they loped through the camp, a ragged cheer followed them.

The elders were all on their feet. Euan was last—deliberately.

The high king halted in the middle of the circle. His broad breast heaved, gleaming with sweat. His teeth were bared in a cheerful snarl. "Good day to you all," he said. "Are you making a war without me?"

"We wouldn't dream of it," Euan said.

"I'm sure," said the high king. "You, brother. Come with me."

The elders nearest Euan moved slightly but distinctly away. Euan shook his head at their cowardice. The Ard Ri was watching, smiling.

Euan smiled back as sweetly as he knew how. He fell in beside the high king and walked through the camp, easily, matching his stride to the bigger man's.

"You have ambitions," the Ard Ri said after a while.

"Doesn't everyone?"

"Not everyone acts on them," said the Ard Ri.

"Not everyone gets to be a king." Euan clasped his hands behind him and lightened his step a fraction. "You're here early. Have you had word from the imperials? Are we finally going to have a real battle?"

"I heard a rumor," the Ard Ri said. "Have you been indulging in fits of magic?"

"Hardly," said Euan, sternly suppressing his memory of the seeing-stone. "What is this? The yammering of my enemies?"

"I would like to think so. You don't have a pack of imperials, then, doing your bidding?"

"They're hardly doing mine," Euan said, "but I can't deny I'm getting some use out of them."

The high king grinned. "I like your honesty. What are they doing, then? Dancing for that cousin of yours, the emperor's by-blow?"

"They dance like priests," Euan said. "Exactly like priests. For the glory of the One and the honor of oblivion."

That made the Ard Ri's eyes widen. He made a sign as if he had been a child or a woman, to avert ill omen. "That's a deadly weapon you're playing with," he said.

"It is," Euan agreed, "to the empire. We're safe enough as long as we keep a grip on it."

"Better you than me," said the high king.

"I'm glad you approve," Euan said, "my lord."

"Would it matter if I didn't?"

"You are the Ard Ri," said Euan.

"I rule by consent of the people," the high king said, "and

the grace of the kings. Remember that when you make your move, boy. You can probably win it, you're clever enough, and you fight well enough for a pup. But then you have to keep it. There have been nine-day kings before. You'll want to watch that you don't become another."

"I do plan to be watchful," Euan said, "and I thank you for your advice."

"Ah, well," said the Ard Ri, shrugging, "you'll forget it as soon as I'm out of sight. But the people will remind you. So will this hot coal you've taken in your hand. Maybe it will win the war for us—and maybe it will be the end of you. Either way, you'll get the blame but I'll get the glory."

"That's always so with kings," Euan said coolly. "I'm not challenging you—yet. I have too much to learn first."

"Good lad," said the high king, slapping him on the back so hard he staggered. The Ard Ri barked laughter and left him standing in the middle of the camp, alive and more or less intact.

Euan walked back through the stares of the people. Most had warmed into respect. He would have to cultivate that. Respect was even better than fear for keeping a king in power.

Halfway back to the circle where the young men were still dancing, Euan stopped. The earth felt as if, just for a moment, it had shrugged.

He looked around him. It was still a blazingly hot, brilliantly sunny morning. People were going about their business as if nothing had happened.

The trickle of sweat down his back meant only that the air was hot. Its coldness was his imagination. A breeze had come up, that was all, gusting through the camp and taking the edge off the heat.

Clouds were brewing overhead. They often did in summer.

They could boil like this, turning from purest white to blue-black and breeding lightning.

Euan turned away from the dance toward the priests' tents. The breeze was stronger. It pushed against him as he walked, until he had to push back or be blown aside.

Gothard's captives were sitting in a circle in the center of the tents. Priests surrounded them, making no attempt to interfere.

Gothard sat in the middle with the starstone in his cupped hands. His eyes were shut. He looked as if he was asleep.

The clouds were raging overhead. The wind had freshened. It swirled in the circle, catching at the ends of plaids and tangling the boys' hair into knots.

Euan could see the strain in their faces. One or two had tears running down their cheeks. Whatever was happening behind those eyelids, it was as grueling as any battle on the field.

The storm had begun to turn slowly, like an eddy in the river. The wind rose to a scream. Gothard's face was still expressionless, but his fingers twitched, tightening on the stone.

It was trying to break his control. If it succeeded and the storm broke over them, it would flatten the camp and everyone in it.

What Euan was going to do was either madly brave or absolutely foolhardy. He would lay bets on both. He stepped between two rapt and motionless mages and stood in the center of the circle.

He did not look up. He did not want to see what swirled there. He took Gothard's face in his hands and spoke without raising his voice. "Gothard, stop it. You're alerting the enemy to our exact position. Send your storm somewhere else."

Gothard neither moved nor opened his eyes. The storm was growing. Euan could no longer see its edges.

Euan held himself steady and kept his voice quiet. "Shift the storm," he said. "Send it over the river."

He could not tell if he was even heard. All he could do was keep saying it, until maybe the words would sink in.

Was the wind shifting?

"Yes," he said. "Across the river. Away from here."

Gothard tensed. Euan braced for an eruption. None came.

One of the boys was gasping for breath. Euan dared not take his eyes off Gothard. There was no magic in what he did—it was plain human will. He willed Gothard to take the storm in his hand like the ball in a child's game, and toss it into Aurelia.

It was not that easy. Euan did not care. Whatever the mage had to do, let him do it—and do it now.

"Now," he said.

The wind died to a brisk breeze. Scraps of sunlight scattered across the circle. The boiling mass of cloud, spitting lightnings, rolled off toward the river. Veils of rain trailed beneath it.

Euan stepped back carefully. One of the boys was down, with priests hovering over him. From what Euan could see of him, he was blue and cold.

The rest were coming out of it, some less slowly than others. They had priests to look after them. Gothard could look to himself.

He was awake—his eyes were open. They were as black as the storm he had sent across the river. "Next time you do this," Euan said to him, "be sure you do it when the emperor is in reach. Otherwise you're wasting power."

"Now you're a master of the magical arts?" Gothard covered the starstone and laid it away. "We'll be ready when the battle comes. I have the way of it now. We'll give them such a storm as the world never saw."

"Leave us a few men to fight," Euan said. "There's no glory in sending armies to oblivion."

"Even if it wins you an empire?"

"I'd like to have a hand in winning it," Euan said.

Gothard rose and shook himself. "I'll take the emperor and leave his armies to you. Will that content you?"

"Admirably," Euan said.

Thirty-Six

Past the fort the banks rose steeply and the river narrowed, roaring between the high walls. The next ford was miles downstream.

Trees closed in. The plain was ending, giving way to a forest of oak and beech and maple. On the far side, invisible in the dark but perceptible to Valeria's senses, the land began to rise. The trees there were dark and tall. Faintly across the water, she caught the clean sharp scent of pine.

The road ran as close to the river's edge as it dared. The stallions set a fast pace, surefooted in the dark.

It was cooler under the trees, and their speed woke its own wind. Even so, as the night passed, Valeria felt a change in the air. When the branches opened enough to see, there were no stars.

Daybreak was quiet, still and very hot. The sky was like hammered brass. They stopped for an hour to rest, then went on. None of them asked to stop longer.

The storm broke near noon. The wind came first, roaring through the trees and shrieking in the gorge. Thunder followed, crack after deafening crack, then blinding flashes of lightning. Woven branches sheltered them for a while—until a tree crashed down across the road, nearly taking Rodry with it.

There was no shelter—no convenient cave, and nowhere to get out of the wind or the sudden torrents of rain. The road was blocked in front of them. It was no safer to turn back, and certainly not to go off the road into the deep woods.

The fallen tree was all the shelter there was. It was an oak, riven with age and old lightning, and it had fallen solidly, braced on the spread of branches and the remains of its roots. The riders pulled saddles and baggage off the horses and scrambled under the rough-barked roof, just as the skies opened.

Valeria was wedged between her brother and Kerrec. Past the arch of Kerrec's nose she could see Sabata's cream-white tail and wet grey rump, and past that, a wall of water.

It was not too horribly uncomfortable. The storm had broken the heat—her face was cold though the rest of her was warm. The wind had died. The rain came down in torrents.

Rodry was snoring gently. It must be true that people said about soldiers. They could sleep anywhere.

Kerrec's eyes were shut, but his body was stiff beside her. A shudder ran through him.

Valeria's arms moved without her willing it, to pull him close. He did not fight her off. She held him until the shuddering stopped.

The rain came in waves, each as fierce as the last, through most of that day. The road had turned to a muddy river. The tree diverted it or they would have been swimming.

Late in the day, at last, the gusts of rain began to weaken. The clouds broke. The sun peered through.

Rodry yawned noisily. His elbow dug into Valeria's ribs. She had been dozing, but that brought her sharply awake. Kerrec's head was heavy on her shoulder.

They untangled themselves from each other and the tree, emerging stiffly into a wet and glistening world. The horses had wandered off in search of grass, but they were still within sight.

More trees than this one were down. The road was washed out. The riverbank had collapsed a bare three furlongs past where they had waited out the storm. It looked as if something vast and voracious had bitten into the cliff. Valeria could hear the river roaring below.

If they had gone on, they would have been caught in the fall. "The gods are angry today," Rodry said, "but not with us."

"You don't think so?" said Kerrec. "There's no road left."

"We'll make one," Rodry said. "I'm thanking the gods we're alive to do it. We'd best start now, while there's daylight. There is—or used to be—an old way station a few miles on. We can spend the night there."

Kerrec turned slowly, sniffing the air. He was scowling. "Yes. There's another storm coming. The horses should be under cover for that, if it's cold as well as wet."

Valeria was no weathermaster. She could smell rain and mud and far too much water, but she could not see where that promised another siege of wind and rain. Still, if Kerrec was right, she would far rather be sleeping under a roof than half inside a fallen tree.

The road was as difficult as Valeria had feared. It was washed away in too many places. Even where it survived, it either hung precipitously above the river or was blocked by slides of mud or rock.

They slipped and struggled and scrambled. More than once they had to shift trees that were too high or tangled for the horses to jump or climb over. They led the horses more than they rode.

The sun hung low when at last they found the way station. It was built of earth and wood and stone, and seemed to grow out of the steep slope beside the road. The roof had held and the hillside did not seem likely to let go quite yet. Better still, it was a good furlong from the cliff's edge.

There was room inside for a dozen horses and a troop of soldiers. For three of each, it was a palace—and it was dry. Wood was stacked against the far wall, more than they would ever need. A barrel stood just outside, brimming over with rainwater.

Rodry built a fire in the stone hearth. Valeria and Kerrec tended the horses, rubbing them down and feeding them handfuls of barley that they had brought from the cohort's stores. Grass grew on the hillside, but there was a rick of hay in the station, well cured and still fresh.

"The legions think of everything," Valeria said as the horses lined up at it, settling in for a long night's browse.

Kerrec responded, which surprised her. "They've been preparing this war for years. There are people whose whole life is the pursuit of tiny details—even to the provision of hay for scouts and outriders. That's how the empire runs, you know. Not on princes and councils and the occasional Dance."

"'The fate of every war is in the clerks' hands,'" Valeria quoted from one of her lessons in the school.

"Quartermasters, too," Rodry said as the fire caught hold. He fed it bits of tinder. "Supply clerks. Keepers of the roster. People who count every bean."

"So what are we?" Valeria asked.

"Extraneous," Kerrec said.

There was a glint in his eye. It nearly knocked Valeria flat. Kerrec—joking, however grimly. Who would have thought it?

Rodry caught the flicker of humor, too, but he had no way of knowing how rare it was. He grinned. "That puts us in our place, doesn't it?"

Kerrec warmed his hands over the rising flames. Valeria shivered. It was hard to believe it had been breathlessly hot only this morning. The fire was more welcome than she could have imagined.

The thunder came back as they shared a surprisingly pleasant dinner, followed quickly by the rain. Dry and warm and almost guiltily comfortable, they ate their bread and dried meat and sharp cheese and shared a packet of honeyed figs, rich and sticky and sweet.

Sabata came to the scent of sweetness. Valeria shared her figs with him. When they were gone, he licked her hands clean, then sighed and groaned and folded up beside her.

She propped herself against his large warm bulk. Rodry was watching her. His eyes had gone wide again. "I keep forgetting," he said. "What you are. What he is."

"Try to remember," she said with a hint of sharpness. "Then forget it matters. I'm still me. I haven't turned into anything different."

"No?" Rodry made tea with a mix of herbs that Valeria knew well. It was her mother's. It smelled of her. Mint and chamomile, rose and vervain, to calm the mind and encourage sleep.

He steeped it as Valeria had learned to do when she was a child, then strained it and poured it into cups. Valeria's heart was eager but her hand was slow to take it. It was redolent with memories.

Kerrec sniffed it suspiciously. His brow rose a fraction. He sipped with care but with evident pleasure. "A wisewoman's brew?" he asked.

"One of Mother's," Rodry answered. "It's safe—don't worry."

"I'm not worried," said Kerrec. "It's good."

Valeria set her cup down untasted. "It is good, but someone has to stay awake."

"Why?" Kerrec asked. "We'll set wards. The stallions will watch for trouble."

She shook her head. He was right, of course, but she was feeling contrary. "I don't like this storm. It's not aimed at us, but it might as well be."

"It's aimed at the army," Rodry said. His usually good-humored face was grave. "Sir, do you think—?"

"Stone magic is bound to earth," Kerrec said. "He, or any stone mage, could have brought down the hillside, but he has no power over air and water."

"This isn't a natural storm," Valeria said. "Can't you feel the power that drives it? If it's not your brother, it's another mage— or one of the barbarians' priests. They all claim to hate and fear magic, but their priests use it freely, from all I've seen. They'll Unmake the world if they can."

She should not have said that. Deep inside her, the Unmaking stirred.

Sabata sighed in his sleep and snorted softly. The distraction was enough, just, to quell the Unmaking. She closed it off behind doubled and trebled wards, with Sabata mounting guard outside.

The others had gone on talking, as ignorant as ever of what she carried inside her. Rodry said, "With this much rain, the river's already swollen. We may have to wait for it to go down before we can cross the ford."

"How far is the ford from here?" Kerrec asked.

"When the road was still there, in good weather it was maybe half a day's ride downstream. In this, with the road in gods know what condition, I can't tell you how long it will take us. The banks drop down toward the ford. If that's flooded, we'll have to find a way around, then hope for better chances farther on."

"And hope, as well, that we don't run into the army before we can cross." Kerrec hissed between his teeth. "Damn. If they could only have held off their storm-herding for a day, we'd be across by now."

"Are you sure it was mages?" Rodry asked. "Maybe it's not a magical storm at all. Maybe the gods are telling us something."

"I am going across the river," Kerrec said. "I am hunting down my brother before he kills my father and my sister and destroys the whole of Aurelia, then tries to take the rest of the world with it. The wind may rage and the gods may laugh, but I will do it. I will not stop until it is done."

Valeria caught Rodry's eye. It was not the words Kerrec said. It was the way he said them. Calm. Matter-of-fact. Absolutely unbending.

They should have knocked him down and bound him and hauled him back to Aurelia. But if Valeria had no power to do such a thing, how could Rodry? All they could do was stay as close as they could and protect him as best they might—and pray they found Gothard before Gothard raised the Unmaking.

Thirty-Seven

Valeria lay with Rodry and Kerrec in a thicket of bracken, looking down on what had been a shallow ford. It was a roaring flood now, overwhelming the banks and spreading far over a tumbled landscape of field and forest.

The road was deep underwater. Valeria could see where it had been, descending the long hill and disappearing into the muddy torrent. It ascended again on the other side, no longer the straight paved way of the imperial armies but a narrow rutted track winding upward into the trees.

"A pity the gods don't fly," Rodry said, with his eyes on that unattainable country.

Kerrec's face was closed. "There's another ford, you say?"

"The flood will go down," Rodry said. "Where we need to go is south of here in any case. We'll travel more of it on this side, that's all."

"And the army? Where is that?"

"West of the ford," said Rodry. "It was camped at Tragante, two days' ride from here, as of a week ago. If it's moved, my wager would be that it's gone farther south. The land's better there for a battle. It's rougher country here, and those trees up there can hide whole nations."

"That's where they are," Valeria said. "Up there."

Rodry nodded. "The emperor will try to lure them into the open."

"Will he do it?"

"Eventually," said Rodry. "They can't resist a battle."

"My brother can," Kerrec said. "He'll stay where he's safe, and wage his war from a distance. Where did you say the Calletani camp was?"

"We'll make our way south to Oxos ford," Rodry said. "Be careful now. We're a long way from the army, but there will be patrols. If you can raise that spell of yours again—can you work it by daylight or should we travel by night?"

"Night's better," Kerrec said, "but I'll do what I can."

Neither had asked Valeria what she could do. She bit her tongue. She was there because she insisted on it, not because they thought she could be of any use.

She could raise wards, at least, to keep mages from finding them. And she could see patterns—how the wind blew, how the light fell. There was war downriver, and a tide of death running even stronger than the flood.

It took them three days to skirt the flood. By then the river was still running high, but it flowed inside its banks again. On the fourth day, once more, the three of them looked out from a covert to a ford. Once again, there was no crossing it.

The river was down, the ford clear. There was an army camped beside it.

The emperor had not gone south from Tragante. He had brought his army north.

Kerrec had no words to say. Rodry's shoulders sagged. Valeria did her best to keep the relief from showing on her face.

The gods were speaking clearly, but Kerrec refused to listen. "Tonight," he said. "After dark. I'll get us across."

Rodry swallowed, then nodded.

Valeria opened her mouth to object, but the words would not come. A dart of bitter cold had pierced her.

The Unmaking. Someone was toying with it—tempting it. It felt like a mage testing his powers. Somehow he had touched what was inside her.

Dear gods. If that was Gothard, and if he realized who she was—if he tried to use her—

She had to trust her wards and hope they would be enough—just as she had to trust that Kerrec was right. He could lead them to Gothard and stop him before he turned this new power on the army.

They waited out the day in an oak grove that grew on a hill above the river. It had a strange feel to it, as if gods had walked here long ago.

The stallions were completely unperturbed. They grazed in the clearing at the grove's heart and drank from the spring that bubbled on its edge. The water was as cold as snow. It tasted of earth and greenery and a faint but distinct sharpness of magic.

Rodry slept like a sensible soldier. Kerrec sat on a flat stone that lay in the middle of the clearing, face turned to the sun. He looked as if he were drinking sunlight.

Valeria dozed for a while, but her dreams were strange. They seemed to belong to someone else. She saw people walking in the clearing and heard faint chanting. The words were like the grove, ancient and long forgotten.

She opened her eyes on Sabata grazing in the sun. He cropped grass as any horse would, switching his tail and shaking his ears at the flies. He was more real than anything in the world.

The sky lost its clarity as the sun sank. By evening the clouds were thick, though no rain seemed about to fall. It would be a dark night, without either moon or star.

Kerrec's satisfaction tingled on the edges of Valeria's perception. She was inside Petra and Sabata and even, in a dim way, Rodry's gelding.

She woke from a light doze and found her awareness spread like mist through all the horses. Whatever they felt or heard or smelled or saw, she felt with them.

She was not alarmed. It was a pleasant sensation, as if she were more a part of the world than any human could be. She could walk and talk and eat, and neither of the others looked at her oddly.

Kerrec had strengthened his spell of mist and confusion. The look of strain was back on his face. Valeria wondered if she should worry. The stallions were unconcerned, but they were not human enough to understand how close to the edge Kerrec could walk.

All she could do was watch him and be ready for whatever came. After nightfall, they waited for the army to settle for the night.

It looked as if it was under discipline, as Rodry's cohort had been. That meant half rations of wine and ale, and men in their tents and asleep by an hour after sundown.

The sentries were still awake, and many of those were mages.

There were wards on the camp. Valeria saw them as a glimmer in the gloom.

Kerrec skirted them as he led the others away from the grove, flowing like a mist toward the river. Through Petra, Valeria felt the effort in him, the struggle to keep his spell from scattering.

She had to be careful herself or she would be lost in the working. She kept a part of her awareness inside of Petra and therefore Kerrec, but drew the rest into herself. The world was less wondrous because of it, but her focus was clearer.

The horses picked their way down the hill toward the river. Once they came to the bank, they had to pick their way along the edge of the camp toward the ford.

There were guards, magical and mortal, and protections against intruders. Kerrec's spell and Valeria's wards had to hold. If they failed, the whole army would come down on them.

Valeria turned her mind away from fear. She had to remember to breathe. Sabata trod softly in Petra's wake.

Rodry was between them. He was mage enough to know what they were doing. He said nothing and clearly tried to think nothing.

Whatever mud and flotsam the flood had left, the emperor's troops had cleared away. The ground was bare and level. On their right hands, the earthwork rose above their heads.

Every imperial camp had such a wall, even if it was only for a night. Here, where three legions together prepared for battle, it was buttressed with stone. Guards walked the rampart, peering into the dark.

None of them saw the riders passing below. There was a mist on the river, dank and chill, and no moon to cast a shadow.

Mages were watching, clear-sighted in the dark. None sounded the alarm.

The ford was closely guarded. Archers who were mages were

stationed at intervals along the bank. The shimmer of wards caught their faces and the gleam of their helmets.

Mortal eyes could have seen nothing. To Valeria, seeing as the stallions saw, the world was dim but clear. Wherever magic was, there was light.

The riders slipped between two of the archers. One of them shivered with a breath of cold air from the river. The other stood still, staring out in the dark. He was watching with more than eyes.

He never saw or sensed their passage. Just past him, Kerrec paused, gathering strength before he sent Petra into the water.

A small wind had begun to blow, stirring the water. Waves lapped the bank, a soft whisper and sigh. Reeds rustled. Leaves whispered.

Valeria's nose twitched. The wind was blowing from the farther bank, bringing the scent of pine from the forest beyond.

On this side of the river, magic had laws. Mages gathered themselves in orders, each divided according to its arts and skills. The world was not a tame place, but it was an orderly one.

No such law ruled beyond the border. Magic ran wild. The tribes worshipped a god of blood and reveled in disorder. Chaos was holy. The Unmaking was divine.

Valeria was shaking. Sabata was calm under her. She pressed her hands to his warm, massive neck and bent, burying her face in his mane. The familiar warmth and the tickle of coarse hairs steadied her.

Petra stepped softly into the water. Rodry's gelding hesitated, but the stallion's will drew him onward. Sabata was close behind.

The wind was blowing briskly now. Valeria glanced up. The clouds were breaking. Moonlight glowed behind them. Stars glimmered through the tatters.

Kerrec's spell was holding. His power was stretched thin, worn down by wind and water, but he held on.

They were a third of the way across the river. The army's wards were behind them. They were already looking ahead to the wilderness beyond and the forest into which they had to vanish before the sun came up.

The moon's light grew stronger. The sky was black and silver. A white glow swelled over the water.

Valeria had heard of the moon's road. Mages could walk it, people said, if they were strong enough. It was eerie to see Kerrec wading through it, leaving no shadow and no ripple on the water.

She blinked. There was a shadow and a shimmer after all. Was Kerrec swaying?

He was as straight as ever. It was the moonlight shifting and swelling and the water flowing. They were halfway across now. The far bank was dark and quiet. No guards stood there. Wherever the enemy was, he was not watching over the river.

The clouds tore. The moon cast the world in silver.

Petra halted in the middle of the river and raised his head. Light gathered in him, blazing up to the moon and turning the water to white fire.

Thirty-Eight

Kerrec had no warning. One moment he was holding the spell of mist and darkness, drawing strength from the wild magic beyond the empire's edge. The next, he stood in a blaze of light.

Petra had turned traitor. There was no time to hate him for it. Arrows were flying. One sang past Kerrec's ear, so close it stung.

Kerrec gathered himself to urge the stallion forward. Petra erupted. For the first time in more years than he could count, Kerrec flew off that faithless back into icy water.

It was shallow, hardly more than knee-deep, and the current was not particularly strong. He came up gasping into a circle of cold-eyed archers, each with an arrow aimed at his heart.

Valeria and Rodry were still mounted but likewise surrounded. Kerrec knew better than to expect either of them to resist. He could taste Valeria's relief beneath the bile in his mouth. Who knew? She might have had something to do with this betrayal.

He had vowed not to be bitter, but that was not easy. His captors bound his hands, then the others', pulling them off their horses and half carrying them out of the river.

The stallions submitted to being led like common animals, plodding meekly beside soldiers who had no inkling of what they were. The blaze of light that had betrayed them had vanished as quickly as it came. Men's minds being what they were, they quickly forgot what they had seen, ascribing it to a trick of moonlight on water.

Kerrec had by no means given up hope. He would be seen by the captain of the archers first, surely, then passed up through the ranks to one of the legionary commanders. It would be hours if not days before they were done with him—more than enough time to plot an escape.

He had not included blind chance in his reckoning. The emperor had escaped from the press of clerks and counselors just in time to see the light on the river. It brought him from his tent in the center of the camp, down to the ford.

He was waiting by the rampart as captors and captives approached the gate. There was no escort with him. He was dressed in the working uniform of a legionary commander, without mark of imperial rank. But Kerrec would always know his father.

People said they looked alike. Kerrec did not see it. For one thing, he did not grow his beard, whereas Artorius did. For another, Artorius cultivated good humor. Kerrec considered it a useless indulgence.

There was no smile on that face tonight. Artorius recognized the stallions—Kerrec saw how his eyes widened, then took in the captives. As they fell on his late and unlamented son, they went cold.

He said nothing to Kerrec. His glance slid away toward Kerrec's captors. "Bring them in," he said.

Valeria and Rodry were mute. Kerrec's jaw ached with clenching. His captors were not unduly rough, but they were not gentle, either. They quick-marched him through the gate into the camp.

The Emperor Artorius sat in his tent. Witchlight glowed brightly, dazzling eyes accustomed to moonlight. He had dismissed his servants. Except for a handful of guards, he was alone with the captives.

The guards had unbound them—not altogether willingly, but they were obedient. They were none too pleased to share the tent with three horses, either, though, gods knew, there was room enough. A cohort could have formed ranks here and been only slightly crowded.

Artorius studied his odd assortment of guests. He looked well, Kerrec thought randomly. His magic was restored and his body recovered from the ravages of the drug that had nearly killed him before the Great Dance. He was lean, fit, and bronzed by the sun. War suited him.

He leaned forward in his carved chair, searching each of their faces. None of them flinched. Valeria went so far as to smile.

He smiled back, if briefly. "Now," he said. "Suppose you tell me why we find you here, breaking the ban and crossing the river, instead of safe on the Mountain."

Valeria opened her mouth. Kerrec spoke before she could begin. "We're on an errand for the gods."

"Indeed?" Artorius said. "Is that why the gods laid you open to us all?"

"The gods are incalculable," Kerrec said.

"So we're often told. It doesn't answer my question."

"There is no answer," Kerrec said.

"I could have you interrogated," Artorius said coolly. "I would prefer not to. I've had word from your sister that you were missing—she hated to confess it, but she could hardly avoid it. I must say, neither of us expected you to fall into my lap."

"There was a flood," Kerrec said. "This was the first ford that we could cross. You were in Tragante. Why didn't you go south?"

"Am I required to explain myself to you?"

Kerrec's chin lifted. "This is a terrible place for a battle. You have open land behind you, there is that—but there could be fifty thousand of the enemy in the trees yonder, and you would never know it."

"So now you are a general," Artorius said. "A moment ago, you were a captured spy. Are you going to tell me what you really are?"

"The gods' plaything," Kerrec answered.

"I think you're trying to play the gods," Artorius said. "What is it? Where do you think you're going?"

"He wants to find Gothard," Valeria said before Kerrec could stop her. "I suppose then there will be blood and entrails and magic spewing everywhere."

"And you let him go?" said the emperor.

She met his hard stare. "It wasn't a matter of letting," she said.

"I am supposed to be across the river," Kerrec said tightly. "Can't you see how it calls me? Sire, in spite of all that is between us, please try to understand. This renegade is a great danger to all of us—greater than anyone seems to see. I have to find him before he unleashes whatever it is that he's got hold of. He'll do worse than lose the battle for you. He'll destroy everything on both sides, and laugh while he does it."

Artorius seemed hardly to hear him. "Why you?" he asked—without anger, at least. "Why can't you trust me to find him, with all the resources at my disposal?"

"I believe this task is given to me," Kerrec said. "Will you help me? It's no loss to you if I fail. If I succeed, there's one less threat to your victory—and your life."

"No loss?" said Artorius. "You think so?"

"I'm dead already," said Kerrec.

He was mildly gratified to see how his father's face tightened at that. "There are fates worse than death," the emperor said. "I would rather not see you suffer any more of them."

"You concern is commendable," said Kerrec, "but please, sire. Think."

"I am thinking," Artorius said. He nodded to the guards. "See to their comfort. Treat them as guests. I hope they will agree not to escape until morning."

"We'll stay," Valeria said. "Thank you, sir."

"Sire," Kerrec said. "Every moment we waste—"

"You will rest tonight," his father said, cool and firm. "In the morning I'll speak with you again. Good night."

That was as polite a dismissal as Kerrec could have asked for. It made him feel fourteen years old again.

He bit his tongue before he said anything that might confirm his father's opinion of him. He bowed stiffly and turned on his heel.

That was not the wisest thing he could have done. A wave of dizziness struck him. For a moment he was sure he would fall flat on his face.

Somehow he kept his feet and his balance. No one seemed to notice his sudden weakness. It was gone as quickly as it had come, leaving a dull headache behind.

They were taken to a smaller room within the larger tent. There were carpets on the floor, rich and soft, and beds made up, one for each of them. Valeria was not given her own prison—Kerrec found that interesting. Did the emperor remember who she was?

Of course he did. Artorius never forgot a face. Either he was paying her the courtesy of treating her like a rider, or it simply did not matter to him what she did or where she slept.

Kerrec rubbed his aching forehead. He had stretched the boundaries of his magic to sustain the spell of mist and shadow. Its breaking had come too fast.

There was a basket on a table, covered with a cloth. Under the cloth were loaves of legionaries' bread, flat and floury, and wedges of hard yellow cheese. There was a jar of wine and another of water.

Those were soldiers' rations, deliberately unpretentious. Kerrec found he was ravenous. The bread tasted much better than it looked. The cheese filled him admirably, and the water tasted like the spring in the oak grove.

The horses were still in the outer room. Kerrec heard them eating—the steady grinding of jaws—and smelled hay and straw. They were being stabled in the emperor's hall.

That would destroy any chance Kerrec had of secrecy. White horses in the imperial tent—any fool would know what that meant. But he could not leave the room to visit them, let alone escape. When he tried, he met wards that he was too worn down to break.

He would wager Valeria could have broken them. She seemed content to eat a few bites of bread and take a sip or two of water, then lie down and close her eyes. Rodry, as usual, was already asleep.

Kerrec's clothes were no longer dripping from his fall in the river, but they were clammy and cold. He stripped them off and wrapped himself in the blanket from the one remaining bed.

He meant to sit up, searching for ways to escape, but his eyelids drooped in spite of all he could do.

For this one night, he gave way to weakness. He lay on the bed, which was surprisingly soft. Sleep swallowed him in a rush of cool darkness.

Thirty-Nine

The prisoners were left to sleep for as long as they wished. Kerrec was the last to wake, with morning well advanced and the smell of breakfast in his nostrils.

Valeria and Rodry were up and bathed and dressed in fresh clothes. They were eating a considerably more elegant meal than they had shared last night. There were sweet cakes and exotic fruits and a concoction of eggs and sausage and cheese that made Kerrec's mouth water.

He had no will to resist. He left the bed, remembering almost too late to wrap the blanket around him, and reached for a plate and a spoon.

Valeria seemed in excellent spirits. Rodry looked somewhat pale around the edges. He must be waking to the reality of what he had done. He was a deserter in the emperor's camp. A court-martial was the least of what he could expect.

Kerrec had given the boy his word. He did not mean to break it. As far as he could, he would protect him.

Kerrec would not have been surprised to wait days for a second audience, but the emperor, like his son, was a man of his word. It was much nearer noon than morning when the summons came, but it did come.

Last night's audience had been a conversation. This was a trial.

The emperor was not alone this time. There was a legionary commander with him, wearing the crowned eagle of the Valeria, and a pair of Augurs in white, and a quiet man in brown whose magic made Kerrec's bones hum. He wore nothing to indicate which order of mage he was, but there was no doubt of his power.

They sat in the central room, where the horses still were. All three were asleep, with the gelding lying down while the stallions stood over him.

Kerrec had nothing to say to the horses, least of all Petra. The men required at least a greeting. A rider bowed to no one, but he might bend his head in freely offered respect.

The emperor and the legate and the mages bowed in return. Petra began to snore.

Out of the corner of his eye, Kerrec saw Valeria bite her lip. There were times when she reminded him all too vividly of the stallions.

He set his teeth and straightened his back. He was losing focus, and he could not afford that. He had broken an imperial ban and caused the desertion of a legionary. He could be put to death for what he had done.

He could not find it in himself to be afraid. He looked his father in the face. "Let the others go," he said, "and I'll pay whatever penalty you exact."

Artorius was perfectly expressionless. It was the elder of the two Augurs who said, "The omens, sire—if our strategy is to continue—"

The emperor raised his hand. The Augur fell silent. "Master Pretorius?"

The man in brown stroked his close-clipped greying beard. His eyes were bright with good humor, but there was steel beneath. "They are meant to be here. Whether that is safe for us or for your war—that, I can't tell you. But it would do no good to pack them home. Worse things would come to take their place in the pattern."

"You are sure of this?" Artorius asked.

The mage shrugged, spreading his hands. "I can only tell you what I see."

"If you have true sight," Kerrec said, "you must see what danger my brother represents. He cares nothing for tribes or empire, only for his own ambition. He will use any means possible in order to achieve it."

"Yes," said Master Pretorius. "He will. We are aware of him, my lord. We understand what he is and what he may be moved to do."

"Do you?"

Master Pretorius smiled. "I believe we do. We have taken precautions. If he does in fact attack us, we'll be ready for him."

Kerrec wanted to believe him. It would have been so easy to lie back and let the emperor's mages take the burden he had carried for so long. All he had was hate and a certainty that amounted, in the end, to mere obsession—that he must be here. This was his fight.

The obsession would not let him go. The mage's smile was too easy. He was indulging the poor broken mage and disregarding his fears.

No one except possibly Valeria could see what Kerrec saw.

No one wanted to see it. They all wanted this war to be simple and sane, with no greater fear than a barbarian invasion and no greater danger than a bit of outland sorcery.

They could not even begin to imagine what Gothard wanted to bring down on them all. They should have seen it when he broke the Dance—but they had been as blind then as they were now. None of them would see until it was too late.

Kerrec set his lips together. The mage's smile widened. He bowed to Kerrec as if he could have had any honest respect for what Kerrec was, and said, "It will be seen to. Trust in that."

The emperor shifted in his seat, a rare confession to impatience. "That is well and we are reassured. Nevertheless, all other matters aside, we have a deserter and a ban."

"Please," Valeria said so meekly Kerrec's hackles rose. "This soldier is my brother. It's my fault he's here."

"We'll take that under consideration," Artorius said. His voice was stern but his eyes were warm. "And you, soldier? Have you anything to say?"

"Only that I'll pay my own penalty, sir," Rodry said. "They didn't force me to come. I saw what they were doing and I made a free choice."

"Indeed?" said Master Pretorius. "Why would you do that?"

"Because, sir," Rodry said, "those patterns you see—I don't have that kind of sight, but I feel things. I have to be here, just like the rest of them. The patterns—or the gods, if you like—brought us here to you. We have something to do. The gods will tell us when it's time."

"Your faith is admirable," Master Pretorius said. "You're aware, surely, that it leaves you open to court-martial and a deserter's sentence."

"I know that, sir," Rodry said.

For the first time the legionary commander spoke. He was

older than the emperor but not as old as the Augur, a sturdy man who looked as if he had spent more time on the battlefield than in a palace. "This rider is your sister, yes?"

"Yes, sir," Rodry said.

The commander nodded. His eye came to rest on Valeria. "I saw you in the Great Dance," he said. "I'm no mage, but I'm not a complete fool, either. You are something this empire hasn't seen before. I'm going to assume that this scout, who has never had so much as a reprimand for being late to morning muster, has blood as well as fate calling him. He's still a deserter. That charge can't be evaded."

"Sir," she said, "I don't want him dishonored because of us. If there's anything you can do—"

"I'll do what I can," he said.

"For the moment," said the emperor, "we have a battle to plan. You three are confined to quarters. I hope your word will be enough. If not, my mages will bind you."

"We'll stay," Valeria said without glancing at the others.

Kerrec held his breath, but his father did not press the others to give their word. He simply nodded. His mind was already elsewhere, focused on his war.

The gods had no mercy, but sometimes they could let a bit of luck slip past their guard. Kerrec pushed it a step further. "The stallions can't stay here. They need free air and room to run. If you could—"

"We'll look after them," the brown man said.

"Thank you," said Valeria.

That was not what Kerrec had been going to say. He shut his mouth with a snap.

They were dismissed. Guards surrounded them, herding them toward the door. Kerrec contemplated blasting the lot of them.

He let himself be led, not back to the room they had all slept in, but to a tent beside the emperor's. It was wide and high and there was a room for each of them, with servants as well as guards.

There were books. There was ink and parchment. There was a board for chess, a set of knucklebones, and a servant who said, "Whatever you wish, lords and lady, only ask."

Our freedom, Kerrec knew better than to answer.

Valeria was investigating the books. She held one up. Kerrec recognized it. It was the same history of the empire from which Valeria's year had been reading.

The rest were a mingling of dull, didactic, and diverting. Valeria laid claim to a volume of poetry from the court. Kerrec considered forbidding her—some of those verses were hardly fit for a young woman to read—but Valeria was not the usual sort of young woman at all.

He retreated to the sleeping room farthest from the door. Outside in the larger room, he heard Valeria and Rodry talking in low voices.

They sounded calm enough. Valeria would protect her brother—or force the stallions to do it. Her determination was warm and solid inside of Kerrec, close by the magic that had been growing steadily since he left the Mountain.

The master stone was safe in its pouch around his neck. None of them had been searched or their belongings taken.

That was careless of his father's guards. At least one of the guards was a mage, but he was not a mage of stones. The wards he raised were not badly made at all—if he was keeping in the ordinary sort of power.

It was all an afterthought. The emperor was planning a great battle to end this long war against the barbarians. There was no time to spare for his scapegrace sons—either the one who had betrayed him or the one who had hunted the traitor.

In spite of everything, Kerrec caught himself smiling. Maybe he could forgive Petra after all. He had brought Rodry and Valeria here, where they were as safe as they could be in the middle of such a war. The emperor would look after them while Kerrec went where he had to go.

The great weakness of a tent as a prison was that its walls were canvas—and they were not mortared to the floor. There was the matter of the tent's being in the center of a large and watchful camp under manifold magical protections. But Kerrec could walk invisible, and the master stone gave him power over wards and defenses.

There were hours of daylight left. He took advantage of them to rest and gather his strength.

Valeria looked in on him once. She was hardest of all to deceive, but she seemed to accept that he was asleep.

He went as still as he could, inside and out. The earth was quiet beneath him. The camp's buzz and clamor dropped away. The deep, growling roar of war retreated from his awareness.

The patterns had come back. The intricate levels of his power were restoring themselves one by one. He was not whole, not nearly, but neither was he broken.

Good. The more nearly himself he was, the better chance he had of destroying Gothard. It did not matter if he went down with his brother. No one would be terribly unhappy to be rid of him.

The moon was only slightly less bright than it had been the night before. Kerrec was ready for it as he slipped out under tent wall and wards. He was a shimmer of moonlight rather than a curl of mist above the river.

There was no Petra to betray him, and he was not about to risk it again. He went on foot. Surely, once he was across the river, he would find a horse to ride—somehow.

He passed like a breath of wind through the camp. It was settling late tonight. Councils were meeting and runners dispensing orders. Men were polishing their armor. Battle was close.

Where it would be or how it would be waged, Kerrec neither knew nor cared. Close by here, he supposed, in a place where the legions could fight in the open.

Gothard had never been a man for open battle. He would stay hidden in the trees if he could, and let others die for him.

The ford was guarded as before. Kerrec's powers were fresh tonight, and stronger than they had been in a long while. He slipped through the lines of archers and set out once more across the river.

Halfway, he fought every instinct that cried out to stop. The moon's light was constant. His spell was unshaken. The world was perfectly still.

His foot touched the far bank. No alarm sounded. No arrow flew. The gods might not love him, but tonight they were indulgent.

Again he resisted the urge to stop. He could not do that until he was well away from the river, hidden in the forest.

He was barefoot as he had gone into the water, with his boots hung by their straps around his neck. He stopped to dry his feet and pull them on, sighing a bit. They were made for riding, not for walking.

They were all he had. He took a deep breath and sprang up the slope from the river into the shelter of the trees.

Forty

Euan was ready to start the battle himself, and to hell with the Ard Ri. They were playing at negotiations again, sending messengers back and forth and pretending either side wanted anything but a good, solid fight.

The men were losing their edge—again. Boredom made them unruly, and reduced rations did nothing to improve their mood. There were too many of them now to feed off the land—and this country was nearly empty of towns and villages to raid.

There had to be a battle, or else they had to retreat without a fight. There were no other choices. The one some of the men were muttering about, to move farther upriver and start raiding all over again, would only prolong the agony. The only way to win this war was by backing the legions into a corner and cutting them to pieces.

The night he decided to confront the Ard Ri and be damned to what came of it, he was stopped on the way to the council

fire by one of Gothard's traitor princelings. The boy was babbling, but Euan slapped a little sense into him. His babble
shifted to more or less coherent words.

What sense Euan made of it sent him off at a run. The boy
trailed behind, wheezing for breath.

Gothard had had the same thought as Euan. The Ard Ri
dwarfed him as they stood face to face just outside the priests'
circle. The moon washed their faces with a deathly pallor.

As Euan loped to a halt, the Ard Ri's finger stabbed at two
of the boys behind Gothard. "Those two are sons of an imperial general. I need them to bargain with."

"And I need them to win the battle," Gothard shot back, "if
there ever is one."

"There will be a battle when I say there is a battle," the high
king said. "I'm leaving you the rest of them. These two I take."

"I need them all," Gothard said.

"We'll win with or without you," said the Ard Ri. He lifted
his chin. Four of the men behind him, burly warriors all, moved
toward the boys.

Euan's skin prickled. He flung himself backward.

The blast caught him and flung him sprawling. Men were
screaming. He smelled burning flesh.

When the world stopped rocking under him, he staggered
to his feet. The Ard Ri's warriors lay in smoking ruin. The high
king was alive, but his face and chest were scorched and his eyes
were wild.

Gothard stood untouched amid the carnage. He smiled at the
high king. "The time for games is over. Let your men off the
leash. Or are you afraid? Is that why you keep them so long in
camp? Is it cowardice? Weakness? A simple inability to act?"

"You know nothing of what it is to be a king," the Ard Ri said.
He was not a coward if he could say that to the man who

had just blasted his best men to cinders. He was a fool, then—a fool with a death wish.

Gothard clearly shared the thought. "I may never have been a king," he said, "but, sir, from all you've done or failed to do, neither have you."

There must be a dizzy freedom in saying what one pleased, to whomever one wanted to say it. Gothard had a starstone. He paid homage to no one.

The Ard Ri's expression was so bland that Euan's nape prickled. "You may not answer to me," he said, "but you will answer to the One."

"I have every expectation of so doing," Gothard said. "Go on, rally your men. You'd better do it quickly—because if you won't lead them, someone else will."

"One of your puppets, I suppose," said the Ard Ri.

Gothard smiled. "You have puppets. I have allies. They think for themselves."

"Like these?" said the Ard Ri, darting a glance at Gothard's captives. They stood in their circle, swaying slightly on their feet, with eyes that had long since seen through the world to something unimaginable.

"These are priests of a new order," Gothard said, "an order that strives for the purity of the One. They are bound together in soul as in body. They will teach the empire to bow to the One and to worship oblivion."

The Ard Ri held himself stiffly, as if to keep from turning and bolting. "That had better be the truth," he said. "We're moving in the morning. If you're not ready, you'll be left behind."

"We'll be ready," Gothard said.

The high king swallowed hard, then spat. Then he seemed to find the courage to turn his back on that nest of mages, priests, or whatever they pleased to call themselves.

* * *

Euan was gone almost before the Ard Ri. By the time the call to arms went out, he had his men rousted out of bed or away from their jars of mead and ale. Not one of them grumbled once he knew the reason why. Some actually sang as they gathered and packed and stored their belongings. Every now and then, one or more of them would erupt into a brief war dance, leaping and spinning.

Euan caught a dose of their excitement, though his was leavened by what he knew of Gothard and the starstone. Gothard was touching on things not meant for mortals. Maybe he had promised to keep the people safe, but he would have some difficulty doing that from the depths of endless night.

No risk, no glory. There would be no sleep tonight. Tomorrow would be a long day's march down to the river. The day after, the One willing, it would all, finally, come to a head.

Win or lose, Euan welcomed it. His blood was already running high at the thought of a battle. Good, clean, and bloody— that was the life for a man. And that was the death, too, if so it was meant to be.

Forty-One

Kerrec strode as swiftly as he could through the keen scent and whispering stillness of pines. Tall trees marched away into the dark. The undergrowth was thin, bracken mostly, with here and there a dead branch or a fallen tree.

When he was out of sight of the river, Kerrec stopped under an overhang of rock and ferns and uncovered the master stone. It lay in its leather wrappings like a pool of darkness. Moonlight and starlight were swallowed in it.

Magic here was wild, with no mages to bind it in structures of magic and discipline. Patterns crowded around him, tangling and untangling.

The stone kept him from reeling with the complexity of it all. He pressed it to his lips, whispering the name he hated. "Gothard."

The air he breathed was sharp and clean, but it was underlaid with something dark, like mold and old stone. Moonlight dazzled him. The patterns flickered, shaping and re-shaping.

Gothard was in them. The taste of him was like clotted blood. The heated bronze of his anger, so deep and abiding that it had come to define what he was, struck Kerrec with such intensity that he nearly let go of the patterns.

They strained against his will, but he held on. One more moment, just one, and he would know—

There.

Eastward away from the river, deeper into the forest. Kerrec slipped the stone back into its pouch. He was a little dizzy, and his head ached. He needed rest.

He should be much closer to Gothard before he gave in to the urge. If his brother shifted camp, he would have to perform the working all over again. He was not sure he had the strength for that.

He walked where the patterns led him, which was turning into its own exercise in strangeness. He had never traveled afoot in his life. His feet were insulted. It took an unbearably long time to cross an unbearably short span of ground.

It was the only choice he had. Somewhere ahead, there had to be a horse. He would walk until he found it.

Valeria snapped awake. Something was—not wrong, no. Different. The patterns of the world had changed.

The stallions were quiet, but she did not trust them. There was a distinct air of smugness about them.

They were up to something.

She rose and dressed and ran her fingers through her hair, tugging out a tangle. She could hear Rodry breathing in the room next to hers. From Kerrec's on the end, she heard nothing.

The skin tightened between her shoulder blades. She glided

silently toward the flap of canvas that was his door. There was no sound beyond.

The room was empty. She found the place where he had slipped out. The memory of his presence led away from it, as clear to her eyes as the moon's road.

As quickly and quietly as she could, she ran back to her room, gathered her belongings and stuffed them into their bag. She slung it behind her and returned equally quickly to the room Kerrec had abandoned. His track was as distinct as before. She slipped beneath the heavy canvas of the tent and followed where he had gone.

He had eluded the wards and the guards with exquisite ease. She followed his pattern exactly, and the wards slipped over her and the guards saw through her. It was a beautiful thing, a magical thing, the work of a master.

He had gone nowhere near the stallions. None of the mortal horses was missing, either. Kerrec had walked away from his captivity.

A rider on foot must be a most unhappy beast. Valeria, who had walked everywhere until hardly more than a year ago, was better suited for it.

Past the river, his trail was harder to follow. The patterns were different there. Still, if she narrowed her focus, she could see him clearly.

He was moving quickly for a man who never walked where he could ride. His magic was strong, but it felt somehow frayed. He was expending strength without regard for the cost.

She quickened her pace. The moon was sinking. Dawn would come soon. She would wager Kerrec did not know how close to the edge he was. That part of his judgment had never quite come back.

She was almost running. Her legs ached and her lungs burned.

Hooves thudded behind her. She turned, purely by instinct, and caught flying mane. The horse's speed carried her up onto a broad back.

Her arms clamped around Rodry's waist. The mane she gripped was black, and the back she sat on was bay, gleaming darkly in the moonlight. The power of the spirit within was so strong that it nearly flung her to the ground.

Rodry was riding Briana's bay Lady, who had been safe in Aurelia the last Valeria knew. What that meant—what it promised—Valeria was almost afraid to ask. A Lady in Aurelia was unheard of. A Lady across the frontier, outside the empire, in the middle of a war and the very real threat of Unmaking…

"Rodry," she said in his ear. "How—"

"Later," he said tersely.

She bit her tongue. The Lady's gallop slowed. The stars were fading. The patterns were shifting too fast to follow.

If Valeria had learned nothing else in her year on the Mountain, she had learned to flow into the patterns. If she was inside them, she could understand them.

Magic was swirling, rising like mist out of the ground. Power was drawn to power, and Kerrec with his broken magic and his conquered stone was irresistible. Strange things were creeping toward him, distilling out of the air and oozing up from the earth.

Valeria knew where he was. It was a sudden knowledge, as if an eye had opened and seen him lying in a bed of bracken.

He looked as if he had fallen there. He had managed to raise wards, and his spell of concealment was tattered but still serviceable. To the eyes of Valeria's magic, it was like a swirl of smoke around the fitful glow that was Kerrec.

The Lady halted so abruptly that Rodry and Valeria lurched onto her neck. She shook her head irritably and shrugged them back where they belonged, then stamped. The earth rang under her hoof.

The wild magic went perfectly still. The mist paused in its ascent. The moon hung motionless in the sky.

The Lady breathed out sharply. The world began to turn again.

The wild magic sank back under the earth. The patterns were still blindingly complex, but there was order and reason to them.

Valeria slid to the ground. Kerrec was close, almost underfoot. Her eyes could not see him at all—she had to look for him with her other senses.

She pulled him out of the bracken. He was conscious and, though he swayed dizzily, he could stand. He looked at her with eyes that had gone beyond bitterness. "Will I never escape you?"

"Not in this life," she said.

"You and the Ladies," he said. "There's no hope for any of us."

Was he smiling? It must be a trick of the light.

If Valeria did not take control of herself soon, she was going to kiss him—and where *that* bit of foolishness had come from, the gods knew. She was already swaying forward. She stiffened her spine and said, "Here, mount."

He shook his head. "I'll walk."

"On those feet?" She leveled a glare at Rodry. He had already dismounted, which was wise of him. He held the Lady's stirrup and waited.

The glare wheeled back toward Kerrec. "Mount," Valeria said.

However stubborn he was, Kerrec could not resist a horse's back. He bowed to the Lady first. She flattened ears at his silliness, but she would have been even more annoyed if he had not done it.

He took a deep breath and swung onto her back, then held out his hand. "You, too," he said.

Valeria shook her head, but Rodry said, "Get on. I can run with her. Can you?"

"I'm sure I could if I tried," she said.

"Stop that," said Kerrec. "Either you ride with me or we leave you behind. There's no time to waste."

Valeria might have kept on resisting if it had been only the two men, but the Lady's eye rolled at her. That and the restless heel convinced Valeria as nothing else could. She ignored Kerrec's hand and lifted herself onto the Lady's rump once more.

Even as she found her seat, the Lady bucked lightly. Valeria found herself pressed against Kerrec's back. She had to fling arms around him or be pitched to the ground.

The Lady's satisfaction thrummed through her. So did a sense of pressing urgency.

Rodry stood at the Lady's stirrup, smiling up at Valeria. This was not real to him, she thought. He had wandered out of the world he knew into the realm of gods and magic.

So had they all. They rode in the rising dawn, trusting the Lady to take them where they needed to go.

Not only the powers of earth were stirring around them. Men were moving in clans and tribes, marching toward the river. Something had roused them and brought them all together. Battle was coming.

When the sun was well up, the Lady stopped. She had brought them to a stream that flowed down a sudden hill into a clear pool. There was grass for her and water for them all, and in a bramble thicket, sweet blackberries that they shared with one another and a flock of birds.

Rodry caught a fish in the pool, tickling it with his fingers until it lay stunned. He cleaned it and rubbed it with salt and herbs and packed it in clay, and built a tiny fire that sent up no smoke at all.

While the fish roasted and the Lady grazed, Valeria planted herself in front of her brother and said, "Tell."

He spread his hands. "What's to say? I woke up and you were both missing. I thought you might be with the horses. I found Her instead—" he said it exactly like that, with overtones of awe "—and She told me to get on her back and ride."

"She *told* you?" Kerrec asked. Valeria had thought he was asleep.

"I heard her, sir," Rodry said. "It wasn't words, exactly. It was more that I knew she wanted me to ride, and I had better be quick about it. She's one of Them, isn't she? Though she's not a stallion. Or white."

"They aren't all greys," Valeria said.

"Or all stallions, either," said Kerrec. "I thought I had seen everything. An army scout riding a Lady as if she were a common horse—ye gods, if the riders only knew."

"Why?" said Rodry. "Have I done something wrong?"

"Nothing is wrong if a Lady allows it," Kerrec said. "But it is unheard of."

Rodry ducked his head. "I won't ride her again," he said. "It was only—she was so insistent. I couldn't say no to her."

"Nor should you if she asks again," Kerrec said. "At ease, soldier. It's obvious we're in the gods' hands—or hooves if you will. All we can do is go where they lead us and do what they ask of us."

"Are they leading you?" Valeria muttered. "Or are you forcing them to accept whatever you please?"

Of course he did not answer that.

Rodry prodded the fish in its casing, which was now baked hard. He wrapped his cloak around his hand and lifted it gingerly from the coals, laying it on a flat rock that he had brought from the pool. With the hilt of his dagger, he cracked it open. Steam hissed forth, with a delectable scent.

The fish was cooked perfectly. Valeria savored her share of the sweet flesh, washing it down with water from the pool.

She was the last to finish. The others were ready to break camp. Rodry doused and buried the fire, and Kerrec smoothed the ground they had trampled. Valeria saddled the Lady once more.

"He's close," Kerrec said.

Rodry nodded. "We're not far from where the camp should be. They've been hunting these runs—there's no game left. They'll have to move either ahead or back."

"Are we in time?" Kerrec asked. His voice was cool, but Valeria felt the urgency behind it.

"We should be," Rodry answered. "We'll be there by morning. I don't think the battle will be tomorrow. The day after, maybe, or the third day."

"Soon," said Kerrec. He mounted with casual bravura, without touching the stirrup.

Valeria chose this time to mount in more mundane fashion, setting foot in the stirrup he had scorned and holding out her hand. He arched a brow, but he swung her up behind him.

Forty-Two

Rodry was scouting. Kerrec was sustaining wards. Valeria had nothing to do but offer strength if they needed it.

She caught herself dozing off with her face buried between Kerrec's shoulders. The familiar smell of him, the movement of the Lady under them and the warmth of the sun shining through the trees, lulled her to sleep.

Her dreams at first were peaceful and inconsequential. Even while she was in them, she knew their memory would be gone when she woke.

Gradually they changed. This sunlit forest, this summer warmth, twisted little by little. The Unmaking stirred.

It was not the wild magic that woke it. That was strange to her senses, but it was real and solid and completely in the world.

Beneath it was something else, something dark and old and cold. Words came to her. *The roots of the One.* In her mind she saw the roots of trees digging deep into black earth. Blind things crawled on them. Dissolution was caught in their knotted tendrils.

She clawed her way out of the dream. The sun had shifted distinctly westward. The Lady stood motionless in the shadow of trees. Rodry crouched just in front of her. His whole body was alert.

Kerrec's head turned slowly. Valeria heard the passage of at least a dozen men. They were moving quietly but not stealthily, slipping through the trees.

"Cymbri," Rodry breathed, "from over the mountains. This weapontake has reached far."

Valeria wondered how he knew. She could glimpse them now, flashes of bright hair and bright metal and the dizzying patterns of their mantles. They were moving quickly, loping like wolves on a fresh trail.

After they were gone, Rodry waited a long while before he would leave the covert. The Lady was patient. Kerrec sat quiet on her back, but Valeria dismounted.

Rodry frowned. She scowled back. She crept away, slipping around the trunk of a huge tree.

No barbarian lay in wait for her there. She relieved herself as quickly as she could. As she set her clothes back in order, she paused.

This country was a tracery of brooks and streams and little rivers. They had had to cross at least a dozen since the day began. One trickled past the tree, murmuring to itself. The sun sparkled on it. Tiny fish danced in the water.

Patterns shifted and flickered. She should turn her eyes away and go back to the others, but the flash of light on water held her just a moment too long.

The streambed transformed into a wide and rolling field. The fish became armies on it. The emperor's legions marched in their armor. The enemy came on in hordes, naked and painted blue and red and yellow, with torques of gold or bronze or copper. They fought with great axes and swords so heavy they needed two hands to lift.

That was as beautiful and terrible as battle always was. But Valeria's eye was drawn into the darkness of the forest. Old things crouched there, cold things, dark and strong. Their power focused on the legions' heart.

The emperor held all the threads of war and magic in his hands. His mages and generals worked his will. If he fell, the army would flounder. The tide of battle would turn.

Valeria watched him fall. The power that struck him down felt familiar. It was Gothard, but he had changed.

The Unmaking was part of him now. It lodged in something that he kept close, a stone, she supposed—but heavier and colder and darker than any stone she had known before. It felt like the darkness between stars, utterly empty and yet filled with power.

Kerrec had seen this. He was obsessed and probably mad, but he saw the truth. Gothard's power, bound by blood to both the emperor and the princes of the Calletani, was the key.

The emperor fell. The armies fought on, but the heart had gone out of them. Two legions retreated. One, the Valeria, stood its ground. The enemy rolled over it and destroyed it.

Then came the Unmaking.

"Valeria!"

Kerrec's voice flung her out of the vision. His hands gripped her shoulders painfully, shaking her until she squawked in protest. His eyes were blazing. "Gods help you, woman! If I lose you—"

"If you lose me, what? You'll sing a rite of thanksgiving?"

He let her go so suddenly she dropped to her knees, and stood glaring down at her. He was not going to answer.

She pulled him down to face her. "We have got to stop this," she said. "You don't have to hide anything from me any more. If we're both going to be whole and strong for what's to come, we have to—"

"I don't care if I die," he said, "but I refuse to be the death of you."

"That's not your choice to make," she said.

He sat on his heels. "You are difficult," he said.

"And you are not?"

"I don't know how to be anything else."

"Now that is true," she said. If she did not burst out laughing, she would burst into tears. Since it was not useful to do either, she settled for saying, "Can you at least try to stop breaking my heart?"

She had tried to say it lightly. He looked as if she had knocked the breath out of him. "I didn't—I was trying—"

"I know."

"You're not going to let me be."

"I can't."

"And you wonder why riders never tangle themselves with women." He reached, startling her. This time his grip was much gentler, his hands resting on her shoulders, drawing her to him.

She could have stopped him. He was not holding her tightly at all. But she could no more have done that than she could have stopped loving him—even when she wanted to strangle him.

He kissed her softly. There was passion in it, buried deep and sternly disciplined. She willed herself not to lock arms around his neck and cling.

He drew back. For the first time in a long while, his face was unguarded. It was brief, hardly more than a moment, but it told Valeria everything she wanted to know.

She took his face in her hands. He did not try to pull away. "Stop fighting it," she said. "We're riders. We can't be alone if we try. Our whole art is an art of patterns, danced in twos and fours and eights. Never one by one. One is the enemy."

"I know how to train a horse," he said, "and ride the Dance. This, I don't know at all. I have no art and precious little talent for it."

"It's just like training horses," she said. "Open your mind and listen. Then do what your heart tells you."

"I'm afraid," he said.

All the rest of it had left her deliberately unmoved. Those brief words brought the tears springing. She blinked them back, hissing at her own foolishness. "So is the colt when he comes down from the Mountain. What do you do for him? Do the same for yourself."

He frowned. He always did that when he was thinking. After a while he said, "You're training me."

"Gods forbid," she said. "Great Ones aren't trained. They're educated. Wheedled. Persuaded."

"I'm not a—"

"Sabata is easier than you," she said. She bent forward and kissed him. He responded before he could have known what he was doing.

She did not hold the kiss for long—just long enough to make his blood sing. When she sat back and lowered her hands, he caught and held them.

He kissed each palm and folded the fingers over it. Then he rose. His head tilted. He was listening.

She had heard it, too. More tribesmen were coming, slipping like wind through the trees.

* * *

Rodry had not moved since Valeria left him. He would not look at either of them. He had heard every word.

Valeria's cheeks were hot, but she was not about to apologize. If her brother was shocked, so be it. Neither she nor Kerrec could help what they were to each other.

This latest arrival of the clans was large enough to be called an army. It took a long while to pass, then a longer while before they felt safe to go on.

In all that time, none of them spoke. Apart from the danger of being discovered, they had too much thinking to do.

Finally they left their hiding place. They did not need Rodry to show them the way—there was no doubt as to where the clans had gone—but a trained scout knew how to travel both fast and undetected. He could read the signs and tell the others when to ride and when to hide.

The vision was still working inside Valeria. Kerrec had distracted her from it, but as she went on, it woke again.

There was more to it than the emperor and his armies or the barbarians in their horde. It hovered briefly above one barbarian, lingering as if to tempt her with Euan Rohe's fine white body, before it closed in on Kerrec's face. Close beside it hovered another that Valeria remembered too well. She would never forget Gothard, however dearly she wished to.

He had been dangerous before. He was worse than that now. The new power he had, the dark stone, turned against Kerrec. Kerrec in the vision was beautiful in his strength, but Gothard was stronger. Kerrec tumbled in ruin.

With his last stroke, he destroyed his brother—but even as Gothard's body and soul shattered, Kerrec was already gone. There was nothing left of him but a drift of ash on the wind.

Valeria's arms tightened around Kerrec's waist. She unlocked them with an effort before he had time to protest.

It had all seemed so simple. The empire was threatened by something much more terrible than a barbarian invasion. The emperor's life was in danger. She would give Kerrec whatever powers he needed to bring down his brother, and so save the empire and hold back the Unmaking.

This vision turned a certainty into a dilemma. Save the empire, destroy Kerrec. Save Kerrec, see the empire fall.

She tried to see a way around it. Maybe there was more to the vision. Maybe she was misreading it. Prophecies were notoriously difficult to interpret.

No matter how she tried, this one was all too clear. She could see the brothers face-to-face, with the same profile after all, though so much else was different. They fought as mages did, with blasts of magic—and they both died. No matter how she tried to shape the patterns, that was the only outcome she could see.

She opened her eyes on rapidly fading daylight. They were at a standstill again. Valeria did not need Rodry to tell her the enemy's camp was just over the hill. She could feel it inside her, in the blight that was the Unmaking.

By then it was nearly dark. They made a fireless camp where trees had fallen together in some long-ago storm. The maze of fallen trunks and tangled branches hid them completely.

For once it was Kerrec who ate his frugal supper and went straight to sleep, and Rodry who held on grimly to wakefulness. "Someone has to keep watch," he said.

"I'll do a turn later," said Valeria. She knew she should sleep if she was going to do that, but she was wide awake.

It should have been pitch-dark in their makeshift shelter,

but the Lady had the same soft glow about her as the stallions. Her bay coat made it redder—more like sunlight, in its way. By that light Valeria caught Rodry darting glances at her, then looking away.

Valeria stood it for as long as she could, but finally she said, "Don't tell me you're scandalized."

In that light it was hard to tell, but Valeria thought her brother turned crimson. "Is it even legal?" he asked.

She laughed—softly, so as not to wake Kerrec. "There's no law against it."

Rodry scowled. "Is he cruel to you? Because if he is, First Rider or no, I'll—"

"He tries too hard to protect me," Valeria said pointedly.

Rodry had grown up in the same family Valeria had. He took the point. But he said, "Tell me you haven't given yourself to a man who can't give back. Because you deserve better."

A day or two ago, Valeria would have agreed with him. Tonight, she said, "He is exactly what I deserve. We both have our obsessions. Outside of those…he's the other half of me."

Rodry chewed his lip. "You really mean that?"

She nodded. "He knew what I was from the first, and he never betrayed me. Before they let me be a rider, he was the only one who would teach me. Don't trust his face, Rodry. He wears it like a mask. Sometimes it even deceives me."

"I hope you're right," Rodry said.

"I know I am," said Valeria.

Forty-Three

Rodry tried to convince Valeria not to take the second watch of the night, but he was out on his feet. She knocked them out from under him and sat on him until he gave in. When she stood up again, he was already halfway into a dream.

She slipped out of the deadfall past the warm and breathing bulk of the Lady. The stars were out. The moon had risen.

At first she thought the world was perfectly still. Then she heard it, a deep pulse like the earth's heart beating.

It was a drum. She glanced back. The Lady flicked an ear.

Rodry and Kerrec would be safe. Valeria crept through a tracery of moonlight and shadow, moving as softly as she knew how. That was very soft—Rodry had taught her.

Near the top of the hill, she dropped onto her belly and crawled to the summit.

The trees were thinner here. There was a wide clearing beyond the hilltop, sinking into a shallow bowl.

It was all but empty. Most of the clans camped under the trees. She could feel them—thousands, maybe tens of thousands. Their fires were banked and their voices silent.

In the clearing was a standing stone. Human figures stood around it, swaying gently. She could not see the drum, but its beating filled her body.

A low chant rose up out of the clearing. The sound of it raised the hairs on the back of her neck. Something was bound to the stone. She could not—in truth would not—make out its shape, but it glistened wetly in the wan moonlight.

She clung dizzily to the tilting earth. They were chanting the battle chant and performing their sacrifice of blood and bone, glory and pain. They were calling up the One—raising the Unmaking.

New shapes moved toward the priests and the sacrifice. They were all men, and naked. Their white skin gleamed in the moonlight. Their hair was long and loose, flowing down their backs.

She could not see their faces. They wore masks without features, with blank slits of eyes.

These could not be Brothers of Pain. That was an imperial order. But they wore the mask.

They spread in a circle. Their arms locked. Their feet stamped. The chanting swelled from pulsebeat to another, equally familiar rhythm.

It throbbed in Valeria's body. So much bare and glistening flesh, long muscled backs, taut buttocks, phalluses erect and thrusting into the yielding air—she bit down hard on her tongue.

The pain helped her focus. Her skin felt as if a touch would ignite it. Her center was melting.

She had never known they did *this*. The blood and pain, yes, she knew of those. Torment for the tribes was a sacrament.

She could shrink from that in all good conscience. But this called to instincts far deeper and far less easily resisted.

The chanting deepened to match the drumbeat. Through blood and pain and hot desire, they were opening the gates of the earth. Valeria knew too well what waited on the other side.

The power of priests raised this working, but the power of a mage controlled it. Valeria had no need to wonder who that mage was. Gothard must be one of the shadows around the standing stone.

The stone itself was the drum. Something else, something enormously powerful, was beating on it from outside.

This was stone magic as it had never been intended—magic made purely for destruction. It created nothing. It preserved nothing. Even under potent restraint, it shook apart the bindings of things.

The air blurred around it. The earth crumbled.

It took every scrap of will Valeria had to crawl down the hill and make her way back to the others. The Lady was awake, watching as she came. She looked into the dark and liquid eye. It calmed her, though it did nothing to lessen the sense of urgency.

She touched Rodry's foot. He came awake all at once, hand to knife hilt. The sight of her, glowing with witchlight, did not seem to reassure him. She beckoned him outside.

The Lady followed them into the starlight. The sky was growing pale in the east. "Rodry," Valeria said, "you have to go back and warn the emperor. They're raising something more than battle magic. All those men and armies are a feint. The real attack will come from the priests—or from something worse than priests."

"He must know that," Rodry said. "He has a whole battalion of mages."

She shook her head sharply. "You heard what his mage said to Kerrec. They think they know what's coming, but they aren't looking far enough. Kerrec is right, Rodry. This is stronger than anyone expects, and it's aimed at the emperor—at the heart of his bond to the empire. Once they have him, no mage's power will be able to save him or anyone who owes allegiance to him. They'll Unmake us all."

"If I go back," he said, "I won't get near his majesty. I'll be arrested and hauled off to a hanging."

"Not if you go with her," Valeria said, tilting her head toward the Lady. "She'll take you where you need to go."

"But—"

"Save the emperor," Valeria said. "I'll do what I can to save his son."

Rodry eyed the Lady. She moved between them, presenting her back. He half turned, probably to fetch the saddle, but she blocked him.

Valeria laced her fingers. Rodry looked dubious, but he set his foot in them and let her toss him astride. There was just enough time for him to find his seat before the Lady wheeled and sprang away.

Valeria let out a slow breath. The Lady would keep him safe. Now there was only Kerrec left, and a battle that might kill them all.

She was still standing there when Kerrec came out beside her. The stars were fading. The drum had stopped. The tribes had resumed their march toward the river.

She wound her fingers with his. He did not pull away. "So," he said. "You sent your brother to safety."

"Someone has to warn the emperor," Valeria said. "What's

coming is worse than they want to imagine. They need to know how much worse."

He turned her to face him. "You believe me now?"

"I always have," she said. She rested her palm against his cheek. "It comes down to us, doesn't it?"

"It often does," he said dryly. He caught her hand before it dropped, then turned his head and kissed it. "Are you ready?"

"As ready as I can be."

He nodded. "Will you eat? There's the last of the bread."

"I think we need to do this fasting," she said, "all empty and clean."

He took a deep breath. With no more warning than that, he set off toward the hill.

Valeria followed. Now that there was no turning back, she was calm.

It was a white calm. The stallions were in her, below even the Unmaking. She could see the circle of them, the long white faces and the dark eyes.

They might let her die or worse. Still, she was glad they were there. They helped her find strength, and steadied her steps as she made her way back up the long slope.

It was a harder journey than it had been in the night. The powers that the priests had raised were awake and moving. Other powers were advancing against them. The emperor's mages had begun the battle even before the armies met. War raged in the heavens and rampaged across the earth.

None of it had anything to do with a pair of horse mages separated from their horses. Whatever buffets they took to their magic, none of the blows was meant for them.

It was an advantage, in its way. They could not have asked for a more effective diversion.

By the time they reached the hilltop, Valeria felt bruised inside her skull. Blasts of magic and countermagic raged overhead, roaring like thunder or howling like wind. Lightnings cracked, now from one side of the sky, now from the other.

The clans had left their camp. The forest was still. Down in the clearing, the stone stood by itself, with nothing bound to it. The earth had swallowed the blood of the sacrifice.

The camp was not deserted. The priests were still there. So was the power Kerrec had come to find.

Kerrec had been right in everything. Gothard had not gone to the battlefield. He was fighting from this safe place, surrounded by lesser powers that fed the greater one.

"He has a starstone," Kerrec breathed in Valeria's ear as they paused on the summit.

She looked at him.

"A stone that fell from the sky," he said. "A gift of the gods. I'm an idiot for not having realized it sooner. No wonder he has all his power back. Even a master stone is a small thing beside that."

"Then you don't think we can—"

"We're not stone mages," he said.

He stood up. She snatched, meaning to pull him back into hiding, but he was already out of reach, walking coolly down the hill.

Gusts of random power tugged at him. He held steady. Clouds raced above him. Lightning danced its wild dance.

A bolt struck near enough to make Valeria's hair stand on end. She choked on the acrid reek of it. Kerrec never faltered.

He had the master stone in his hand. She could barely pick out its presence amid so much warring magic. She hoped—prayed—that none of the other mages noticed it.

Prayer was hard. So was walking. The Unmaking was singing.

* * *

There was a tent pitched on the edge of the clearing. Two circles of men sat in front of it. The ones on the outside were all naked. There was no hair at all on their bodies. Their skin was blue-white but their eyes were as dark as oblivion. They made Valeria think of blind things that crawled in caves.

The men in the inner circle were dressed like tribesmen, but most were slight and dark—imperials, and nobles from the look of them. They were much less repellent than the others, but they had the same eyes. If anything, the darkness in theirs was deeper.

She had no trouble recognizing Gothard. He wore leather leggings and a gaudy plaid, and his hair was plaited down his back. He had grown a soft reddish mustache since she last saw him. He still had the curved nose and dark eyes of an imperial noble, and the look of profound and inborn discontent that Valeria remembered too well.

He sat cross-legged in the center of the twofold circle. His hands cradled a black stone no larger than a baby's fist.

The stone's color was dull black, but there was more to its darkness than that. Dark light rose from it.

Gothard raised his eyes. He was staring straight at Valeria. For a long moment she was sure she was safe, that Kerrec's spell concealed her.

Then she knew there was no concealment, not from the Unmaking. It was not only inside her. It was all around her.

Gothard's eyes opened wide. Valeria snatched desperately at the rags of her magic.

They were already out of reach. Nothingness had swallowed them. She could not find the stallions anywhere. They were gone.

She had no weapon to fight him off. Her hands would not obey her will.

Her body stumbled and fell. All her power swirled away into the dark.

Forty-Four

At long last, the second dawn after Gothard provoked the Ard Ri into calling out the muster, the tribes crossed the river. They left the priests—of the old order and the new—behind in their previous night's camp. That was close enough for the working, Gothard said, but far enough to be safe if it failed.

Euan Rohe did not believe anywhere would be safe if Gothard lost his grip on the starstone. Every day that he and his pack of boys wielded it, it came closer to the heart of the One. And the heart of the One, as any tribesman knew, was annihilation.

They were all in a wild mood—even wilder than usual before a battle. None of them had slept since the weapontake began. The night had been one long roaring tumult of thunder, shot through with bolt after bolt of lightning. No rain had fallen and no relief had come, until morning brought a brazen light and the call to battle.

Somehow, below thought or reason, they all knew what the

stakes were this time. More than death would fall on the field that day. More than a pair of worlds hung in the balance.

They marched as they lived, in loose order. Even those who had horses chose to go on foot as the people had done since the dawn of time.

There were no ranks or columns. Clans and tribes held together by the cut of their plaids. They flowed like water through the trees, pouring down toward the river.

The imperials were waiting. They had deliberately left the ford unguarded. It was open like a gate, luring the tribes onto the field that they had chosen.

The Calletani, with the royal clan in front, took their time coming out of the trees. For once the Ard Ri led his people—his warband was first to reach the river. Clans of Prytani and Mordantes and Cymbri swarmed in his wake. The Galliceni and the handful of Skaldi hung back behind the Calletani.

Euan's heart was with the first crossers, but the part of him that was king was minded to wait a bit. He knew the land well by now, with and without the seeing-stone—every tree and stone on both sides. The imperial camp with its high palisade and square towers lay just upriver. There were men on the palisade—he saw the flash of helmets.

The imperials' greatest advantage was their discipline. Their legions fought in ironclad ranks, with every place accounted for and every eventuality taken into consideration. He had read that in their officers' manual when he was in the School of War. He would wager he remembered the details better than most half-baked young tribunes just out from Aurelia.

Discipline made the legions a terrible machine of war. It did not make them unstoppable—though it came close. A legion almost never lost a battle.

There were three legions down there, close on fifteen thousand men. Euan would reckon the massed horde of the tribes at half again that, maybe more. His people were not much for lining up men or numbers, any more than they were fond of fighting in ranks and squares, all straight lines and sharp corners. Their world was one of circles and curves.

The first swarm of tribesmen was nearly over the river. The legions were waiting. They were drawn up in ranks behind a wall of shields. Archers and cavalry flanked them and waited in reserve behind. It was all neat and orderly like game pieces on a table.

The emperor stood on a low hill behind the central legion. The banner of sun and moon snapped in the wind over his head. His golden helmet flamed in the morning light.

At first Euan thought it was the sun in his eyes, or else a bird—hawk or vulture—hovering in the sky. A speck of darkness hovered above that dazzling helmet. The longer Euan looked at it, the clearer it became. It was growing larger.

The Ard Ri set foot on the farther bank. His men shrieked and yowled, swarming over and past him. The clans still in the water picked up speed, splashing headlong to shore.

A gap was opening between the Calletani and the last of the leaders. Euan loped down the hill with his men behind him.

With each step, his broad view of the battle shrank. By the time he came to the river, he was part of the flood that fell on the legions. He could see the men on either side and in front and hear the ones behind. The rest was feel and instinct.

The first wave of tribesmen crashed against the shieldwall. Arrows flew and men fell, but further waves roared behind them. They battered the wall of shields, hewing at it with axes and great swords.

The imperial ranks held. The tribes had no ranks to hold. They ran past the shieldwall, aiming at the cavalry and the archers. Few of them cared that arrows rained down on them and hooves trampled them. They were lost in a trance of battle.

When the mages began their work, the result brought them up short. Spells lost strength halfway to their target or slipped aside or, if the mages were very unlucky, rebounded on those who cast them.

Euan laughed as a mage-bolt turned sand to glass just in front of him. Call it priestwork, get one of Gothard's boys to lay a blessing on it, and even the most suspicious clansman would take an amulet against the pollution of magic.

It was mostly the Calletani wearing river pebbles in pouches around their necks, but they were numerous enough to keep the imperial mages both busy and frustrated. Battle magic was not much use if the worst damage it did was to one's own side.

The battle was clean because it had to be. Clean sweat and clean steel. At least Euan had found a use for magic—to negate itself. The One ought to be pleased with that.

Euan took his axe to the shieldwall of the Valeria as if it had been a thicket of trees. Spears thrust at him. He hacked off their heads.

The shield in front of him splintered. The man behind it stabbed with his short sword, aiming for Euan's gut. Euan's axe split him in two.

Another little dark man in armor tried to close up the wall. Euan thrust his bigger, heavier body against the smaller man, pressed in so close that even the short stabbing sword was useless. Euan's belt dagger opened the legionary's throat between the cuirass and the helmet strap.

The whole world had narrowed to this tiny piece of it. Inch by inch, stroke by stroke, Euan's Calletani broke down the wall of shields.

The enemy gave as good as he got. The ground was a mire of blood and entrails. Bodies rolled underfoot.

Not all of them were dead. Few of them were intact. Axes and great swords took a terrible toll on limbs and extremities.

So did spears and short stabbing swords, arrows and lances and charges of cavalry. The Aurelians contested every step and held off every charge against them. Every time their ranks broke, they re-formed, as straight if not quite as numerous as before.

The only way to win that the people had ever found was to wear them down—keep on coming until the last legionary fell to wounds or exhaustion. There was a high price on victory, but the glory that went with it was worth dying for.

Euan broke through the ranks and found himself face to face with the cavalry—the cataphracts in their heavy armor on their massive horses. They were powerful but they were slow, and they needed room to build up the momentum of a charge. There was no such room here.

His Calletani swarmed over them like ants over a carcass. Their long lances were useless at close quarters, and their horses floundered. One by one, horse by horse, they went down.

Euan laughed. After a while he began to sing. This was a beautiful day, a glorious day, a grand day to die.

Forty-Five

Kerrec advanced through a maelstrom of warring magics. The master stone protected him somewhat. So did his sense of the patterns that composed the world. Something was trying to rise from beneath and destroy them, but for the moment they were holding.

In the darkness behind his eyelids, he could see and hear and feel and even smell the battle by the river. The barbarians were still swarming across, an endless horde of them. The whole north must be stripped of its fighting men.

They were falling on the legions like a storm surge against a bastion of rock. Battle magic did not touch them—they had something, some power or warding, that protected them against it. But that was not what nearly flung Kerrec out of the working.

The emperor's command post stood on a hill just beyond the limit of the fighting. A triple wall guarded it—cataphracts on their great horses, picked footmen of the imperial guard, and a battalion of mages. Nothing on that field could come near him.

None of them had thought to protect against the sky. It had been clear at sunrise, but clouds were gathering now, tall white flotillas that would breed thunder later.

One cloud had taken shape directly over the emperor's head. It looked like a natural cloud—unless one could see it with eyes of the spirit. Those eyes saw a core of nothingness within the billows of white and grey and silver.

It hung like a sword above the emperor. The thread on which it hung grew thinner with each moment that passed.

Just as Kerrec began to understand how great the danger was, Valeria collapsed. He nearly lost the vision and all the power that went with it. Valeria—he had to—but his father—the empire—

That paralyzing confusion was an attack of its own. He beat it back. Focus, above all he must focus.

The master stone throbbed. He raised it in his hand. The starstone shrieked.

Kerrec reached for any power that would come to his call. He no longer cared what it was or where it came from, if only it did his bidding. He would have welcomed the Unmaking itself, if it won him this battle.

White power flung the thought aside. White magic wrenched him back into focus. Petra and Sabata thundered toward him through the madness of magics.

The priests could not move. The circle of mages was locked fast.

The working bound them. That was the weakness of their art—that it needed so many and held them so helpless.

Gothard was stronger than they, or else the ruler of that dark dance could keep his wits about him when the rest had given up every scrap of will and volition that they had. He struggled to draw the sword at his side, but he moved with dreamlike slowness.

Kerrec had taken him completely by surprise. If he had expected any attack, it had been from the imperial mages. He had never expected his brother, poor broken thing, to come hunting him.

Gothard always had been prone to underestimate his enemies. Kerrec reached in, ah, so easily, and caught him by the throat.

Never trust anything that comes easily.

Kerrec had forgotten who first told him that. His father? One of his instructors on the Mountain?

Gothard smiled. Whether he had planned this or whether it was a gift of the One, he was in a kind of bliss. One devastating stroke, and both his father and brother would fall. And he could watch them do it.

The starstone's shriek had soared beyond the threshold of hearing. All the patterns were unraveling.

Kerrec met his brother's eyes. There was no kinship there, no memory of the blood they shared. There was only death. It opened a mouth as vast as the sky.

Kerrec hovered between life with all its pain, and the sweetness of oblivion. All he had to do was let go.

So easy. So very, very easy.

There was only one thing left for him to do. Everything else he could forget, but that, no. Never.

He brought the master stone down upon the starstone.

There was no fear in him at all. He did not care if he died. It did not matter if his soul vanished like mist in the sun. All he cared for was that the stone should break, and Gothard with it.

Stone struck stone. The roar was soundless. The flash was dark—all light swallowed in void. The stones shattered.

They had Unmade one another. There was nothing left of either, not even a puff of dust.

Gothard sprawled at Kerrec's feet. His face was stark with shock.

Kerrec read his thoughts as easily as if they had been written on a page. He had been absolutely certain that he had the victory. He had felt it in his hand, as sharply potent as the stone. All that stood in the way was his weakling of a brother.

Not so much a weakling, Kerrec thought. His fingers were numb with the force of the stones' breaking, but they obeyed his will. There was a scabbard at Gothard's belt. The knife hissed as Kerrec drew it.

The traitor's breast was bare. Kerrec heard the heart beating hard beneath the breastbone. If he shifted his sight just so, he could see it, clenching and unclenching like a fist. He knew exactly where to thrust the knife, up beneath the ribs, hard.

Petra's large and breathing warmth loomed behind him. His focus wavered. In Gothard's staring eyes, he saw the battle on the field, blood and slaughter and a living darkness stooping like a hawk upon the emperor.

Come, the stallion said.

Never in all their years together had Petra condescended to offer a human word. It froze Kerrec where he knelt. Gothard was helpless, with the knife pressed against his ribs.

Kerrec could not make himself thrust it home. Not, he told himself, because after all he loved his brother. Gods, no. His hate was as strong as ever.

Even to destroy his worst enemy, he could not commit murder in cold blood. If that made him a coward, so be it.

Kerrec left Gothard where he lay. He was nothing now. He no longer mattered, even to put out of his misery.

Kerrec turned slowly. They were all down, priests and mages.

Most of them were dead. If anyone survived, he was a husk, empty of will or understanding.

There was nothing left here—and yet that, like Gothard, did not matter at all. Kerrec's great working and the victory he had thought so complete had failed to do what he meant them to do. Without Gothard and his circle of mages, the powers that they had raised had not fallen. If anything, they were stronger.

Gothard had laid traps within traps. Each one that Kerrec uncovered only concealed the one beneath. Here maybe was the real trap, the reason for all the rest.

Gothard's working had opened a gate. The powers he had summoned were swarming through it.

Mortal will had no power over them. They were free, and they had their target. They roared down upon it.

The cloud of dissolution was nearly upon the emperor. There was no way Kerrec could stop it. The battlefield was an hour's hard ride away. He could not—

Sabata stamped. There was something lying at his feet, perilously close to that furious hoof.

Valeria.

She was alive. She sat up, hand to head, then staggered to her feet. Sabata offered his shoulder. She pulled herself onto his back.

Kerrec should not have succumbed to temptation. He cast one last, burning glance at Gothard.

His brother bared teeth at him. "You always were weak," Gothard said.

Kerrec's sight turned briefly bloody. But the cold part of him, the part that saw patterns and foresaw futures, recognized this latest of so many traps. If he gave way to provocation, Gothard might die—but so would Artorius.

After all his maunderings about Gothard's insignificance, it was bitter to let go. His stomach heaved. It was well for Gothard it was empty, or he would have had a faceful of the consequences.

Kerrec stabbed the knife hilt-deep into the earth beside Gothard's staring eye and flung himself onto Petra's back.

The stallion was already in motion. Sabata ran ahead of him, mane and tail streaming. Valeria clung to his neck.

They sped away from the dregs of Kerrec's obsession. Trees flashed past. Kerrec could not begin to guess how fast they were going. Faster than a mortal horse could gallop—faster than the wind.

He set his teeth and held on. Whatever he was going to do when he came to the battle, he had no master stone to feed his power. All he had was himself.

And Petra. And Valeria. And Sabata. No rider was ever alone. She had said that. She was often right—as little as he liked to admit it.

The battle was in full spate. Kerrec had no time to make sense of the surge and flow of forces across the field, except to note that all of the enemy had crossed the river. The farther bank was empty of any but a scattering of corpses, all barbarians.

The ford was full of them, lying side by side with men in imperial armor. Some were still moving. The stallions surged through them. Bloodied water sprayed high, but it never stained those moon-white coats.

Kerrec heard the hiss of Valeria's breath behind him, a gasp sharply cut off. His heart twinged. She was as strong as any man he knew, but she was terribly young. She had never seen so much blood or so much death all in one place.

He had, years ago, but he was long out of practice. He could only bear it by closing off his heart and focusing on what he had come to do.

The emperor's mages were holding off the assault, but they were weakening fast. Already some of them had fallen. Artorius was wielding sword and spear against tribesmen who had broken through the ring of his guards, fending off lances and arrows with a shield that bristled with them, and sustaining wards against the constant barrage of hostile magic.

There were two armies locked in combat between the river and the emperor. Petra slowed as he reached the bank, bucking slightly, tossing his head with uncharacteristic ill humor.

Sabata, whose fits of temper were notorious, half reared and loosed a bellow. It was barely to be heard above the battle's clamor.

Away on his hill, the emperor swayed and his banner nearly fell. A bolt of pure destruction hurtled down.

Artorius flung up his shield. Wards blazed blue-white.

The bolt struck them and shattered. Shards flew wide. Mages fell—maimed or dead.

There was nothing human or mortal or even comprehensible in the thing that hovered above the emperor. It could have been a cloud or a pall of smoke or a memory of terror. It existed to devour him whole.

It was as blank and empty of mortal malice as the storm that had kept Kerrec from crossing the river. There was no use in raging at it. It merely was.

Kerrec shook his head, tossing it like one of the stallions. This was raw formlessness, power without conscious will—but it had a purpose. That purpose was to destroy everything that Kerrec lived for.

He called on power of his own. Up from the earth, down from the sky, through the bodies and the immortal spirits of the stallions, he summoned it into his hand. He shaped it into a weapon—a spear, for choice—and cast it into the center of the cloud.

The cloud howled. He had wounded it, but it was not destroyed. It was growing as he watched, sucking warmth from the air and light from the sun, swallowing lives and souls of imperials and barbarians alike.

His father was still on his feet. His wards were holding—though barely. His legions were overrun. Here and there, the victory chants had already begun.

Kerrec gathered himself for a new muster of magic. He was losing strength. He could feel the raw edges and mended places more keenly than he had in days.

He was still strong. He could strike another blow—and another if he must, and another after that.

"Wait." Valeria's voice was quiet. He should not have been able to hear it through the tumult of the battle.

She rode up beside him. The bay Lady was with her—and Rodry on the Lady's back, greenish pale and wide-eyed but remarkably steady.

Rodry's magic was clear and strong. Though it was not horse magic, it fit well with the Lady's deep and singing power. She was using it to anchor herself to the mortal world, drawing strength through it and giving strength in return.

The last few stragglers of the melee had moved away from them. They stood alone in a broad expanse of trampled grass and mud and stony earth, littered with yet more of the fallen.

The emperor's wards were fading fast. The enemy poised to swarm up over his hill. Nearly all of his guards, as well as his mages were down. The few who remained fought desperately against a rising tide of barbarians.

Valeria looked Kerrec in the face. "Dance," she said.

He opened his mouth. "What—"

Petra turned his head and bit Kerrec's foot. The pain focused his mind wonderfully. He had no reins to gather and no saddle to settle deeper in, but was he not supposedly a master of riders?

He drew a breath and sat a fraction more erect. Petra came into balance beneath him. The purity and subtle beauty of it made his eyes fill with tears.

Rodry got a grip on the Lady's mane and held on. "Just stay with her," Valeria said to him. Her glance at Kerrec said a great deal more, but none of it needed words.

Sabata pawed once, sharply impatient. Valeria freed him to flow into the first movement of the Dance.

Forty-Six

War was hell. Valeria's father had often said that, and she had heard stories enough. But the reality—the blood, the crushed and severed limbs and trampled entrails, the screams of the wounded and dying, and over it all the numbing clangor of metal on metal—was worse than anything she had imagined.

She had no time to be sick. The legions were losing the battle, and the emperor was barely holding on against the tide of Unmaking.

She was barely holding on herself. If the stallions had not come across the river, she would still be lying with the fallen priests, and her soul would have gone into the dark. The stallions and the Lady were all that stood between Valeria and dissolution.

It was the Lady who put in her mind the thought of the Dance. The part of Valeria that had been trained as a rider did not want to listen. How could there be a Dance with three instead of four or eight? What hope did they have of succeeding? What if the Unmaking was waiting for exactly that, to break the Dance once more and end what it had begun?

The Lady's ears flattened to her skull. She snapped her strong yellow teeth in Valeria's face. *No questions. Stop thinking. Dance!*

Sabata's back coiled beneath her. He could as easily buck her into the river as accept her guidance.

The others were waiting. Rodry might not know her wits were wandering, but Kerrec did. He had had his own fit of the I-can'ts—and been bitten for it, too.

Completely unexpectedly, she laughed. The Unmaking recoiled. Sabata tossed his mane and stamped.

She sent him forward. He was not the great master that Oda was. She had to guide him. But she knew the patterns. They were as clear as words on a page, written on the earth in front of her.

The Lady moved ahead of Sabata. Rodry was motionless on her back.

There was no gate and no hall. No Augurs stood in their gallery to interpret the Dance. The ground they danced on was not perfectly raked and groomed sand but trampled grass, slick with blood.

Nevertheless this was a true Dance. With the first step that the Lady took, the power woke.

It drew the Unmaking away from the emperor. Valeria knew she should not do it, but she looked up. A black tumble of cloud hung over the Dance, swirling slowly. Its heart was darkness absolute. At first it was no more than a pinpoint, but as the Lady marked the limits of the Dance, it opened wider.

A fierce wind began to blow, buffeting Valeria. She dared not stiffen against it—that would unbalance Sabata. He had to be perfectly steady.

There was a moment when she knew that neither of them could do it. They were both too young. They had the power but not the art. She could not guide him. He could not carry her. They would fail.

She brought herself up short. The Unmaking was working inside her, sapping her courage, even while it sucked the light and life and soul out of the world. She would be strong enough, Sabata would be steady enough, because they had to be.

The Lady set the pace. Petra, behind Sabata, anchored them to earth and all its powers. Sabata was the balance between them.

Valeria had never known a Dance like it. Not only were there only three of them, and not only did they dance directly under the maw of the Unmaking. The Lady's presence changed everything they did. It went deeper and rose higher.

The powers that came to this Dance were stronger than Valeria had seen before. Everything that the full quadrille of stallions was to the Dance, the Lady was, alone, in her single self—and more.

The stallions in the Dance were submissive to the riders' will. They performed the movements as their riders instructed and raised their powers under the riders' guidance. They were the living incarnation of their magic, but that magic was an instrument in the riders' hands.

The Lady did not submit. She drew on the riders' power and discipline, but the Dance was hers.

The whole world was the power and the Dance, but Valeria was aware in her bones that the battle had gone still. Somewhere in the ranks, a drum began to beat.

She faltered and almost dropped Sabata out of the Dance. But this was not the drum that had beaten for the priests of the One. This one throbbed with magic, but its heart was mortal.

It fell into the rhythm of a human pulse. The Lady's satisfaction brushed past Valeria like a breath of wind.

The Lady was not afraid of the Unmaking. It could Unmake her—of that she was certain. But like all horses, she did not trouble herself with what might be. There was only what was—now and always.

It was the gift and curse of mortals that for them time was a running stream and not a perpetual present. That was their power, but it was also their greatest failing.

The Lady needed that failing. She needed even the fear. It shaped a pattern, and that pattern strengthened the bonds of the world against the Unmaking.

Kerrec gave her his fear, and his hatred, too, and bitter disappointment that he could not commit murder when he most needed to do it. That was a strong pattern, dark and clear. Into it he wove other, brighter strands, too many and swift for Valeria to follow. She was in them, and Briana, and even his father, whom in spite of their long war, he truly loved.

She spun her own threads into the pattern. As they wove through Kerrec's, she realized that she could see them with her mortal eyes as well as her magic. They were taking shape in the world, an intricate tracery of light and shadow. It spread across the field of the Dance and rose up over the dancers, raised like a shield between the Dance and the Unmaking.

The Dance both traced the pattern and created it. This was a Great Dance, but it opened no gates and shaped no future but the one directly before them. The gate that was open, the gate of Unmaking, must be shut. If it was not, there would be no future. The world would be swallowed in nothingness.

The image in Valeria's mind was altogether mortal. It was ridiculous, maybe. A man might laugh at it. She saw the many-colored threads and the void beyond, and thought of mending a torn shirt.

The Dance was the needle. Each movement drew the edges closer together.

It was an enormous working. Without the Lady she could never have done it.

When she tried to stop, to let the Lady control the Dance, the Lady would not allow it. This was for her to do. It needed mortal eyes and mortal sense of the world.

Valeria gave in to it. She drew ruthlessly from the others—shrinking a little from Kerrec until he opened his magic wide and laid it in front of her. It was not perfect, but even roughly mended, it was a potent thing.

Its greatest strength was not the raw power but the order and discipline he imposed upon it. He was a master of his magic, and he gave it all to her, to use as she would.

There had never been a greater gift. The Lady and the stallions came together within it, and Rodry with his bright, sunlit, utterly mortal magic. That was the world as it should be—the world they must save.

Valeria fixed on it. It was beautifully simple, like one of her mother's herbal teas, or a Word spoken to kindle a fire. That simplicity was the greatest power that mortals knew. It swayed even the gods.

With the others' help, Valeria bound the Unmaking. She closed the gate. It strained against her—but she held fast.

The Dance wove its last figure. The intricate pattern hung in the air. The sky was clear, the cloud of oblivion gone. Slowly the pattern melted and flowed until it was part of all that was.

The drumbeat stilled. The horses danced to a halt. Sabata's neck was dark with sweat, and his breathing came hard.

The battle of magic against Unmaking was ended. But the

armies had declared no truce, and neither had surrendered. As if the long pause had been no more than a breather, they clashed with a roar of renewed fury.

Valeria hissed. Sabata snapped and kicked at air. Neither of them needed to ask what the others would do. With Sabata in the lead, they plunged into the melee, aiming for the emperor's hill.

Forty-Seven

Between the tribesmen's amulets and the cloud of oblivion hovering over the emperor, the imperial mages were completely and successfully occupied. It was axework on that field, and the legions were falling like trees.

Euan Rohe knew exactly when the tide of battle turned. There was a moment when the legions no longer stood fast and no longer tried to advance. They were falling back—step by step.

It was slow, but there was no doubt of it. The people were advancing and the legions were retreating. Up on his hill, the emperor's circle of defenders was growing smaller.

Euan gathered as many of his Calletani as he could find. They stopped for a breather, sipping from waterskins and eating a bite or two if they had rations with them.

The legions were retreating faster now, trying to draw together around their emperor. Most of the tribesmen harrying them did not seem to notice that they were following rather than herding their prey.

If the imperials closed up their wall again, the fight would still end in their defeat—but it would drag on much longer than it needed to. Not that Euan minded, but there was a gap and he had just the men to make it wider. There was much more sport in hunting legionaries in ones and twos than in hammering away at their blasted shieldwall.

He whirled his axe around his head and howled—and his Calletani howled back. So did a straggle of outlanders, clansmen who had lost their chieftains or been cut off from their people. He swept them all together into the gap between legions.

The flanks of both were auxiliary foot—outlanders in imperial pay. They were notoriously loyal and famously deadly, and they were not about to lie down and accept defeat. They would die first. Euan was happy to oblige them.

Up to now he had felt like a woodman hewing trees. This was a real fight. Some of the auxiliaries were as tall as he was, and they fought like men—one by one instead of in a box of shields.

He went axe to axe with a great golden bear of a man. He was faster but the auxiliary was stronger. They traded blow for blow, the auxiliary's smashing strokes against Euan's lighter, quicker assault.

After the first parry that nearly shook his arms from their sockets, Euan ducked and darted rather than take the blows on his axe. He had to hope the other man would run out of strength before Euan ran out of speed—and then hope he had enough strength left to strike the deathblow.

The auxiliary's axe whistled past his ear. He slid aside before it hacked through his shoulder. His lips peeled back from his teeth. He whirled, letting the weight of his axe carry him, aiming at the auxiliary's neck.

Euan's axe clove empty air. The auxiliary sprawled on the bloody grass with the Ard Ri's great sword in his skull.

The high king grinned at Euan. His face was spattered with blood and brains. Blood ran down his arms. He looked as if he had been bathing in it.

Euan could have—ah, so easily—let his axe continue its circle and sever the Ard Ri's head from its neck. Maybe he was a fool for letting the weapon fall and leaning on it, grinning back. They exchanged no words. Side by side, they threw themselves back into the fight.

They were nearly through the gap and ready to surround the fragments of both legions when the light changed. Euan knew better than to let anything distract him when he was fighting for his life, but this had the too-familiar stink of magic.

Something new was on the field. It did not feel at all like Gothard. It felt like—

He nearly lost his head to a legionary's sword. He cut the man down, barely even aware of what he did. For the moment at least, everyone else was absorbed in killing one another. He turned and looked out across the field.

The battle had long since left the ford, leaving only flotsam behind. There were three horses in the middle of it—two greys and a bay. They looked common enough, and their riders looked like imperial couriers, or maybe scouts. None seemed to be armed.

They must have come with dispatches from the empire and found themselves on the edge of a battle. Except that they seemed to have come across the river rather than up it. And the way they were standing there, drawing all the light to them—that was not so common.

Then they moved and the world went still, and he knew.

Had Gothard known about this? If he had, would he have bothered to tell anyone? There were riders on the battlefield, materialized from who knew where, and they were pacing through the movements of a Dance. Euan could almost see their pattern distilling out of air, a twining, circular shape like one of the intricate brooches of his people.

For a dizzying moment he wondered if they were more of Gothard's allies. But that dream did not last long.

Whatever they were doing, there was nothing Euan could do about it. He could have sworn on his father's barrow that one of those riders was a woman—and that woman was Valeria. If Valeria was here, the One alone knew what would happen.

Maybe not the One, Euan thought as he looked up. He had been perilously slow to realize what was different. The sun was shining through a tumble of clouds—just as before. But the cloud over the emperor, the cloud of Unmaking, was gone.

So was the stink of magic. There was none left on this field—anywhere. Gothard's sorceries had failed.

Euan breathed deep of the wonderful, living, mortal stench of a battlefield. The emperor was still alive, but the tribes were taking his hill. His legions were all but fallen. What could his gods do now, if they had not done it already?

An auxiliary's axe nearly cut Euan in half while he stood grinning at the empty sky. He blocked it at the last instant and turned it on the man who had struck it. The white gods and their oddest servant sank far down in his awareness. It was kill or be killed here. The end was close enough to taste.

Forty-Eight

The only weapon among the three riders was Rodry's long knife. He was clinging too tightly to the Lady's mane to draw it. Valeria had too little magic left to raise wards, and Kerrec was barely hanging on. Speed was their only defense.

Men were fighting in cohorts and clans, the strict order of imperial battle broken down before the barbarian hordes. The emperor was free of the magical attack, but he was still the enemy's dearest target. The tribes were doing their best to take him.

The press of men and weapons was tighter, the nearer they came to Artorius. The fighting was fiercer. Imperials and barbarians fought sword to sword, body to body, driving against each other with brute strength.

Most of the archers on both sides had long since given up shooting and resorted to coarser weapons, but a few were still sending flights of arrows into their enemies' ranks. As they started up the hill toward the emperor, one such deadly rain fell on the riders.

Valeria crouched low on Sabata's neck. Petra shouldered to the lead. The Lady pressed on at Valeria's knee.

The armies were parting more slowly for them than before. As arrows fell all around them, men dropped, wounded or dead. One bolt slit the leather of Valeria's breeches as if it had been gauze. She ducked another before it pierced her throat.

She turned to Rodry, meaning to warn him—as if he could not see for himself. He was crouched as she was, making himself as small as possible. She started to breathe a sigh of relief.

An arrow sprouted between Rodry's shoulder blades. It was a black arrow fletched with glossy black feathers—raven, she thought. The tribes loved the beasts of battle, the wolf and the raven and the kite that fed on carrion.

Maybe it was not sunk as deep in him as it seemed to be. Maybe it had only pierced the skin. He was still clinging to the Lady's back. He was alive and riding.

His fingers loosened. His body began to slide. Valeria lunged toward him, wheeling Sabata about and then sidewise.

She was too late. Rodry tumbled to the bloody ground, eyes wide, staring blankly at the sky.

There was a small space around him, a zone of quiet. The fight was thick all around it. Most of the fighters were barbarians. The emperor's troops were fighting desperately, but they were outnumbered.

Valeria had a great deal of difficulty understanding what that meant. She should move. She should fight—somehow. But there was Rodry, white and still. How could he be so still?

A warrior burst out of the melee and stopped short almost on top of him. It was a barbarian, a big man with an axe nearly as tall as he was. Her numbed mind took in a blur of gold and plaid and coppery red.

He had not killed Rodry, but he was an enemy. He would do. She drew up magic from depths of rage that she had not known she had. It gathered in her hand, a bolt of bloodred light.

She looked into the enemy's face. His eyes were golden amber like a wolf's. He was a little taller and a good deal wider that she remembered—a man now rather than a rangy boy.

Euan Rohe stared at her as if she had risen from the dead. He was not only alive, he was clearly prosperous—his torque was gold, as were his brooches and rings and armlets. A mob of men fought behind him, hacking off heads and spilling the entrails of the emperor's soldiers.

Maybe she knew some of them, too. She did not look to see. His face transfixed her.

It was her fault he was here. She had helped him to escape from the ruins of the Great Dance and his grand conspiracy. If she had not done that, he would be safely dead or locked in one of the emperor's prisons.

He could have raised his axe and killed her and Sabata together. She should have loosed the mage-bolt that was still in her hand, straining against the bonds of her will.

Deliberately he lowered his eyes and turned away. Equally deliberately, she flung the mage-bolt at random, far away from Euan Rohe and his warband.

There would be a price to pay for that. Twice now she had had him in her power and let him go. But he was part of her— her first lover and once, in spite of the worlds between them, her friend. She could not bring herself to kill him.

She wrenched her mind back to the battle. Rodry was still dead. Nothing in the world could change that.

The Lady whirled suddenly into motion. She mowed a swath

all around his body, felling tribesmen in bloody ruin. Then she darted through the mass of warring mortals.

Petra ran in front of her, with Kerrec still on his back. Sabata sprang after the others.

The suddenness of the leap nearly flung Valeria to the ground. She clamped legs to his sides until he bucked in protest. Prudently, if without apology, she loosened her grip.

Kerrec had stopped just ahead. His head turned, scanning the field. His back tightened, then relaxed—as if he had seen a difficult choice and made the only one possible.

Valeria could make no sense of the confusion, but it seemed he could. He sent Petra onward again—not toward the emperor but in a sweeping arc across the field.

Sabata followed. The Lady, riderless, curved in the opposite direction. She was herding men—driving tribesmen on imperial swords and bringing the remnants of the legions together into a new wall of shields.

Kerrec was doing the same on the other side. Instead of hooves and teeth, he wielded his voice, calling out commands. Men obeyed him.

The enemy were not fools. They could see what the rider was doing. A swarm of them turned against him.

Valeria smote the ground in front of them with a mage-bolt born of anger and grief. The wall of fire drove them reeling back.

Kerrec took no notice. He was bullying, coaxing, cajoling, turning a jumble of scattered cohorts into a disciplined army.

The enemy battered them again and again. They wavered, but then they steadied. Shield locked on shield. The sound of it made Valeria's skin shiver.

The barbarians howled in rage—and then in terror, as they realized what the rider and his hooved allies had done. Two walls of shields hemmed them in. The third wall was the open field and the river, now full of archers and spearmen and swordsmen. The fourth was the emperor's cavalry and mounted auxiliaries, regrouping and launching the latest of innumerable charges.

The cataphracts in their heavy armor bore down on the mass of the enemy. The lighter auxiliaries darted in and out, shooting arrows or hurling spears with deadly accuracy.

The enemy might be crazy in their courage, but they were sane enough to know when they were done for. They broke and ran.

They overran the defenders on the field, swarmed over and through them without heed for the weapons raised against them. Archers and cavalry pursued them, taking a terrible toll—but no small number won free and fled across the bloodstained water.

Petra halted on the edge of the ford, with Sabata close beside him. The last of the clans had disappeared into the trees. Some of the mounted archers and the remains of the Valeria would have gone after them, but Kerrec stopped them with a raised hand.

"Let them go," he said. "They're broken. They won't be a danger to us for a long while."

"We should break them completely," said the commander of the Valeria. He had lost his horse and was limping badly, but he had refused to withdraw from the fight. "It's the only way to be rid of them."

"Ah," said Kerrec. "You would track every last one of them to his hole and destroy him. That's wise."

The commander eyed him dubiously. Valeria had heard the irony, too. She opened her mouth to say something, but a runner halted panting beside Kerrec.

The boy's eye rolled at Petra, but he was too desperate to be afraid. "Sir! The emperor—he's calling for you."

Kerrec's face went still. If he had been anyone else, he would have looked stricken. There were tears running down the dust and blood that caked the runner's cheeks.

Kerrec barely paused to say to the commander, "Take command here. Do what you will." The last of it was flung over his shoulder as Petra wheeled and galloped toward the emperor's hill, with Sabata close on his heels.

The hill was barely visible above the mass of dead and dying. The imperial banner still streamed in the wind, but the hand that held it was rigid in death.

At first Valeria dared to hope Artorius was only exhausted, sitting up against the stump of a blasted tree. Then she saw the blood. There was a great deal of it—more than she would have thought a single body could hold.

Kerrec flung himself from Petra's back and dropped to his knees. The emperor opened his eyes. They were clear and empty of pain. "You do realize," he said, "that you are guilty of escaping imperial custody."

"I said I would pay the penalty," Kerrec said stiffly. He looked around him. There was only Valeria standing within earshot. "Find a Healer," he said. "Quickly."

"Don't trouble," said Artorius. "He won't get here in time. Both of you listen. Tibullus of the Valeria is the most capable of the generals. Put him in charge of the army and have him see to the mopping up. My clerks know what other arrangements to make. Master Pretorius—trust him. He owes allegiance to no one order of mages, but he's sworn indelibly to the empire. And Briana—tell her—" He stopped. He had run out of breath, but there was more to it than that. His eyes were full of sadness. "Tell your sister she'll do no worse than I ever did."

"I'll tell her," Kerrec said. "Who should take my surrender? Tibullus or Pretorius?"

"Neither," said his father. "Gods, you're a stiff-necked thing. Was I that bad when I was young?"

"Probably," Valeria said. Her eyes were dry, but her throat kept trying to close.

Artorius smiled at her. "You're good for him," he said. "Don't let him trick you into forgetting it."

"I'll try," she said. She took his hand. It was already cold. "I'm sorry we couldn't save you. We did everything we could."

"You did a very great thing," the emperor said. "That Dance—I'm glad I lived to see it. There's never been anything like it."

"It failed," said Kerrec.

Artorius shook his head. "It succeeded. It's not only the One who takes blood sacrifice. When the need is greatest, our gods exact the utmost price, as well. It's fair. Blood and flesh belong to earth. Our souls we keep."

"There is nothing fair about this," Kerrec said. His voice was raw.

Artorius's free hand reached for his, gripping it as hard as his failing strength would allow. "Child," he said, "I love you, too— as poorly as I've ever been able to show it. Maybe it would have been better if I hadn't loved you so much. Then I'd have been less outraged when you chose a herd of fat white horses over me."

"Did you ever think it was easy?" Kerrec said.

"I made it easier, didn't I? I drove you away."

Kerrec did not try to deny that. He said, "I did my share. If we had only—" He bit off the rest. "Damn it. Damn you. You weren't supposed to die."

"You can't always get your way," his father said. "I'm leaving you with a ruddy mess—war always is. Tell Tibullus not to go after the tribes. He'll want to—he'll be convincing, too. But stand your ground."

"I already did," Kerrec said.

Artorius laughed—breaking into a fit of coughing. There was a thickness to the sound, a gurgle that made Valeria's heart clench. When he swallowed, she knew he swallowed blood.

He forced words through it. "Good! Good. You'll know what to do with the rest, then. Gods, I've missed you. Briana is a better heir than I ever deserved, but you and I—you know why we fought so much. We're exactly alike."

"So people say," Kerrec said. He bent his head and kissed the hand in his. Tears fell on it. "I'm not going to forgive you for this. Or myself."

"Don't be ridiculous," his father said. "All I regret is that we waited so long to be civil."

"Better late than never," Kerrec said.

Artorius smiled. He was letting go. "My dear," he said. "There's one last thing."

"Yes?" said Kerrec.

"Closer," Artorius said. "Come closer."

Kerrec bent down, nose to long arched nose. Both of Artorius's hands gripped his.

Kerrec met the wide grey eyes. His own were the color of rain.

Artorius let it all go.

Kerrec's body spasmed. He fought to pull away—but his father held him fast. All that Artorius had been, all that he had known and seen and wrought, poured into him. All the magic, the manifold powers, the gifts and arts and skills of a thousand years of emperors, filled him until surely it would burst him asunder.

He tried to stop it. "Father! You can't—this should be—Briana—"

"This is for you," his father said. His tone was gentle, but there was no yielding in it at all.

He gave it all to Kerrec—every scrap of magic that had ever been in him. When it was gone, he gave all that was left, his life and soul and the love he had so seldom been able to express.

Kerrec was crying like a child, great gulping sobs that rocked his father's body. Its emptied eyes stared up at the sky. Though its lips were growing cold, they smiled.

Death was seldom peaceful, no matter what the songs said. But this truly was peace.

Valeria reached to close his eyes, but Kerrec was there before her. His storm of weeping had passed quickly. The eyes he raised to her were preternaturally calm.

He was whole. She looked into him, searching out his scars and mended places—but there was none. He was all healed, all but his heart.

Forty-Nine

"Damn him," Kerrec said.

There was no rancor in it, which Valeria found encouraging. He looked down at his hands as if they belonged to a stranger. That gave her a moment of cold fear. Then he raised his eyes, and the fear drained out of her.

He was still Kerrec. His magic was as beautiful as it had been when she first met him—and more. How much more, she did not know yet, but he was no image of the walking dead.

He looked out across the field. He had changed after all— his face was not the perfect mask it had been. She saw the pain and the deep shock.

Battle was ugly. Its aftermath was uglier. And there was so much of it.

People were picking their way across the devastation. Most of them were rescue parties, soldiers guarding Healers who would try to find the living among the dead. Others had begun to gather and sort the fallen. Valeria had no doubt there were looters among them, scavengers who would rob the defenseless corpses.

Kerrec rose with his father's body in his arms. Petra knelt. He stepped astride. The stallion straightened and began to descend the slope, picking his way down the hill.

Valeria followed on Sabata. Others joined them as they went, the wounded limping, half carrying one another. No one spoke.

It was a long slow way across the battlefield, and a long procession, pacing in silence. The healers and the burial parties paused as it went past, bowing low before the royal dead.

The gate of the camp was open. Guards stood on either side. As the emperor passed, they performed the full salute. Weapons clashed, armor rang. Then at the last, they smote spears on shields, beating out the pace of the death march.

In front of the emperor's tent, Petra halted. People were waiting to take the body—embalmers in their robes and cowls, faceless and voiceless.

Kerrec surrendered his burden reluctantly. Once it was gone, he sat motionless on Petra's back. His face for a moment was empty, as if he had given up his spirit as well as his father's body.

Then life came back into it, and grief, and a steadiness Valeria had not seen in him before. He caught her eye.

There was no need for words. People were standing, numb or helpless, waiting for someone to tell them what to do. Kerrec on his glimmering white horse, with his father's face and now his father's magic, drew them irresistibly.

He drew himself up. He was exhausted—they all were. Grief lay heavy on him. But he could not run away and hide and cry himself out in peace, any more than Valeria could. There was too much to do.

"If you're wounded," he said to the men around him, "go to the Healers' tents. If you're walking sound, find your cohorts. Clerks will run the tallies—dead, wounded, whole."

It was simple common sense, but they bowed to him as if he had dispensed the gods' own wisdom. Valeria doubted that he saw it. He was already riding through them, heading back toward the field.

They opened the way in front of him. Hands rose here and there, yearning toward the stallion, but no one quite dared touch.

Their awe made Valeria's stomach hurt. It fell on her, too, because of Sabata and the Dance. Generals and commanders were ordinary if exalted mortals, but riders who had come out of nowhere to win the battle for them were as close to gods as made no difference.

Once he was past the camp's walls, Kerrec turned Petra toward the nearest general's banner. Sabata would have followed, but Valeria was done with running the gods' errands—or, for that matter, Kerrec's. She set her leg to his side and shifted her weight. He veered off toward the river.

The masses of the dead were greater the nearer Valeria came to the ford. Barbarians lay on their faces, hacked down from behind. Legionaries lay in battle order, many of them headless or with their right hands hacked off. The carrion birds were coming down to feed, going for the eyes and the soft bellies, snaking their heads in under armor and helmets.

There was nothing in her stomach, but it did its best to turn itself inside out. Sabata stood patiently while she leaned over his neck.

After a while the fit passed. Valeria straightened slowly. She was not going to find her brother—not among so many dead.

She had to try. She owed it to him. He had anchored the Lady to earth and shown her the way through the Dance. Maybe he had been no horse mage, but he had done a thing that no rider had ever done. Because of him, the empire was still standing, and Valeria was still alive.

She steeled herself to ride on. It did not get easier. She made herself focus on what she knew. Rodry had not worn armor—that excluded almost every imperial on the field. He had obviously not been tall, fair-haired, or painted blue.

If she had been a seeker as he was, she could have set a spell to find the one man in plain riding clothes among thousands of dead. But in spite of all her power, she had not been given that gift. She had to hunt as mortals did, step by step and body by body.

She refused to give up. Maybe the sorting parties would find him first. Probably they would not. They were on the other side of the field. It would be a long while before they came this way.

It occurred to her that Sabata did not need to endure this. It was slow, and she had to stoop over every heap of bodies. But when she tried to dismount and go on foot, he spun and sidled and bucked.

He wanted her on his back. She sighed. He went on, stepping carefully.

She found Rodry on the far side of a heap of barbarian dead. There was a ring of green grass around him, with flowers springing in it. Their scent was eerily sweet amid the stench of death.

He did not look as if he was sleeping. He looked dead. Whatever had healed the earth had done nothing to bring him back to life.

The Lady stood over him. Valeria had not seen her coming. She was simply, suddenly there.

"You," Valeria said. "Bring him back."

The Lady's head drooped.

"I don't believe you," said Valeria. "You let him die. Now make him live. You're a god, aren't you? You can do whatever you please."

The Lady sighed heavily. Some things were not to be undone.

"Undo it," Valeria said. "He earned it. Give him back his life."

The Lady turned her back. Valeria dropped to the ground and stooped and pitched a stone at her.

She flinched strongly under the blow, but she neither kicked nor bolted.

The grass was growing. A moment ago it had been a furze of green over the raw ground. Now it was fetlock-deep on the horses.

A vine unfurled over Rodry's body, putting forth buds that bloomed into sweetly scented flowers. Their petals were waxy white, but their centers were the color of blood.

Death was transformation. Valeria had heard priests say that.

She knew nothing about it. Her brother was dead. She wanted him back.

She was not being reasonable. Why should she be?

Because you have to be.

The Lady had turned to face her again. Valeria had another stone in her hand, but she clenched her fist before she threw it. The eyes in the long horse-face were dark and sad and ineffably wise. They understood grief—which Valeria found difficult to believe—but they did not indulge it.

Valeria's magic was the highest and strongest of all, because it could open the gates of time and change the course of the world. It could not change this. Worlds and empires could shift under the power of the Dance. One life was too small for it to change.

She sank to her knees. The grass and the flowers were swallowing Rodry's body. The earth was accepting the sacrifice, turning it into new life.

Rodry's soul was gone. The Unmaking had never touched it. Wherever it was, she could not follow.

His body was a low mound in a spreading expanse of green. The tide of grass and flowers flowed over the heaps of the fallen.

When Valeria looked back, the Lady had vanished. She had heard no footfall. The Lady was simply and completely gone.

So was Rodry. There was a bank of flowers where he had been, and a seedling rising out of it. She recognized the leaves of an oak, tiny but perfect.

Tears were streaming down her face. Her first instinct was to swallow them. She never cried. Tears were a weakness. She could not afford to be weak.

Who would know? There was only Sabata, cropping grass with a singular lack of concern. He knew exactly what she was, to the tiniest detail. No one else was within sight. Even the dead were gone, sleeping under a blanket of grass.

It reached all the way to the river now, and halfway to the camp. The burial parties had stopped to stare at it. It must be dawning on them that they would be left with nothing to do.

Something huge was rising in Valeria. For a few moments it swelled, caught under her breastbone. Then it broke free. She lay in the grass and cried herself out.

Fifty

The fortunes of battle were notoriously fickle, but as turn-abouts went, this was neck-snappingly sudden and appallingly complete. One moment the tribes were victorious—the emperor was down, most of his guards and mages were dead, and the legions were a few broken remnants on a bloody field. The next, three fat cobby horses and two tattered and nondescript riders created an army out of nothing and drove the tribes back over the river.

Bloody imperial gods and their bloody imperious servants. Euan Rohe had had Valeria within his reach. He could have hewed the blocky white head off that stallion of hers. And he had gone on past. He had let them go—and now it was all lost.

He would pay for that. For now he rallied his Calletani as best he could, along with anyone else who would listen to his voice. They crossed the river more or less together and scrambled up the far bank, slipping in mud and blood.

They caught up with the remnant of the Ard Ri's warband between the river and the trees. They were going slowly, carrying the high king.

He was conscious and his mind was clear. He greeted Euan with a fair imitation of his old, fanged grin. "Bloody imperial axe," he said, glowering at the leg that had bled through its mass of bandages.

The blade had nicked the great artery, from the looks. He must have got a bandage on it as soon as the blow fell—probably killed off the man who struck it, too. Whatever failings he might have as a warleader, the Ard Ri could hold his own in a fight.

Euan's Calletani lent a hand with the Ard Ri. There was no pursuit—yet—but they judged it wise to make as much speed as they could. Once they were well into their own woods and hunting runs, the legions would have to work to find them.

They swept through the camp they had left only this morning—and it was still barely past noon. A double circle of priests and imperial renegades lay dead on the camp's edge.

Gothard was not among them. Not all of his Aurelians were there, either. At least one was missing from the count of the dead—the tall fair one with the priest's eyes.

No need to ask what had happened there. Hooves had trampled among the dead—big and round and unshod. Euan would wager that three gods from the Mountain had been here.

He would also wager that the starstone was gone—destroyed. He felt an odd emptiness when he thought of it, as if part of him was missing.

He shrugged it off. He was in a better state than he had been the last time his stroke against the empire fell disastrously short. This time he went home as king, with a growing mob of clansmen behind him. Remarkably few had died, considering how badly they had lost the war.

* * *

By nightfall they were a long way from the river. The walking wounded were dragging. The men who were carrying the worst wounded were walking in their sleep.

They made what camp they could, with what they had been able to bring from the old camp. Euan decided to risk a fire. It might draw pursuit, but he had a feeling the legions would not be looking far tonight. They had a victory to celebrate.

He had wagered well. People did come to the light and warmth—but they were warriors from broken clans or tribesmen who had lost the rest of their people in the rout.

The legions had called off pursuit, they said. The last to come in declared that the old emperor was dead and there was a new one already—a man on a white horse who rode back and forth through the imperial camp, and the legions did as he told them.

"I thought the emperor's heir was a female," the Ard Ri said. He was bleeding whiter by the hour, but he clung fiercely to consciousness.

"She is," Euan said. "They must have misunderstood."

The Ard Ri nodded. His latest bandage was soaked through. The shieldbrother who had been looking after him was standing by with fresh bandages.

Euan moved away to give him room. He was not feeling anything yet, and if he had any sense he would wait a long while before he did, but he could think clearly enough. He knew who the man on the horse had to be—and that one had been born to be emperor. Now he had won the battle, who knew what he might decide to do?

A horse mage on the imperial throne. That would be interesting. Would he make Valeria his empress?

Euan did not like what his stomach did when he thought of

that. He was not feeling anything, of course not. He was only seeing her face every time he closed his eyes.

That was shock, of course. He had fallen out of a pitched fight into a circle of quiet, and there she was, sitting on her fat white horse. Even though he had half expected her once he saw the horse gods on the field, he had not been prepared for the blow to the heart.

Damn her. She had got under his skin. Now he owed her a double defeat—and he could no more hate her than he hated the air he breathed.

The Ard Ri died in the dark before dawn. He was clear-headed to the last, and he was unafraid. Late in the night, when he was nearly bled out, he said to Euan, "When they have the kingmaking, don't be a fool. Let someone else have it."

"Are you telling me I should try for it?"

The high king's eyes on him were dark with irony. "I'm telling you you shouldn't. A tribal king—now that's a free man. The high king is slave to everyone in the tribes."

"What if I do it in spite of you?"

"The One knows," said the Ard Ri, "I won't care."

"There's not likely to be anyone else," said Euan. "Galliceni king is dead. Prytani king may be. Mordantes king hasn't been seen since the battle. They'll all be making kings of their own—never mind a high king."

"Victory can be hollow, can't it?" said the Ard Ri. "We're broken badly. We've lost more men than we can spare, and the legions are going to come after us, demanding tribute. Be careful you don't find yourself an imperial vassal, boy. That's what they'll want. They'll do everything they can to trap you into it."

"I'll be careful," Euan said. It was better than arguing with a dying man. He knew about traps—and about treachery, too.

He stayed with the high king through the night, not just because the Ard Ri wanted him there. It seemed the right thing to do.

When the night reached its darkest point, the time most sacred to the One, the Ard Ri let slip his spirit. Euan closed his eyes for him, giving him to the dark. Already the keening had begun, the death chant for the high king of all the people.

Fifty-One

Kerrec had taken the army's reins because no one else seemed able or willing. The generals, even Tibullus, were numb with the emperor's passing. It was as if he had laid a spell on them, and now that it was broken, they did not know what to do.

Kerrec made what order he could. For the most part the troops knew what to do after a battle. They simply needed a touch here and a tug there. Kerrec on Petra, riding back and forth across the field, served well enough.

When the tide of green began to roll over the dead, he paused. The Lady's power thrummed in the earth. He tasted her sorrow, like bitter herbs.

Petra went on of his own accord, carrying Kerrec toward soldiers who had never seen such magic. They needed to see and hear him and touch Petra, to be sure of their place in the world. Then there was a flurry of clerks and a matter of supply wagons and a long hour among the wounded.

Whispers followed him. Some of it he expected—that he was a First Rider, that he had been the emperor's heir once and had died to that world. Some of it took him slightly aback. People were marveling that he had stopped a war without laying his hand on a weapon.

Magic was a more terrible weapon than any sword or bow. He was full of magic, overflowing with it. He could swear it was dripping from his fingers.

It fed him strength. He fed it in turn to the men of his father's legions. There seemed to be no end to it.

Sunset caught him by surprise. It had seemed as if this day would never end. When he stopped to think, he realized that the battle had been won before noon. As battles went, it had been mercifully short.

By then the army was settled in camp, with fires lit and the evening meal eaten. Tibullus had ordered a double ration of wine. Kerrec would not have done that, but he lacked the common touch. Maybe Tibullus's order had been wise.

It certainly raised the army's spirits. They were singing and shouting and dancing victory dances. Any grieving they meant to do for fallen comrades was put off until tomorrow. Tonight they would give themselves up wholeheartedly to rejoicing.

Petra was tired. He might be a god, but he lived in flesh, and his body needed to rest. Kerrec found a place for him in the emperor's horselines. The grooms bowed low before him.

When Kerrec left him, he was buried to the eyes in sweet hay. He barely acknowledged his rider's farewell.

Kerrec's own stomach was growling ominously. But seeing Petra fed and cared for reminded him that he had not seen either Sabata or his rider in some time.

He pushed fear aside. If either of them was in trouble, Petra would know. Still, there were other kinds of danger than an arrow in the dark.

The last thing Kerrec wanted to do after a long day on horseback was trudge across the battlefield looking for a strayed rider-candidate. He commandeered a horse—a plain and sensible chestnut who responded to his touch with a contented sigh—and fended off the flock of people who were trying to get him into his father's tent to eat and rest.

A few of them trailed after him, but they were a minor nuisance. The sky was still full of light. The battlefield had transformed into a long rolling meadow.

All the dead had been taken into the earth. Valeria's brother was there somewhere, asleep under a carpet of flowers. People were saying this great magic had come from him, or from the Lady who had deigned to carry him.

The burial parties had long since returned to camp. There was a watch on the river but not on the farther reaches of the field.

Kerrec found Valeria where the grass gave way to a thicket. Sabata was grazing not far from the trees. Valeria lay on a bed of flowers, staring up at the sky.

Kerrec dismounted near Sabata, tied up his gelding's reins and let him loose. The beast was delighted to graze in the white god's shadow.

Kerrec sat a little distance from Valeria. The temptation to stretch out beside her was overwhelming, but if he did that, he would fall asleep. "I'm sorry," he said.

"So am I," said Valeria. Her voice was steady, but he could hear the dregs of tears in it. "It's true, you know. All this is because of him."

"So I heard," said Kerrec. He had a powerful urge to move closer to her and take her in his arms, but something about the way she was lying told him that would not be a good thing to do.

"He'd be annoyed," she said. "All this fuss and magic, when all he wanted was a quiet grave somewhere, and maybe a little glory to carve on his stone."

"We could still give him a stone," Kerrec said.

She shook her head. "That's not what this is about. He helped us win. I'm proud. And I'm so angry I could spit. His death was stupid. Stupid and bloody random."

Kerrec held his tongue. Anything he could say would only make matters worse.

She did not seem pleased by his silence, either. "You're annoyed with me, I suppose. I didn't help you. I did a little—there were wounded who needed taking in and soldiers wandering around confused—but it wasn't much. I abandoned you."

He shook his head—though she was not looking at him. "You were there when we needed you most. The Dance succeeded because of you."

"Don't indulge me," she said.

"That's the last thing I'd dream of doing," he said. "I saw you on the field all day. It was more than a few wounded and the odd lost trooper. You were working as hard as I was."

"Was I? It didn't feel like it."

"Battle is ugly," Kerrec said.

She shot a glance at him. "You must think I'm acting like a silly girl."

"Not likely," he said. "The young troopers, the first-timers, have been puking their guts out."

"I did that," she said.

"Then you got up and went to work." He moved closer. "I saw my first battle before I was Called. I had to learn, you see, because someday I'd be emperor. I lasted an hour before I fainted. They had to carry me off the field."

"You never fainted in your life," she said.

"Like a lady in a corset," he said.

"So it gets easier," she said. "Should I be glad?"

"Not easier," he said. "You learn to swallow it, that's all, then carry on. I think you've already learned that."

"And yet," she said, "if you listen to the songs, war is all pride and glory. Warriors live for it."

"Warriors are madmen, fools, or soldiers who count the hours until they're home and safe and far away from the field."

"I wish I were home," she said.

"Believe me," he said with heartfelt honesty, "so do I."

"Can we go back soon?"

"Yes," he said. "As soon as my father's body is ready, we'll take it to Aurelia. Then we'll go."

"I'll make you keep that promise," she said.

She said no word of leaving without him. He found that he was glad.

He rose, pulling her to her feet. "Come back to camp. You need to eat. Then sleep."

She let him toss her onto Sabata's back before he mounted the gelding. He eyed her warily, but she seemed well enough, all things considered. She was tired, that was all. Tired and very young.

Kerrec refused to sleep in the emperor's tent. Instead he claimed the one that for a few hours had been his prison. The servants had opened up the rooms so that they were all one airy space, and brought in a curtained bed that would have done justice to an imperial duke.

Either they were seers or the rumor was true—servants really did know everything. They had laid out a feast, which Valeria barely touched. She was out on her feet.

Kerrec slipped the cup of heavily watered wine from her

hand before she dropped it, then lifted her in his arms. She was a solid weight. He laid her in the extravagant bed and stood looking down at her.

He would not have stopped her if she had asked to go back to the Mountain before all his duties were done, but when she made it clear that she would not even think of it, his heart had leaped. He did not want her to go. He wanted her with him, close by, completing him in the same way Petra did. Somehow, without his even knowing it, she had come to mean the world to him.

He lay beside her. She was deep asleep. He drew her to him, cradling her, breathing the fragrance of her hair. She sighed and murmured and burrowed into his chest.

"My lord?" The voice was soft, a little hesitant, but determined.

Kerrec opened an eye. Valeria was still asleep, curled against him. The chief of the emperor's servants, whose name was Marius, was standing over them, taking great care not to stare.

Valeria barely stirred when Kerrec left her in the bed, except to curl tighter and fall deeper into sleep. He hoped Marius took note of the fact they were both fully clothed. "What is it?" Kerrec asked. "What's happened?"

"The sun's up, my lord," Marius said, "and the generals are demanding to speak with you. Since they do outrank all of us who are standing in their way…"

"I see," Kerrec said. "Fetch a bath and clean clothes—the plainer the better. Tell their lordships I will summon them as soon as I am ready."

Marius's eyes glinted. "I'll be pleased to obey, my lord."

"First Rider," Kerrec said. "That's my title. I'm not—"

"First Rider," said Marius. "Yes, my lord."

Clearly he was incorrigible. Kerrec shook his head but let it be.

Clean, shaved, fed, and dressed in elegant but acceptably plain riding clothes that had been his father's, Kerrec received the generals in the common room of the emperor's tent. He would have preferred another place, but it had to be this one. They would not accept any less.

Not only the three legionary commanders had come at his summons. A handful of mages and priests attended, as well, with Master Pretorius prominent among them.

The ravages of the battle were still on them all. Some seemed honestly to be grieving for the emperor. Kerrec took note of those.

They were studying him as he studied them. He hoped they were sufficiently disappointed.

When the silence threatened to crush them all with its weight, Master Pretorius said, "Yesterday's battle will never be forgotten. Not in a thousand years has a war been won in that way. Because of it, the tribes are broken. It will be a long while before they challenge us again."

"I still say we should wipe them out," Tibullus said. "Maybe they're driven into their holes now, but they breed like rats. They'll be back in a year, raiding our borders, and back at full strength in ten, with a whole new war for us to fight."

"Maybe," said Kerrec. "The empress may find ways to prevent it."

"The empress," said Viragus of the Seventh Corinia. He was a fine soldier or he would not be here, but he had the air of an imperial fop. His uniform was perfectly cut and fitted, its every bit of metal polished. He sighed delicately. "She is that, by the emperor's will. Pity she can't be with us today."

"Oh?" said Kerrec with lifted brow. "Why is that?"

"Why, my lord," Viragus said, "war is not for the faint-hearted. A woman's tenderness, as much as it is to be valued, is perhaps out of its depth where the harsher realities are concerned."

"By which you mean to say," said Kerrec gently, "that my sister, the emperor's chosen heir, is unfit for the office."

"Oh," said Viragus. "Oh, no. Nothing so coarse, let alone so insolent. I was merely reflecting on…realities."

"Ah," said Kerrec. "Realities. Such as that the empire requires a regent when the emperor is away in his wars? And that the war itself, however vital to the empire's interests and indeed survival, is in strict truth a clash of isolated armies on the far edge of the world? And that while we wage this war, the rest of the world needs care, feeding, and administration of its provinces? Those realities? I do happen to agree with my father that his heir is well chosen."

"Chosen?" said the third general, Baruch of the Sixth Gregoria. "What choice did he have? She's all that's left of the line, except a traitor and a—" He broke off.

Kerrec looked him in the eye. "Say it," he said.

Baruch shook his head. He was older than the others, tough and wiry, with a ruined eye and a distinct hitch in his gait. He had won his laurels in the deserts of Gebu.

He had the harshness of the desert about him, and a darkness that Kerrec would investigate when he could. There was a rumor that two of his sons had been found among the barbarian dead.

For now, Kerrec would let that be—but not the rest of it. "A traitorous bastard and a prince who died rather than accept his destiny," he said for Baruch, since he would not. "Did I say it was his choice? The gods chose for him."

"Maybe," said Master Pretorius. "It's always perilous to second-guess divinity. Even Augurs acknowledge that their interpretations can be wrong."

"So," Kerrec said with a distinct chill in his tone. "Is this mutiny? Are you refusing his choice?"

"We are considering the empire's needs," Viragus said. "Women have ruled before, some well, some badly—but in these times, will a woman's touch be enough? She can't credibly lead the legions."

"Are you sure of that?" Kerrec asked. "My sister has been trained to fight. She's studied tactics with the best the empire has to offer."

"My lord," said Master Pretorius, "your loyalty to your sister is admirable. But think. What you did yesterday—and the ease with which you did it—made clear to us how badly we need a true heir of his late majesty."

"No," Kerrec said flatly. "Don't say it. Don't even think it."

"My lord, we must," said Master Pretorius. "Your art, your training, your discipline—no one else has what you have. And he gave you his magic. I see it in you, so strong it nearly blinds me. He meant for you to take the throne."

"He did not," said Kerrec. "The law forbids, and I will not break it—which he well knew."

"The law can be changed," Viragus said.

"Not for me," said Kerrec. He rose. "If you have nothing useful to say, then this meeting is ended. You, Tibullus, are commander here by his will. I trust you will do as he would wish. The rest of you are free to choose. Stay and accept Sophia Briana as your empress—or tender your resignation. Any other choice will constitute high treason."

Viragus's nostrils flared. "My lord! You cannot—"

"I cannot," Kerrec agreed, "but the law can. And will."

He left them sputtering among themselves. He should have stayed and talked them around, but he could not stand it. Their proposition was inevitable, all things considered. It made him ill.

Master Pretorius found him on the horselines, brushing Petra until he shone. Kerrec felt him coming, but he had no desire to be polite. He kept his back turned and his mind on what he was doing.

After a while, Master Pretorius said, "Please accept our apology. We realize that this is difficult and your grief is fresh, but our need is so great and our fears so overwhelming—surely you can forgive us."

"Do not," said Kerrec, "attempt to manipulate me. You want an emperor who is indebted to you, whom you think you can control. Do you know what my art is? Do you understand what it does?"

"I thought I did," said Master Pretorius, "but suppose you enlighten me."

Kerrec turned to face him. Pretorius was at ease, smiling, but his eyes were wary. He was not as confident as he pretended.

"You don't want me as emperor," Kerrec said. "Believe me. If my father was intractable and my sister threatens to be— I would be worse. How much worse, you would do well to reflect."

"You have a poor opinion of yourself, my lord," Master Pretorius said. "The troops can't get enough of you. They love you."

"If they love me, it's because I look like my father," Kerrec said. "And because you won the battle and set them in order and proved that not only can you command armies, you can win their hearts."

"I train horses," Kerrec said. "It's no more complicated than that. It doesn't make me fit to rule an empire."

"With all due respect, my lord," Master Pretorius said, "I don't believe you are qualified to make that judgment."

"And you are?" Kerrec turned back to Petra, bending to pick a stone out of his foot.

"I think you know that I am more than the usual run of mages."

"I made inquiries," Kerrec said. "Your talents were equally coveted by Augurs, Dreamweavers, and Astrologers—so you took mastery in each. You're a prodigy." He moved on to the next foot. "Read the omens, Master Mage. My throne is my stallion's saddle."

"That's a choice you may regret, my lord."

"I think not," said Kerrec.

Fifty-Two

The full work of the embalmers' art needed eighty days, but four days were enough to prepare the emperor's body for its journey home. Valeria spent most of that time keeping Kerrec from throttling the army's commanders. They were after him to push Briana aside and take her place—and no amount of refusal on his part seemed to sway them.

No one was gladder than Kerrec, on the fourth morning, to see the cortège take shape on the field by the river. One legion, the Gregoria, would stay in this place, to turn the camp into a permanent fort and keep watch over the border. The Corinia would ride with them for a while, then turn toward its usual posting in the south of Elladis. The Valeria would escort the emperor to his funeral in Aurelia.

The legion's namesake was more than ready to go. As beautiful as the Lady's magic had made the battlefield, the memory of blood and slaughter was strong.

Valeria had slept for a night and a day and most of another night after the battle, but she had barely closed her eyes since. When she did, she saw horrors. The only relief she had was Kerrec's warm and solid body in her arms and his beautiful new magic all around her. In that, she could rest.

The cortège formed ranks in the grey light of dawn. The legions had built the bier out of shields and legionary cloaks, so that it glittered in bronze and scarlet. The wagon it rode on was newly made of oak, and the coffin was oak and cedar. White oxen drew it. A white canopy protected it from rain and sun— white for mourning. The emperor's banner rode in front of it and the banners of the legions behind.

The Gregoria and its commander saw them off, beating drums and blowing trumpets until they were long out of sight.

There was an honor guard in front of the bier. The rest of the legions marched behind. Kerrec rode beside it, with Valeria just behind him.

They marched or rode in silence. Later the legions would relax into their usual marching songs, but that first morning, the weight of their sorrow was too great. The only sound was the tramping of feet and the rumble of the cart.

Kerrec was shut inside himself, but for once he had not closed Valeria out. His grief washed over her. It felt cleansing somehow, as if she bathed in cool fire.

His heart was mending slowly. He had so many regrets and so much old anger—it would be a long time before he worked through it all. Still, the healing had begun. This long ride in the heavy heat of late summer was teaching him the beginnings of acceptance.

The news had gone ahead of them. Each village and town they passed was hung with white banners. People in white followed the cortège, weeping and singing hymns of sorrow. That for Valeria would be her clearest memory of that long march, voices swelling as they drew nearer to a town, then fading as they made their slow way past.

At night they made camp outside the walls of towns or in open fields beside the road. People came far into the night to pay their respects, or appeared in the early morning, pausing by the bier and offering a prayer or a candle or a garland of flowers. After the cortège left each camp, candles and flowers remained as a remembrance.

The nightmares did not stop simply because Valeria had left the battlefield. The first night, while Kerrec kept vigil by the bier, she dared to sleep—and woke shuddering.

She tried to stop, but the harder she tried, the worse it was. She sat up, groping for the jar of water by the cot. Her hands shook so much she could barely lift the jar to her lips.

The water was cool and sweet. It steadied her a little. As she lowered the jar, the tent's flap opened. Kerrec slipped through.

She almost burst into tears. She thought she caught herself in time—but his face changed.

She did not see him move. One moment he was at the flap. The next, he knelt beside her cot.

Half of her wanted to drive him off with harsh words—lashing out at him for her own weakness. The other half pulled his head down and kissed him, then froze, waiting for him to drive her off.

He did no such thing. He returned the kiss so freely and with such eager passion that she caught her breath. That made her hiccup, which made her laugh, which set him back on his heels, affronted. And that made her laugh even harder.

He scowled, but his lips were twitching. It was not true he had no humor—he only wanted people to think so. She abandoned the cot, which was too narrow in any case, and bore him backward on the worn carpet.

This time the kiss did not veer off into silliness. It went on for a long, delicious while. Somehow or another, their shirts got lost, and then their breeches.

Valeria's body was afire, and yet she was in no hurry. She wanted every moment to last as long as it possibly could. His hands on her skin, the taste of his lips, were blissfully sweet.

She tangled fingers in his hair, then ran them down his back past the familiar knots and interruptions of scars. He shivered lightly under her touch. The world's patterns took new shape around and within them. Where they had been two fiercely, sometimes painfully separate beings, now they were flowing into one.

It had been a long while since they had done that. There were dark places, thoughts and secrets that they would not share, but it did not matter.

She lifted herself above him. His eyes were dark in the lamplight, thinly rimmed with silver. "I missed you," he said.

"Whose fault is that?" But she did not say it with anger. She dipped down for another kiss. "Never shut yourself away from me again. Promise."

"By my heart," he said.

He was smiling. That was so rare she almost did not recognize him. He looked years younger with all the stern lines gone.

There was such sweetness in his smile that it made her heart melt. "Gods, I love you," she said. "I don't know why. I can't help it."

"Some things are beyond reason," he said.

She kissed him again, and then again. Reason had nothing to do with it. It was not his pretty face, either, though that was a distinct advantage. It was everything about him.

She took him inside her, just as he rose to take her. The dart of pleasure was so strong it was almost pain. She cried out softly.

He paused, alarmed. She locked ankles around his hips and held him tight, driving him deeper. He gasped in shock and piercing pleasure.

Kerrec kissed her awake. His face was somber as usual, but his eyes were smiling. As she sat up blinking, he set a steaming cup in her hand. The scent of herbs wafted from it.

He was dressed, all but his boots. He sat cross-legged on the floor beside her and set a laden tray between them. There was more tea and bread and early apples and sharp cheese. "Hardly elegant," he said, "but it's filling."

"It's perfect," said Valeria. "You're perfect."

It was hard to tell in the dimness of the tent, but she thought she saw a flush on his cheeks. "Not as perfect as you," he said.

She grinned. "Well, no. But you'll do."

He startled her by grinning back. He saluted her with his cup, and bowed as princes did. His happiness bubbled over.

There was sorrow in it for his father and for his brother who was still alive somewhere beyond the river. Those in his mind were failures, and he would not easily or quickly forgive himself for them. But as long as he was with her, he could let the dark things fade from his mind.

By the time they were done with breakfast, ranks were forming outside and the legions were preparing to march. Kerrec went out while Valeria dressed. When she emerged into the early-morning mist, he was saddling Petra. He wore the same face as always, but as she passed him on her way to Sabata, he warmed her with a smile.

During the day, nothing was different. At night, everything was. Valeria felt as if her heart had been buried deep in cold earth, but now it had sprouted and bloomed.

She felt a pang of guilt that she was so happy and this was the emperor's funeral march. She still grieved for him. He had ruled well, as far as she was qualified to judge. She had liked him—loved him, maybe, as so many of his people did.

It occurred to her that he would not mind. He had struck her as a man who knew how to love. Maybe he would even approve of the lover his son had chosen.

On the fourth day of the slow march, Baruch took the Corinia off to the south. The Valeria stayed to escort the emperor home.

Baruch made a point of saying goodbye to Kerrec. "Sir," he said, "you may want to forget what you are, but the blood remembers. If you need me, send a message. I'll come."

Kerrec thanked him, but Valeria could tell he had no intention of securing himself a legion. Baruch left, riding at the head of his troops. They were chanting a death chant of the desert, a slow rolling dirge shot through with sudden, piercing cries of grief.

It was a deeply disturbing song. The memory of it stayed with Valeria for hours after.

Later that day, she rode up beside Tibullus. He was riding with the honor guard, mounted on a sturdy brown cob. He greeted Valeria with an inclination of the head. "Rider," he said.

"General," she said in return. "I have a favor to ask of you."

"Ask," he said. "I'll grant it if I can."

"I hope so," she said. "You remember my brother who rode with us across the river. He had to break the emperor's ban to do it."

Tibullus's face darkened. "Yes. I remember."

"He died," Valeria said, "in the battle." That was harder to say than she had thought it would be. "What happened to the field, happened because of him. He rode in the Dance. He was the rider on the Lady, the bay mare. Without him, we would have lost the battle."

"So I've been told," Tibullus said.

Valeria raised her brows. "Then you'll agree that he's suffered the utmost penalty for his desertion?"

"He sacrificed his life for the legions," Tibullus said.

"Then," said Valeria, "he's not dishonored, is he? His name won't be struck from the rolls. He's honored dead."

"He is honored dead," Tibullus said. His face softened ever so slightly. "Yes, rider, we'll send his shield home."

"That's what I was going to ask, sir," Valeria said. "Can I be the one who takes it?"

Tibullus's brows went up. "That's not traditional."

"I know," said Valeria. "It's just that he died because of me. I was there and I couldn't stop it. I have to be the one who tells our mother what happened. It can't be anyone else."

Tibullus studied her for some time before he said, "It's a worthy honor for his shield to go home with one of the white gods' servants—especially since he died one of them."

"He wasn't a horse mage," Valeria said. "That's why he could do what he did. His magic was earth magic—mortal magic."

"I'm sure," said Tibullus, "there are niceties of the magical arts that I'm not aware of. He was serving the gods when he died. The least they can do is send his shield home with one of their own."

His eyes warned her not to argue any further. She had what she wanted—what she dreaded, but she had told him the truth. She had thought long and hard, in between the nightmares, and there was no choice. She had to do it.

Fifty-Three

From the battlefield at Oxos Ford to the gates of Aurelia was forty days at the pace of eight white oxen. They marched from summer into autumn, from the season of sudden, explosive storms to golden days and nights that hinted ever so subtly of winter's cold.

As the days went on, Kerrec began teaching Valeria her lessons again. He had all the books in his head, and all the patterns back again, every one. He recited each lesson, then asked her to recite it after him, teaching her the art of memory. In a way he was learning it all over again for himself, bringing it to the front of his mind and making it more solidly a part of him.

She was a quick study, but he had always known that. What he had not expected was to find his own power and knowledge growing as he taught her the arts and skills that would, once she passed the testing, make her a Fourth Rider.

That was his father's magic putting down roots and spreading branches through his mind and body. It was intricately ordered and breathtakingly strong. Now that it had finished healing him, it was transforming him in ways that he could not yet fully understand.

He supposed he should have been afraid. But there was no more danger in what was happening to him than there ever was with magic of that level and intensity. That was a great deal—but it was danger he understood.

No doubt he was being arrogant. Arrogance was his besetting flaw. And yet when he felt the magic growing in him, he felt a kind of singing excitement. He wanted it. He had no desire to refuse it.

Artorius had known his son better than Kerrec knew himself. Maybe it was part of the magic that Kerrec did not hate him for it.

Another part of the magic made him deeply happy. The reticence that had been such a curse was not exactly gone, but it was much diminished. With Valeria it was almost not there at all.

The night before they came to Aurelia, the crowds of mourners went by in slow procession all night long. From the tent Kerrec could hear their passing, the slow shuffle of feet and the catch of a sob.

Valeria had fallen asleep. Her face in the lamplight was still faintly flushed from loving, her hair tousled, lying in curls across her forehead. He stroked it softly back from her cheek and brushed her lips with a kiss. She smiled in her sleep.

He dressed quickly and slipped out into the chill of midnight. Torches flared around the bier. The line of people was not quite as long as it had been in daylight. He joined it quietly.

No one recognized him. It was dark and he was plainly dressed. He looked ordinary enough—no blazing mark of imperial blood on his forehead, and no white stallion to betray his rank and art. Petra was safely and contentedly asleep on the horselines.

Something had been happening as he drew closer to Aurelia. It was so gradual that at first he did not even notice it. In the past few days however, he had begun to realize that his senses were changing.

He could feel the land. It had always been there in the back of his awareness, part of the gifts that came to him from his blood and breeding, but this was stronger. It was like the sense of patterns that made a horse mage, deepened and strengthened until it sang in his bones.

Standing here in this slow procession of his own people, almost within sight of the imperial city, he felt as if the whole of the empire was contained in his body. From the far south of Gebu to the far north of Toscana, from Eriu to Parthai, it was all there inside him. He could tell where it was thriving and where it was ill—though not quite yet how or why.

"Sir, are you sick? Do you need to sit down?"

Kerrec blinked and shook his head to clear it. Somehow he had come as far as the torches. A woman was standing in front of him, with a much younger man behind her—her son, he supposed. She had a broad weathered face and a knot of greying hair, and she stood foursquare on solid feet. Her eyes were shrewd but kind. She had magic, not a great deal but enough to dazzle his newly altered sight.

She would have been a Beastmaster, he realized, if she had gone into any of the orders. She petted him as if he had been one of her animals, and offered him a flask that turned out to be full of deceptively innocuous cordial. The first sip was sweet and pungent with herbs. The second set him back on his heels.

His benefactor grinned. "Wakes you up proper, doesn't it?"

"Very proper," said Kerrec once he remembered how to breathe. "I may actually live to see the morning."

"Good," the woman said. She tilted her head toward the bier. "It gets you in the heart, that. Even if you never knew him to talk to, he was there, being good at what he did."

People behind them nodded and murmured. One said, "The young one, the heir, is just like him, they say."

"I've seen her riding out," said someone else. "She's a little thing, and a beauty, but there's steel in her. She rides as well as a man."

Kerrec held his breath, but no one mentioned the late heir who was a rider. They were all focused on Briana and on the emperor who lay under the pall. Kerrec was almost in front of the bier now.

He had been riding beside it for well over a month. He had kept vigil over it for part of almost every night. Tonight was different. All these people who had never known the emperor and yet loved him, and the sense of the land inside Kerrec, came together into a pattern he had not seen before.

This was Aurelia—not courts and princes or legions or gods on the Mountain. These people coming from far away, most of them on foot, to pay their respects, were the heart of the empire. They tilled its fields and tended its cattle and marched in its legions. Aurelia was a living thing because of them.

Kerrec had always set himself above them. Even as a rider-envoy, mingling with the common people, he had kept his distance. He was not one of them. His world was altogether different.

Tonight he was part of them and they were part of him. They shared his sorrow. They looked after one another, as the woman had done with him.

It was a new world. He was not sure that he was comfortable in it, but neither could he turn his back on it.

The bier was in front of him. The white pall glowed faintly—dawn was coming. He laid his hand on it.

There was no life or spirit inside it. That had gone long since. Still, there was memory, and the magic unfolding inside of Kerrec. He bowed to that and gave it a tribute of tears.

After the last of them passed by the bier, they dispersed in ones and twos and fours. Kerrec slipped aside and watched them in the slowly swelling daylight. He wanted to remember their faces. Then when he thought of Aurelia, he would remember them and this night and the way the land had come alive inside him.

Fifty-Four

The city of Aurelia was waiting for its emperor to pass for the last time through its gates. All of its walls were hung with white. Its people were dressed in white and carrying sprays of white flowers, strewing petals on the processional way as the honor guard and then the bier entered the city.

The legion would not come into Aurelia. That was a very old tradition from the days when emperors were made and broken by the legions, and any adventurer with a mob of rebels could call himself a general and storm the imperial city. Now as in those days, the Valeria withdrew to the old barracks and parade grounds that lay eastward along the shore.

The dead did not enter the city walls, either, except royal dead. Everyone who died in the city or in the barracks was buried in the city of tombs beyond the legionary camp. But the emperor would lie in the crypt of the palace, in the royal chamber directly beneath the hall of the throne.

Every living emperor or empress ruled above the bodies of his forefathers. That was the custom. There was power in it, binding whatever magic the living ruler had to the combined magic of the dead.

Kerrec had been taught this while he was still his father's heir. It struck him vividly as he rode beside the bier into the city he had declined to rule. If it had not been for the stallions and Valeria, he might have broken and run, fleeing toward the Mountain.

They kept him where he was, part of his father's honor guard. It was by no means traditional for the emperor to go to his burial with white gods and their riders in attendance, but it seemed fitting.

Briana, by tradition, could not meet the bier at the city gate or beyond. She had to wait at the palace gate, dressed from head to toe in white silk, with her own guard and the loftier notables of the court around her.

Kerrec saw her down the length of the processional way. She seemed very small, standing erect and still under the great arch of the gate. He could not make out her face from so far away, but he could feel her in his heart. Grief for her father, fear of what she had taken on herself, determination not to let it overwhelm her—all of those mingled inside him, matching his own emotions almost exactly.

If he had had a fraction less discipline, he would have bolted past the crawling oxen, burst through the honor guard and galloped toward his sister. She could see him as he saw her, in his simple rider's uniform on his shimmering white horse. Her relief and gladness almost broke his resolve.

This was the last imperial ceremony that would be celebrated in Artorius's name. Out of respect for him, they had to let the rite unfold in its proper order. If that meant standing painfully alone in a flock of courtiers or riding at a maddeningly slow pace from the gate to the palace, then that was the way it had to be.

Step by crawling step, the bier made its way toward the palace. The crowds that lined the road were silent. There was no music and no singing. The cart rumbled and creaked. The oxen snorted, grinding flowers under their hooves. The scent of bruised roses and jasmine was almost overwhelming.

Kerrec held his breath as much as he could. Petra shook his head and sneezed. Kerrec stroked his neck in sympathy.

It only seemed that this march would take forever. It would be over soon. There was still the funeral to endure, but that would not take place until tomorrow. Tonight, Petra at least could rest.

Petra snorted wetly and coiled his back, dancing for a moment—enthralling the part of the crowd directly in front of him—before he settled again to his scrupulously disciplined, meticulously cadenced, teeth-grindingly slow walk.

At the palace gate, Briana's attendants parted for the honor guard and the bier, then fell in behind. Briana was on the other side as Kerrec rode past. He glimpsed her face over the bier, but her eyes were not on him.

The oxen hauled the emperor's bier straight up to the great hall. Then the honor guard lifted it out of the wagon in which it had traveled for so long and carried it through the golden doors.

The oxen were led away to a well-deserved rest. Petra and Sabata went in with the bier. Their riders' choice had little to do with it. Once it was laid in the center of the hall where it would remain for the night, they took station on either side of it.

Mages were waiting to build wards, and priests were ready

to begin the long rite of the emperor's burial. The stallions disconcerted them severely.

Kerrec dismounted, with Valeria half a breath behind. This was not their vigil. They unsaddled and unbridled their stallions quickly, rubbed them down—to the scowling disapproval of not a few watchers—and retreated in as good order as they could.

"Carry on," Briana said when the shocked stillness continued. Her voice was quiet but clear.

The Chief Augur started as if he had suddenly come awake. He raised his staff. The Master Cantor recovered his wits and drew breath to begin the chant. The priests remembered themselves and their places.

Kerrec might have continued his retreat until he was completely gone from the hall, but he found he could not do it. He put saddle and bridle in Valeria's charge and sent her off to Riders' Hall—glaring down her objections.

Luckily she was in as biddable a mood as she was capable of. She did as she was told. She would come back, he knew, but not for a while.

The first rite, the rite of welcoming the dead to his hall for the last time, was a mere hour long. It required the heir to play acolyte to the chief priest of Sun and Moon. Any other living imperial offspring was expected to wait on the mages. As First Rider, Kerrec should have been accepting their service instead of giving them his, but in this rite he was no more or less than his father's son.

There was comfort in ritual. When he had to share duties with Briana, they moved together as smoothly as in a dance. She offered him the flicker of a smile, which he returned.

The mages raised their wards and the priests welcomed the dead. Then the layfolk were free to go, except for the first watch of the emperor's guards. The night's vigil was a matter for magic and the gods.

Earth must be placated and the powers of air comforted. For three and thirty years Artorius's power had lain over his empire. Now it was gone, leaving a void that hostile powers would be eager to fill.

"It's only ritual," Briana said in the sanctuary of her library. She had retreated there from the hall, dismissed guards and servants, and ordered a light supper for herself and her brother.

She dropped to the low and much-worn couch that lay under the eastward window. Daylight was fading, the clouds turning crimson. She lay back and sighed so deeply her body shook. "You settled it all at Oxos, didn't you? There's no gap in the patterns. All our magic is whole and safe."

"I'm sorry," Kerrec said. "We weren't thinking about protocol at the time."

She shot him a glance. "Why are you apologizing? You did a magnificent thing. Sit, eat. I'll be up in a moment."

Kerrec was not hungry, either. He went to stand over her, hooked a stool with his foot and pulled it to him and sat on it. "He gave me his magic. I couldn't stop him. I know it was supposed to go to you. I—"

"I have it," she said. He stared at her. She nodded. "The land, the empire—I had them before he left. It goes with the regent's office. The powers were given for use but not to keep. When he died, they changed. All the gates opened and the wards went down. That was how I knew, long before the message came, that he was dead."

Kerrec studied her for a careful moment. "You're telling the truth. Then how—what—"

"What happened to you? I don't know. Maybe the mages do."

"I think mages are long past making any sense of me," Kerrec said dryly.

"Maybe so." She sat up and leaned forward, hugging him hard. Then she held him at arm's length, looking him up and down. "You look wonderful. I've never seen you this well or this comfortable with yourself. You look—you look like Father."

"I am not growing a beard!"

She laughed much harder than his poor display of wit warranted. When she finally stopped, she sat grinning at him, with tears drying on her cheeks. "Oh, my dear, I needed that so badly. I needed you. Would you believe I'm scared? I'm terrified. What if I'm not good enough for all of this? What if I can't do it?"

"You'll do it because you have to," Kerrec said. "He said as much, you know. 'She'll do no worse than I did,' he said."

She laughed, a sound half like a sob. "I don't suppose you'd take my place?"

"Not in this life," he said. "Don't try to coax me, either. I've had enough of that already."

The laughter left her face. "I suppose you would have," she said. "Did they lean on you very hard?"

"Not so much hard as persistent," Kerrec said. "What is it with men that they would rather bow to anything male, however unwilling and unsuitable, than to a woman?"

"I don't know," she said. "I'm not a man."

"I am, and I still can't understand."

"That's because you're a prodigy of nature—a male with the capacity for reason. In a way I wish you had given in."

"I don't," he said. "I have gifts enough and magic beyond the usual, but I was never meant to rule this empire. To help, yes, and protect it with my life and soul. I'm a rider, that's what I was born for. I'll never be an emperor."

She took his hands, drawing him up and toward the table with its trays and jars and covered bowls. "Do you know how much alike we are? I have the calling to be a rider, but I belong to the empire first and always. You would have been a very good emperor, but the Mountain keeps you. I think we're meant to be in this together."

"I believe we are," he said as she sat him down and took the chair opposite. "I only wish everyone else could see."

"They will," Briana said. "Some may need years and the gates of death to come to it, but they will."

Fifty-Five

Valeria would have carried both saddles and bridles out of the hall herself, but a pair of servants insisted on doing it for her. She did not resist too strenuously. It was a fair trudge to Riders' Hall.

She had not known what to expect when she came there. Dust and cobwebs would not have surprised her, but she had underestimated the servants whom Briana had given to Kerrec. They were not only still in residence, the house was spotless and the rooms were ready for guests. Savory smells wafted from the kitchen.

Smells of a different and to Valeria equally pleasant kind emanated from the stable. Briana's mares were still there. So was Quintus. From the evidence, the boys were still coming for instruction—the saddles were clean but with the look of regular use, and the mares were glossy and muscled, with the soft eyes of horses who were worked well and often.

There was another reason for that softness, too. Every one of them was in foal.

Petra's innocence was genuine, glowing in Valeria's heart. Sabata tried to pretend, but he was a terrible liar—and terribly smug. Foolish humans had never guessed what he did at night when each mare was in season.

Valeria suspected that Briana had hoped for just such an outcome. If Sabata had been in the stable and not playing statue in the emperor's hall, Valeria would have kicked him. As it was, she let him know just how presumptuous he had been. He barely wilted under her disapproval.

"Men," she said in disgust. The mare she had been examining agreed heartily, with flattened ears and restless heels.

One more blow to tradition, Valeria thought. The white gods did not breed outside of their own kind.

Clearly Sabata did not care for such niceties. These were mares, and beautiful. He had only done what any sensible stallion would do.

"What does sense have to do with it?" Valeria wanted to know. She fed the mare a bit of honey sweet and left her to eat her dinner in peace.

Valeria's own dinner was waiting in the small dining room she had sometimes shared with Kerrec before they both ran off to end a war. She thought she would eat and then go back to the palace, but by the time she had worked her way through a bowl of soup brimming with bits of fish and strange delectable things in shells, she decided not to go. Briana needed her brother tonight.

Valeria ate a little too heartily. The soup was like nothing she had tasted before. There was fresh white bread with it, and the soft herbed cheese that she was inordinately fond of, and a tart of almonds and cream and eggs and sweet spices that needed two servings to do it justice.

She went to bed alone in the room she had slept in before. Her stomach was unpleasantly full. She had been eating soldier's rations too long—she was out of practice.

Her sleep was fitful, her dreams dim and formless. She was aware of the stallions on guard and Kerrec keeping vigil with his sister beside their father's bier. Sometimes when she woke, she felt him beside her, but that was a dream. That night he belonged to his family.

Morning came early, with bells tolling from all the temples. Valeria sprang out of her first deep sleep of the night, stumbled to the privy, and lost most of her overly ambitious supper.

Once she was rid of it, she began to feel better. She could not look at breakfast without feeling her stomach heave all over again, but a little herb tea with honey went down and stayed down.

By the time she was bathed and dressed, she was almost herself again. The clothes she was wearing were new, a rider-candidate's uniform in white. It fit well, though the coat was a whisper tight across the chest.

She went back alone to the palace, eluding any servants who might have tried to escort her. The solitude of the riders' passage was welcome. Wards protected it from magical attacks and shielded anyone inside it from awareness of the world.

She could be tempted to stay there, but the emperor's burial rite would not wait for her. She quickened her pace.

The great hall was full, with people spilling out of the doors and gates and into corridors and courtyards. There was a space around the bier, with the stallions guarding it. The Lady stood with them, her deep red coat drinking the early sunlight.

Briana and Kerrec stood in the space the gods had cleared. The priests of Sun and Moon surrounded them, all in white vestments. Mages stood to the north and east and south and west.

Valeria recognized the Chief Augur and the Master of Stones. One of the others must be the Master Cantor in black and crimson, startling amid so much white, and the last would be the Mistress of the Sea Magic in a gown that shimmered like water. Valeria could have sworn she saw schools of tiny silver fish swimming in it.

The door through which Valeria had entered was hidden in the wall. She would have stayed near it, but Sabata's summons brought her across the hall. It reshaped patterns so that each moment as she made her way through the crowd, a space opened, then closed behind her.

She would have liked to study that, to see how he did it, but they both had too much else to think about. Just as she slipped around the bier and into Sabata's shadow, the burial rite began.

The Cantor invoked the powers of air and darkness and the wings of the storm. The Sea Witch sang of water springing from the earth and falling from the sky and roaring in the sea. In a voice like boulders shifting, the stone mage woke the strength of earth. Last of all, the Augur called on the sun's fire and the moon's cold light.

The priests took up the chant from the Augur. Its slow rolling cadences crept under Valeria's skin. She rested her hand on Sabata's neck to steady herself.

He curved his head around to blow sweet breath in her face. She rested her cheek against his for a moment before he straightened into immobility again.

The hymns the priests sang were older than the empire. They called on elder gods than Sun and Moon and the gods of the Mountain—gods of the elements and powers of earth and rulers of the deep places. They were only remembered in the rite of burial, when they were invoked to receive and cherish the dead.

Valeria's mind followed the intricate weaving of voices in the chant, tracing the pattern that took shape there. It was a strange pattern, no little bit disturbing. Something in it made her hackles rise.

She glanced around her. No one else seemed troubled. Neither Briana, whom she could see standing with the Lady at the head of the bier, nor Kerrec, who was on the other side but who was also in Valeria's heart, showed any sign of alarm. The stallions and the Lady were quiet.

It must be an aftershock of the battle and her nightmares since. She forced her breathing to slow and her heart to stop pounding. She would not have said she was exactly calm, but she was less unsettled than she had been.

Mercifully, the chant ended soon after. The Master of Stones stepped forward. He had a ring on his finger with a stone like an ember, and a rod in his hand, tipped with another fiery stone.

He bowed to the bier and paused. Valeria felt the gathering of power from below. The Master's stones caught fire.

He lowered the rod until it touched the paving in front of the bier. For a long count of breaths, nothing happened. Then, so slowly at first it was imperceptible, the floor opened.

Valeria had expected the breath of cold stone and the smell of tombs. That rose up out of the opening, to be sure, but there was also the heated-metal scent of magic wielded strongly and often.

The tombs of the emperors were warded as strongly as anything she had seen. Even the Mountain's defenses were no stronger than this. But for Sabata, she would have fallen, struck down by the power of it.

She wondered what was down there that needed such protections. Emperors were mages more often than not, and some had wielded powers that rivaled the Unmaking. But they were all dead long since.

Or were they?

It was odd how much that shook her world. She had seen more of the imperial family than she would ever have believed possible, and gods knew she had studied their history and lore. But this was out of her reckoning.

While she dithered inside herself, the honor guard had come forward to take up the bier. Steps descended directly in front of it, down into darkness lit by a cold light. It was fitting illumination for the journey of the dead.

Sorrow pierced Valeria so suddenly that she gasped. Artorius had been a warm man. He loved plain daylight and the taste of good wine and the sound of laughter. It seemed peculiarly horrible that he should be laid in so chill a place.

The bier began its descent. Briana and Kerrec walked slowly behind it. The mages and priests followed.

Valeria would have loved to run away into the sunlight, but she could not bear to lose her lover or her friend to the darkness. She gathered every scrap of courage and forced herself to go after them.

The Lady and the stallions stayed in the hall. Oddly, that comforted Valeria. They were on guard as they had been since the bier came into the palace. Between them and the massive structure of wards, whatever was imprisoned below could not break loose.

After so much dread and creeping terror, the reality was rather disappointing. A long, wide stair descended into a vaulted hall. Tombs lay along the curve of its walls and had begun to work their way inward to the center in rays like the sun on the emperor's banner. Some were starkly plain, with nothing on them but a carved name, whereas others were elaborate works of art crowned with effigies of the deceased. Those effigies were often painted in the colors of life, so that there seemed to be a small crowd of men and women in antique dress standing in a circle, watching the arrival of their latest descendant.

Artorius's tomb had been built for him through the years of his reign. It was neither as stark as the simplest nor by any means as elaborate as some of the tombs from three and four hundred years ago. It was made of alabaster, moon-pale and translucent. Images were carved on it in bas-relief, a legion marching toward a fort and a river, a troupe of dancers at a banquet, a company of nobles on a hunt.

Its lid was ornamented with the beginning of the Dance, the entry of the stallions into the hall. Sun and Moon shone above them. A forest of woven trees lay below, with patterns in their weaving that Valeria committed to memory. Later she would try to understand them.

Mages opened the tomb with a Word and a working. Priests blessed it and sweetened it with incense. The honor guard laid down the bier and uncovered the coffin. It was made of oak and cedarwood lined with lead, its lid brushed with gilt to honor the royalty within.

When the guards lifted it from the bier, Kerrec was there with Briana to lend a hand. They helped raise it over the tomb and then lower it carefully.

Valeria held her breath. No one's fingers slipped. The coffin made no move to escape the hands that held it. It slid down smoothly into the tomb.

There was a pause. Briana rested a hand on the coffin's lid, near where the heart would be. Kerrec's hand covered hers. They stood for a moment, then drew back.

Slowly the lid came down over the tomb. The priests sang a hymn of rest and farewell. Their voices were soft in the deepening gloom. The cold light was fading little by little.

Just before it sank into dark, torches leaped to life. The priests had brought and lit them. Their light was smoky and unsteady and not particularly bright, but it had a mortal warmth that the other had altogether lacked.

Briana bowed low to her father's tomb. "Good night," she said. "Sleep well. May the gods grant you peace."

Fifty-Six

The floor of the hall was closed again. The dead were warded below. The priests blessed the now hidden gate and cleansed the hall with chanting and incense.

Then the air was clean again. The emperor was dead. The empress would not be crowned until winter had passed and spring had come with its brighter omens, but the power was hers—as it had been from the moment her father died.

Briana had to sit through the whole of the funeral feast, with its twenty-four courses and intricate entertainments and endless memorials to the late emperor. Kerrec lingered only through the fourth course, when he could honorably plead indisposition and make his retreat.

Valeria might have stayed longer because the patterns forming in the court were so fascinating, but Kerrec was a stronger lure. She had missed him badly last night. Even if he only wanted to sleep, he would be there with her.

* * *

He wanted to do more than sleep. He startled her, and maybe himself, with how much he wanted it. In saying farewell to the dead, he had reminded himself that he was alive—and nothing spoke more strongly of life than this.

Valeria's mind emptied of thought. The world was pure pleasure. When she swam out of it with her body singing, he was lying beside her, propped on his elbow, smiling.

She smiled back and ran her fingers down his cheek. "Pretty," she said.

He hated when she did that, but tonight he only frowned a little and brushed his own fingers across her lips. "Beautiful," he said.

"You're still prettier." She wound her fingers in his. "Will we be going home soon?"

"I think so," he said.

"You won't stay? The boys are still coming to ride. They're keeping the school going."

"So I heard," he said. "I suppose you know the other thing, too."

"Sabata and the mares." She sighed. "He's horribly smug."

"So is my sister," said Kerrec. "She's getting half a dozen prodigies of nature."

"She's devious," Valeria said admiringly. But she had not forgotten what else they had been talking about. "So? Are you staying to carry on with your school?"

"I do intend to carry on," he said, "but first I have to go back to the Mountain. If it will accept me—if it doesn't try to break me again."

"That wasn't the Mountain," said Valeria. "You know that. You're whole again. I've never seen you stronger."

"I feel strong," he admitted. "I'm ready for the test. But I should warn you—"

"Nothing is going to happen to you," she said.

"I'm thinking of you," he said. "You realize you could be expelled for what you did. If you want to stay here—at least until the furor dies down—I'll understand."

"I have to go," she said. "If there's a punishment to face, I'll face it."

"Even if you're expelled?"

"Even then," she said steadily. It was hard, but she was telling the truth. She could choose to stay here and teach the boys until Kerrec came back—but she could not do that. If she had been a nobleman instead of a farmer's daughter, she would have said it was a matter of honor.

Kerrec nodded. He could follow her thoughts if he was minded, and these were no secret. "I would do the same. I promise, whatever happens, I'll stand by you. It was my fault you left at all."

"We'll let the other riders lay the blame," she said with a touch of dark humor. Then she paused. After a while she said, "There's something else."

He raised a brow.

"There's somewhere I have to go on the way home. If you want to stay longer here, or ride ahead, I won't mind."

"Imbria?" he asked.

She blinked. "How did you— Who told you? Have you been talking to General Tibullus?"

"I know what's done when a soldier dies honorably," Kerrec said, "and I know you. You wouldn't let a stranger do it. I'm not going to ask if you think you're up to it. I know what you'll answer. But I will ask this. Will you take me with you?"

"Why would you want to do that?"

"Because it's not something you should have to face alone. Even if I camp outside the village and pretend we have nothing to do with each other, I should be there."

Valeria drew a breath. She wanted him with her—desperately. But that same desperation made her mistrust her judgment. "You don't get to hide," she said. "If you go, you go beside me. I won't lie, either, about what we are to each other. My mother may not be merciful."

"All the more reason for me to stand at your back."

Valeria smiled crookedly. "Well, then," she said, "we'll face our demons together. Though if you're not sure—if you would rather not go—"

"You followed me to the ends of the earth," Kerrec said. "Should I do less for you?"

"Just remember," she said. "Once you're committed, you're bound. You don't get to back off when you meet my mother."

"I'm sure your mother is perfectly charming."

Valeria gaped, then burst out laughing. "If a she-bear in the spring is charming, then that's my mother."

"Surely she's not as bad as that."

"You'll see," Valeria said darkly.

The funeral feast and the festival of the emperor's passing lasted eight days. The first day had been the burial. The following seven saw a new feast each day in the city as well as the palace, for the people to share.

The festival ran in and around the feasting. There were games and dances and sacred dramas, but no Dance. Artorius's future was ended. There was nothing to foresee.

On the eighth night, Briana dined privately with her brother and his rider-candidate. She should properly have been concluding the days of feasting in hall with the court, but she had made a brief appearance there and then withdrawn.

"There is a slight advantage in being empress," she said. "If I decide to break protocol, no one can stop me."

"No one but the whole empire," Kerrec said, pouring wine for them all.

"The empire isn't here tonight," said Briana. "You're sure, then? You're leaving in the morning?"

"It's time," Valeria said.

Briana nodded. "You know that if the worst happens, you have a place here. Both of you. We'll found a new school if we have to."

"I don't think we will have to," Kerrec said. "We've both committed serious offenses against order and tradition, but the school can't afford to lose us—especially now. The war between legions and warbands might be over, but the Dances have made it clear. Something else is coming, and the Mountain will be part of it. For that, the school will need every scrap of power it can find. Whatever penalty we have to pay, it won't be as dire as expulsion. We'll still be riders."

"For your sake I hope so," Briana said. She raised her cup. "Travel safe, prosper well, come back as soon as you may."

They bowed to the blessing and then drank to it, murmuring thanks.

Briana shook her head. "You deserve more. No one knows or understands what you've done. I wish—"

"It's better this way," Kerrec said. "Mages know what we do, and there are stories enough in the markets. People understand well enough that we have power to protect the empire. They don't need to know exactly what we've done or how."

"Thank the gods for that," Valeria said. "None of us could stand being followed everywhere we go, or having songs sung about us. When we ride the Dance, we should be invisible. Watchers should only see the stallions."

"As a target born and bred, I envy you," Briana said. "Still, it seems less than fair that you should have saved Aurelia twice, and no one knows your name."

"Maybe there should be fewer mysteries about us," said Kerrec, "but some things are better left alone. We aren't in it for the glory."

"You are all very frustrating," Briana said.

Valeria laughed. Kerrec frowned, but his lips were twitching. "That's our greatest gift," he said.

"I'm going to miss you," she said.

"I'll be back by spring—the Master permitting. I'll hope to ride the Coronation Dance. Then, if I'm given leave, I'll continue what I've started. There should be another school besides the one on the Mountain—a real one, with real magic and real stallions."

"Yes," Briana said. "And maybe, if it does well here, we can open others elsewhere. Instead of a single beating heart, the empire will have strong and capable branches all through its provinces."

"Some will argue that the more diffuse a power is, the weaker it becomes," Kerrec said.

"We'll deal with that as it comes," said Briana. "Drink up now, and eat. We have a long night ahead of us. There's so much you haven't told me—all your adventures, and the battle, and the long ride here. How *did* you win the battle? I heard it was a Dance, but it couldn't have been anything like the ones we've seen here or on the Mountain."

"It was a Dance," Kerrec said. "Two stallions and a Lady, two horse mages and a wisewoman's son. There was never a Dance like it."

Valeria sat back while Kerrec told the story, sipping wine and nibbling bits of dinner. Her stomach was still intermittently unsettled. It seemed to be behaving itself tonight, though she would not be surprised if she regretted it again in the morning.

Kerrec's voice soothed her into a drowse. Now and then it paused, then Briana asked a question or told a story of her own. Their ease together, the comfort of blood kin, reminded Valeria of how she had been with Rodry.

She was far enough along in her dream that the pain was blunted, but it was still so sharp she caught her breath.

Neither of them seemed to notice. She slid deeper into sleep. As long as Kerrec was here, there were no nightmares that she remembered. She smiled and rested her head on her folded arms, falling the rest of the way into soft darkness.

Valeria was sound asleep. Kerrec paused in answering another of his sister's questions. "Do you think—"

Briana beckoned to one of the servants who stood discreetly by the wall. The man bowed and lifted Valeria in his arms, carrying her to the next room, where there was a bed and servants to see to her comfort.

"She's worn out," Briana said. "Have you been working her too hard?"

Kerrec flushed. It was not work that left them both so short of sleep, but he was not about to tell his sister that.

Briana paid no attention to his silence. "She's terribly young. She's so strong and can do so much—we all forget. But she's hardly more than a child."

"She and her stallion." Kerrec shook his head. "We need her so badly and use her so ruthlessly—we'd never do such a thing to one of the horses. I'm as guilty as any. But have you ever tried to stop her from doing something she felt obligated to do?"

"The stallions can."

"They're even more ruthless than the rest of us. Whatever they're trying to do, she's a key to it—and every door it opens is more disconcerting than the one before."

"Poor tormented rider," Briana said with no perceptible sign of sympathy. "At least you value her. The others will learn in the end, I suppose. If they turn out to be difficult, send her back here. We can use her—and protect her, too."

"She belongs with me," Kerrec said gently. "If she comes back, I come with her."

"You would be more than welcome."

Kerrec frowned into the wine he had barely touched. "Half of me wants to stay. There's so much to do, and the center of it all is here. But the Mountain is calling us back. It sent us out to do what was needed. Now it needs us close again."

"Your heart needs to heal," Briana said. "The Mountain can do that, now your body and your magic are whole."

He nodded. Rather unexpectedly, he smiled. "Have I ever told you how fortunate I am to be your brother?"

"Never," she said.

He leaned across the table and kissed her on the forehead. "Don't take undue advantage of it."

"But of course I will." She grinned at him. It was a very comfortable moment amid so many uncomfortable ones.

He relaxed into it. That was an art he was learning, slowly and painfully. Someday he might even be good at it.

Fifty-Seven

Valeria woke in a strange bed with Kerrec stretched out beside her. For a long few moments she could not imagine where she was. Then she recognized the carving and gilding of the ceiling.

She was in the palace. She had fallen asleep, ignominiously, over dinner. Someone had undressed her and clothed her with a fine linen gown and put her to bed.

Kerrec was still in the shirt and trousers he had worn the night before. He was sound asleep. She eased herself out from beside him and padded barefoot to the door.

The dining room was directly outside. It was empty, lit with early sunlight. From somewhere she heard a bird singing, a sweet, mournful call that repeated over and over.

Obviously they were not going to leave at dawn today. Valeria found her clothes neatly folded at the foot of the bed. They were clean and brushed, and her boots stood at attention on the floor, freshly and impeccably polished.

She dressed quickly. Bright though the morning was, it was cold. Autumn was here for certain, and the autumn Dance was already past. She had fair hopes of being in the school for Midwinter Dance.

As she perched on a stool and reached for the first boot, she felt Kerrec's eyes on her. There were remnants of a dream in them, but he was more or less awake. He smiled, then frowned—which was perfectly like him.

"Good morning," she said.

He sat up, yawning. "It's late."

"The sun's barely up," she said. "We can be on the road in an hour."

"Two," he said. He looked around for his coat and boots. She handed them to him. For thanks he gave her a preoccupied stare. "You wouldn't wake up," he said.

He sounded only faintly aggrieved. "You could have had me carried home," she said.

"It was easier to wait," he said. He pulled on his boots and shrugged into his coat. "Bath. Breakfast. Riders' Hall."

"Yes, sir," she said with a soldier's salute.

That won her a grim stare, but he kept the reprimand to himself. He was already halfway to the door. She had to run to catch him.

Bath and breakfast were waiting in Riders' Hall, in that order. Their bags were packed, and the stallions were brushed until they gleamed. Quintus was just bringing out the saddles when they came down to the stable.

Valeria took Sabata's saddle from him. He smiled and bowed. She smiled back. It did not seem necessary to say anything. She would see Quintus again—maybe not always in the way or time that she expected, but the patterns around him touched hers more than once down the passage of years.

As she finished girthing up Sabata's saddle and turned to retrieve the bridle from its hook, she found herself face-to-face with half a dozen silent and staring boys. She had not felt their coming. She had been focused too far away, on what might happen in a year or two or more.

They had been coming to Riders' Hall every day, even through the funeral. Kerrec, intent on his father's death and his sister's grief, had not seen or spoken to them. Nor had Valeria, what with leaving every day by sunup and not coming back until well after sundown.

This morning they were early. From their expressions, that was deliberate. They had screwed up their courage to face the riders, and they were not going to let either of them go without saying what they had come to say.

The door of Petra's stall swung open. Kerrec came out leading his stallion, saddled and bridled and ready to ride. The boys flinched a little but stood their ground, blocking his way to the door.

"Sir," Maurus said, "we have to ask you something."

Kerrec's brow arched. He looked impossibly haughty. "Ask," he said.

Maurus took a deep breath and let it out all at once. "Sir, are you coming back? Will you keep on teaching us?"

"I am coming back," Kerrec said, "but not likely until spring."

"How are we supposed to hold on that long?" Tatius demanded, then added belatedly, "sir."

"Quintus will keep on teaching you," Kerrec said. "If you grow past him, ask the horses. They're better teachers than any human."

"Horses can't talk," Darius said. "How can they teach us?"

"Humans can listen," Kerrec said.

"But—" said Darius.

Maurus cut him off with an elbow in the ribs. "We don't understand, sir," he said.

"When you're ready, you will."

"You always say that," Vincentius said, but he was only whining a little.

"Listen," Kerrec said, "and learn. I'll be looking for you to be much better riders when I see you again."

"That won't be hard," Maurus muttered.

The others hushed him, not gently. He bared his teeth at them and said to Kerrec, "Sir, we'll do our best. You won't be disappointed."

"I don't expect to be," Kerrec said.

They drew back like an honor guard. He saluted them without irony and led Petra past them, with Valeria close behind.

For her there were smiles and grins and whispered goodbyes. She returned them as best she could, but Kerrec was moving too fast for her to stop. He was in the yard and mounted before she reached the stable door.

The boys streamed out behind them and followed them into the street, running after them for some distance before Quintus's bellow called them back. It was as grand a farewell as Valeria had ever needed.

"I hope we do come back," she said as she rode up beside Kerrec. The street was deserted—unusual at this hour. Apparently they were not the only people in Aurelia who had slept late this morning.

Kerrec kept his eyes focused straight ahead, but he answered her amiably enough. "I do intend to come back and teach them," he said, "or at the very least send someone who can take them past where Quintus leaves off. I took them up and then abandoned them. I owe them the best instruction I can find."

Valeria was not going to argue with his judgment of himself. It was a little harsh, but it was accurate.

Sabata was fussing. He had been locked up for days—he was jumping out of his skin. She let him stretch his legs, even allowed a judicious buck or two, before a rising tide of passersby brought his exuberance to a dancing, snorting halt.

The city was waking around them, stumbling out to greet the day. Merchants had set up shop and vendors opened their stalls in the markets. Most of the traffic was aiming toward the various gates, funeral guests and mourners leaving in a swelling flood.

That was exactly what Kerrec had hoped to avoid, but he suffered in silence. It took them well over an hour to travel a distance that on other days would have taken a quarter of that. Then there was the crush at the east gate, with supply wagons coming in while what seemed like half the city tried to get out.

If they had been on foot they might have given it up for fear of being trampled. With the stallions, they endured jostling and tedium but no danger to life or limb.

Eventually—very eventually—they rode through the gate. The road beyond was crowded with foot traffic and wagons, but the greenway for riders was almost clear.

Sabata was not the only one to take advantage of it. Petra showed him a fine pair of heels. They raced one another down the greenway, dodging the priest on his mule and the pair of nobles on extravagantly pretty but otherwise undistinguished horses. The nobles were offended, but the priest cheered them on.

They ran neck and neck for the last few furlongs, away from the worst of the crush and toward the legions' encampment.

Gradually the stallions slowed to a canter, then to a walk. Sabata was still inclined to dance and fret, but Petra returned to his deceptively phlegmatic self, plodding down the greenway like a plowhorse coming in from the fields.

Valeria had not faced the purpose of this particular errand yet today. Now she had no choice. The encampment loomed in front of her, with guards at the gates and along the top of the wall.

They were expected. The guards saluted them as they came toward the gate, and an escort was waiting to take them to the commander. No one tried to separate them from the horses, which was well. Sabata was not in an obliging mood.

Every legionary camp had quarters for the various cohorts, with tents laid out in a square. In the middle was the parade ground, a wide open space fronting on the commander's tent.

That space was full this morning, with all the cohorts standing in ranks. They wore full battle armor. Their shields were slung behind them and their spears were upright and grounded. The general and his staff stood in front of them.

This was a full review. Valeria would have hung back and waited for it to be over, but Kerrec rode straight down the center toward Tibullus on his platform.

As he rode, with Valeria hesitant behind him, the marching drums began to beat. Petra and then Sabata began to dance in time with the rhythm.

Valeria could be terribly slow-witted, but once she caught sight of the white mule standing to one side, she understood. The mule was wearing a pack saddle and carrying the full armor, spear and shield of a legionary.

Rodry's legion was giving him full honors—general's honors. The banner of the legion came down as Valeria approached, and the battle standard lowered. The standard-bearer wound the banner around the staff and held it until Sabata came to a halt in front of the platform. Then he laid it in Valeria's hands.

It was surprisingly heavy. The staff was a spear, and it was hung with badges of honor.

Her throat had locked shut. She had been expecting Rodry's shield and a salute from his cohort, and maybe a commendation from his general. This was beyond anything she would have dared to hope for.

She did her best to commit it all to memory. The glitter of sunlight on helmets and the bristle of spears, the weight of the standard in her hands, Tibullus's measured tones as he named Rodry and his cohort and his legion and then spoke of his commendations and his service, sank into her remembrance and set as if in amber.

"At the end of his service," Tibullus said, "he broke the emperor's ban and crossed the river, guiding a pair of riders into the enemy's country. For that he would be counted a deserter and so dishonored. But the gods had chosen him. Through him the enemy was destroyed and the battle won. He redeemed himself a hundred times over, and transformed dishonor into great honor. His name will be remembered among the great ones of the Valeria. Whenever the names of heroes are recited, his will come high among them. He served his empire well. He did honor to his legion."

Then he granted Rodry the salute, and every man of his legion followed his lead. The sound of stamping feet and clashing armor, multiplied almost five-thousandfold, rocked Valeria in the saddle and made her ears ring. Last of all they beat spears on shields, hammering out the rhythm that had made their enemies' blood run cold since the first emperor led his armies into battle.

With Kerrec leading the mule and Valeria still cradling the

standard, they bowed their heads to the general and his legion. Then they rode slowly out of the camp. The sound of spear on shield followed them for a long way, until finally they had ridden out of its reach.

Valeria had to stop then. The tears did not last long, and Kerrec did not reprimand her for them. His own cheeks were wet.

"I never dreamed they would do so much," she said. "I wish my father could have been there. I wish he could have seen it."

"He can," Kerrec said. "There is a way."

Valeria stared at him. "What—"

"It's a kind of pattern magic," he said.

"Can you teach me?"

"When you're ready," he said—damn him.

Fifty-Eight

They were three days on the road to Imbria. They could have done it in two without mortally offending the mule, but Valeria suffered a collapse of courage. The closer she came, the slower she rode, until Sabata dribbled unhappily to a halt.

Kerrec very carefully said nothing. She was well aware that he was restraining himself. He rode in silence behind her, with the mule plodding alongside.

If he had suggested they give it up, send the mule to Imbria with a courier and head straight for the Mountain, she would have hit him—and done just that. She would have hated herself for it and blamed Kerrec, but it would have been easier than facing her family and telling them Rodry was dead.

Valeria had never taken the easy path in her life. That got her out of bed on the third morning, her stomach so knotted she lost last night's supper and turned away disgusted from breakfast.

The landlady of the posting inn was, rather surprisingly, unoffended. She insisted on wrapping up the uneaten bread and eggs and stewed apples and sending them with Valeria when she left. "You'll be hungry soon enough," she said. "Watch yourself on that horse, now."

"I will," Valeria said. "Thank you." It seemed rather strange, but some people were odd about stallions.

It was no more than half a day's slow ride from the inn at Bari to Imbria. Halfway there, the road divided. The wider way led to Mallia and eventually to the Mountain. The narrower road, rutted and unpaved, wound through hills and patches of woodland.

The day had begun bright and almost warm, but by midmorning it had turned grey and cold. The wind had an edge that made Valeria think of snow. It was early in the year for it, but in these parts, not impossibly so.

Out of sight of the main road, open country gave way to fenced pastures and harvested fields. Away in the hollows, she could see the low shapes of farmsteads. If Kerrec had asked, which he did not, she could have named the farmers who held them. They were all old soldiers out here, retired legionaries who had taken the grant of farmland and a mule and gone to make something of it.

Her father's farm was farther off the northward road but closer to the village. The nearer she came to it, the slower she wanted to go. Everything here was familiar to the point of pain.

She glanced back at Kerrec. He was wearing his favorite mask, the haughty, princely face that could make him seem so far above the rest of the world. There was no telling what he was thinking, and Petra was not in the mood to let her look behind the mask.

Probably he was wondering what he had got himself into.

Valeria's first urge was to draw deeper into herself. Her second was to ride up beside him and slip her hand into his.

His warm fingers closed around her cold ones. He raised her hand to his lips and kissed it.

The tightness inside Valeria did not let go completely, but the worst of it opened up and poured away. She sat straighter in the saddle, to Sabata's manifest approval.

They rode on past familiar lanes and paths that led to houses she knew. Not long before noon, they came to the runepost that marked the boundary of her father's farm. It was freshly painted and the wards newly set—her mother renewed them every year after the harvest was in. It was old habit from when she had been a centurion's wife on frontier postings. Winter brought wolves, two-legged as well as four-legged, and sometimes things came in off the snow, seeking warmth and mortal blood.

The wards prickled on Valeria's skin, but they raised no alarm. They were set to recognize family. Petra sneezed as he passed them. Kerrec stiffened, then frowned.

He should not have been surprised. Valeria had warned him about her mother.

Sabata moved ahead of Petra, leading him down the hill and over the stream. As they rounded the bend, they paused.

Her father's farm filled a shallow valley. The house and its outbuildings stood secure in their palisade above the pastures and the plowed rectangles of fields. All the barley and wheat were in, and the winter-wheat field was ready to be planted. There were still apples in the orchard up beyond the house.

People said that one's old home always looked smaller after one had seen the world. Titus's farm looked exactly the same as Valeria remembered. The barn had a new coat of lime wash and the house roof was freshly thatched. Like the runestone, that was an autumn ritual.

Valeria's youngest sister, Gwynith, was playing in the yard in front of the house, tumbling in the dirt with the dogs. She bounced up staring—people on horses were a vanishing rarity in this place—and let out a long wail. "Pa*paaa*!"

She turned and fled into the house. The dogs were much less appalled. They leaped and fawned around the stallions, licking Valeria's hands in an ecstasy of recognition.

Titus came out of the barn with a pitchfork in his hand and her younger brothers looming unexpectedly behind. Niall was taller than his father, and plump little Garin had grown into a tall, narrow young thing with a voice that cracked as he said, "By the gods! It's Valeria."

"On a horse," Niall said. His voice had been cracking last year. It was almost comfortable with itself now, though he looked as if he did not know what to do with his body yet. "A *white* horse. Do you think—"

"I see that," Titus said. His tone was mild, but it silenced his sons. He lowered his pitchfork. "You, dogs. Down. Come here."

The dogs did not want to obey, but not all of Valeria's gifts came from her mother. When Titus spoke, the dogs did as they were told. They backed away from Valeria, still wagging their tails, and crouched at Titus's feet.

His eyes fell on the mule. The shield and armor were covered, but their shape was unmistakable. His face went still. "Garin, fetch your mother. If she's not still at market with Murna, find out where she is and go there. Bring her back."

Garin looked as if he might have argued, but when Titus spoke in that particular tone, no one crossed him. Garin ran past the stallions—darting a wild glance at them as he went—and vanished down the road to the village.

"Niall," Titus said, still with that terrible quiet, "see to the horses."

"We had better do that," Valeria said. "They're not—exactly—horses."

Titus barely paused before he shifted stride. "Help them, then," he said to Niall.

Kerrec dismounted and led Petra and the mule toward the barn. Valeria was trying to keep her chin up, but whatever coldness she had expected from her mother, she had at least thought her father would be glad to see her.

"It's as if he recognizes me," she said to Kerrec in the barn as they unsaddled and rubbed down the stallions and the mule, "but he doesn't know me at all."

"Maybe he thinks he doesn't," Kerrec said.

"It makes me feel cold."

"Mother says it will snow tomorrow," Niall said. He had bedded three of the plowhorses' stalls with straw and was pitching hay into the mangers. He flushed, conspicuously shy. "I know, that's not what you meant. It was hard when you left. You were always his favorite."

"I was not," Valeria said.

"Were, too," Niall said.

Valeria bit her tongue. Now was not the time for that familiar fight.

Sabata was unsaddled and clean. She led him into the middle stall, where he settled himself with hay and water and a handful of barley. Petra was in the end stall. Kerrec and Niall were unloading and tending the mule.

Valeria went back out into the grey daylight and the blustery chill. Titus was in the house—she could feel him there. She almost turned and ran back to Kerrec, but she had given up cowardice when she took the turn toward Imbria.

* * *

The house was warm. Titus had stirred up the fire and hung the pot to boil, and was lowering one of the hams from the rafters. Valeria reached up to steady it as it came down.

He nodded his thanks. "You've grown," he said.

"A little." She set the ham on the big, scarred table. Titus fetched the knife and set to work carving off thick slices.

Valeria let herself fall into the old familiar rhythm. It was strange to go down into the root cellar in search of turnips and potatoes and find it as it had always been—minus the bed that had made it a prison for a daughter who could not possibly be hearing the Call to the Mountain. She came back up again as quickly as she could.

She and her father worked side by side, scrubbing and peeling and chopping. Potatoes, turnips, an onion, a handful of ham chopped fine.

Gwynith reappeared from wherever she had gone to hide and think things over. Clearly she had reached a conclusion. She wrapped her arms around Valeria's leg and clung as she had done when she was barely old enough to walk.

Valeria tossed the last handful of potatoes into the steaming pot and sat on the bench by the wall. Gwynith climbed into her lap. She smelled of dust and dogs and warm child.

Niall brought a gust of cold wind into the house. Kerrec followed in much more contained fashion.

Valeria saw how he took in the room, sweeping a glance over it that caught every detail. It was a big room for a farmhouse, and high, coming to a peak around the chimney. Compared to a room in the palace, it was tiny and smoky and crowded with people and furniture.

Kerrec did not think that way. At first Valeria could not tell where the thought had come from—then she recognized the flavor of Petra's presence. Kerrec saw things for what they were.

Valeria was duly chastened. She started to stand up for belated introductions, but Niall was taking care of that. "His name is Kerrec," he said to his father. "He's a First Rider. That means he's a master mage. He's had his stallion for ten years. The stallion picked him, not the other way around. He's been bucked off six times. He said—"

Obviously, while Valeria had been trying to mend matters with her father, Kerrec had been seducing her brother in the barn. He had told Niall more in half an hour than Valeria had got out of him in a year.

Gwynith lifted her head from Valeria's shoulder and peered at Kerrec. "Pretty," she said.

That shocked laughter out of Valeria. "My sentiments exactly," she said. "You like him, then?"

Gwynith nodded. "He's shiny."

She could see magic. Valeria smoothed her tangled curls. They crackled a little. It was not just seeing, then. Maybe Morag would have a proper heir, after all.

As if the thought had conjured her, Morag herself appeared in the doorway, with Garin and young Murna behind.

Valeria's father had not changed a bit. Neither had her mother. Morag was still as tall as a man and as straight as a steel blade, and there was still no sign of grey in her glossy dark hair with its red lights. Her eyes were the same odd color as Valeria's, neither green nor brown, flecked with gold.

She was beautiful. Valeria had never seen that before, though she had heard it often enough. Beautiful and terrible.

Morag's glance across the room reminded Valeria vividly of Kerrec's not so long before. Her eyes took in the stranger with the prince's face and the accent to match, and leaped from him to Valeria.

Valeria braced for the blast, but none came. Morag went as quiet as Titus had. She hung her cloak and hood on the hook by the door and sent Murna to fetch the good lamps from the bedroom. Then she greeted Kerrec with civility that would not have shamed a court lady. "Sir. You're welcome in this house."

Kerrec bowed. "I'm honored to be here, Mistress," he said.

Valeria rose, lowering a protesting Gwynith to the floor. "Mother," she said.

Morag did not go blind as Titus had seemed to. She saw Valeria perfectly clearly. "You're too thin," she said. "Aren't they feeding you?"

"Mostly I feed myself," Valeria said.

"Feed yourself better," Morag said. "Those horses in the barn are sturdy enough. They can carry a bit more of you."

"Mother," Niall said, "those horses are—"

"I know what they are," Morag said. "And you, too, sir—past and present. So a woman can be Called, after all?"

"So it seems, Mistress," Kerrec said.

"Has she acquitted herself well?"

"Extremely well, Mistress," said Kerrec.

"Good," Morag said. "You'll eat with us, of course."

Kerrec inclined his head. The boys and Murna watched wide-eyed. They would be imitating his every gesture for days. Like Rodry, they were in love with him.

Maybe it was a disease of their blood. Valeria was the worst of them all.

Fifty-Nine

Dinner was by no means a silent meal, with the children chattering brightly and Kerrec answering their spate of questions. Valeria said hardly a word. Titus ate in silence. Morag watched and studied and ignored the food and drink in front of her.

When the boys had devoured their third helpings, Morag sent all the children to bed—over their loud protests. A solid glare put an end to those. They tumbled and clamored their way out of the room, with many glances back.

Valeria went with them because Gwynith begged her. She tucked her in tight beside Murna in the big wooden bed. As she laid a Word of sleep with the kiss on each sister's forehead, she looked up to find her mother watching from the doorway.

"I'm sorry," Valeria said. "I shouldn't have—"

"They're still your sisters," Morag said, "whatever else you may be."

"I'm glad you think so," Valeria said.

Morag did not rise to the bait. She stood back, leaving room for Valeria to slip past her through the door.

Titus was as silent as he had been all evening, sitting with Kerrec by firelight, nursing a mug of ale. Valeria sat on the bench beside Kerrec, a little defiantly—if anyone cared.

Morag stayed on her feet. "Now," she said. "Tell us. Rodry or Lucius?"

Valeria let go her breath in a long sigh. "Rodry," she said.

"How?"

Valeria had rehearsed for days, until she had the story perfectly straight and thorough enough to pass scrutiny in one of her classes on the Mountain. It was all gone from her head, lost in her mother's stare.

Kerrec spoke beside her, softly, but his words were clear. He began with the meeting in the inn in the town of Valeria Victrix, and told the rest in order. As he spoke, the words took shape. It was like living it all over again, with all the sights and sounds and smells and Rodry's living, laughing presence.

Kerrec had turned the words into living memory. Everything that Rodry had seen and done that Kerrec could know, he laid before them. The battle, the Dance, the stark and sudden ending, they were all there. Then at the last, he gave them what Valeria had asked for, the legion's great honor and splendid farewell.

For a long while after he was done, no one spoke. The fire danced and flickered. The wind wuthered in the eaves.

Kerrec sat with his head bowed and his hands folded. He had wrought a great working, as powerful and yet as subtle as any work of magic Valeria knew. He had taken words and memory and woven them into patterns that made them real in the minds of everyone who heard.

It was no wonder he had declined to teach her the trick of

it. This was First Rider's art. It needed strong discipline and indelible memory, and control of patterns that for all her strength, she had not yet mastered.

The stallions humbled her constantly, but it was not often she bowed in deference to a rider's magic. She was too sure of her own strength. She tended to forget that her magic was art, not brute craft.

After a moment or an hour, Morag stirred. "Thank you, sir, with all my heart. You've given us a great gift."

"I would rather have brought him back alive," Kerrec said.

"That was in the gods' hands," Morag said. "You know what they say to soldiers. 'Come back with your shield or on it.' He chose his way. It won him honor. The rest is for us to live with."

Kerrec rose and bowed. It was a princely gesture, and it nearly knocked him flat.

"You're exhausted," Morag said. "Come, you need to sleep."

"I'll bed down in the barn," he said. "If I could borrow a blanket or two…"

"You will not," said Morag. "I realize that there are gods in our barn tonight—gods who eat hay and sleep in straw and have thick coats against the cold. You need a little more pampering than they do, especially after such a working."

Kerrec opened his mouth to argue, but he was no more able to resist Morag's will than one of her children. She bore him off to her own bed. She and Titus would spread a pallet in front of the fire, she said in a tone that brooked no opposition.

Valeria was no doubt expected to sleep in her old bed with her sisters. There was more room than there used to be, with Caia married off to Wellin Smith. Gwynith and Murna would be glad. They were happy that she had come back, though their parents were not.

She almost gave way. But she needed Kerrec tonight after reliving so much pain. She left her parents to their makeshift bed and retreated to the strange-familiar room.

It felt most peculiar to stand in that space. It had always been her parents' kingdom, with the enormous carved bed that filled most of it, and Titus's old army chest at the bed's foot, and the nursing chair that Morag had brought from Eriu. Children only came here on sufferance.

The sheets were fresh and smelled of cedar from the press. They were the best sheets, the wedding sheets, woven of creamy linen and embroidered along the edges. Morag must have had a premonition of important guests and—Valeria had no doubt—sudden sorrow.

Kerrec had managed to undress and fold his clothes tidily before he slipped under the down-filled coverlet. Valeria did the same. His skin was blissfully warm. She wrapped herself around him.

Neither of them was in the mood for more tonight. Kerrec fell asleep in the middle of a kiss. Valeria lay awake while the lamp burned low.

The room was warm—one wall was the kitchen chimney. Faintly, with a bit of an echo, she heard her parents' voices on the other side. She made no particular effort to catch the words. It was clear enough what they were talking about.

She fell asleep listening to their voices rising and falling, murmuring through the cry of the wind.

"Are you going to get married?"

Valeria opened one eye. Murna's face hung over her. The weight bouncing on her was Gwynith's, and Niall and Garin were hovering beyond.

Murna had asked the question. It was Niall who said scornfully, "Riders don't marry, stupid."

"They do, but it's not very common." Kerrec was awake and apparently undismayed to find the room full of curious children.

"So are *you*?" Murna demanded. She was nothing if not persistent.

"No," he answered before Valeria could stop him.

"Are you going to?"

"Caia is having a baby!" Gwynith announced loudly.

Murna was still young enough to be easily distracted. "Yes! Mother says it's a girl. Caia thinks it's a boy. Wellin Smith doesn't care as long as it's healthy."

"Wellin Smith is a wise man," Kerrec said, sitting up. Gwynith transferred her bouncing self to him. "She isn't having the baby today, is she?"

"Today!" Gwynith sang. "Today!"

Niall plucked her out of Kerrec's lap. "She's crazy," he said. "Mother says breakfast is ready whenever you are."

Valeria glowered. "She sent you?"

"Just Murna," he confessed. "The rest of us came to help."

Valeria threw her pillow at him. "Get out! *Out!*"

It took a while, but they roared and tumbled out, all four of them.

Kerrec fell back in the bed. He was shaking with laughter.

Valeria was still furious, but she could not help but see the humor in it. Her face cracked into a smile. In a moment she was laughing as hard as he was.

When the last gust of giggles was gone, they were in each other's arms. Kerrec was grinning. He looked no older than Niall. "Now that never happened to me before," he said.

"You're lucky," Valeria muttered.

"Oh, no," he said. "You are. These children—they're wonderful. Your mother and father have their terrifying aspects, but they've raised you well."

"They're none too happy with me," Valeria said.

"They don't know what to say," he said. "They're not sure they know you any more."

"And you know them well enough to tell me what they're thinking?"

"Sometimes the view is clearer from outside."

"So what would you have me do?"

"Whatever's in your heart."

"My heart wants to get up and get dressed and go to the Mountain."

"Does it?"

He was using his teaching voice. She hated when he did that outside of the schoolroom.

She particularly hated it when he was right. "My heart, damn you, wants to make them see I'm still Valeria. Maybe I cut my hair and left my skirts behind, but I didn't change my blood."

"Tell them that."

"Because you told me to?"

"Because your heart told you."

"You are my heart," she said, "damn you."

"Your heart-damn-you is grateful for the honor." He sat up again and stretched. There was art in it, deliberate stretching of each limb and muscle, a dance of suppleness and strength.

She hated to get up and brave the cold air and the icy floor, but it was either that or stay in bed until spring. The prospect was terribly tempting.

A storm was raging outside, a white blast of wind and snow. Breakfast lay on the table. Everyone was out—storm or no storm, there were stock to feed and stalls to clean, cows and goats to milk and wool to spin and clothes to make and mend.

Valeria eyed the pot of porridge and the jug of cream and the bread and soft cheese and apple butter, and swallowed. Later, she thought. She took a deep breath instead and opened the door.

The wind cut like a sword. It ripped the door out of her hand and wrestled with her as she fought to pull it shut again. Snow mixed with sleet lashed her face.

She almost gave up and fled back into the house, but she was not one to quit once she had begun. She crossed the yard, blinded and buffeted by the gale, and dived into the warmth and relative quiet of the barn.

The boys were in the loft, pitching hay down for the cows and the horses. Valeria found Titus outside the mule's stall, kneeling in the aisle. He had uncovered Rodry's armor and propped the shield against the wall. Now he was unwrapping the standard.

It was a heavy, awkward thing for one pair of hands. Valeria lent him hers. He did not order her away. They unfurled the banner together, uncovering the eagle and thunderbolts of the Valeria.

Titus smoothed it, then touched the standard with its tokens of bronze and steel and gilded lead. "I fought in some of these battles," he said. "That one there—that's Morrigu, where we broke the back of the Mordantes and took half the Calletani royal line hostage."

Valeria brushed the token with a finger. It was silver, not steel, she realized—a disk as large as her palm, stamped with an odd, angular bird perched on top of a skull.

"The high king wore that as an amulet," her father said. "That's the raven of battles that always brings victory. We took it that day, with its owner's head. The emperor had the skull cleaned and sheathed in gold and sent back to the tribe."

"That was a great gesture," Valeria said.

"Artorius was good at that." Titus angled a glance at her. "You've learned a thing or two since you left here."

"I'm still Valeria," she said.

"You'll always be Valeria," Titus said. "I like your young man."

That was not as abrupt a change of subject as it might have seemed. "I don't know if he's mine," she said. "He's not a tame creature."

"He's yours," Titus said. "He looks at you the same way your horse does."

"Sabata isn't my horse, either. I belong to him."

"Yes," Titus said. "It goes both ways. When his eyes are on you, he doesn't see anything else."

"Is that a good or a bad thing?"

"If he doesn't break your heart, it's good." Titus began to roll up the banner again, carefully. "There's enough of that in the rest of life—and death."

"I wish Rodry hadn't died," Valeria said.

Titus paused in rolling up the standard. He was blinking rapidly.

He had looked the same to Valeria for as long as she could remember, foursquare and weathered, with flecks of grey in his tightly curling hair. He was shorter than her mother and much broader, and famously strong. As he liked to say, he was built to last.

Even so, he was not a young man. He must be as old as the emperor had been. He was much older than Morag, Valeria knew—Morag's family had taken a long time to forgive their daughter for running off with a centurion old enough to be her father.

Valeria never had asked exactly how much older he was. He was just Papa, as immutable as the earth and as solid to lean on.

For the first time she understood that he was human. It was a deep shock, deeper in its way than her brother's death. One's father was supposed to be a lofty and forbidding figure, not an aging man in a barn aisle, mourning the loss of his firstborn.

Valeria stopped waiting for him to come to her. She wrapped her arms around him and held him tightly.

He was stiff at first. Men did so hate to be seen for the fragile things they were. Then he relaxed little by little. His arms closed around her and tightened.

She let go first. Titus held her at arm's length. "We thought we'd never see you again."

"Did you think I was dead?"

He shook his head. "No. Just lost to us."

"I'm sorry," she said. "I should have written a letter. It was just—"

"Anger's a hard one to get over," Titus said. "Your mother's been regretting what she did since she found the root cellar empty and you gone out of reach. She honestly thought it was for the best."

"I don't believe you," said Valeria. "Mother was never sorry for anything in her life."

"There's a first time for everything," her father said. "She loves you more than she loves herself. If she's hard on you, it's because she's afraid for you. She's seen you flying so high—but the higher you go, the farther and harder you can fall."

"I'm scared, too," Valeria said, "but I can't give it all up for that."

"Nor should you," Titus said. "But try to be a little more understanding of your mother. She's only doing what mothers do."

"Mothers and lovers," Valeria said with a heavy sigh. She

hugged him tightly but briefly, then pushed herself to her feet. There were still stalls to clean and cows to milk.

The crooked-horned cow was lowing her discomfort. Valeria set to work with bucket and stool.

She heard the door blow open at the end of the barn. A blast of cold air set loose straw swirling and roused a squawk from one of her brothers.

"Valeria!" Murna shrilled. "Mama wants you!"

Valeria thought of pretending not to hear, but that had never worked in her family. She rose with a faint groan. "Come here and finish milking the cow."

Murna groaned, too, but she took Valeria's place on the stool.

"What does Mother want me for?" Valeria asked her.

Murna looked up from the cow's side. "Caia's having a baby," she said.

"What, now?"

Valeria saw the start of Murna's nod. She did not wait to see the rest.

Sixty

Morag was in the stillroom in the smaller barn, filling her midwife's bag with packets and vials. Valeria had brought her mother's heavy cloak from the house, and one for herself—the old legionary's cloak she had worn every winter since she grew as tall as her father.

"She's having this baby early," Morag said as she fastened the bag tightly and wrapped herself in the cloak. "I was sure we'd have another half month at least."

It was as if Valeria had never been away at all. She dug in her heels. "Mother, I can't stay here and be a wisewoman."

Morag regarded her in what seemed to be honest surprise. "Did I ask you to? You were never particularly focused, but you had wonderful hands. We may need them. If there's another reason for this than the baby's impatience—"

"I'll go," Valeria said. "I just need to be sure you know. As soon as the roads clear, I'm going back to the Mountain. That's where I belong."

"I know that," Morag said. "Are you coming?"

Valeria wound the cloak tighter around herself and pulled up the hood. Morag nodded, took a deep breath, and forayed out into the storm.

Valeria had been out in storms as bad, on similar errands with her mother. She had never been out in worse. She had to trust to Morag's sense of direction—she was deafened and blinded by the wind and snow.

Something loomed up in front of them. After a blank moment she recognized it as a cloaked human figure—then as Kerrec.

He did not say anything, but turned and went on in front of them. The air behind him was notably quieter, the wind less overwhelmingly strong. As Valeria's mind came back into focus from the confusion of the storm, she felt the tingle of the working.

Kerrec was full of surprises. It made sense enough if she remembered her lessons—everything he was doing was part of a horse mage's power. But she had not realized how much there was to it, or how useful some of it could be.

It was still a hard road, whipped by wind and drifted with snow. Sometimes they had to stop and cling to one another, waiting out a particularly powerful blast. Valeria's feet went numb. Her face felt like a block of ice.

Wellin Smith's house stood on the edge of the village. A huge oak tree stood in front of it. In the summer people brought horses or mules to be shod in its shade.

There were still leaves on the branches, though the wind was ripping them to tatters. The door of the smithy was unbarred, the smithy deliriously warm. A brawny boy was tending the fire.

"Upstairs," he said when he recognized Morag. He took no

particular notice of the others. They were cloaked, plastered with snow and ice and barely recognizable as human.

Valeria had never been in the smith's house before. The stair in the back of the forge led to a surprisingly large and luxurious space. There were carpets on the floor, and one wall was painted with scenes from a harvest festival. The table in the middle of the room was longer and heavier than the one in Morag's kitchen, with chairs drawn up to it. A silver wine service glimmered at one end.

Caia had married even better than Valeria thought. Valeria was happy for her.

It would not matter how rich she was if she did not survive this birth. Morag shook the snow from her cloak and spread it on the bench in front of the hearth, where a fire was burning strongly. Kerrec and then Valeria quickly did the same, then followed Morag through a doorway and up a short stair.

The bedroom had its own hearth, burning applewood with its sweet scent. Wellin Smith's bulk seemed to fill the room, but in front of Morag he shrank into a frightened boy. "Mother-in-law! Thank the gods. How did you know we needed you?"

Morag did not answer that. She pushed him aside as if he had been no bigger than Gwynith, and bent over the bed. Valeria, from near the door, could see her sister's dark hair in an uncharacteristically untidy braid, and hear her quick, light panting.

She was not screaming, which rather surprised Valeria. She would have taken Caia for a screamer.

Morag spoke without looking away from Caia. "Wellin, go down to the forge and make yourself useful. Eat on the way, if you can. It's going to be a while. First Rider, can you boil water? I need these packets brewed into tea. Valeria, help me undress her."

Kerrec took the packets Morag handed him and followed the smith out of the room. With the men gone, Morag stood a bit straighter and breathed a little easier. She folded back the coverlets—muttering at their number and heaviness.

Caia was drawn into a knot around her pregnant belly. She was conscious, but she was so lost in fear and pain that she did not even realize her mother was there. She was swaddled in three layers of linen shifts, with more laces and ribbons and furbelows than Valeria had seen since the last time she helped Briana dress for a state occasion.

Morag shook her head at the foolishness of it all and set her hand to the first of many laces. Together she and Valeria got Caia out of her stifling clothes and laid her naked on a fresh sheet.

Caia unfolded while they did that, and came to herself a little. "Mama?"

"Yes, child," Morag said with the brisk matter-of-factness that had soothed many a terrified new mother.

"I fell down cooking breakfast," Caia said. "It came so fast. Is it supposed to be that fast?"

"Sometimes it is," Morag said. "What were you doing cooking for yourself? What happened to Brigid?"

"Her mother is sick," said Caia. "It was just supposed to be for a day or two. I didn't expect—"

"Neither did I," Morag said. "Here, sit up. Valeria, the folded linen from my bag, please."

That unfolded into a much plainer shift than the ones Caia had been wearing. Just as they smoothed it into place and laid Caia down again, Kerrec appeared with a pot and a stack of cups. He had brewed the tea—perfectly, Valeria happened to notice.

Caia squinted at him. Then she peered at Valeria. "Valeria? I'm not dreaming you, am I? And who is *that*?"

"You're not dreaming," Valeria said. "That is Kerrec."

"Who is—"

"First Rider," Morag said pointedly, "a cup of tea, if you please."

He poured it obediently and held it to Caia's lips for her to sip. She was staring at him as if she had never seen a man before.

"If you say 'pretty,'" he said, "I'll be forced to retaliate. And you, madam, are beautiful."

"So are you," she said in a tone more fit for a dream-dazzled girl than a wife in childbed. "Wherever did she find you?"

"In a hedgerow," he said.

The cup was empty. He lowered it. Her hands caught his.

The pains struck just then. Her fingers clamped tight. His breath hissed, but he did not pull away.

"Good," Morag said as if to herself. "Don't move." She lifted the shift and reached up beneath.

Caia gasped but did not scream. Morag's face emptied of expression. She was searching with more than hands. Magic hummed in the room.

"It's backside first," Kerrec said. "You'll have to turn it."

Morag raised her brows. "You're a midwife, too?"

"I can see."

"Can you?" Morag wasted no time in amazement. "Well, then. Tell me exactly what you see."

Kerrec nodded. His eyes closed. Valeria, focused on him, saw the patterns forming and re-forming around him. Her eyes followed them downward from his hands through Caia's body.

She caught her breath. It was like looking through a smoky glass. She could see the beating heart and the intricate tracery of veins, the glistening curves of organs and the white scaffolding of bones.

There was the baby, tiny and complete, curled in a tight ball as if fighting the compulsion to be born. It was a boy—Caia would have her wish after all—and he had magic. It glowed in him like an ember.

"I need your hands," Morag said in her ear. "Rider, tell her—"

"I see it," Valeria said. She whispered a Word that she had learned for calming horses. Caia sighed and relaxed and stopped trying to push out the baby.

Valeria reached up inside. It was eerie to see her hand passing through those translucent shapes, sliding up and around the baby and carefully turning him until he lay head down, angled as he should be to be born. He had stopped fighting. The Word acted on him, too, and mercifully so.

"Now," she said to Caia. "Wake up and push."

Caia wasted no time whining. She gritted her teeth and let instinct have its way.

Morag moved in past Valeria. Valeria was glad to leave her to it. She was feeling the aftereffects of strong magic, with light head and heaving stomach.

She found the privy behind the kitchen, a real room with heat from the chimney and running water. It was much simpler than what she had learned to take for granted in the school, but for Imbria it was the height of luxury.

She was grateful for it, as her empty stomach registered its objections to everything she had been doing to it. Eventually the spasms stopped. She washed her face in icy water, gasping and spluttering.

When she came out, she surprised herself with hunger. There was bread in a cupboard in the kitchen, along with a round of her mother's sharp and savory cheese. She found a slab of beef in the cold cupboard, too—half-frozen in this weather— and a bag of onions and a barrel of cider.

She could do something with those. She hunted up a pot and a box of spices, raided the herbs drying in bunches along the ceiling, and came across a trove of dried fruits.

Caia was still in labor. Valeria left the pot simmering and went up to see. Kerrec had shifted until he was sitting on the bed with Caia in his lap, propped up against him. Morag sat by the fire, as calm as she always was when things were going as they should.

Valeria did not try to see inside. Even with bread and cheese in her stomach, she was a bit weak still. She trusted her mother to know when to worry.

Kerrec's eyes smiled at her. He seemed quite at ease serving as a birthing chair.

Valeria could imagine what the riders would say. She perched on a stool beside him. Caia was resting, but woke as another spasm took hold of her.

This one was strong. Valeria laid a hand on the swell of her belly. "Cool," Caia said. "That feels cool."

Morag brought another cup of tea. Caia dashed it out of her hand. "I'm sick of tea! I want to have this baby!"

"Then have it," Morag said.

Caia sucked in a breath and pushed until the cords sprang out on her neck and her face went crimson. "I…can't…*do* it!"

"Again," Morag said, merciless.

Valeria frowned. Caia was losing strength. Something inside her wanted to break. Valeria smoothed the pattern that tried to turn jagged and held it in place while Caia gathered herself for one last bitter fight.

Caia pushed as hard as she had ever pushed in her life. Valeria pushed with her. Kerrec fought the battle, too, and Morag refused to let her slacken. Then for the first time Caia let out a scream: a long roar of absolute rage.

A much shriller cry joined it, with the same horrendous temper and the same indomitable will. Morag raised her grandson into the light, wet and glistening and howling at the top of his substantial lungs.

Sixty-One

It was just as hard to birth a baby as it was to save the world.

Valeria helped Kerrec extricate himself from Caia. He was so stiff he could barely move, but he insisted on lifting Caia with the baby in her arms while the others spread fresh sheets and made the bed clean again. Then he laid her down. The only sign of strain was a slight catch in his breath.

Caia smiled up at him. "I was going to name him Titus," she said, "but now I'm thinking—"

"Titus is a wonderful name," Kerrec said quickly. "My grandfather's name was Titus."

"Oh," said Caia. "Well, then. Maybe he can have two names. Other people do."

"You want him to get above himself?" Morag asked.

"Why not?" said Caia. "He's my baby. He can be anything he wants."

Morag sniffed. Caia rocked her son and cooed to him, then

looked up with an expression that made Valeria stop worrying about her infatuation with Kerrec. Wellin Smith was standing in the door, looming and hulking and trying not to do either. Caia loved to feast her eyes on a handsome face, but her husband, she simply loved.

Maybe she was not such a shallow idiot, after all. She certainly was stronger than Valeria had given her credit for. She had fought this fight as well as anyone Valeria had seen.

"This is your son," Caia said to Wellin. "Look. His name is Titus."

"That's a very good name," Wellin said, lowering himself to the stool Valeria had been perching on.

He leaned forward and kissed his wife, then peered into the nest of blankets. Valeria could tell when he found the tiny red face. His own big red one went all soft.

She pulled Kerrec with her out of the room, down the stairs and into the dining room. Her pot was bubbling gently, wafting out fragrant steam. She filled bowls and broke a loaf of bread and sat down with him.

She was ravenous. So, she saw, was he. He ate two bowls and mopped the second clean with the last of the loaf.

"I should cook for you more often," she said. "I've never seen you eat that much at a sitting."

He smiled. "That's part of a woman's dowry in these parts, isn't it?"

"A box of spices, a barrel of ale, and her mother's arts in the kitchen," Valeria said. "A woman isn't ready for marriage until she can do the whole festival dinner, from eggs to apples, in sixteen courses."

"Now there's an art to conjure with," he said.

She kissed him, savoring the spices. "Someday I'll make it for you."

"All sixteen courses?"

"Every one."

He held up his empty bowl. "Is this part of it?"

"For you it can be."

They grinned at one another. They were still grinning when Morag brought cup and bowl with her from the kitchen and sat across the table to eat.

"All's well?" Kerrec asked her.

She nodded. "If you're done here, you can go back to the farm. Titus will want to know he has a namesake."

"Are you sure you won't need us?" Valeria said.

"I'm sure," said Morag. "Wellin's boy went to fetch the maid. She's a midwife's daughter, that's why I talked Caia into hiring her. Once she gets here, I'll come home myself."

"I'll tell Father," Valeria said.

"Go on," Morag said. "You've just enough time to get there before dark."

It was still daylight and still snowing, but the wind had died down. The air was bitter cold.

The snow was knee-deep but light, and not unbearably difficult to wade through. They went arm in arm, which kept them from slipping.

Valeria's heart was as light as the snow. Rodry was still dead and there was terrible uncertainty in front of her—maybe even expulsion from the school—but there was great power in the birth of a baby.

The light was fading when they came into the farmyard. There were lamps lit on either side of the door, and yellow light shone out of the windows onto the snow.

Her father and brothers and sisters were at dinner. She could hear them from outside, the familiar uproar of a large and boisterous family. When she walked through the door, warmth and light and noise struck her like a welcome blow.

They were all yelling at once, even her father. She held up her hands until they quieted down. "It's a boy," she said, "and his name is Titus. Mother will be home by morning."

Titus let his breath out in a long sigh of relief. The children were clamoring for the whole story.

Tonight it was her turn to tell it while Kerrec listened and nodded. She could not make it real—not yet—but none of them cared. The words were enough.

For once sleep was welcome when it came. The battle Valeria dreamed of was the battle to birth a child. In her dream, it was her in Kerrec's lap, fighting the pain, but it was still her mother on the midwife's stool. The baby was a girl. She opened eyes the color of rain, so full of magic it dripped from her like water, and smiled.

Morag came walking through the farmyard just as Valeria came out of the privy. The snow had stopped in the night. The early-morning sky was clear and so cold it looked as brittle as ice.

Valeria was feeling a little green still. She hoped her mother would not see, but Morag's eye was too sharp for that.

She herded Valeria into the silent house. Titus and the boys were long gone about the morning chores. Kerrec was in the barn, seeing to the horses. The girls were still asleep, having stayed up well past their bedtime.

Valeria would have excused herself and gone to lend someone a hand, but Morag sat her down firmly and brewed up a tea that made Valeria's nose wrinkle. "Red raspberry tea? What are you feeding me that for?"

"What for indeed?" said Morag. "How long have you been sick in the mornings?"

"How long have I—" Valeria stopped short. "No. Oh, no. That's not possible."

"Don't lie to your mother," said Morag. "I'll wager he knows. It wasn't only Caia he was seeing yesterday."

"He didn't say a word," Valeria said.

"He doesn't usually, does he? Not about matters of the heart. He's as bad about that as you are."

"But I *can't* be," Valeria said rather desperately.

"Why not? You're healthy, young, and mad in love with a healthy young man. There isn't a ward or an herb or a protection in the world that will stop nature from taking its course, if it's determined and the gods are paying attention."

Valeria drank her tea numbly, because the cup was in her hand and her mother was expecting it. She liked red raspberry tea—that was not the trouble. It was what it meant that made her go all strange.

She shrank from looking inside herself as she had looked inside Caia, but she had to be sure. She had to know. She opened her eyes in that particular way.

It was very small yet, but there was no doubt that it was there. It had been there, she judged, not quite two months—since that first night on the road from Oxos to Aurelia.

The gods had wasted no time. They were laughing, she was sure. What she felt...

She did not know yet. The tea settled her stomach. It would make her womb strong, too, and ease the birth.

"My dream last night," she said. "It was true. Kerrec was with me. It was a daughter. And...you were there."

"Of course I was," Morag said. "You think I'd let anyone else birth my grandchild?"

"This doesn't change anything," Valeria said. "I still have to go back to the Mountain."

"Then I'll go to the Mountain."

Valeria almost choked on the last of her tea. Master Nikos and Morag together in the same citadel—the earth would shake.

The earth was going to shake badly enough once the riders discovered what Valeria had been doing while they pretended not to notice. She could hide it, she was sure, at least until after Midwinter. Then—

"Valeria," her mother said in the tone she resorted to when her daughter's mind had wandered off the edge of the world, "I'm going to tell your father. But not until after you leave."

"Thank you," Valeria said, "I think."

"You are welcome," her mother said. "Now go let your man know you're not as hopeless an idiot as he might be thinking."

"Kerrec knows I'm an idiot," Valeria said. "We're both idiots. That's why we match so well."

Morag burst out laughing—so suddenly and so completely unexpectedly that Valeria sat gaping. She could not remember ever having heard her mother laugh like that. It was the most joyful sound she could imagine.

"Go on," Morag said through it. "Go tell him."

"But if he already knows—"

"Out! Go!"

That was more like the mother she knew. She half ran out into the cold, clutching her cloak around her.

Sixty-Two

Kerrec was tending one of the plow horses, the grey who was the tallest horse in six villages. Kerrec had the platter-sized hoof in his lap, trimming it, while the horse bent his head down to watch. As Valeria paused, Kerrec stroked the big arched nose and murmured something that made the beast sigh blissfully.

Valeria had hoped one or more of the children would be there, adoring him as utterly as old Nimbus did. But she was not going to get that excuse to keep from telling him. He was alone.

He looked up and smiled. She could not see any difference in him, at least not since his father's magic broke down the worst of his walls.

Had he known *that* long?

Oh, no. That would be unbearable.

She planted herself in front of him. "This is your fault, you know," she said.

"I'm told it takes two," he said.

"I don't care. I'm blaming it on you."

"I suppose that's fair enough," he said. He set Nimbus's hoof down and slapped the rump that rose well above his head.

"Are you angry?" she asked him.

"Do I look angry?"

"You always look angry," she said.

"Even when I'm smiling?"

She lunged at him, bearing him backward into the straw. Nimbus stood perfectly still when Kerrec fetched up against his forelegs.

"You can't tell anyone," she said. "They'll never let me back if they know. Once I'm in, when there's no longer any hiding it—"

"Stop," he said. "Just stop."

She stared at him.

"Do you really hate me for this?" he asked. "Because if you do, there are ways to make it go away. No one has to know."

"Except us," she said, "and Mother. And the innkeeper in Bari. And who knows who else?"

"Even so," he said steadily.

"You would let me do that?"

"It's not a matter of letting. It's your life this will change."

"And not yours? You don't even care?"

"Of course I care!"

She had never heard him raise his voice before. It rocked her back on her haunches.

"Of course I care," he said in his usual tone. "But if you truly can't go through with this, and if you truly foresee that it will destroy any hope you had of being a rider, I can't stop you. I may not forgive you—but I won't stop loving you. I can't ever do that."

His face was as transparent as it could be. That was not very, but Valeria was learning to read it. He meant what he said.

"What if I go through with it?" she said. "Can you live with what's going to happen? I doubt there's been a scandal like it since—"

"Since a woman was Called to the Mountain?" He shifted smoothly. She slid off him. He stood and held out his hand.

She got up without his help. "Don't take it so lightly," she said. "It's going to be bad."

"You might be surprised."

"I would like to be," she said without much hope.

"You have more friends than you know," he said, "beginning with the gods and the Ladies. Don't you think they had something to do with this? We both had wards up. They shouldn't have failed. I'd have said they couldn't, if it wasn't so obvious that they have."

"The gods are going to get a piece of my mind," Valeria said with a baleful glance toward the stallions.

Neither of them appeared to be listening. Sabata was nibbling hay. Petra was asleep.

She turned back to Kerrec. He should have looked tired— he had been working harder than he ever worked on the Mountain, on somewhat less sleep—but he had never looked better.

He set his hands on her shoulders, searching her face. "Are you really unhappy about this?"

"No!" she said sharply. "No. I should be. This is more trouble than I ever thought I could get into. I'm terrified. But when I look inside and see—you know how they say in stories, 'Her heart leaped'? I never knew it could. But that's exactly what it does."

"You want it?" he said. "You want this baby?"

"Do you?"

He nodded as if words had failed him. His heart was full, brimming over in his eyes.

"So do I," she said, "in spite of everything."

* * *

By the second morning after the storm, the cold had begun to loosen its grip. The sun was warm on Valeria's face as she brought Sabata out into the farmyard.

Morag and Titus were standing with the children in the drifted snow. The young ones were silent for once.

Gwynith had cried herself out when Valeria tried to explain why she had to go away. She had only stopped the flood by promising to come back as soon as she could.

The others had better control over their tears, but they were also more difficult to soothe with promises. "You'll only come back if someone else dies," Niall had said with the bitterness of the young.

He was still refusing to look at Valeria, though he could not take his eyes off the stallions. They were, for reasons best known to themselves, letting these mortals see a little more of the truth than anyone usually saw outside of the Dance. Even Valeria was dazzled.

Morag's eyes were narrowed against the brightness, but her mind was as practical as it always was. "Are you sure you won't stay for the baby's naming ceremony? It's only two more days."

"I wish we could," Valeria said, "but there's another storm coming. If we wait, we'll be caught in the mountains."

Morag nodded. She had enough weather witchery to see it, too. "I'll see you on the Mountain in the spring."

"If we're not there," Kerrec said from Petra's back, "we'll be in Aurelia. Look for us in the palace. If we're not there, either, they'll know where we've gone."

Morag barely blinked at that. "You'll be on the Mountain," she said with conviction. She clasped Kerrec's hand, looking him in the face as a free woman of Eriu could do even to a high king. "Look after her until I get there. Keep her out of trouble."

"I'll try," Kerrec said.

She patted his knee. "Good. I'll hold you to it."

Valeria turned from her father's long, rib-creaking embrace toward Sabata. Morag was standing between. Her embrace was shorter but just as strong.

Morag pushed Valeria away with a visible effort and straightened her face—though not before Valeria saw a glint of moisture in her eye. "Go on now. That storm's not going to wait for us to finish dragging out our goodbyes."

Valeria hugged her one last time, quickly. "Until spring," she said.

Morag nodded, pushing her toward her stallion. "Until spring," she agreed.

Valeria looked back once as she rode away. They were all standing together, huddled close against the cold. For a moment she could see what they must see, two dark figures on white horses, dwindling down the snowy road.

Her heart contracted. She wanted to go back to the Mountain—more than anything in the world. And yet she wanted them, too, in all their maddening familiarity.

These days had been a gift. They had given back a part of herself that she had not even known she was missing. It hurt to leave them, but her heart knew she could come back. Or they could come to her.

A wall had broken down. Rodry had died to make it happen—she would mourn him for the rest of her life. But she would thank him, too, and honor his spirit.

Icy wind whipped the tears from her cheeks. She turned resolutely and focused on the road ahead of her. The Mountain was at the other end of it, and a reckoning.

She was not afraid. Whatever price she had to pay, she knew she could pay it. She was going home.

Sixty-Three

Euan Rohe came back to Dun Eidyn at the gates of winter—a year, near enough, since the last time he had crawled home in defeat.

This time he had the royal clan at his back. They had fared better than any of the other clans, having lost only a dozen men and gained almost a dozen times that in new allies and clanless men. The high king's funeral rites were behind them, with a clan gathering made bitter by grief and loss.

In the spring there would be a new high king. Euan meant to cast his axe into the circle and lay claim to the title.

That was months away. This raw and rain-sodden evening, he found the hall clean and swept and the fire burning. A fat ox turned on the spit, and a feast was waiting.

Euan had the luck, people said, seeing how strong the Calletani still were. They did not know whose fault it was that the battle was lost—or what Euan had failed to do that would have kept the tide from turning. That was not a secret he intended to share.

Tonight he let himself be glad he was home. Dun Eidyn greeted the winter with its storehouses full. With so many new mouths to feed, they would be tightening their belts before spring, but with some more of Euan's fabled luck, they would not starve.

He was not in the mood for an all-night roister. Simple people could celebrate a homecoming and forget what had brought them to it. He kept remembering a battle won and then suddenly, devastatingly lost.

As soon as he sensibly could, he slipped away. He meant to sleep, but he was too restless. He climbed the tower instead.

The stars kept their places tonight. The air was still and bitter cold. He circled the tower, treading carefully on the crumbling floor.

Near the yawning darkness that was the ladder to the lower hall, he nearly stumbled over a lump of shadow. It unfolded, raising a small, pale face and eyes that glinted in the starlight. "Good evening, Da," said his son.

"What are you doing here?" Euan asked—softening his voice at the last instant. He did not want to send the child screaming back down the ladder.

Conor did not even blink. "I like to come up here," he said. "It's quiet."

"So do I," Euan said, squatting beside him. "It's a cold night to be up on the roof."

"I like cold," Conor said.

"Still," said Euan, "come down where it's warm. I hear your amma made some honey sweets."

"I know that," Conor said. "I had six." But he let Euan lift him and carry him out of the cold.

He was warm and comfortably heavy in Euan's arms. Euan

was oddly reluctant to surrender him to his grandmother. A child of his age belonged with the women, learning to behave properly and be obedient to his betters, but surely one night would not undo his training.

Conor offered no objection to being taken to his father's rooms instead of his grandmother's. Euan thought he might be asleep, until Euan paused in front of his door. Conor raised his head from Euan's shoulder and said, "Don't go in there."

Euan stopped with his hand on the latch. "What's wrong? Did you put a snake in my bed?"

Conor shook his head. "Just don't go in."

Euan frowned. Children had odd fancies. He sniffed, but there was no stink of magic around the door. He opened it and paused, senses alert.

The room was dim and quiet. Only one lamp burned in the cluster by the bed. Two broad-shouldered shadows lurked by the wall—but they were only empty armor and legionary standards long since won.

Someday Euan would bring in new trophies to outshine the old. These were dusty and faded, like the glory they recalled.

Conor's arms were tight around his neck. Euan's own grip tightened on the child. With an effort he pried Conor loose and set him on his feet. "A warrior is brave," he said, "and he's never afraid of the dark."

"It's not the dark," Conor said. He pointed with his chin toward the far corner.

There was a tall chest there, another piece of imperial loot, in which Euan kept his war cloaks and plaids and a few oddments. One of those oddments, which Euan would have liked to forget, was a small box lined with silk, in which he had hidden the seeing-stone Gothard had made for him.

He had not looked into it since well before the battle. Maybe he should have—then he might have seen the horse mages coming. But his love for magic had grown even less the longer his alliance with Gothard went on. He had used what Gothard had, hoping to win the war—and he nearly had—but he had decided that for his own self, magic was a foul and deadly thing.

He should have dropped the stone in the river when he could. Why he had kept it, he did not know. Maybe because a wise man never discarded a weapon.

Conor could not know it was there. Euan had told no one. But he was staring at the chest as if it held a venomous snake.

He tugged at his father's hand. "Let's go see Amma. She has honey sweets, remember?"

Euan would have been happy to be diverted, but now his hackles were up. "Stay here," he said, lifting Conor and setting him back on his feet near the door.

He did not stop to see what the boy did. If he ran to his grandmother, so much the better. Euan approached the chest carefully, feeling a little ridiculous—a king of the people, stalking a wooden box.

He opened it slowly. The rich smell of cedar wafted out. His clothes were tidily folded. There was no viper nested in them, and the cedar kept moths at bay.

He moved to shut the door and turn, meaning to say, "You see? There's nothing there." But his hand persisted in reaching under the pile of folded wool to the small hard lump of the box. It was purely his imagination, but his fingers stung when he touched it.

His hand snapped back. He gritted his teeth and reached in again. This time there was nothing to shock him.

The box was Calletani, carved with twining shapes that were both pleasant and intriguing to the touch. The thing inside buzzed like a nest of bees.

It was all Euan could do not to fling it across the room. He set it down hard. He meant to slam the door, but again, his hand did something other than what he commanded. It dropped the box.

The lid fell open. The stone slid out, lying on the bright plaid. It looked like the maw of Unmaking.

He stepped back sharply and nearly fell. Conor was directly behind him. He swung the boy into his arms and kept on backing up.

More than the stone was humming now. Conor was shaking in time with it. "Stop," Euan said fiercely. "Stop that."

"Can't." Conor's voice was breathless.

Euan's back struck the door. He slid along it, reaching behind himself for the latch.

The humming stopped. Conor gasped, then went limp.

Two men were standing in the room. They were stark white and staring like apparitions of the dead. One of them sucked in a breath and collapsed. The other looked around him, blinking eyes that had swallowed oblivion, and smiled.

Conor gasped again and cried out. Euan held him as close as he could without choking the breath out of him.

Gothard's smile widened. "I see I have you both to thank for bringing me safely home."

"I've told you before," Euan said low in his throat. "I'll tell you again. Hands off my son."

"Believe me, cousin," Gothard said, "I wouldn't dream of harming him."

Euan tossed that off as the lying nonsense it was. "What are you doing here? How did you get in?"

At Gothard's feet, his yellow dog twitched and rolled onto his face, raising himself to his knees. The boy looked even madder than Euan remembered.

His eyes rolled. Had they been that pale before? Now they were almost white. They might be blind, though when they came to rest on Euan, they stayed. "We came through the gate," he said. "The maw of the Unmaking."

Euan had thought him mute. Clearly not. He spoke the language of the people rather well, which was not surprising considering his face and coloring. He must, like Gothard, be some imperial nobleman's by-blow on a captive woman.

"He means the stone," Gothard said. "What, did you think I'd run for it on foot after the last time? I've learned a little since. Not to put all my power in one stone, and to leave myself a way out. It was good of you to keep my gate. I was afraid you'd lose it."

"I wish to the One I had," Euan said bitterly. "You're a curse on all our tribe."

"Am I? Are you starving? Hunted? Stripped of your young men? How many of the Calletani did you lose?"

Euan's teeth clicked together.

"Indeed," said Gothard as if Euan had managed an answer. "How long has it been? It is spring yet?"

"Not nearly," Euan said, though his throat wanted to close. "It's the dark of the year."

"Earlier than I wanted," Gothard said as if to himself, "though it will do. I'll be taking this stone, if you don't mind."

"Where?" Euan demanded. "Where are you taking it?"

"That depends," said Gothard. "We still have a bargain. Unless you're already high king? Is the Ard Ri still alive?"

"He died after the battle," Euan answered. He considered not doing it, but that would serve no purpose. This was still his ally, he could suppose—though what he felt for Gothard was rapidly changing from dislike to outright hatred.

"So, a kingmaking in the spring," Gothard said. "Meanwhile,

there are plans to make—things to do. I take it the legions didn't press the advantage too hard, since you're here and not in a prison in Aurelia. How much tribute have they demanded? Are you intending to pay it?"

"There's been nothing," Euan said. "There's a legion camped at Oxos still, but it's just standing guard. No one's come to take our surrender."

"Excellent," said Gothard, rubbing his hands together.

If Euan's arms had not been full of a very quiet but blessedly alert Conor, he would have gutted Gothard where he stood. It would have done the people a great service.

Gothard was watching him, still half smiling, as if he could follow every turn of Euan's thoughts. He no longer looked dead. He merely looked as if he had not seen the sunlight in months. He must be feeding on air—or on the power of the stone—because Euan had deliberately not offered him either food or drink.

"Do think," said Gothard. "Not too hard now, but let it grow in you. What is the real power of the empire? Not its legions. Not its merchants, either, or even its mages. Where is the empire's heart?"

Euan shook his head. "I'm not going to listen to you. Go down to the hall, claim the vagrant's portion, then leave. I don't care where you go as long as you swear on that stone to stay away from my people."

"First your son, then your people," Gothard said with an exaggerated sigh. "You're a very proper tribesman. And here I'd been thinking there was more to you. Don't you want to break the Aurelian empire?"

"The Aurelian empire is succeeding rather well in breaking us," Euan said.

"Yes, and why? Or rather, who? Who has blocked us at every turn? Who lost us the battle when we had it won?"

"We had it won," Euan said sharply. "You had already failed."

"I let the starstone break," Gothard said, "because I was done with it. What I set in motion should have swallowed the whole army. Who stopped it? Answer me that."

Euan refused. Gothard said it for him. "We thought that if we broke the emperor's Dance, we could change the future and give ourselves the victory. We were half-right. It wasn't the Dance we needed to break. It was the dancers."

"You're going to take on the Mountain." The words escaped before Euan could catch them. "That's insane. No man can—"

"I already have," Gothard said. "The Mountain is stone. That's my power, cousin. Stone, and Unmaking. It only takes a little—that's the beauty of it. A little magic, a tiny working, and it grows. It's growing already. If we Unmake the Mountain, how long will the empire last? Will you wager on it?"

He was as seductive as pure evil always was. And yet, Euan thought, he could be right.

The empire was built on magic. Take away the magic and what was left? A federation of warring states—that was what they taught in the School of War on the Mountain. They were rather proud of it.

With the emperor dead and a young and untried woman in his place, a war won but at no small cost, and the horse mages themselves weakened by the attack on the Dance, Aurelia was not in much better state than the tribes. If there was a way to weaken it further…

"It won't all happen in a day," Gothard said, "or in a year, or maybe even ten years. But each step brings us closer to the victory. So far we've lost on the face of it—but they've fared worse. We'll win in the end. Their gods are strong, but the One is stronger. That's always been so. It always will be."

Euan looked at him, hating him but hearing every word.

Conor was silent in Euan's arms. What he made of this, only the One knew.

In the end it was very simple. A man needed sons. Sons needed places of their own, realms to rule and people to follow them. What better inheritance for this child than an empire?

"We still have a bargain," Euan said.

Gothard bowed to him in the imperial fashion. "Your hand on it, my lord king?"

Euan snarled at him. "You have my word. That's enough."

"Surely," said Gothard. Maybe there was anger deep in those eyes. Maybe it was merely mockery.

Whatever he thought of it, it was done. Euan turned his back on his dearly hated but inescapable ally. His son needed rest, and so did he. He had another war to plan—another stroke against the people's ancient enemy.

This time, the One willing, he would win it. Then...

Time enough to ponder the rest once he had his victory. He shifted Conor in his arms, settling the child more comfortably, and left Gothard to his plotting.

* * * * *

Don't miss Caitlin Brennan's new title in her
White Magic *series,*
Shattered Dance,
coming in September 2006.
What will happen when Euan and Valeria meet for the third time?
Take a peek…

The Mountain slept, locked deep in winter's snow. Far beneath the ice and cold and the cracking of frozen stone, the fire of its magic burned low.

It would wake very soon and send forth the Call. Then young men—and maybe women—would come from the whole of Aurelia to answer it. But tonight it was asleep. One might almost imagine that it was a mortal place and its powers mortal powers, and gods who wore the shape of white stallions did not graze its high pastures.

Valeria leaned on the window frame. The moon was high, casting cold light on the Mountain's summit. It glowed blue-white against the luminous sky.

"Has anyone ever been up there?" she asked. "All the way up past the Ladies' pastures, to the top?"

Kerrec wrapped her in a warm blanket, with his arms around that, cradling the expanding curve of her belly. He kissed the place where her neck and shoulder joined, and rested his chin lightly on her shoulder. His voice was soft and deep in her ear. "There's a legend of a rider who tried it, but he either came back mad or never came back at all."

"Why? What's up there?"

"Ice and snow and pitiless stone, and air too thin to breathe," he said, "and, they say, a gate of time and the gods. The Great Ones come through it into this world, and the Ladies come and go, or so it's said. It's beyond human understanding."

"You believe that?"

"I can't disprove it," he said.

"Someday maybe someone will."

"Not you," he said firmly, "and not now."

She turned in his arms. He looked like an emperor on an old coin, with his clean-carved face and his narrow arched nose— not at all surprising, since most of those forgotten emperors had been his ancestors—but lately he had learned to unbend a little. Even as sternly as he spoke, he was almost smiling.

"Not before spring," she conceded. She kissed him, taking her time about it.

The baby stirred between them, kicking so hard she gasped. He clutched at her. She pushed him away, half laughing and half glaring. "Stop that! I'm not dying and neither is she."

"Are you sure?" he said. "You looked so—"

"Shocked? She kicks like a mule." Valeria rubbed her side where the pain was slowly fading. "Go on, go to sleep. I'll be there in a while."

He eyed her narrowly. "You promise? No wandering out to the stable again?"

"Not tonight," she said. "It's too cold."

He snorted softly, sounding exactly like one of the stallions. Then he yawned. It was late and dawn came early, here at the far end of winter. He stole one last kiss before he retreated to the warmth of their bed.

After a few moments, she heard his breathing slow and deepen. She wrapped the blanket tighter.

Inside her where the stallions always were, standing in a ring of white faces and quiet eyes, the moon was shining even more brightly than on the Mountain. Power was waking, subtle but clear, welling up like a spring from the deep heart of the earth. The world was changing again—for good or ill. She was not prophet enough to know which.

She turned away quickly from the window and the moon and dived into bed. Kerrec's warmth was a blessing. His voice murmured sleepily and his arms closed around her, warding her against the cold.

Kerrec was gone when she woke. Breakfast waited on the table by the fire, with a Word on it to keep the porridge hot and the cream cold. Valeria would rather have gone to the dining hall, but she had to smile at the gift.

She was ravenously hungry—no more sickness in the mornings, thank the gods. She scraped the bowl clean and drank all of the tea. Then she dressed, scowling as she struggled to fasten the breeches. She was fast growing out of them.

Her stallions were waiting for her in their stable. She was not to clean stalls now, by the Healer's order—fool of a man, he persisted in thinking she was delicate. But she was still riding, and be damned to anyone who tried to stop her.

Sabata pawed the door of his stall as she walked down the aisle. The noise was deafening. Oda, ancient and wise, nibbled the remains of his breakfast. The third, Marina, whickered beneath Sabata's thunderous pounding.

She paused to stroke his soft nose and murmur in his ear.

He was older than Sabata, taller and lighter boned, with a quiet disposition and a gentle eye. He had been the last stallion that old Rugier trained, a Third Rider who never rose higher or wanted to—but he had had the best hands in the school.

Rugier had died after the Midwinter Dance, peacefully in his sleep. The next morning, Marina moved himself into the stall next to Oda's and made it clear that Valeria was to continue his training.

That was also the morning when Valeria confessed to Master Nikos that she was expecting a child. She had planned it very carefully, and rehearsed the words over and over until she could recite them in her sleep. But when she went to say them, there was a great to-do over Rugier's passing, and then there was Marina declaring his choice of a rider-candidate over all the riders in the school.

"I suppose," Master Nikos said after they had retreated from the stable to his study, "we should be thinking of testing you for Fourth Rider. You're young for it, but we've had others as young. It's less of a scandal than a rider-candidate with three Great Ones to train and be trained by."

"Are you sure I'm ready?" Valeria asked. "I don't want to—"

"The stallions say you are," Nikos said. "I would prefer to wait until after Midsummer—if you can be so patient."

"Patience is a rider's discipline," Valeria said. "Besides, I suppose it's better to wait until after the baby's born."

For a long moment she was sure he had not heard her. His mind was ranging far ahead, planning the testing and no doubt passing on to other matters of more immediate consequence.

Then he said, "That is what I had been thinking."

Valeria had been standing at attention as was proper. Her knees almost gave way. "You—had—"

"We're not always blind," Nikos said.

She scraped her wits together. "How long have you known?"

"Long enough to see past scandal to the inevitability of it all," he said. "The stallions are fierce in your defense."

"They're stallions," she said. "That's what they're for."

Master Nikos sighed gustily. "You, madam, are more trouble than this school has seen in all its years. You are also more beloved of the stallions than any rider in memory. Sooner or later, even the most recalcitrant of us has to face the truth. You are not ours to judge. You belong to the gods."

Valeria's mouth was hanging open. She shut it carefully. "Do the other riders agree with you?"

"Probably not," he said, "but sooner or later they'll have to. We all profess to serve the gods. That service is not always as easy or simple as we might like."

"I'm going to keep and raise this child," she said. She made no effort to keep the defiance out of her voice. "I won't give her up or send her out for fostering."

Master Nikos neither laughed nor scowled. He simply said, "I would expect no less."

He had caught Valeria completely off balance. It was a lesson, like everything else in this place. People could change. Minds could shift, if they had to. Even a senior rider could accept the unacceptable, because there was no other choice.

In this early morning at the end of winter, three months after Master Nikos proved that not everything a rider did was predictable, the stallions were fresh and eager. So were the riders who came to join Valeria in the riding hall. The patterns they transcribed in the raked sand were both delicate and random—deliberate in that they were training exercises, random in that they were not meant to open the doors of time or fate.

Valeria could see those patterns more clearly the longer she studied in the school. She had to be careful not to lose herself in them. The baby changed her body's balance, but it was doing something to her mind, as well. Some things she could see more clearly, others barely made sense at all.

Today she rode Sabata, then Marina, then Oda—each set of figures more complex than the last. Her knees were weak when she finished with Oda, but she made sure no one saw. The last thing she needed was a flock of clucking riders. They fussed enough as it was, as if no other woman in the history of the world had ever been in her condition.

It was only a moment's weakness. By the time she had run up the stirrups and taken the reins to lead the stallion back to his stable, she was steady again. She could even smile at the riders who were coming in, and face the rest of the morning's duties without thinking longingly of her bed.

This would end soon enough—though she suspected the last of it would seem interminable. She unsaddled Oda and rubbed him down, then turned him out in one of the paddocks. He broke away from her like a young thing, bucking and snorting, dancing his delight in the spring-bright sun.

Imagine not knowing if your next meal may be your last.

This is the fate of Yelenda, the food taster for a leader who is the target of every assassin in the land. As Yelenda struggles to save her own mortality, she learns she has undiscovered powers that may hold the fate of the world.

Available wherever trade paperbacks are sold.

Luna's Night Sky
© Amoreno 2005
www.DuirwaighGallery.com

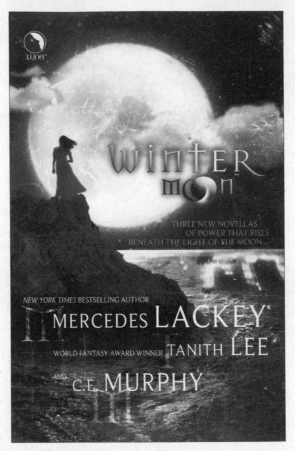